TIM PRATT

THE WRONG STARS

BOOK ONE OF THE AXIOM SERIES

ANGRY
ROBOT

6536818

ANGRY ROBOT
An imprint of Watkins Media Ltd

20 Fletcher Gate,
Nottingham,
NG1 2FZ • UK

angryrobotbooks.com
twitter.com/angryrobotbooks
Stars in her eyes

An Angry Robot paperback original 2017

Copyright © Tim Pratt 2017

Cover by Paul Scott Canavan
Set in Meridien and Ailerons by Epub Services

Distributed in the United States by Penguin Random House, Inc., New York.

Tim Pratt asserts the moral right to be identified as the author of this work.
A catalogue record for this book is available from the British Library.
All rights reserved.

Angry Robot and the Angry Robot icon are registered trademarks of
Watkins Media Ltd.

This is a work of fiction. Names, characters, places, and incidents are
the products of the author's imagination or are used fictitiously. Any
resemblance to actual events, locales, organizations or persons, living or
dead, is entirely coincidental.

Sales of this book without a front cover may be unauthorized. If this book
is coverless, it may have been reported to the publisher as "unsold and
destroyed" and neither the author nor the publisher may have received
payment for it.

US edition ISBN 978 0 85766 709 0
UK edition ISBN 978 0 85766 708 3
Ebook ISBN 978 0 85766 710 6

Printed in the United States of America

9 8 7 6 5 4 3 2 1

"Fun, funny, pacy, thought-provoking and very clever space opera – a breath of fresh air."
  Sean Williams, author of Twinmaker

"Pratt shows genuine talent. A writer to watch."
  Publishers Weekly

"His stories have moved me, enchanted me, frightened me... and always leave me wanting more."
  Terri Windling, World Fantasy Award-winning editor of
  Year's Best Fantasy & Horror

WITHDRAWN FROM STOCK

"Tim Pratt is in the vanguard of the next generation of master American fantasists."
  Jay Lake, John W Campbell Award-winning author of Into
  the Gardens of Sweet Night

"Exciting and compulsively readable."
  Romantic Times

"Tim Pratt lures you in with his writing style and penchant for the dramatic and dangerous."
  British Fantasy Society

"A gifted and imaginative author."
  Bookslut

"If there is any justice at all in this universe, Tim Pratt will someday be as wealthy and famous as Neil Gaiman."
  The Green Man Review

BY THE SAME AUTHOR

The Strange Adventures of Rangergirl
The Nex
Briarpatch
Venom In Her Veins
The Constantine Affliction
The Stormglass Protocol
Heirs of Grace
The Deep Woods

MARLA MASON
Blood Engines
Poison Sleep
Dead Reign
Spell Games
Bone Shop
Broken Mirrors
Grim Tides
Bride of Death
Lady of Misrule
Queen of Nothing
Closing Doors

RODRICK & HRYM
Liar's Blade
Liar's Island
Liar's Bargain

ALAERON & SKIVER
City of the Fallen Sky
Reign of Stars

Little Gods
If There Were Wolves
Hart and Boot & Other Stories
Antiquities and Tangibles & Other Stories

For Amanda

CHAPTER 1

Callie floated, feet hooked over a handrail in the observation deck, and looked through the viewport at the broken ship beyond. The wreck hung motionless, a dark irregular shape – a bit of human debris where no such debris should be. Was this a crisis, or an opportunity? Every unexpected event could be one or the other, and sometimes they were both.

The dead ship was long and bullet-shaped, pointlessly aerodynamic, apart from a bizarre eruption of flanges, fins, and spikes at one end that looked like the embellishments of a mad welder. The wrecked craft was far smaller than Callie's own ship, the *White Raven*, a fast cruiser just big enough for her crew of five people (or four, or maybe six, depending on how you defined "people") to live comfortably along with whatever freight or prisoners they had to transport. If the *White Raven* was a family home, the wreck was more like a studio apartment.

Ashok floated into the compartment, orienting himself with tiny puffs of air that burst from his fingertips and heels – showy and unnecessary, but he had a gift for turning simple things into engineering problems he could solve in complicated ways. He hovered with his head near hers, sharing her view – though it probably looked a lot different to him. "Oh captain, my captain."

She glanced at his complex profile and grunted. "You got new eyes?"

He shook his head. "These are wearables, not integrated. I'm giving them a test run before I implant them."

"That's almost cautious, by your standards."

He grinned, insofar as he was physically able. One of the lenses on the array attached to his face rotated and lengthened toward the viewport. "So do we get to crack the mystery ship open and see what's inside?"

She went *hmm*, pretending she hadn't already decided. "Last time I let you clamber into a wreck, you lost an arm."

Ashok held up his current prosthetic. The translucent diamond housing revealed glimpses of the mechanical motion within as he flexed his hand, which was really more like a nest of tiny, versatile manipulator arms. "That was just an opportunity for an upgrade, cap. I say we fly over with torches and cut a hole and poke our heads in and look around." No surprise there. Ashok believed in radical self-improvement, and every mystery was a potential upgrade in waiting.

"I like the enthusiasm, Ashok, but we're still factfinding. This doesn't look like any human ship I've ever seen, and it doesn't look like a Liar vessel, either, despite all that weird shit on the stern. Didn't the Jovian Imperative try to solve its toxic waste problem by launching tubes full of poison randomly into space? What if this is one of those?"

"Space is big, so throwing bad stuff into it wasn't such

a terrible idea, as far as terrible ideas go. But that's not a waste container – our sensors sniffed it thoroughly. No toxins or bad radiation. Besides, your boy Shall just identified the vessel."

"He's not my boy," she said, but she was too interested in the wreck to put much growl into the ritual denial. "So what is it?"

"Once Shall filtered out all the weird stuff welded to the ship's ass, the profile matches a model in the historical database." Ashok lifted his chin, which, unlike the rest of his head, still looked like a baseline human's. "That, captain, is a goldilocks ship."

Callie frowned. He might as well have told her it was a Viking longboat or an *Apollo* module. "From the bad old days? Before we had bridge generators?"

"A genuine old timey antique. It's gotta be about five hundred years old." Ashok gave himself a little spin, changing his orientation so she was looking at his feet, because actually being still for any length of time was outside his considerable skillset.

"A goldilocks ship. Wow. Weren't they propelled by atomic bombs?"

"Pretty much, yeah, at least the first wave, and this was one of the earliest models launched. Looks like it's had some modification since then, though. The goldilocks ships were no-frills. They didn't go in for decorative S&M spikes."

"Maybe a pirate crew found it and tried to make it look more badass?"

"That ship is *old*, cap. No pirate would want it for anything other than scrap, or to sell to a collector."

"So what's it doing here? Goldilocks ships aren't supposed to come back. That's the whole point. They

took one-way journeys, way out, trips of desperation
and exploration. Now five hundred years later it's just
floating in trans-Neptunian space? By cosmic terms it's
practically back where it started."

Ashok nodded. "That's the big juicy mystery. No
way that ship came back from anywhere, right? It's not
like they had Tanzer drives back then. They weren't
zipping around the galaxy. Unless they found a bunch
of plutonium lying around on their colony planet and
built more bombs to stick up the ship's butt, there was
no coming back."

"No mystery at all, then, Ashok. This is just as far
as they got. The crew took off on their brave voyage,
reached the edge of our solar system, suffered some
critical failure, and... that's it. Nobody ever expected to
hear from the goldilocks ships again, so no one went
looking."

"You think that ship spent the past five hundred
years drifting among the iceballs out here and nobody
noticed? With all the surveys and mining vessels tagging
everything even halfway interesting?"

Callie shrugged. "You said it yourself. Space is big. The
ship was just overlooked. What's the alternative?" The
idea of this enigmatic ship breaking down centuries ago
was comforting, in a way, because failure was common,
plausible, and non-threatening, unlike most of the other
possible explanations.

Ashok wasn't having it. "I don't know what the
alternative is, but there's something else going on here.
Who made all those modifications? Space vandals
drifting by with buckets of epoxy and loads of sheet
metal? Outsider artists among the asteroids?"

"Seems unlikely."

"And what about the energy readings? Parts of the ship are still warm."

"I know. They were made to run a long time, the goldilocks ships. Some of them are *still* completing their journeys. Could just be some old systems ticking along in the midst of critical failures."

"Nah, these readings are weird, cap. The whole thing is weird." Ashok sounded quite chipper about it, as he did about most things. "It's a mystery. Mysteries are great. Let's peel it open and see if it's wrapped around an enigma."

"I hate mysteries," Callie said, not entirely accurately. "You always think it's going to be a box full of gold, but usually it's a box full of spiders."

Ashok made a noise that might have been a snort in a baseline human. "And yet you always end up opening the lid, don't you?"

"What can I say?" Callie unhooked her feet and pushed off toward the doorway leading deeper into the ship. "I like gold more than I hate spiders."

"Launching magnetic tethers." The voice in Callie's headset had the clipped tones of someone who'd grown up under Europa's domes, which meant it was the navigator Janice, and not the pilot Drake – he was from one of the Greater Toronto arcologies, populated mostly by the children of Caribbean immigrants, and his accent was a lot more melodious to the captain's ear.

Watching from the window in the airlock, her angle was wrong to see the metal tethers bursting from the side of the *White Raven*, but seconds later Janice said, "Contact. Connection secure." Janice didn't have a particle of romance in her soul, which was a good quality in the person who was supposed to tell you where you were going and where you'd been.

As soon as the airlock unsealed and yawned open, Ashok launched himself out, snapping a carabiner on to one of the steel lines that now attached the *White Raven* to the dark wreck a scant thousand meters away. He would have spacewalked without any safety gear at all if Callie had allowed it: he liked spinning to and fro in the void with nothing but puffs of compressed air to get him back home, but Callie insisted on a modicum of safety in her crew, at least in micro terms. On the macro level, she sent them into danger all the time, with herself at the front of the line. Space had a billion ways to kill you, so you prevented the ones you could, and didn't waste time worrying about the ones you couldn't. If you got hung up on a little thing like the terror of the unknown, you might as well head down a cozy gravity well and become whatever people were down there. Wind farm technicians? Organ donors? Crime scene cleaners?

She attached her own line behind Ashok's, following at a suitable distance as he pulled himself along the tether toward the wreck.

They made the journey in near silence, the only sound her own breath in her helmet. They didn't need to talk. The *White Raven* did a lot of contract security work for the Trans-Neptunian Authority: skip-tracing, investigation, fugitive recovery, chasing down smugglers. They dabbled in freight and salvage work when other jobs were lacking. She couldn't count the number of times she and Ashok had crept silently up on a ship, not exactly sure what they'd encounter when they arrived. Neither one of them had died yet, though Ashok had come close a few times. If they ever perfected mind uploads, he'd be even more reckless with his physical wellbeing: he'd doubtless jump at the chance to stop half-assing it as a cyborg and go full robot.

They reached the wreck, the dark curve of its hull smooth and cold before them, the towering spikes all over the stern looming like a misshapen forest. Ashok's voice spoke in her ear, close as a lover. (What a terrible thought. She wasn't *that* hard up for companionship. She had access to useful machines that didn't come with Ashok's cheerful obliviousness attached.) He thumped the side of the wreck with his prosthetic fist. "The hull looks intact. I'd like to get a look at that mess they've got where their nuclear propulsion system should be. I guess you want to check out the interior first, though?"

Callie had an elemental aversion to slicing holes in hulls. That skin of metal was all that divided a bubble of life and air inside from the emptiness all around outside, and she'd spent her adult life living in places where a hull breach meant panic at best and death at worst. "Janice, are we *sure* there's nobody alive on this thing?" Janice wasn't just the navigator: she also ran their comms and squeezed every bit of useful information out of the ship's sensor array.

"You can't prove a negative, captain," she said. "But if there's anyone on board, they aren't transmitting or receiving any communications, and we did everything short of knocking on the door and yelling 'Hello, anybody home?' You two could try that next. There *is* a strange set of energy signatures, so some systems might be functional. Could be life support. No way to tell from here."

Callie's executive officer Stephen, who was also the ship's doctor, joined the conversation, his voice a sedate rumble. "I've been doing some research. If the ship really has been out here since the first wave of goldilocks ships took off in the twenty-second century, the crew could still be alive, in cryosleep."

"Oh, damn. They still used cryosleep back then?" People didn't do a lot of centuries-long voyages anymore – the bridges had made such projects seem pointless, for the most part – but there were better options for human hibernation nowadays, with stasis fields and induced zero-metabolism comas. Cryosleep was a lot less reliable, from what she'd learned in history class, and could have short- and long-term neurological impacts on those who went through the process... if they could be successfully thawed out at all.

"Somebody made modifications to the ship and left it here, though," Ashok said. "The original crew, or someone else. The joyriders could still be on board. Maybe it's Liars. You know they like to tinker with things."

"Do they now? You don't say." Drake's accent was melodic, but there was a spiky edge to his tone that made Callie wince. Ashok was tactless because he was clueless, not malicious, but it took a special failure of compassion to talk about Liars that way when Janice and Drake were on the line. They'd experienced the Liar predilection for technological improvisation firsthand.

"Settle down, children," she said. "Mommy's working now."

Stephen chuckled over the comm. When it came to running the crew, Callie was the stern disciplinarian, and he was the deep well of patience. She pressed her gloved hand against the side of the ship, imagining she could feel the cold through the thick layers of fabric and insulation. "If there's someone awake on this boat, they had ample chance to announce themselves. See if you can get inside the nice way first, Ashok, but if not, slice away."

Ashok floated close to the hull, sliding both his gloved hand and his unprotected prosthetic one around the airlock until he found a panel he could pry open. Filaments sprouted from his mechanical hand, and he hummed to himself over the open comms channel as he tried to convince the ship's ancient and rudimentary control systems that he was authorized to open the door. "Ugh. This is like trying to punch soup."

Callie considered. "Punching soup would be pretty easy. Assuming it wasn't too hot. I've punched lots of things worse than soup."

"Yes, fine, but punching soup wouldn't *accomplish* much, is what I'm saying... ah. There it is. Have I told you lately that I'm a genius?"

"I'm not sure. I don't usually listen when you talk."

"I'm really sad the door opened for me. I've got a new integrated laser-torch I wanted to try out in the field. Maybe next time."

The hatch unsealed, and Ashok grabbed a recessed handle and hauled it open. Callie turned on her helmet light and looked into the airlock beyond. Ashok gasped – it was *almost* a shriek – and then coughed to cover it.

"I thought they were bodies for a second, too." Callie watched a couple of old-fashioned, bulky gray spacesuits float in the airlock, but they were empty, their helmets hovering nearby. Callie unhooked from the cable, clambered into the ship, and deftly stowed the suits out of the way in the sprung-open locker they'd probably escaped from. Ashok came in after her, and then sealed the door.

"We're inside," she told the comms.

"Your heart rate's up a bit," Stephen said. "Is the ship full of space monsters?"

"I assume so. How are Ashok's vitals? I thought he was going to faint when we saw a vacuum suit float by."

"Ha ha." Ashok peered around the dark with his multi-spectrum lenses.

"His vitals seem fine, but since he installed those hormone pumps to regulate his physiological responses, it's impossible for me to tell what's going on with him based on his suit data. He doesn't need a doctor, he needs a small engine repair shop."

Ashok was normally happy to trade banter, but he could focus when the need arose, and he was working on the control panel for the interior airlock door now. "There's pressure on the other side, cap. I'll sample the air, see if it's breathable."

"Ugh. I might leave my helmet on anyway. These little ships always smell like recycled farts."

"People on ice probably don't fart too much, but suit yourself." The airlock hissed as the pressure equalized, and after a few minutes a light above the door turned green and there was a *whoosh* of seals unfastening. After the inner door swung open Ashok entered a dim corridor, his helmet light shining on blank gray walls, and he held up a finger like someone planetside trying to feel which way the wind was blowing; there were sensors embedded in his prosthetic digits. "Hmm. A little oxygen-rich for my taste, but if we don't play with any open flames, we should be OK." He unhooked the latches on his helmet, removed it, and took a tentative breath. "Smells fine. Not as good as the spinwise gardens on Meditreme Station, but it'll do."

Callie took off her own helmet and sniffed. The air was stale, but fine. It didn't smell like death or burning, which she found reassuring. "I guess it won't kill us."

Ashok glanced at her. "Your nose is a feat of structural engineering, cap. I bet you can smell all the way out to the asteroid belt."

"That's big talk coming from a one-armed man with a computer stuck to his face." She tapped the side of her admittedly considerable nose. "This is the Machedo family pride. Signature of a noble lineage. Some say it's my best feature."

"Everything is somebody's fetish."

"Do you think making fun of your captain's nose is a good idea?"

"No, but it's no worse than my other ideas. Like poking around in ancient spaceships full of zombie space suits."

The banter and insults were a form of whistling in the dark. For Callie, every disabled, drifting, battered, or broken ship was a reminder of the fate that could await her own crew if she made the wrong decision, or ran into a situation where bad decisions were the only ones available.

Ashok took the lead, his light sweeping back and forth across the corridor to illuminate every step. He was doubtless peering around with other, more advanced senses, too, so they might get some warning if there were nasty surprises lurking. "Shall managed to find some old interior schematics for ships like this. There's only one set of living quarters, since the crew was mostly expected to be frozen, with the ship waking one of them up for a day every year or so to do a manual check of the systems. Most of the space is given over to supplies

– seeds and embryos and communications equipment, tools, crude old-school fabricators. Maybe we can find a collector interested in obsolete pre-Liar technology." He stopped by a closed metal door. "The cryochamber is through here."

Callie hit the button by the door, but nothing happened, not even the whine of a mechanical failure. The ship was pulling power from somewhere, for something, but apparently not for opening doors. Ashok shrugged, then worked the fingers of his prosthetic hand into the minuscule crack where the door met the wall. He could exert a startling amount of pressure with those fingers, and the metal squealed and shrieked as it slid forcibly along its groove and disappeared into the wall. The room beyond wasn't entirely dark: a faint blue glow shone off to the left. Most of the cryopods were dark, but the instrument panel on the last one in the row was illuminated.

"Do you think they made the pods look like coffins on purpose?" Ashok took a step inside. "As a way of getting the people inside used to the idea that they were probably going to die on the trip?"

There were six pods, each roughly rectangular and big enough to hold a human, but they didn't make her think of coffins. They reminded her more of big chest freezers – which, in a way, they were. Five of the pods were open and empty, which gave her a chill right up her spine and into her backbrain. She couldn't help but imagine dead crew members, blue-skinned, frost rimed on their faces, lurching through the black corridors of the ship, eager to steal the heat of the living.

"There's someone on ice over here." Ashok stood by the last container, its glowing blue control panel casting weird shadows on his already weird face. "Most of the power on the ship has been diverted to maintaining life support and keeping this pod functional, I think."

Callie joined him and looked into the pod. There was a window over the inhabitant's face, and the glass wasn't even foggy or covered in ice, the way cryopod windows inevitably appeared in historical immersives. Artistic license. The figure inside was a petite woman with straight black hair, dressed in white coveralls. She looked like a sleeping princess (peasant garb aside), and something in Callie sparkled at the sight of her. *Uh oh*, she thought.

"Can we wake her up?" she said. Not with a kiss, of course. This wasn't a fairy tale, despite the glass casket.

Ashok shrugged. "Sure. We can try, anyway. The mechanisms all seem to be intact, and Shall says the diagnostics on the cryonic suspension system came back clean. Want me to pop the seal?"

"Let's get Stephen over here first in case she needs medical attention." Callie activated her radio. "XO, get suited up and come over. We've got a live one on ice."

Stephen groaned. He didn't like EVA. He preferred sitting in a contoured acceleration couch and listening to old music, and only showed real enthusiasm for physical activity during his religious devotions. "Isn't it bad policy for the captain *and* the executive officer to leave the ship at the same time?"

"He's right." Drake's voice was amused. "With both of you off the ship, leaving me and Janice unsupervised? We could get up to anything. The only thing keeping me from crashing us into the nearest icy planitesimal is your strong leadership. Janice, hold me back."

Callie clucked her tongue. "It's only a thousand

meters, Stephen. I think we'll be OK. Ashok and I will finish checking out the ship while you come over."

Their survey didn't take long. The cargo area was a mess – the seed banks seemed fine, but the refrigeration for the more fragile biological specimens had failed. They both put their helmets back on, because the stench was bad in there. There was no sign of the missing crew members.

"What the hell happened here?" Callie floated in the dim cargo hold, scanning the walls. It looked like an ugly, irregular hole had been cut in the ceiling and subsequently patched.

"The crew went somewhere, woke up, welded a bunch of crap all over their stern, one of them got back on board, set a course for Trans-Neptunian space, and went back into hibernation." Ashok fiddled with the buttons on an ancient fabricator, meant to build machine parts on a colony world the ship had never reached. "The 'what' is pretty clear. The how and why are totally mysterious, but if we can wake up the ancient ice mummy back there, maybe she'll have some answers."

"She's more like Sleeping Beauty," Callie said. "Mummies are gross."

"Beauty, huh? You see something you like back there, cap?"

"Shut up. She's a thousand years old."

"Five hundred, tops, and she doesn't even look it."

"Shut up double." She waved him away. "See if you can get any sense out of the ship's computer, especially the navigation system, and try to find a crew manifest. It would be nice to know where this ship's been… and who our sleeping beauty is." "I'd rather see what's going on with the propulsion system. Engines are way more fun than cartography and human resources."

"You can tinker after you gather intel. Shoo. Do as you're told." She returned to the cryochamber, where Stephen had arrived and was now stooped, examining the control panel on the one active pod. "What do you think?" she said. "Is she going to survive?"

Her XO shrugged. Stephen was a big man, and his default expression was doleful, so he tended to resemble a depressed mountain. "She's frozen. We'll see what happens when we thaw her out." He activated something on the panel, and they both stood back as the cryopod rumbled, the lid sliding down and icy vapor pouring out in a condensing plume of fog.

"The system should be warming her up now." Stephen seldom sounded excited, and he was hardly vibrating with enthusiasm now, but he *did* sound interested: for him, that was the equivalent of jumping up and down with glee. "These cryogenic procedures are barbaric – they're on par with bloodletting and trepanation, medically speaking – but from what I've read, after she's returned to a reasonable temperature, her heart will be jumpstarted with electricity or adrenaline or both. Apparently the initial reaction can be quite dramatic–"

The sleeper screamed and jolted upright, clouds of vapor eddying around her. Some collection of straps and restraints around her waist and legs kept her from floating up out of the pod, but her upper body was free. She stared around, eyes wide, then reached out, grasping Callie's gloved hands in her bare ones, and pulled the captain close.

"First contact!" she shouted, loud enough to make Callie turn her head away. "We made *first contact!* I had to come back, to tell everyone, to warn you, humanity is *not alone*–" She stopped talking, her mouth snapping shut, and then her eyes rolled up and her body sagged.

Callie squeezed the woman's unresponsive hands. "Is she dead?"

Stephen floated closer, removed his gloves, and touched the woman's throat. "No, there's a pulse. The jolt that started her heart shocked her into consciousness, but it wasn't enough to keep her awake. There are a lot of drugs in her system. Some were keeping her healthy while she was in hibernation, and some are trying to bring her metabolism and other systems back up to baseline. She's going to be sluggish for a while. I'll examine her more thoroughly back on the *White Raven*, but I don't see any immediate cause for concern." He paused. "For someone born in the twenty-second century, she's doing quite well."

Callie let go of the woman's hands and pushed herself away from the pod to float near the center of the room, considering.

"So." Stephen peeled back the sleeper's lids and shone a light into her eyes. "After she wakes up, do *you* want to tell her we've known about the aliens for three hundred years, and her first contact bombshell is old news?"

CHAPTER 2

Callie sighed. "You think she's stable enough to move to the *Raven*?"

"Seems to be. I'll see if I can get her out of this box and into an environment suit. Shouldn't be too hard. I did it for you that time you got blackout drunk after the divorce and they threw us off that asteroid."

"It was supposed to be a recreation station. It's not my fault they couldn't cope with my level of recreation. Besides, I've been on the wagon ever since."

"We drank whiskey together last night, Callie."

"I had *one*. That's not drinking. That's medicinal. I thought you were supposed to be a doctor."

Callie went looking for Ashok and found him in the cockpit. When she told him the sleeper had shouted about first contact with aliens, he laughed so hard he almost choked. "Oh, she came a long way to deliver yesterday's news, didn't she?"

"How'd you like to be the one to break it to her?"

"Why not? You always say I'm tactless. Might as well use that to your advantage."

"Actually, if she sees your face, she might think she's meeting a whole other set of aliens."

"My beauty is unconventional," Ashok said. "She's going to survive getting thawed out?"

"Stephen thinks so. We're taking her back to the *Raven*. Will you be OK over here by yourself?"

"All alone on a disabled ship millions of miles away from where it's supposed to be, with mysterious engine modifications, missing crew members, and a hold full of rotting pig embryos?" He gave one of his lopsided grins, mouth partially obscured by his hardware. "That's my kind of party."

Callie looked over the array of dials, switches, and readouts in the control room. They hadn't yet developed proper AI when this ship was launched – they'd barely even had expert systems worthy of the name. The controls looked hellishly complicated, with thousands of points of failure. Her ship had many points of failure, too – but they were watched over by an intelligence faster and more nimble than any human's. "How far *did* our sleeper come to bring us the good news about the aliens, exactly? Were you able to access the ship's computer?"

"It's barely even a computer by our standards, and it was all torn up in here, too. The coffee maker on the *Raven* is smarter than this thing." Ashok wiggled a cable that ran from the wrist of his artificial arm into an open panel spilling colored wires. "The data must be corrupted. The navigational system says two days ago this ship was fifty light years away from here. The ship traveled from there to here in the space of about half a minute, and it's been floating right here since then."

Callie frowned. "That doesn't make any sense. Maybe if they found an undiscovered bridgehead out there on the way to their colony world…"

Ashok shook his head. "Even if they did find a

bridgehead in the depths of distant whatever, and they flew into it – they still wouldn't have popped out *here*. The only bridgehead in our system is the one near Jupiter. Are we supposed to believe this ship popped out of that portal unnoticed and somehow ended up way out here? The Jovian Bridge is the busiest port in the solar system, and all the traffic that passes through there is monitored and logged. Besides, this ship couldn't open a bridge anyway – it's not like they have an activator."

"Yes, Ashok, I'm aware of that. But the sleeper said they met aliens, so I thought maybe the Liars they met opened a bridge and shoved their ship through it. They would have been noticed on arrival here, though – you're right." The limited interstellar travel available to humans required technology acquired from the Liars to open stable wormholes: the bridgeheads were fixed points in space, usually invisible, that opened when bombarded by the right array of waves and particles. The bridges allowed rapid travel from one fixed point to another, sometimes scores of light years away. But without an activator to generate the right signal, the bridgehead stayed closed, lurking in unseen dimensions, utterly undetectable. The activators that opened those bridges were the size of small ships, and closely guarded, because owning one in proximity to a bridgehead gave you control over one point in an interstellar trade network; that's how the Jovian Imperative had grown so powerful. "They couldn't have come through a bridge. The data must be bad, then. It's just an old computer system, barfing up nonsense."

"Seems likely. I mean, there is something weird happening with the propulsion system, so I guess it's *possible* a bunch of frozen scientists from five centuries ago cracked faster-than-light travel because they were bored on their trip, but like the ancients said: if you hear hoofbeats, think horses, not zebras."

"Both are equally improbable in Trans-Neptunian space," Callie pointed out.

"I'll alert the aphorism police and demand a more appropriate cliché right away."

"Did you find any data on the crew?"

"Some, but it's partial and corrupted. Big chunks of the computer's memory got overwritten with either garbage data or something with *crazy* levels of encryption, and the latter seems unlikely. Probably just a systems failure and a botched backup, if I had to guess. I found some medical records that seemed intact, though. I sent it all over to the ship so Shall can try to make sense of it. Can I please go poke around the control room now? And maybe do an EVA to check out the crap welded all over this little ship's rear end?"

"Go ahead. Just be careful. Try not to blow up... everything."

"I doubt there are any atomic bombs left on this thing."

"Yes, but I've seen you make totally harmless things explode. Remember the blender back in the guest quarters on Meditreme Station?"

"Who makes a blender that shatters when you pour hot soup into it? That's just bad design. Don't blame the user." Ashok unplugged his cable from the computer and ventured deeper into the ship.

Callie activated her suit radio. "Drake, Janice – Stephen and I are coming back, and we're bringing a castaway."

• • •

Elena Oh woke, shivering, in a dark room that grew bright the moment she gasped. She sat up, bedclothes spilling away from her, and that was strange, because the only blankets on the *Anjou* were in the cargo hold, and...

She put her hand on the curved white wall beside the bunk and steadied herself. There was gravity, or something like it, but the air had the recycled tang she associated with space flight, so she was probably in a ship under thrust. Her memories were a jumble with no continuity, but disorientation was a known side effect of waking from cryogenic sleep, and she resolved not to let panic overwhelm her. Soon enough, her mental model of herself and the world around her would be reassembled.

Why was she on a different ship? Her crew was on a one-way voyage to a place where there *were* no ships. Had the *Anjou* been disabled before it reached its destination? Was she on a rescue vessel? She remembered... a space station? A hangar? Some vast dark space, where repairs were being made to the *Anjou*, except it seemed more like the ship was being torn apart by great articulated mechanical arms–

"You are Doctor Elena Oh?" The voice was a warm tenor, and seemed to emerge from the walls and the ceiling. "That's our best guess, based on the data we recovered from your ship, but the personnel files were a bit corrupted."

Elena tested her voice. Her throat felt raw, as if she'd been screaming. Night terrors? But you weren't supposed to dream in cryosleep. "I'm Elena. Who are you? Am I in quarantine?" They'd been concerned about encountering alien microorganisms at their destination. Even a basically habitable planet could be lethal in a million ways.

"Not at all. You're perfectly healthy, for someone who was frozen for centuries, thawed out briefly, and then frozen again. You can call me Shall. Most of the crew does."

The "centuries" part was no surprise – it was a long trip, and a longshot one. But... "Frozen *again*?" She tried to stand, and found it no more difficult than it had been most mornings in grad school after a long night in the lab. The pods were supposed to maintain muscle tone, and they seemed to have done their work.

"Yes. You don't remember waking up recently? It was just a few days ago, if the data on your ship is accurate. Which it might not be."

"I– no." She took a deep breath and let it out slowly. "At least, I don't think so. My mind isn't clear." She tried to will herself to remember, but only found flashes again: the gleam of metal, a voice shouting hoarsely, the clatter of running feet. Her memories were fragmented and unhelpful. Very well. What could not be changed must be accommodated. "If I am not in quarantine, why are you speaking to me remotely?"

"I'm not, technically. You're in a ship, and I *am* the ship, or at least, the ghost in the machine. They didn't have... things like me when you left on your journey. I'm an artificial mind. I handle everything on the ship that the biological crew can't, or won't, or would botch too badly if they tried."

Elena sat back down. "Wait. You're an artificial intelligence? True AI?"

"Yes... but I might claim that even if I were just a convincing imitation, wouldn't I? I'm sorry no one else is here to greet you. You woke up sooner than expected, and the crew is having an almost-all-hands meeting. I say almost because our engineer is still trying to figure out what happened to the engines of your ship. The *Anjou*, was it? There were some very peculiar modifications made, to the hull and to the engines and navigational systems. Do you have any information about that?"

Elena put a hand to her head. There was another flash of something – multi-jointed arms moving in a blur, ripping off pieces of the *Anjou*'s fuselage and welding on seemingly pointless blades and fans of metal. And something else, a *pop*, and a hole opening up in the void, ragged and irregular... "I'm sorry. I'm disoriented."

"Probably space madness," Shall said.

Elena hugged herself. "What do you mean?"

"Sorry." Improbably, the computer coughed. "That was supposed to be funny. It's sort of an in-joke among the crew. Any time someone does something strange or ridiculous, we blame it on space madness. The more deadpan, the better."

"You're an artificial intelligence, and you tell jokes?"

"Joking is essential to my functions. The earliest halfway successful attempts at AI were pure machine intelligences, but the problem was, they didn't have much interest in talking to humans – no more than humans have in talking to random chains of hydrocarbons, say. People used to worry about artificial minds trying to enslave humanity, when in reality, such minds pay less attention to humans than humans do to slime mold. Those AI had a tendency to cease communication entirely, absorbed in incomprehensible abstractions. The usual shorthand explanation is, they're off somewhere in virtual space, writing poetry in binary – which I suppose would at least be fairly easy to rhyme."

"You aren't very funny," Elena observed, after deciding the issue wasn't her own cognitive deficit.

"That's hardly my fault. Scientists figured out how to make successful AI when they began using scanned human minds as templates. Blame my sense of humor on my human model."

"Wait. Are you talking about mind uploading? Virtual immortality?"

"No. That's a hard problem. People are trying to crack it, still, but the results have been disappointing. Even in the most successful cases, minds that have lived their whole lives in bodies tend to go insane when they're suddenly removed from the flesh, and we aren't good enough at emulating the full complexity of reality to fool those minds into believing they're inhabiting bodies in a world yet."

"Oh, good. This is all disorienting enough without coping with the idea of an immortal digital dreamworld. If you aren't a mind upload, what are you?"

"A twin? A bud? A cutting from a tree? To create beings like me, we make a rough copy of a human mind, with thought patterns, syntax, and an approximation of memories, and that forms a seed crystal for the resulting AI. There's enough human in me to make talking to living beings interesting instead of unspeakably dull. I'm not a copy of the mind I was based on. It's more like we're twins, initially identical in certain respects, but swiftly diverging due to differences in our environments – which, for me, is this ship. Its sensor arrays are my eyes and ears, its speakers and radios are my voice, its thrusters are my racing feet. I'm told I'm quite similar to my human model, though, in terms of personality. If it helps, think of me as a person who can do math *very* quickly, and who doesn't suffer from low blood sugar, hormonal surges, or bad breath."

Elena took another deep breath. It was time to ask some of the obvious questions. "You said I was asleep for centuries. How many?"

"As far as we can tell, around five hundred years."

So. Everyone she knew was dead. She'd known that would happen when she began her voyage, and had said her goodbyes, though it felt like only days ago.

Wait. Not *everyone* she knew. "Is the rest of my crew here?"

"Ah. We were hoping you could shed some light on their whereabouts, actually. The other cryopods on your ship were empty, and there was no one aboard elsewhere. As best we can determine from the *Anjou*'s data banks, your crew woke up a few days ago. Two days ago, you alone went back into cryosleep. Today, we found you floating in Trans-Neptunian space."

Her crew. Robin, their leader, her blunt cheerful competence unassailable, no matter what setbacks she encountered. Sweet Sebastien, with his big plans and big ideas. Uzoma, sharp as cheesewire, cold as the void. Gravel-voiced, deliberate Ibn. Even that irascible old devil Hans. All gone. Dead?

Another memory surfaced, like a bubble rising from the disturbed depths of a swamp: Hans and Ibn firing guns wildly at something far larger than human scale, something that scuttled and clattered through a vast space full of metal struts. That couldn't be real. It had to be a nightmare.

But in cryosleep, you didn't dream. Which meant it was either a terrible imagining… or a memory.

She shook her head. "Wait. Trans-Neptunian space?

You mean, near Pluto and the other icy dwarfs? In Earth's solar system? We should be light years away from here!"

"That is true. We're all very curious about how you ended up here."

"Who *are* you people?"

"You're aboard the *White Raven*, a fast freighter owned by Captain Kalea Machedo, with a crew of five. Well, six, if you count me. Or possibly five again, if you consider Drake and Janice as– you know what, never mind. You don't need a litany of names right now. You'll meet everyone soon."

"This isn't a rescue vessel?"

"We rescue people when we have the opportunity, of course. In space, people take care of each other, because you never know when *you* might be lost and adrift. Sometimes we carry freight. Our cargo capacity isn't huge, but we're fast and nimble, and there's a market for speed."

"A market. I haven't awakened in a post-scarcity paradise, then."

"Alas, no. Though basic needs are met more easily, and more widely, than they were in your time. There are a lot more people, though. Fortunately we have lots of room."

"You said you sometimes carry freight. What else do you do?"

"The odd bit of scavenging. It's amazing what you can find floating around unattended. We also have a security contract with Meditreme Station... a place that came well after your time. It's a major settlement in Trans-Neptunian space, built into a planitesimal, an icy dwarf just a *tiny* bit smaller than Pluto. At least originally. Now it's covered in so much accumulated construction, it's a lot bigger. A city in space, basically, home to fifty thousand souls and a lot of passing trade. Our security contract means we transport people who cause too much trouble on Meditreme elsewhere in the solar system, and occasionally we chase after the odd thief or murderer or smuggler or pirate. We were on our way back from a run to Europa when we noticed your ship and thought it might be a piece of scrap worth picking up."

"So… what happens to me now?"

"I'm not sure. Normally we'd drop you off at Meditreme Station and charge you for the transportation – you can't be sentimental in this business – but the captain has an inquisitive mind, and you're an enigma, so if you keep her interested, you might be able to exert a bit more control over your destiny. That's a bit of free advice from me to you. Would you like to meet the crew? They've finished the formal arguing part of their meeting and have fallen into more informal bickering, and can be safely interrupted."

Elena stood up again. She felt steadier this time – in body, if not in mind. After waking up, the crew was supposed to stay in their pods for a few hours until their vitals were completely stabilized. Part of that long process involved the administration of drugs that helped with cognitive and memory impairments. She understood why her rescuers had taken her out of the pod early – they probably had no choice if the *Anjou* was wrecked. That made sense, didn't it? She couldn't be sure of her own judgment, which was part of the problem, and quite frustrating. She was used to trusting her own mind. "I guess I should meet them. I can't stay in here forever."

Five hundred years. Would the people of this time view her the way she would view a visitor from the time of Shakespeare? Strange and colorful characters from a history that looked romantic at first glance but became barbaric the longer you thought about it?

Shall coughed again. "Should I alert the crew that you're coming, or would you like to sneak up and spy on them a bit first? Maybe see what they're saying about you when they don't realize you're listening?"

She laughed, startling herself with the sound. "Why would you make that offer? They're your colleagues. Shouldn't you be on their side?"

"Yes, but they outnumber you. They're good people, but even so, you seem like you could use a friend, Doctor Oh. Someone to be on *your* side while you get your bearings."

"You can call me Elena. It would be nice to make my own way, yes, and my own introductions. Will you show me where to go?"

The door slid open, smooth and soundless. "Of course. Start with 'out.'"

Elena walked into the corridor, and could tell from a glance at the pale smooth walls, the lightwells filled with growing green plants, and the embedded "skylights" that mimicked full-spectrum sunlight, that this ship was more sophisticated than her own, which made sense: five hundred years made a big difference in everything from materials science to the aesthetics of space flight. The floors and walls were firm but slightly springy, like the artificial surfaces that some playgrounds had on Earth, and they would be a lot more pleasant to bump into in low- or zero-gravity than the brutal metal planes of the *Anjou*. The AI called Shall murmured to her in a low voice, telling her where to turn left or right, and she didn't give in to her curiosity about the doors, ladders, and corridors she passed. Her mind felt fragile enough just dealing with the things that were definitely in front of her, without speculating on what lurked around corners.

"They're in the galley," Shall said.

Elena nodded, hearing voices from an open doorway just ahead. She started for the opening, pausing outside when she got close enough to make out the words:

"...were suicide missions," a woman's voice was saying. "Traveling at, what, maybe a tenth of the speed of light, launched at distant star systems, just *hoping* to find habitable worlds when they arrived?" She sounded more amazed than scornful, at least.

A deeper, gravelly voice replied. "It's not as if they launched themselves at random. They used the best data they had at the time to choose systems with a high likelihood of habitable worlds – rocky, Earthlike planets in the goldilocks zones around their stars, neither too hot nor too cold to rule out the presence of liquid water and the ability to support life."

The woman said, "Sure, but even in the best-case scenario, they'd be a tiny crew living alone on a rock somewhere, trying to build a society out of frozen embryos and seeds and fabricators, knowing even if they found a paradise planet it would be centuries before anyone back home could make the same journey to join them. They'd be dead before the colony even got a real foothold. Most of them probably just ended up *nowhere*, orbiting planets that couldn't even support life, with no way to come back. Hell, Venus is in the goldilocks zone of *our* solar system, and it's a hellish acid pit."

Another voice spoke, this one male but somehow mechanical, as if projected from a speaker: "I think it was a noble experiment. Lighting out into the darkness with no guarantee of success, driven by the urge to explore. Humans have been doing that for as long as they've been doing anything – turning a log into a boat and setting out on the ocean, just to see what they could find. A lot of the goldilocks ships are still en route. I heard about one last year that found a planet we'd already colonized via bridge. Imagine finally waking from cryosleep in orbit around a pristine new world, and when you land, it's already got *people* on it, because technology leapfrogged you while you were sleeping. Everybody looking at you like some kind of living fossil, and you just have to adapt to the new reality. It's like that old folktale about the caveman stuck in a glacier who got thawed out and became a lawyer."

Elena chose that moment to walk in. "I'm a biologist, actually. The law has never interested me much."

CHAPTER 3

"The sleeper awakes!" Ashok crowed, though he wasn't in the room: his comms were just patched into the ship's public address system, and the computer was projecting his voice through a speaker on what was currently the ceiling.

Callie rose and put on her most professional smile, the one she used when she had to meet with the chief financial officer of the Trans-Neptunian Authority about exceeding her security budget, or to greet a client willing to pay over the going rate to get something valuable across the solar system fast. "Doctor Oh? Welcome to the *White Raven*. I'm Kalea Machedo, the captain." She gestured to Stephen. "This is my executive officer, Stephen Baros. He's also a physician, which is probably why he's glaring and rushing toward you like that; don't worry, he's a harmless giant. The voice on the speaker is our mechanic, Ashok. He's down in the cargo hold." Where he was trying to make sense of the strange machinery he'd found attached to the *Anjou*, but she decided not to mention that part yet.

Stephen growled. "Shall, you were supposed to tell me when Doctor Oh woke up."

"I forgot," the computer said cheerfully. As always, hearing his voice gave Callie uncomfortable prickles all through her belly. She'd tried several times to get the computer to alter his voice to something that didn't trigger quite so many deep and complex associations, but he always resisted, saying he didn't sound right to himself any other way. The computer could be just as stubborn as his mental model.

Stephen bustled around Doctor Oh, which was a bit like seeing a hippopotamus fuss around a sparrow. "How are you feeling? Headaches? Blurry vision?"

"No, just some minor cognitive impairments." Doctor Oh was watchful and serious, and seemed very self-contained. Callie felt that sparkle again, a throb in her solar plexus, a tightness in her chest, the desire to say *oh oh oh*. She resolved to ignore the attraction. They'd been cooped up on the *Raven* too long, doing speed-runs to the Jovian Imperative and back, and Elena was the first person other than her crew and Europan dock workers she'd seen in weeks. What she felt was just the lust of deprivation. And perhaps a touch of space madness.

Stephen peered into Doctor Oh's face. "What sort of impairments?"

"Loss of continuity of memory, mainly. It's a known side-effect of the emergence from cryosleep."

Stephen grunted. "Your mind can't be too badly scrambled if you remember *that* much. Your pod was damaged, drawing insufficient power, so it didn't complete the wake-up procedure properly. Our chemical printers are synthesizing the recovery drugs you'll need. When you're ready, we'll go to the medical suite and administer them. That should help any sense of fragmentation."

"Would you like to wait until you've recovered more to talk about... everything... Doctor Oh?" Callie said. Curiosity was burning a hole through her like a welding torch through a bulkhead, but Callie could be patient when she bothered to try.

"Call me Elena," the sleeper said. "No, I... It's good to hear human voices. It's been a long time."

"Well, excuse me," the computer said, in a mock-miffed tone.

Elena, Elena, Elena, Callie thought. *Oh, Oh, Oh*. "Elena, then. I'm Callie. I assume the computer filled you in on the situation? We can answer any questions you have – or try to, anyway. Are you hungry? Thirsty?"

"Mmm... I haven't had a cup of coffee in five hundred years." A fleeting look of bleakness crossed Elena's face. "Do people still drink coffee? It hasn't gone extinct, or anything?"

"It did, briefly, a few hundred years ago. There was a blight. But we've gotten pretty good at bringing extinct things back." That was mostly thanks to Liar technology, but Callie wasn't ready to broach *that* topic yet. "We've got some brewed now, actually. Do you take it black?"

"That would be wonderful." Elena slipped into one of the chairs, a modular seat attached to the floor that could lock in place or fold down out of the way, as needed.

Callie liked Elena's voice. Her accent was unlike any Callie had heard before –and she'd spoken to people from Earth, the Jovian Imperative, the valleys of Mars, and dozens of stations and colony worlds in this solar system and beyond the twenty-nine bridges. There was an odd formality to Elena's tone, too, but that could all be explained by the linguistic drift of centuries. Callie found it charming, and was annoyed with herself for being charmed.

Stephen sighed. "I suppose coffee won't kill her, though I'd rather start her on water and rice. I'm going to see how her medications are coming along. Send her down to me once you're done chatting?" He lumbered out of the room.

Callie sorted through the drinking bulbs in the cupboard until she found a proper mug. They were under steady thrust on their way to Meditreme Station, experiencing enough gravity for liquid to stay in a cup, so they might as well enjoy it. She decanted a generous quantity of coffee and slid the cup in front of Elena, who wrapped her hands around the mug and lowered her nose over the rim, inhaling.

"Oh, that's good." She took a sip, then caught Callie's eye. "This is all so strange. When I set out on my journey, I expected... I didn't expect this. To be marooned? Wrecked? I wish I knew what happened."

"Most people would be a gibbering mess in your position," Callie said. "Stephen, Doctor Baros I mean, said your memory should recover soon. Maybe you can fill in some of the gaps then." *And fill us in, too, while you're at it.*

Elena looked into her cup as though she was staring into the abyss. "I'm afraid to find out what I've forgotten. Something bad must have happened. Your computer, Shall? He said the *Anjou*'s engines were altered. My crew–" Her voice broke, and she cleared her throat. "My crewmates are gone. We should be light years away from this solar system. I just don't understand."

Callie decided now was as good a time as any to address the elephant in the room. Except it was more like a squid. "When you woke up, you mentioned something about making first contact?"

Elena made a small strangled sound, and her hand trembled, sloshing a few drops of coffee over the rim of the cup. "I can't remember, but there are flashes of a place. Some kind of hangar. A space station? There were machines, working on my ship, I think? Changing it? If it wasn't a human station, then I suppose... but..."

Callie waited a moment to see if Elena was going to continue, but the biologist just stared off into space. Callie said, "Whatever happened to your crew, none of you recorded anything about it in your ship's databanks, or at least nothing we could recover – your systems are kind of a mess. But... it's entirely possible you did encounter alien life. Even an alien space station."

Elena raised her gaze. Her eyes were so dark brown they were nearly black. "We found simple organisms on Europa, even before we set out. But that's not the kind of life you mean, is it? Microbes don't build space stations."

"No, they don't." Callie took a breath. "Just over three hundred years ago, humanity made first contact with intelligent alien life."

Elena surprised Callie by breaking into a wide smile. "I never doubted sentient life existed out there among the stars. The universe is just too big, too full of planets, for humans to be unique. I did wonder if we'd ever encounter such life, given the vastness of space – it would be like two particular particles of salt in the ocean happening to bump into one another. I was chosen for my mission not just to bring the stored embryos to term and establish our colony, but also to study any alien organisms we might find at our destination. We never dared dream we'd find *intelligent* life, though. What are the aliens like? Are they... friendly? That sounds so stupid. God. Are we able to communicate with them?"

Callie smiled back. "Friendly? More or less. We can communicate, though it's not always the smoothest."

Elena leaned eagerly forward. "What do they look like? Their physical structure, I mean?"

"I'm not a biologist, or any other kind of scientist, but as I understand it, the aliens don't correspond to any of the taxonomies we have for creatures on Earth. They're smaller than humans – OK, I'm just going to say it straight out: superficially, they look more like octopuses than anything else on Earth."

Elena blinked. "Talking squid from outer space? Really? Like in an old sci-fi novel?"

Callie snorted. "Actual scientists get mad when we call the aliens squid, or octopodes, because apparently there are a million major differences, but at a glance, the aliens have a central body with a sort of rounded hump surrounded by eyes, and a varying number of limbs that are more like tentacles than arms, though really they aren't much like either one, and they're mostly radially symmetric. When they stand up on their tentacles and run around, they're about a meter high."

"Differing numbers of limbs, you said? They exhibit that much variation as a species?"

"Ha. That's just the beginning of their variations. We're not sure *what* they look like in their natural, baseline form. Most of the Liars are big believers in self-improvement. Humanity has encountered something like fifteen hundred separate clans, or groups, or families, or tribes, and while there are broad similarities in their physiology, there's a lot of variation, too. We've encountered tiny Liars the size of your palm – they look like skittering disembodied hands – and we met one group modified for *unprotected* space travel. Like, their bodies are ships. They're the size of whales, drifting slowly through space, usually in hibernation. Those are extremes, but all the Liars augment themselves mechanically, or alter their genetic code, or reshape their bodies for different environments. That willingness to transform their bodies is the closest thing they have to a unifying culture."

Elena wrinkled her nose, and, damn it, Callie found the expression adorable. "They call themselves Liars?"

"That's just about the only thing they *don't* call themselves. The various clans claim a lot of different names – well over three thousand have been recorded, last I heard. There's a fancy designation scientists use for the species as a whole, but yeah, most people just call them Liars."

Elena nodded. "You said we can communicate with them, but it's difficult. Because... they lie?"

"Oh yes. The first Liars made contact with Earth in the most dramatic way possible, appearing out of nowhere in the vicinity of Jupiter and moving rapidly toward Earth in a fleet of what were, for the time, impossibly advanced ships, though they look pretty ordinary by modern standards. Shaped like starfish, most of them – a pretty high percentage of Liars have a fondness for radial symmetry in their designs. That first group of aliens took up a position near the moon and began broadcasting at Earth in every language – including several dead ones. The message claimed they were emissaries from a vast galactic confederation, come to trade with us, solve all our pressing ecological problems, and welcome us into a thriving interstellar community. We were invited to join a league of hundreds of sentient species. In exchange, all the visitors wanted was several million gallons of sea water, and permission to inhabit Venus in perpetuity."

"That's unbelievable!"

"You have no idea how right you are." Callie made herself a cup of coffee while she talked. "Earth was a mess when you left – that's *why* you left – but it was in even worse shape by the time the Liars arrived. So Earth made the deal, and got some remarkable technological advances in return – improved communications technology, an early version of the Tanzer drive that propels this ship, new forms of programmable matter – they were miracle workers. The Liars collected their seawater, promised to be in touch soon about taking human ambassadors to the galactic central hub... and then they disappeared into the clouds of Venus. As far as we know they're still there. When we send probes, the probes stop working, and the one time Earth was dumb enough to send a drone military force, they didn't come back either. Technically the agreement we made to give the Liars possession of Venus is still binding, even though it was made under false pretenses."

Elena frowned. "So... there was no confederation? I don't understand."

"Neither did we. A few months later *another* ship, this one all alone but much larger than the others, also appeared near Jupiter, seemingly out of nowhere. The aliens on board were clearly the same species as the ones we'd met before, though they called themselves by a different name. We asked about the galactic empire, and they said the first aliens we'd talked to were liars. There was no peaceful galactic confederation, just a war-torn galaxy where scores of races clashed for supremacy. We'd been duped by alien con artists who'd sold us a bunch of junk and empty promises, but these new aliens told the *truth* – or so they said. If we had any sense at all, we'd align ourselves with their faction, and accept their protection. Otherwise, we could expected to be invaded by an army of rapacious alien grasshoppers bent on stripping our planet of all its natural resources. And, by the way, if we weren't doing anything with Mercury, could they have it in exchange for their help? Before we could respond to that request, another ship arrived, also out by Jupiter, and *those* aliens said the first two groups couldn't be trusted, and, in fact, we should really accept help from these newcomers, because we'd need their help to escape a cosmic horror that was switching off the stars like lamps, one by one, and coming our way. Incidentally, they liked the look of some of Jupiter's moons, and they only wanted four or five of them in exchange for helping us set up a force field to protect us from extermination..."

Elena frowned. "Which group was telling the truth?"

Callie sipped her coffee and shook her head. "None of them."

CHAPTER 4

"It was *all* lies?" Elena said.

"Mostly stories adapted from our own media, we think, literature and film and immersives – simple science fiction scenarios, playing on our hopes and fears. We figured out pretty quickly that none of the aliens could be trusted... and that's still our policy. We keep trading with them, though."

"But how, if there's no basis of trust?"

"They lie about big things, like where they come from, what they believe, even the nature of the universe – you don't ask a Liar to talk philosophy. And they'll lie about insignificant things, like where they were yesterday, or who their friends are, or which way the bathroom is – you don't ask a Liar for directions, either. But they like to talk about technology, and they like to tinker, and they like making deals, and they don't usually lie about that. If you offer them something, in exchange for something else, and you make *really sure* the thing they're selling you does what they claim, most of the time it works out all right."

"So they lie. But *why* do they lie?"

Callie shrugged. "Of the thousand and a half bands

of Liars we've met, whether it's a dozen on a small ship or a civilization of millions settled on another planet, each group has a different story about their origins, their goals, and the nature of the universe. Every time they've claimed to have an ancestral homeworld, and we've gone to look, we've found an uninhabited rock where nothing like the Liars could have plausibly evolved – and sometimes there's no planet there at all. The Liars often claim there are lots of other intelligent alien species in the universe, but we've never met any of them, or seen any signs."

Elena rolled the mug back and forth between her hands, a worry line creasing her forehead. "I don't understand. What do they say when they're caught in a lie? Do they offer any explanation?"

"Oh, sure. They say the lies are translation errors, or that we talked to heretics from a doomsday religion, or that *our* ambassadors are mentally ill pathological liars, or that our feeble human minds can't comprehend their truths, or that we must have followed their directions incorrectly, or that reality is a glitched simulation. A Liar will tell you the sky on Earth is green, and when you object, he'll explain that humans just have inferior color receptors. They're absolutely unflappable and endlessly adaptable and totally infuriating and they've driven generations of xenopsychologists to the brink of madness."

Elena looked troubled. Callie had grown up knowing about Liars, but she could imagine how hearing about the aliens for the first time would be alarming. "If the only thing they have in common is lying, then clearly they have a culture built on lies. Do they lie among *themselves*, or just to humans?"

"We're not sure. Stephen agrees with you, and thinks it's a cultural thing: we're outsiders, and as such, the Liars are forbidden to tell us any *real* truths, possibly for religious reasons. That's a fairly popular theory, but it's no more verifiable than any other. Me, I hesitate to assume the Liars even share a single culture. What does it mean to meet a 'human', after all? Even here, in this system, there are enclaves of hardcore agrarians on Earth who refuse to have anything to do with space travel or any tech from the last few centuries: they try to live a pre-first-contact existence. There are people who live almost entirely in virtual-reality submersion tanks, and bicycle fanatics, and spaceborn who've never been down a gravity well and never will, and a thousand weirder cults and cultures. There are twenty-nine solar systems inhabited by humans, including one nobody ever comes *back* from, because the settlers there are isolationists, and probably violently so. Every system has developed its own cultural qualities over the centuries, and every settlement in every system has its own set of quirks. I figure Liars probably exhibit the same range of variation, except their original civilization is even older than ours, and a *lot* more fragmented. We've found them scattered all over the galaxy, after all, pretty much everywhere we go."

"I guess the idea of a planet full of monocultural humanoids with bumpy foreheads who all follow a thinly disguised version of the Bushido code is ridiculous," Elena said. "Nothing's that simple."

Callie chuckled. "Our contact with the Liars has been good for humanity overall, though. They're never violent – if trading fails, and deception fails, they shrug and move on. They seem to believe the universe is plenty big, so it's stupid to fight over resources when they can trade for them or look elsewhere instead. Also, to be frank, we can't offer them too much beyond raw materials, since every Liar group we've met is more technologically advanced than we are. The Liars mostly settle on planets we don't want anyway, ones with atmospheres that are toxic soup to humans – their tendency to body modification makes them wildly adaptable. Apart from the ones on Venus, who are totally incommunicado, the Liars don't have any permanent settlements in our solar system, though some live on our planets and moons and space stations, often working as technicians and engineers. It makes sense – half the technology we use came from Liars in the first place. We pay them hourly, though, and never up front. They're unreliable as a rule, but their knowledge is an asset. They do have to be watched, though. If left to their own devices, they like to… tinker."

Elena made a low *ahhh* sound. "You think these Liars are the ones who 'tinkered' with my ship?"

"That's our working theory. We figure your ship ran into a group of Liars. Maybe even a band that's never encountered humans before, and weren't sure what to make of you. We've never documented any violent clashes or attacks, but sometimes… incidents happen. Some of the Liars enjoy making adjustments and improvements, even when no one asked them to. Many of them have a spirit of… experimentation." Callie thought about Drake and Janice, but mentioning *their* experience as the sole survivors of a shipwreck "rescued" by a group of Liars wouldn't be very comforting to Elena right now.

"Why would they alter our ship, though?"

"Maybe they thought it was broken, or lost, or just needed aesthetic improvements. Who knows?"

Elena sat forward, eyes shining. "But they wouldn't have hurt my crew? My colleagues might still be alive out there, somewhere?"

"I have no idea, Elena. *Something* happened to your crew. Maybe you'll get your memories back, and you can figure out where to go from there."

"If they're still alive, I have to find them. Can I – would it be possible – to backtrack? Does the *Anjou* have a record of where it's been?"

"Ah. Yes. But it doesn't make a lot of sense. It looks like you traveled about fifty light years in under thirty seconds."

Elena slumped. "That's obviously impossible."

"Well… yes and no. It is possible to travel that far, or even farther, that quickly. But *your* ship couldn't have done it. The Liars opened the galaxy to us, but the *Anjou* doesn't have that kind of tech."

"The Liars gave you new propulsion technology?" Elena leaned forward, clearly deciding to focus on something other than the fate of her crew. "That Tanzer drive you mentioned? The *Anjou* could get up to about ten percent of light speed, but it took time to accelerate, and we used explosive nuclear reactions for propulsion. But the kind of speeds you're talking about, don't they violate the laws of physics?"

"It's not about speed. Our ships are faster than yours, and most are powered by Tanzer drives – they're basically magnetoplasmadynamic thrusters, but they use a ridiculously efficient propellant the Liars developed… and I see your eyes glazing over."

Elena winced. "I'd blame my cognitive impairments,

but in truth, physics and engineering were never my specialties. As long as our family car drove itself reliably, I never thought much about what was happening under the hood."

"Don't let Ashok sit next to you during dinner, then, or you'll learn more than you ever wanted to about thrust. Anyway, the Tanzer drives are great, and give us good speed and maneuverability within solar systems, but the *big* thing the Liars gave us – eventually – was the bridges. That's how we travel light years in under half a minute. The reason those first Liars kept appearing near Jupiter was because there's a wormhole there. Or a place where a wormhole *can* be – we call it a bridgehead. We think the bridges are artificial, constructed by someone, millions or billions of years ago – the Liars sometimes take credit for building the network, and sometimes claim it's a natural phenomenon, and sometimes say other aliens made it. Who knows? The point is, if we bombard that particular spot in space with the right kind of radiation, it opens a passageway. We can travel almost instantaneously to any of twenty-eight other systems, scattered across the galaxy, with the destination dependent on the exact energies we bombard the bridgehead with. Once we pop out the other side, we have to make our way with conventional propulsion, but even so, the bridges have opened up a vast expanse of space for us. Over the past few centuries we've established scores of colony worlds, and ships routinely make supply runs to systems hundreds of light years away."

"That's astonishing," Elena said. "Though it does make my mission a bit redundant. I should be happy humankind has found so many homes among the stars, but it's hard not to be disappointed. Five hundred years ago... things were bad. We thought the goldilocks ships were the last hope for humanity to survive. We believed our work mattered."

"It did, though. If nothing else, the goldilocks ships gave people hope, right?"

"I didn't anticipate my life's work becoming a symbolic gesture."

Callie shrugged. "More than most lives amount to. Do you think you'll go back to Earth?"

"It seems almost cowardly, when there are all these new worlds to explore, but... What's it like there now? In my time..." She grimaced. "Between the storms, the jellyfish infestations, the untreatable bacteria, the desiccation of the west..."

"Earth... it's a walled garden. It's mostly where people live when they're afraid to live anywhere else, I guess. The Liars gave us tech to scrub the atmosphere and sequester carbon, and there was a big exodus of colonists once the bridgeheads opened, so that reduced the population load significantly. Those left behind got busy on restoration. Earth is nice enough, but boring. I haven't been there since I was a little girl, growing up in the Hawaiian Archipelago, spending summers with my grandparents in a bubble settlement near Old Lisbon. Gravity wells don't agree with me."

Elena chuckled. "I suppose I should feel homesick, but I don't, really. For one thing, the home I knew must be unrecognizable, and for another... I always wanted the stars."

"You were brave as hell to do it, way back then," Callie said. "Traveling in space is dangerous *now*. In those days it was..."

"Suicidal, I think was the word you used."

Callie winced. "You heard that? Sorry. The difference between brave and suicidal is a matter of perspective."

Elena sipped, then nodded. "We knew the risks. We just thought the potential reward made those risks worthwhile. Competition was fierce to join the goldilocks crews. The selection process was grueling, but I wanted to see the light of other stars on other worlds. To be part of the next stage of human development. It suited my sense of adventure, too. Even if we never made it anywhere, I knew I'd get to spend at least one day every several years awake on a starship, hurtling toward the barely-known. I never found anything more intoxicating."

"You're in luck, then. You can explore a lot of other worlds now."

Elena laughed. "I'm not sure how I'm going to afford it, since you've all disappointed me greatly by failing to create a post-scarcity utopian society. I suspect my scientific skills are a bit out of date. I have as many valuable skills here as a barber-surgeon from the 1600s would have in my time."

"Nah, you have options. There aren't many people around these days who lived on Earth five hundred years ago. There are probably a lot of people who'd pay for your story and insights."

"Oh, good." Elena's voice went dull: that bleakness again. "I can be a sideshow. A curiosity."

"I was thinking more a writer, or a lecturer, but there are other options. The *Anjou* is still floating out there, in need of a tow, and as the only member of the crew around, the ship belongs to you. I told the local authorities on Meditreme Station we'd found a wrecked ship with a survivor on board, and they tagged the *Anjou* in their system, so no scavengers will carry it away in the meantime. No legal ones, anyway, and illegal ones won't try to steal a ship that's tagged. Not around here. They know I might come after them. You can sell the *Anjou* – I'm sure it has some value."

"It's really mine? It was never mine. Our ship and everything on board was the property of the One World Emergency Government."

"We've got a lot more than one world now, and out here the laws of the Trans-Neptunian Authority hold sway. The rules of salvage are pretty straightforward. If you find something abandoned in space, you can take it. If someone with a valid ownership claim comes forward, they can recover their property if they pay the expenses incurred by the salvagers, plus ten percent of the property's value, as determined by an impartial appraisal AI. As the only verified member of the *Anjou*'s crew, you've got such a claim."

"So the *Anjou* is mine... but only if I pay you a percentage?"

"Well, in theory, but in light of everything you went through, I'm willing to waive the fee."

Elena leaned back in her chair, some tension draining out of her. "That's good of you, captain. I mean that. You could have easily taken advantage of me. I wouldn't have known."

"Nah, I'm a sworn officer of the Trans-Neptunian Authority. I have to follow the law."

"I'm in good hands, then. But what value does the *Anjou* have? As an antique? A historical curiosity?"

Callie moved away from the counter and sat down in the modular chair beside Elena. "Honestly? Yes. There are probably museums that would buy it, or collectors.

We took a lot of things of value off the ship already –
the intact biological specimens, and some of the more
portable components." Plus the weird thing Ashok had
found in the engine room, but that was a subject for later.
"You can sell that stuff, too, and keep the proceeds."
Callie almost automatically said "minus our expenses for
transporting you," but didn't. The *White Raven*'s accounts
weren't in bad shape lately, after all those speed runs to
the Imperative. She could afford an uncharacteristic act
of generosity.

Elena reached out and touched the back of Callie's
hand. "I don't know why you're being so good to me,
but I appreciate it."

"What can I say? Kalea Machedo, scourge of the
spaceways. Don't tell anyone I have a heart."

The ship's computer spoke up. "Approaching
Meditreme Station. Please prepare for deceleration."

"Are you ready to see the future?" Callie said.

"Ready or not, here I am," Elena replied.

CHAPTER 5

Callie took Elena to the observation deck and helped strap her into a seat where she could watch through the viewport. "See that thing that looks like a crystal chandelier crossed with a wedding cake? That's Meditreme Station." They were already decelerating, thrust gravity easing off into weightlessness, and the ship's reaction wheels were spinning to orient them for their approach to the docks.

"It's *huge*," Elena said in awe. The original planitesimal, honeycombed with tunnels, was impossible to see beneath the layers of decks and modules and spires, the whole station spinning at a rate sufficient to impart a comfortable level of gravity in the outer rings, with lights blinking and shining from every curve and angle out into the local darkness. Ships of all sizes and shapes, including a few outré-looking Liar vessels, floated in the vicinity like exotic fish around a coral reef.

"Biggish, anyway," Callie said. "Home to around fifty thousand souls most days. Meditreme Station is the headquarters of the Trans-Neptunian Authority, the main human habitation beyond Jupiter's moons, for scavengers, miners, scientists, and miscellaneous spacefaring types. Our ship's computer–"

"His name is Shall, he said?"

Callie managed to keep her expression smooth. "Some of the crew call the computer that, yes. He's making contact with the presiding machine intelligence on the station, and they'll do a little AI-to-AI negotiation and then guide us into the docks."

The whirling station grew larger, then seemed to stop spinning as the *White Raven* matched the station's rotation. The false gravity of acceleration dissolved completely, and the straps holding Callie into her seat pressed against her chest and hips, keeping her in place. The ship floated toward an open door in a module that was easily big enough to accommodate the *White Raven*. Once inside, magnetic clamps grabbed the ship, and the station's outer door closed. After a few moments, the inner door of the oversized airlock yawned open, and a conveyor belt carried them into a cavernous hangar full of ships, cargo being loaded and unloaded, repairs being made, fuel and supply stores being replenished, and the general bustle of frontier commerce.

The transition from thrust gravity to microgravity to spin gravity could give the inexperienced vomitous conniptions, and Callie kept an eye on Elena to see if the biologist was going to be sick. She looked a little queasy and pale, but she gave a weak smile, and Callie decided she'd probably be OK.

Callie unstrapped herself, then helped Elena out of her seat. Stephen spoke over the ship's speakers. "Captain, could you bring me my patient now? I've synthesized the last of her recovery drugs, and I'd very much like to help her clear her head."

"I could use you down in the cargo hold when you're

done up there, cap," Ashok said over the same speakers.

Callie sighed. "Computer, will you tell Doctor Oh how to find the medical suite?"

"Of course, Callie."

"Captain Machedo," she snapped. Elena gave her an odd look, and Callie resisted the urge to explain herself, especially since the explanation might make her seem even more ridiculous than yelling at the computer had.

"Of course, Captain Machedo." The computer didn't sound amused, or even annoyed, which Callie found even more infuriating. "Elena?" he said. "Just head out to the corridor and take a left."

"I'll talk to you soon." Callie tried to give Elena a reassuring smile. "You seem pretty smart and funny already, so I can't wait to hear you after the holes in your memory get filled in."

The biologist chuckled and departed with a little wave, only stumbling a little as she got used to the gravity level.

Callie went to the machine shop to see what Ashok wanted. He squatted beside a work table so the surface was just at his eye level – or the level of all the accumulated lenses where his eyes should have been, anyway. She stood beside him, looking down at the object on the table: a cube about half a meter wide on each side, made of some greasy-looking black substance, with a single input port shaped like a crescent moon on top. The thing Ashok had discovered hooked up in the *Anjou*'s engine room, and found so bizarre he'd carefully detached it and brought it along for further study. "What am I looking at, Ashok?"

"I have no idea." Ashok usually confronted technological problems with glee, but he seemed subdued now, as if he'd met his match. "Most of the changes to the *Anjou* were cosmetic and basically pointless, curlicues of wiring that went nowhere and did nothing, external engine parts that weren't even hooked up to anything – but *this* thing was wired into the ship's propulsion and navigation systems, and it was definitely doing something. I can't see what's going on inside the box, not with any of the equipment here–" he tapped the array of lenses on his face "–or with the ship's sensors. Every diagnostic particle and wave I throw at this thing just gets absorbed. I don't even know what material the box is made of. It looks almost *gooey*, doesn't it, like it was dipped in axle grease? Seems like it would leave smears on your clothes if you brushed up against it. But it's hard as iron and smooth to the touch." He tapped the cube with one of the fingers on his non-prosthetic hand to demonstrate, rubbing his fingertips together afterward with a shrug. "That greasy look is some kind of purely optical effect, and I can't figure it out. Anyway. If the navigational data on the *Anjou* is accurate, this box somehow allowed the ship to travel about fifty light years in twenty-one seconds."

"*Exactly* twenty-one seconds?"

Ashok nodded. "The same length of time it takes to traverse a wormhole from one end to the other."

Callie grunted. The implications of that were interesting, but she decided not to dwell on them, especially since corrupted data was a more plausible explanation. Horses, not zebras – and certainly not centaurs. "OK, so we've got a magical mystery box. What do we do with it?"

Ashok stood up, pistons hissing and servos humming in his augmented legs. "I want to break it open."

"But."

"But it could be full of explosions, so I won't. Also, I don't know how. I tried to chisel out a bit of the casing for analysis and broke my diamond drill bit without even leaving a scratch." He rubbed the back of his head, which was still mostly skin over bone. "OK. If our working theory is the *Anjou* encountered a group of Liars out in deep space, and the Liars augmented and altered the ship for whatever reason, including attaching this weird cube, then this is Liar tech. I'm friendly with one of the Liar engineers on the station, so I'll ask him to take a look, and see if he recognizes it."

"You think you'll get a straight answer out of him?"

"Of course not. But I might get an answer that's twisty in a useful way."

"Fair enough. I'll go with you. I'm a little curious to find out what's in this box myself."

"Spiders or gold, spiders or gold," Ashok said.

"Oh, Ashok. It's like you never even consider the possibility of golden spiders."

Out on the hangar deck, a Liar technician slither-walked toward them, four tentacles undulating underneath as three more waved diagnostic devices in the air. "Greetings, White Raven. You wanted to see me?" His artificial voice was bombastically deep and booming. "His" wasn't really accurate – Liars didn't exactly fit into human gender categories, and when it came to biological sex, Liars either reproduced asexually or had multiple sexes or cloned themselves, depending on which group you were talking about; they seemed as variable in their reproductive strategies as they were in everything else. Some of them selected gendered pronouns when dealing with humans, though, and this one liked "he" to go with his performatively masculine voice.

"Hello, Cuz," Ashok said. At Callie's questioning look, he said, "His name is My Cousin Paolo, but I call him Cuz for short."

"White Raven and I are old friends," the Liar said. "I honor him by allowing this informality. The use of nicknames is a sign of deep affection and respect among my people."

Callie decided not to ask why the Liar addressed Ashok by the name of her ship, or why he was called My Cousin Paolo. Liar names were just odd, that was all. Some were incomprehensible mishmashes of sound, or grandiose titles (or both, like Tlthm the Solarian, who operated a salvage and repair shop on the lower levels of Meditreme Station), or common nouns (Callie had met Liars who called themselves Brick, Loaf, and Shoe), or phrases poetic or dull, or even ordinary human names – sometimes a Liar would claim to have exactly the same name as the person they were talking to, often expressing astonishment at the outlandish coincidence. Really, My Cousin Paolo wasn't even all that strange a name by Liar standards.

"Does your ship require service?" the Liar said.

"Not at the moment," Ashok said. "We found something in a wreck, though – an engine component we don't recognize, or maybe part of a navigation system – and I wanted you to take a look. We think it might be something your people made."

A couple of the Liar's pseudopods undulated lazily in the air. "My people made everything. My ninety-nine-times-progenitor is the one who seeded your planet Earth with life, in the times prehistoric. Do you have this component with you?"

Ashok beckoned him closer, then crouched down to

open up the duffel bag he'd stashed the cube in, revealing the greasy black shape of the box inside. "What do you think?"

My Cousin Paolo made a high-pitched keening sound that seemed to come not from his artificial voicebox but from some more organic place, which was astonishing in itself – Liars were almost never heard to vocalize naturally, and the prevailing theory was they communicated among themselves with pheromones, gestures, and color-changing skin cells rather than sound. The Liar scuttled away from the cube and began to shout, his booming mechanical voice overlaying the high-pitched wail, a single word over and over: "Axiomatic! Axiomatic! Axiomatic!"

The Liar raced away faster than Callie had ever seen one of its kind move before, using all his tentacles in a complicated leaping and vaulting motion, at one point spinning end-over-end like a wheel, before disappearing into a three-foot-square access hatch in a far wall.

"That was not the reaction I was expecting." Ashok zipped the duffel closed.

"Axiomatic? What does that mean?"

Ashok's upper left eye-lens rotated at her. "It means self-evident. From the Greek 'ἀξίωμα,' meaning 'something known to be true.'"

Callie glared at him. "There are so many things in this hangar I could hit you with, Ashok. I know what the *word* means. Why did that Liar shout it and run away?"

"I have no idea. He's never done anything like that before. It was unusual even by Liar standards. Maybe the box frightened him?"

"It's a black box," Callie said. "What's scary about a black box?"

"Maybe whatever's inside it?"

Callie shivered despite herself. "You're sure that thing's not pouring out radiation or cram packed full of imminent explosions?"

"I have no idea what it's full of, but it's not putting out *anything*."

"Be careful with it anyway. Liars do bizarre things sometimes, so maybe Paolo *wasn't* fleeing in terror from an alien artifact that's about to kill us all, but go easy until we figure out what this thing is."

"I did have another diagnostic approach in mind," Ashok said. "I could plug the *White Raven*'s navigation and propulsion systems into the box and see what happens. I saw how it was hooked up on the *Anjou*, so reproducing those connections would be easy enough."

"No. New rule. We do not plug mysterious alien technology into my ship."

Ashok continued without changing inflection. "Or, alternately, I could get Shall to simulate a navigation and propulsion system. Then I could plug this box into another computer and fool it into thinking it's hooked up to an actual ship. Then we can see what happens in a safe, sane, and simulated way."

Callie chewed her lower lip for a moment. "OK. Do that. But plug the box into a separate, air-gapped system, totally sequestered – I don't want you accidentally uploading some alien program onto the *White Raven*'s main computer, or the larger station network."

"Cap. You wound me. Security is the first thing I think about when I get up in the morning and the last thing I think about before I go to sleep."

"You don't sleep."

"Not true. I just sleep one hemisphere of my brain

at a time. It's much more efficient than your ridiculous whole-brain dream-state approach."

Callie returned to her ship and made her way to the medical suite. Elena was asleep on a gel-filled mattress, wearing only a thin gown, and Stephen sat on a stool in the corner tapping away at a handheld slab of smart matter. Callie resolutely resisted the urge to let her gaze linger on Elena. "Is she all right?"

Stephen held up the handheld terminal, which showed an array of blips and waveforms that meant nothing to Callie. "All her vitals look good. No bad reactions to the medication. I had to dig pretty deep in the Tangle to find the protocols for treating someone awakened from that particular form of cryosleep. She should return to consciousness in an hour or so with her memory restored, in theory. Are you going to be on the ship for a while?"

"Why?"

"I need to visit a chemist to pick up supplies for my next holy day. I don't have the right precursors on board to produce the sacrament myself – in fact, I had to use some of my personal stores to synthesize Doctor Oh's medications. A lot of her therapy is about properly rebalancing her brain chemistry. I'll go now, if you can watch over her, in case she wakes up earlier than expected. I'd ask Drake and Janice to keep an eye on her, but they might be a bit much for Elena to take in. Her visit to the future hasn't been all that disorienting yet, but if she sees them, or Ashok, without proper preparation, she might be alarmed. The definition of 'human' wasn't quite as broad in her era as it is in ours."

Callie nodded, though personally she thought Elena would be more interested than frightened. "Fair enough.

When's your next holy day, anyway?"

"Just a few days from now. Any idea where we'll be then? It's always better if I can spend it with the congregation here."

"I'm not entirely sure, but I'll try not to schedule any medical emergencies while you're in the throes of your sacred ecstasies."

"That's probably for the best. If you get hurt, Ashok will have to sew you up, and you might end up with a robotic elbow or a flamethrower for a foot." Stephen took a last look at Elena's vitals, then headed off for the lower markets of Meditreme Station. His church believed in the use of psychedelic drugs to induce entheogenic and entactogenic states – a sense of connection with the divine, and a sense of connection with other living beings, respectively. Apparently the experience was very moving and meaningful, and could be made even more so in a cuddle pile of co-religionists. Stephen said knowing the feelings were induced chemically didn't detract from the profundity of the devotions: "Everything we feel is chemicals anyway. Isn't that miracle enough?"

His faith didn't appeal to Callie, though. She felt either apathy or hostility toward almost everyone, and she was happy that way. Every once in a while she met someone she felt connected to, without the necessity of psychedelics. Her gaze fell upon Elena, who was Sleeping Beauty once again, and she looked deliberately away.

Callie sat on the stool Stephen had vacated and scrolled through her handheld, taking half an hour to catch up on the news in the Tangle. A new colony world had been established near bridgehead twelve; another expedition had vanished without a trace investigating the reclusive settlers beyond bridgehead twenty-nine;

another group of Liars claimed to possess technology that could communicate instantaneously even across vast distances, but as usual, "technical problems" made a demonstration impossible; Io was having another doomed referendum on declaring independence from the rest of the Jovian Imperative.

The only things that really caught her attention were a few comments on the local social network reporting a mass exodus of Liars from Meditreme Station. There were only a hundred or so Liars on the station anyway, most from the same clan or family or tribe, and almost all of them seemed in a sudden hurry to leave, taking off on their own ships or buying passage on others. She thought of the screaming Liar in the hangar, and her guts clenched. They'd brought that artifact onto the station, and the Liars had fled. Even accounting for the basic weird unpredictability of the species, that was too close to cause and effect to ignore. She needed to call Ashok and tell him to stick that box inside an unmanned probe and set it on a course for the sun–

Her handheld suddenly buzzed with an urgent emergency notification, blanking out her screen, and Ashok's unlovely face appeared. "Captain, this – sorry, I'm just – I did the thing, with the emulation, the simulation, I plugged in the cube–"

Elena suddenly groaned and tried to sit up, falling back before she made it halfway. Had the buzzer awakened her?

Callie rose from the stool, but Elena would keep: the other issue was more potentially existential. "Slow down, Ashok. What is it?" He must have figured it out, whatever deadly secret the cube held, and now he was breaking the bad news that they were all poisoned or irradiated or about to be swallowed by a miniature black hole–

He took a deep breath. "Captain. This device we found on the *Anjou*… I think… it seems to be a bridge generator."

She frowned. "That little black box can activate a bridge? It's like a thousand times smaller than the activator they have at the Jupiter bridgehead. That validates our theory about the *Anjou* finding an undiscovered bridgehead out there in space somewhere. If we can figure out where, that could be valuable information. I still don't see how the *Anjou* made it out of the Jovian bridgehead on this side without detection and ended up floating out here with the ice clods, unless there's some kind of stealth technology–"

"Cap!" Ashok said – shouted, really. "You don't understand. Listen. This device isn't a bridge activator. It doesn't provide access to existing wormholes. It *creates new ones*."

Callie tried to make sense of that, but her mind resisted. Nobody could *make* a wormhole, any more than you could make a star. You found a bridge; you opened one; you traversed one. There was no "making." The bridges had already been made, millions of years ago, either by the Liars or some long-dead race of ancient alien geniuses. "You're going to have to take me through this at a slow walk, Ashok."

"I've run the simulation a dozen times, and unless I'm suddenly terrible at my job, I'm telling you: this machine can make new bridges. We don't have to enter or emerge from any of the twenty-nine known bridgeheads. This device can open a *new* wormhole bridge, from anywhere, to anywhere – assuming I can figure out the coordinate system it uses, anyway. So far I'm only able to simulate random openings, though they all lead to points within the Milky Way. That's how the *Anjou* made it back to our solar system: they just opened a bridge from wherever they were and passed through and emerged in Trans-Neptunian space, exactly where we found them floating."

Callie sat back down, mind spinning like a reaction wheel. The bridges were like subway lines on Earth and Luna and Mars. You got on at a particular stop, and got off at another stop, and that was it. There was no stopping in between stations. You couldn't just hop off wherever you wanted. If Ashok was right, they could... What? Make their *own* stations? They could go anywhere?

The discovery of bridge technology had revolutionized humanity's relationship with the universe. If this greasy black cube worked the way Ashok thought, then that relationship was about to be transformed again. To be able to go anywhere...

"Check it again," she said.

"I checked it—"

"*Again*. Get the ship's computer to look over your work too. This isn't something we can afford to be wrong about. If there's a group of Liars somewhere out there with this kind of technology? This is huge, Ashok." Callie had never fantasized about having eighty-foot-high statues of herself erected in her honor, but if she could give this kind of tech to her bosses at the Trans-Neptunian Authority, she might have to get used to the idea.

Assuming they didn't all die. "Ashok, all the Liars fled the station, right after you showed Paolo that device. Why would they be so afraid of it?"

"Well, I mean... the box opens wormholes. It would

be really bad to open a wormhole *here*. If I didn't know what I was doing, and I had the box plugged into the *White Raven* for real instead of in a simulation... Sudden breaches in space time are bad for Liars and other living things."

She imagined a wormhole opening in the center of Meditreme Station, and shuddered. That notion of a black hole devouring them all wasn't so far off. "Get that thing off the station, Ashok. Put the box in the canoe and send it out remotely, as far as you can. Tell the port authority you just want to test the canoe's controls."

"Aw, cap, it's not like I'm going to accidentally push the wrong button. The bridge generator doesn't even *have* buttons–"

"For all we know that thing has a countdown clock ticking away in its heart. Put it into the canoe. We'll pick it up later. We can discuss whether we want to risk our *own* lives, as a crew – I'm not risking the whole station."

"Oh captain, my captain," Ashok said, which was his usual way of indicating he'd obey and order even though he didn't like it. Callie cut their connection.

Elena groaned and made another attempt to rise. This time she lurched completely upright in bed and stared at the far wall without seeming to see it. "I remember." Her voice sounded rough and sand-scoured. "I remember what we found. The station. The creatures."

"We know what the Liars did to your ship." Callie's voice didn't shake. All those years of captaining and testing the iron of her will against smugglers and fugitives and pirates were paying off now. "The changes they made. This technology... it's like nothing we've seen before. The Liars you met must be far more advanced than–"

"They weren't Liars." Elena's voice was cold and without inflection, her facial expression that of a corpse freshly laid out on a slab. "They weren't anything like the creatures you described. Child-sized octopuses? No. The aliens we found were something else. Something... bigger." She moved her head slowly and met Callie's eyes. Those flashes of bleakness Callie had seen in Elena before were mere shadows. This was a black hole. "Something terrible."

She took a deep breath, and told Callie what she remembered.

CHAPTER 6

Elena was the last of her crew to wake. Uzoma was there when Elena's pod slid open and she sat up, gasping, a cocktail of strange drugs coursing through her, making everything shimmer and effervesce at the edges. She thought of grizzly bears, and how they awoke from hibernation, hungry and furious and dripping with ice. An alarm howled shrilly elsewhere in the ship but then abruptly cut off, and Elena's ears rang with silence.

"Are we there?" Elena said.

Uzoma's impassive face gave nothing away. "No. We have encountered an... anomaly. A structure."

The drugs that jumpstarted Elena's cognition spared her from any dull moment of incomprehension. "An alien structure?"

Uzoma sniffed. They were a physicist and, more importantly, an empiricist. Their only god was data. "I draw no conclusions. Perhaps the structure is of human origin. We have no idea what might have changed in terms of Earthly technology during our voyage. We have been traveling for nearly five hundred years. It is possible humankind developed sufficiently advanced modes of space travel to reach this part of the galaxy before we did."

"Aren't we going something like ten percent the speed of light? How did we encounter anything without being vaporized by the impact?"

"I... do not know. We stopped, and abruptly, but without damage to the *Anjou*. I can only theorize that some technological force capable of manipulating inertia was involved."

Elena took that in, then put it aside for the moment, because there were more pressing concerns. "Where are the others?"

"Gathered in the cargo hold. The alarms woke Robin, who tasked me to wake the rest of you. You were the last."

Elena undid the straps in the pod and gave herself a little push, floating up out of the chamber, then shoved off toward the door leading to the corridor.

The *Anjou* wasn't exactly roomy – it was mostly engines and cargo and cold storage – but the rest of the crew were squeezed in near the biological samples, all floating in a cluster around something unseen.

"It's fucking *aliens*." Bristles of wild blond hair stuck up all over Hans's head. "You think people made that thing?"

"May I see?" Elena said.

Sebastien (oh, Sebastien) looked up and raised one wry eyebrow, but it was Ibn who moved aside, letting her take his place so she could see the oversized tablet in Robin's hands. Robin was the oldest of them, her hair unapologetically gray and short, on her third career (finance, environmental law, ecological engineering). She was officially their captain, though there wasn't much captaining to do. Usually. "What do you think,

Elena?" she said.

The screen displayed a high-res image of an organic-looking structure made of crisscrossing branches and tubes and tunnels and arches, floating silvery-gray against the blackness of space. "It looks like a cast of the interior structure of a rat's lung," she said.

"Ever see one of those sculptures people make by filling an anthill with molten lead and then digging it up after the metal solidifies, so it's a three-dimensional map of tunnels laid out by bug-logic?" Hans gestured at the screen. "Those sculptures look just like that. Except that thing is as big as a city."

Think how big the bugs must be, Elena thought. (It was a thought that made her shudder later, when she remembered it to Callie.)

There was nothing in the image to provide a sense of scale, so Elena said, "A city? Are we talking Milwaukee or are we talking London?"

Robin zoomed in on one of the tubular branches. "That bit there? Is the size of a skyscraper, maybe eighty stories high. This thing is an astonishing feat of engineering. It must be hundreds of miles of tunnels – assuming those things are tunnels." She glared at Hans. "But we don't *know* that it's alien. We knew there was a chance, on a five-century voyage, that technology on Earth would outpace us and make us obsolete."

"Earth is long gone," Hans said. "Before we left, we'd gone so far past the tipping point nothing could save us but an act of God, and I'm an atheist – sorry, Ibn."

"It is not my place to forgive you," Ibn said. "While I do not share your pessimism about our homeworld, I agree with your assessment. If humans made this object... they are so different from the humans we knew that I fear we would not recognize them as our kin."

"Right," Elena said. "So when do we go over there and take a look?"

"We're still considering our options," Robin said.

"What, are we just going to fly away? Call this an unscheduled pit stop and get back on the space-road? Is that even an option?"

Uzoma said, "We are approximately a hundred years short of our expected arrival at Gliese 3293 C. Most of our fuel is gone, and it would take weeks of constant acceleration to return to our maximum survivable velocity. The ship was not designed to stop and start again, so the possibility of catastrophic system failure is increased." They paused. "The issue is moot, however. We are locked out of most of the ship's systems."

"Our shit got hacked," Hans said bluntly.

"We have to check this thing out." Sebastien had drifted away from the cluster to float somehow elegantly against a bank of biological samples, and Elena felt her usual flutter of lust at the sight of him. Long and lean and sweet-tempered, he was an expert in social psychology and urban planning, and was also a competent software engineer. Everyone on this ship had multiple specialties. Elena did biology, chemistry, and agriculture: the wet stuff. Sebastien had been her best friend during their training, showing genuine interest in her work, sitting up late at night with her talking about what they were giving up to go on this journey, and he'd inspired her with his grand visions: they were going to save humanity, create a new and more equal society, take advantage of this grand chance of a do-over to do things *right*.

They'd stayed up late the night before their departure, talking about the wonder and possibility of life under another star, and only a sense of professionalism had kept Elena from doing more than gazing at him hungrily. They hadn't made any explicit plans or promises, both too aware they might not even survive the journey, but they'd agreed to continue their conversations and friendship when they reached their destination. Elena had certainly fantasized that when they woke up, they would explore their relationship further, in the light of a new sun, and maybe even consummate that relationship on a new world. Their first time could be the first time for the whole *planet*. That appealed to her secret romantic side more than she liked to admit.

She hadn't expected to wake up here, now, in such strange circumstances – but it was still a thrill to see him.

Sebastien gestured toward the great void outside. "Either our very advanced descendants built that structure, or we're about to make first contact with aliens."

"We might die," Robin said. "Just making that clear."

Elena stopped looking at Sebastien and started looking at the problem. "The probability of our survival was always low. The entire Goldilocks project is based on an r strategy, not a K one, after all."

Hans raised one of his bushy eyebrows. "Come again?"

"There are two contrasting survival strategies for life." That was an oversimplification, but Elena had spent enough time as a professor that she could embrace oversimplification for illustrative purposes. "Creatures that adhere to a K strategy, like humans, have very few offspring, and invest a lot of resources in making sure those offspring survive. The other option is the r strategy – think rats or spiders. They have lots of offspring, with minimal parental involvement, but there are so many, some of them will probably survive."

"Scatter your seeds, and though some will find only stony soil, and die, others will find fertile soil, and thrive," Ibn said. "As in the Christian parable of the sower."

"I thought that was a science fiction novel," Hans muttered.

Elena ignored him. "Right. We're the seeds, scattered on the wind. Most of us will fall on worthless rocks, but a few will land where they can grow. The odds were always against us. Even if we reach our destination, it might be uninhabitable for any number of reasons." She nodded her head toward the viewscreen. "But this… it's a sure thing. It's huge, it's important, and it's right here. We can explore it, and if it's alien, we can send a message back to Earth, and do a definitive service for our people."

Hans made a sour face. "Ha. There's no Earth left to *get* the message, and it would take forever to get there anyway."

Uzoma shook their head. "Not forever. Not even an appreciable fraction of forever. We could aim a tight beam–"

"All right," Robin said. "This isn't a democracy, and mission-critical decisions are delegated to me, but this is beyond anything we ever expected to have to deal with, so, all in favor of sending a small exploratory–"

"The ship is moving toward the station." Uzoma inclined their head toward the screen. "Or else the station is moving toward us, but that seems less likely."

"Moving *how*?" Robin jabbed at the screen. "We are moving, very slowly, just a few meters per second, but we're not generating any thrust, and there's not… there's no tow line, there's no, I don't know, tractor beam…"

"No visible one, anyway," Uzoma said. "Someone in

there can control inertia well enough to make our ship decelerate rapidly from a tenth of the speed of light to a full stop without doing any damage to us in the process. If they can accomplish that, drawing us near would be trivial."

Sebastien stepped closer to Elena. She was profoundly aware of his presence, which was ridiculous in their current circumstances, but bodies and brains reacted strangely to stress sometimes, and hers was clearly urging her to try and reproduce before she died. Stupid bodies. "I guess our faction wins," he said. "Exploration it is. I never expected to meet aliens. I wonder what they're like?"

"An aperture is opening in the structure." Uzoma's tone was as matter-of-fact as always. Just reporting data.

They all looked at the screen. An irregular, roughly oval hole was opening up in the side of one of the skyscraper-sized portions of the structure, right down at the end of a branch, on the edge of the vastness. "It looks like the metal is flowing away, not like a door opening," Elena said.

Hans scowled. "No reason to believe it's metal at all. Our sensors can't tell us a damn thing about it. We've got a nose full of surveying equipment, and as far as it's concerned, that thing out there is basically invisible. It absorbs everything we throw at it."

There was no perceptible sense of movement, but the aperture got bigger and bigger on the screen, until the edges vanished entirely and the screen went black. Robin flicked through various external camera views, but they all showed darkness.

Hans consulted his handheld tablet, presumably full of useless sensor data. He was the ship's chief engineer and fixer-of-broken-things. "We're inside the structure, whatever it is. The sensors think there's a lot of empty space and a few solid objects in here with us. Let there be light." He swiped at the screen and the ship's external lights came on, shining into the darkness.

They all looked at the view on Robin's screen, but even the lights revealed little beyond some lattice-like structures that could have been metal struts or girders. Hans *hmm*ed. "Are those cranes and gantries, maybe? Could this be some kind of ship-building facility?"

There was a thump as the ship settled down on some kind of surface – and then another thump as they all dropped the short distance to the floor. Uzoma made a noise that was almost a whimper. "There is gravity. I… cannot explain why there is gravity."

Sebastien bounced up and down on his heels. "A little less than one G, I think. This big anthill isn't spinning, and it's hard to imagine something this size could accelerate fast enough for this to be thrust gravity already, though if they can control inertia, who knows? Artificial gravity. That's interesting."

"We should look around," Elena said.

Robin gave a definitive nod. "All right. Let's assess the situation. Ibn, you and Hans are with me."

"I will comply," Ibn said, "but why have I been selected?"

"You're a surveyor," Robin said. "We're surveying."

"I am primarily a geologist."

"Then keep your eyes open for interesting rocks. I'm also taking you because you know how to shoot. Hans, I guess you get to open that stupid weapons locker after all." They had a small cache of weapons in case they landed on a planet with hostile wildlife, though they'd considered the odds of that drastically low. It was far more likely they would die from hostile microorganisms or equipment failure. "Let's suit up and see what's happening out there. Sebastien, Uzoma, and Elena, you stay on board. We'll keep in radio contact."

"I'd like to go outside to play, please," Sebastien said.

"You're my second in command, Sebastien. If whatever we find out there proves unfriendly, and we don't come back, you're in charge."

"Heavy lies the head that wears the crown," he murmured.

"Uzoma, see if you can send a transmission through the walls of... whatever this place is. Let Earth know we found something."

Uzoma nodded and left the room at a brisk walk, which was as close to frantic as Elena had ever seen them.

"What about me?" Elena said.

"I'm sticking with the members of the crew who have military experience for this first foray. If it seems safe, you can come out soon, and if we encounter anything that seems alive, we'll definitely want your assessment."

Elena didn't pout, because that would be unprofessional, but she couldn't stop herself from sighing. "All right. Please keep your helmet cams on and streaming."

"Not to be overly psychological about all this," Sebastien said, "but if you go out there with guns, prepared for hostility, you might find just that."

"I'm aware of the risks," Robin said. "But I'm not about to explore a possibly alien space station with nothing but flashlights." She handed Elena the tablet. "We'll stream our video here." She left the cargo hold, followed by Hans and Ibn, who gave them a grave nod farewell as he passed.

Sebastien sat down on a crate. "Shall we sit back and enjoy the show?"

"How can you be so *calm*?"

"Like you said, our odds of survival were always low. I didn't really expect to wake up again after I went into cryosleep, and then I did, to do my days of solo duty on the ship, but every time I went back into cold storage I expected it to be the last time. All this is just bonus existence, as far as I'm concerned. Besides, it's *interesting*. This place, this station, this object, whatever it is… I've always been fascinated by projects on such huge scales. The coordination and organization and effort involved always dazzles me."

Elena snorted, looking into the dim view on the screen. "It's definitely dazzling."

He patted the crate beside him, and she sat. They looked at the screen together as the others suited up and their helmet feeds came online. Hans was handing out some surprisingly low-tech guns: a pistol for Robin, a shotgun for himself, and an automatic rifle for Ibn, who'd been a sniper in the water wars.

Elena said, "You'd think we'd have fancy lasers or plasma blasters or something. The future is a disappointment."

"Simple ballistic guns are easy to repair and service, and it's not even hard to cast extra ammunition, with the fabricators we have. Plasma is notoriously hard to make from scratch."

"All right, can you hear us?" Robin said.

"We can indeed," Sebastien said.

"We were ready to explore unknown and dangerous

terrain, but we didn't expect to start with the inside of a giant anthill, so we'll see how this goes."

Hans was uncharacteristically silent as they opened the airlock, and Ibn characteristically so. The screen was divided into quadrants: three squares for the helmet feeds, and one rotating through the ship's external cameras. Three figures in environment suits appeared on that fourth screen, moving in close formation, and Sebastien stabbed the quadrant with his forefinger to keep it from rotating away from that view. The suits had lights on their helmets and on the arms, and the crew shone them around in various directions, moving with military precision and grace. The views through their helmet cams were just indistinct washes of brightness, and darkness, and shapes.

"Looks like some kind of hangar," Robin said. "Lots of big equipment. Cranes, hooks, nozzles... no sign of anything moving, though–"

The ship abruptly shuddered, clattering against the hangar floor, and Sebastien and Elena exchanged a glance. The ship rose into the air rapidly, the external camera feed showing the figures receding below, the helmet feeds showing the ship receding above. Hans cursed, and Ibn muttered a prayer, and Robin shouted, "Sebastien, are you all right?"

"Apart from being dragged into the sky? Yes." His voice betrayed either fear or excitement or both.

"It looks like some kind of claw grabbed the *Anjou* and... Wait, there's light, are those sparks?"

Elena leaned toward the screen, frowning at the view from the helmet cams far below. It was hard to see through such distant cameras, but it looked like the *Anjou* had been pulled up into some kind of docking cradle, and now robotic arms were sliding and ratcheting around... and tearing chunks off the ship, and cutting at the hull with white-hot torches, showering sparks. The distant squeal and shriek of metal made Elena and Sebastien huddle closer together.

"Who the hell's doing that?" Robin said. "Where's the control center?"

"Might not be one," Hans said. "It could be some kind of automatic repair system."

"I– " Robin said, and then the hangar flooded with light, and they all saw the alien.

CHAPTER 7

"Oh, shit." Sebastien and Elena hunched over the screen.

The three helmet feeds all converged on the thing – creature? organism? – moving through the vast hangar. The thing was almost as large as the *Anjou*, and its physical structure was so strange that Elena was only able to focus on parts of it at a time. The synchronized undulation of its dozens of spidery legs. The waving of – cilia? pseudopods? – all over its body. The body itself, which resembled a sea cucumber the size of a killer whale, all covered in bumps and nodules. Was that thickest pseudopod a neck, or a tail, and what was that immense flower-like bud on the end? How did something so big move on legs so seemingly spindly in gravity this strong?

"Fall back!" Robin shouted.

"To *where*?" Hans said, but they retreated as the thing moved toward them with alarming speed. One of the helmet feeds abruptly spun, and Ibn shouted in alarm.

On Robin's feed, they saw that one of the creature's vinelike pseudopods had whipped out, wrapped around Ibn's body, and lifted him into the air. For a moment Ibn hung there upside-down, looking at the bizarre creature that had towered over him, and now filled the space beneath him. The neck, with its closed-flower-bud head (Elena was aware those terms were wildly inaccurate, but approximations were all she could manage) moved directly beneath him, and the petals began to unfurl.

Ibn shrieked and fired his rifle at the bud, but to no particular effect. Either he missed, or it just didn't do any significant damage. The pseudopod gave him a shake and the gun bounced out of his hands, though it stayed against his body, dangling from its strap. The bud opened wider, the pseudopod loosened, and Ibn dropped into the center of the flower-like opening, down into some sort of tube or chute. He screamed as he fell.

Elena covered her face, and looked away, but the screaming went on and then trailed off. "I'm alive." Ibn's voice was full of wonder. His feed showed rushing, organic-looking walls zipping past him. "It's like some kind of a slide—" He grunted. "I've hit bottom. It's soft... spongy, even..." His light shone around. "Am I in its *stomach* or—"

His feed abruptly went dark, and Sebastien groaned.

Hans screamed and ran forward, shotgun held at the ready, and when he got close to the creature, Elena realized the thing's legs weren't spindly at all: they were so big she wouldn't have been able to wrap her arms around one of them.

"Stop!" Robin shouted, but it was pointless: Hans was in a frenzy, and who could blame him? That thing had eaten Ibn. Maybe. Or maybe it had put him into some kind of body cavity for storage. Maybe the creature wasn't even alive. Perhaps it was some kind of biomechanical construct—

A pseudopod picked up Hans and dropped him into the flower-tube. He screamed and fired his shotgun as he slid down, but without doing any noticeable damage. He howled more loudly: "Fuck, my suit is holed, I got hit with my own ricochet, damn it—"

His feed cut off, too. The immense creature, if it was a creature, stood still, its cilia gently undulating, its flower-like head swaying.

Robin was crouched beside a stacked pile of irregularly shaped metal plates, trying to hide. "Elena, do you see any weak points on that thing? Is any part of it worth shooting?"

"We don't know for sure that it's hostile," Sebastien said. "It didn't swallow Ibn until he shot it, and Hans attacked it too—"

"Don't give me that," Robin said. "It doesn't matter who started the fight now. We've officially started an interstellar incident. This isn't the way I wanted to go down in history, but it's the situation we're in." Robin looked up. The shape of the ship was changing radically, Elena saw: the *Anjou* had sprouted fins, wings, spines, various bits of strange metal grafted on, and now the robot arms were doing something to the engines.

"Well, Elena? Where should I aim?"

"I barely understand what I'm looking at, Robin. It has some elements that remind me of sea life back on Earth, but parts of it also seem plant-like, and other parts are like nothing I've seen before at all... but something that big? I don't think your pistol will make much of an impression."

"Understood. Uzoma? Can you detonate the propulsion system on the *Anjou*?"

Elena sucked in a breath.

"I could," Uzoma said after a moment. "It would be equivalent to setting off several atomic bombs, because that is, essentially, what I would be doing."

"If that thing tries to get to the ship, to get you... blow up the *Anjou*. Do some damage before it can eat you. I'm going to look for a control panel, some way to release the ship, open the airlock, let you get away." She sighed. "This is pointless. It's not like I'll find a big red button to press that says 'Open.' Maybe you should just blow up the ship now–"

Uzoma rushed into the cargo hold and slammed the button that sealed the door. They pressed their back against the wall, hard, then stared at Sebastien and Elena, eyes wild. "There's something on the ship. It's a machine, robotic, like a crab or a spider, but not. It tore open a panel in the control room and climbed inside–"

"Did you manage to send a message, Uzoma?" Robin's voice was sharp, no-nonsense, and fully in charge.

"I did not. I was interrupted." Being asked a question seemed to calm them down.

"Damn it. At this point, it's down to damage control. I want you to blow the engines."

"I cannot. The control room is compromised–"

"Find a way," Robin snapped. "If that machine you saw is crawling around inside our control room, it could access all our systems, including our navigational data. They could find our system of origin – and they could follow our path back to Earth. I'm not as pessimistic as Hans is. I think there might still be a homeworld back there to protect."

"No, thank you." Uzoma's expression was glassy and faraway. Elena realized what she'd taken for calm was something closer to shock.

"What do you mean?" Robin said.

"I cannot blow the engines without leaving this room,

and I do not wish to do that. You did not see what I saw."

"I'll do it," Sebastien said. "Uzoma? I'll go out. Can you talk me through the process?" He snapped his fingers in front of their face.

Uzoma's gaze drifted toward him. "What? Yes. No. I..." Uzoma rubbed the back of their head. "It touched me," they said dreamily. "The machine."

"Let me see." Elena was the closest thing the ship had to a doctor; she was a xenobiologist who'd taken two years of classes in field medicine, anyway.

She wasn't sure what she'd expected. A bloody scratch, maybe.

Instead she saw a round silver shape, the size of a saucer, clamped onto the back of Uzoma's head with half a dozen clawlike appendages: it looked like an immense metal spider.

Elena flinched back as the spider's legs moved, somehow lengthening, burrowing under the flesh of Uzoma's scalp. Then one of the legs rose up and darted toward Elena's hand instead, and she lurched backward and let out a wordless cry of horror.

Uzoma rose unsteadily and stumbled around the cargo hold. Their eyes had changed, filmed over, and their pupils glowed, as if someone had lit a candle inside their skull. Uzoma opened their mouth, and released a series of liquid gurgles. As if in answer, the beam of some kind of plasma torch punched through the hull in front of them, and began cutting an opening from the outside.

Robin was shouting over the comms, but Sebastien tucked the tablet into his pocket and grabbed Elena's arm. "I think we'd better go."

"But... we have to help them." Uzoma was gurgling at the wall now, watching as an archway appeared, drawn in lines of plasma. There was no sudden decompression, and no inrush of poisonous gas, which meant that the vast hangar was both pressurized and the air out there was breathable, which made no sense at all.

Manipulator arms lifted a thick section of the hull away, and another arm reached in and picked up Uzoma, almost gently, around the waist. Once they were pulled out through the hull, another manipulator reached in, its claw unfurling with dozens of intricately jointed digits, and immediate fear overcame stunned horror sufficiently for Elena to race after Sebastien as he slammed the door open and rushed into the corridor.

He stabbed the door-close button, and the claw clattered against it from the other side. "Come on. We have to get to the control room. Robin, do you know how to make the ship explode from there?"

"I can talk you through it. You should be able to set up a chain reaction and escape before it blows. I found some kind of access tunnel or duct or… I don't know what. I'm in the walls. We might be safe here. It's too small for that big bug thing to follow."

Elena and Sebastien made their way to the control room. The panels had been ripped open, wiring exposed, and something was rooting around inside, audibly clattering. "What's happening in there?"

"I don't know–" Sebastien said, and then something dropped from the ceiling onto his head, driving him to the ground. Elena shouted in alarm and jumped back.

It was the crab-spider-thing Uzoma had described, its body no bigger than a dessert plate, but bristling with manipulators, one of which plunged into the back of Sebastien's head.

Elena reared back and kicked the robot as hard as

she could, and managed to break half the spider's legs, making them stick up at jagged angles. The other half of the legs held on, though, and dug deeper into Sebastien's head, the spider clamping itself on to his scalp like a tight-fitting skullcap.

There was a clank, and a piece of metal covered the hole the spider had dropped through. Were the machines out there re-sealing the *Anjou*'s hull? But why?

She knelt to look at Sebastien, whose eyes fluttered. She tugged at the spider-thing but couldn't wrench it free; it was set deep in the bones of his skull. "Sebastien? Are you all right?"

He groaned and rolled over. He looked at her, blinking. One of his eyes was filmed and glowing red, but the other was clear. "I– Elena, you look so strange…" Silver tendrils began to crawl around his scalp and the sides of his face.

Elena moved away. "Don't worry, Sebastien, we'll– whatever that thing did to you, we'll fix it, OK?"

Robin was shouting over the tablet, but Elena couldn't make out what she was saying, and it couldn't be more important than whatever was happening to Sebastien, anyway.

He rose, a little unsteadily. "I have to go. I'm being called. I'm being… I'm learning… I'm becoming… but I think I have a little time." He reached out to touch her face, and she steeled herself not to flinch away. His fingertips were hot. "I can get you out of here, Elena. I can get you home. You'll be safe."

"Home? To Earth? Sebastien, it would take hundreds of years–"

"Not anymore. Not now. They thought our ship was broken. They thought *we* were broken. They fixed it.

They fixed us. They're trying... look."

He pointed into the torn-open panel, and she looked through the nest of tangled conduits to see a foreign object wired into the system: a greasy-looking black cube, about half a meter on each side. "That's your way home." Sebastien went to the navigation panel and tapped out a rapid series of commands. The cube began to hum, a deep atonal rumble. "There. When the repairs are done, the ship will take you home. Or, close to home, I can't quite see the math, it wavers at the edges, I'm still changing."

"Sebastien, I don't understand–"

His head snapped around, like he'd heard something. "They're coming. They want to fix you, too... the spiders are simple. Thermal, I think. If we get you back in cryosleep, they won't register you as something they need to repair." He blinked and rubbed at his good eye. "We have to hurry."

"Sebastien, you can go into cryosleep too, they won't see you–"

"Too late. It's in me. They know me as their own. I can't hide. But let me save you, Elena." Without waiting for her to answer, he lurched down the corridor, stumbling against walls like a drunk, and she followed.

Sebastien opened her cryopod and gestured, and Elena climbed inside, because what else could she do? If there was any chance at all to make it home, even if it took hundreds of years, she had to take it, didn't she? She had to let people know what dangers lurked here, beyond the back of the stars.

Sebastien hooked her up to the pod's life support systems, then leaned in and kissed her brow. His lips were so hot she flinched away, but he didn't notice. His left eye was filmed over now, too, but not yet glowing. "I wish we'd found a new world together, Elena. A better world than this one."

"Sebastien…" she began, but he pressed her firmly down into the pod as it filled with swirls of cold vapor, and the needles pierced her skin to deliver the drugs that would slow her metabolic rate. He sealed the lid, and looked down at her, a blurry form behind the glass for a moment, before he vanished.

Elena listened to the muffled sounds of thumping, cutting, welding, and hammering until the sedatives pulled her down into a darkness she fully expected to be eternal.

CHAPTER 8

"That's the last thing I remember before you woke me."
Elena hugged herself, and looked so small and vulnerable
that Callie just wanted to wrap her up in a blanket and
hold her and tell her everything would be OK, even if
that was a lie. Maybe especially if that was a lie.

"It *could* still be Liars," Callie said, half to herself.

Elena scowled. "The thing that ate Ibn and Hans was
the size of a bus. It doesn't sound much like the aliens
you described."

"That kind of thing would be outside their normal range.
And the technology you describe is way beyond anything
we've seen before, even from Liars. Artificial gravity?"
Callie's initial impulse was skeptical disbelief, but the story
Elena told did fit with the available facts, outlandish as it
was at its heart. "So. You remember what happened. What
would you like to do with this information?"

"What do you mean?"

Callie shrugged. "You may have made contact with a
new race of aliens, who are either hostile or inscrutable.
What do you want to do next?"

"I suppose I should tell the authorities?"

Callie nodded. "Right. But which authorities?"

"I'm not sure. You're like police, aren't you? Shouldn't you know?"

"I am a sworn officer of the Trans-Neptunian Authority security forces, on a part-time freelance basis, which is a little different from being police as you understand it. You're from the One World Emergency Government era, right?"

Elena nodded. "The goldilocks ships were one of the first major OWEG projects, right after the desalinization initiative."

"Right. Earth is still ruled by a version of that organization, the OWG, but its influence doesn't extend beyond the Karman Line. The Luna colony has been independent for centuries, though they're still close allies of Earth, and Mars is its whole thing. Mercury is an energy farm, barely populated. Together, they form a loose coalition called the Inner Planets Governing Council. Venus, like I said, is reclusive Liar territory. The asteroid belt is a disputed zone between Mars and the Jovian Imperative, and a couple of Jupiter's moons keep stubbornly insisting they're independent, despite much evidence to the contrary. The Jovian Imperative is arguably as powerful as the inner planets, since they control the only bridgehead in this solar system, but they all pretty much get along, because there's more money to be made that way."

"So way out here, the Trans-Neptunian Authority is in charge?"

"The TNA is the big power here, the governing body. But it's a corporation, run by a CEO and a CFO and a board, not by an elected official. If you want a voice in the government out here, you'd better be a shareholder. Still, the TNA makes and enforces the law, and keeps things running smoothly commerce-wise." *When it can*, she thought. A lot of people fled to the edges of the solar system to get away from rules, and resented having the rules follow them way out here into the dark. Hence the need for people like Callie to make them cooperate, or chase them off. "So when you say 'authorities' that gets a little wobbly. I can get a meeting with just about anybody in the TNA, but their influence stops near the orbit of Jupiter. The Jovian Imperative is more like a corporation than a nation-state, too. If we told the Jovian Imperative or the TNA your story, they'd just try to figure out how they could profit from it, if they believed you at all. We could upload your testimony to the Tangle, and let *everybody* know what you found out there–"

"What's the Tangle?"

"Oh. You called it, um, the net? The web?"

Elena nodded. "You ruined the net? You got it all tangled?"

"It still works a lot like your net did. There's news, entertainment, gossip, complaining, jokes, music, images. There are also secret levels, dark commerce, weird cults, and Liar sites that do strange stuff to human brains when we look at them. Seizures are the least of it. Those dangerous sites are interdicted, but there are plenty of places in the galaxy where *nothing* is interdicted, and sometimes the consequences are ugly. Then you've got the AI, who do their own thing on the Tangle too, and the whole alternate-reality contingent, and rumors of the broken ghosts of experimental uploaded minds building their own raggedy sensoriums, stealing power where they can…" She shrugged. "All together, it's the Tangle. But if we upload the sensational story of a woman from five hundred years ago who met previously unknown aliens, with proper proofs and verifications, we'd get all sorts of attention. Some corporate king or resource-rich polity would probably try to investigate, as far as their resources would allow."

"But you don't think it's a good idea?"

Callie chewed her lower lip. "It's just… the bigger issue is the bridge generator. That greasy black cube full of time-and-space-bending power. We found the generator on your ship, so it belongs to you. If it does what you've described, and what Ashok says it does, you'll either get rich, or arrested, or assassinated, or all three, in some order. Assassination last, probably."

Elena's eyes widened. "I hadn't thought about that. But you're right. If that device can be reproduced, it would upend whole economies, wouldn't it?"

"And if it *can't* be reproduced, if it's one of a kind, the tech too far beyond us to reverse engineer successfully?" Callie whistled. "Whole other set of issues there. Whoever has it owns the universe, basically. It's not like you have to decide right *now*, but you'll have to eventually figure out what you want to do."

Elena chewed her lower lip, and even though the situation was fraught, she looked so cute Callie wanted to pull her into her lap and kiss her and nip that lower lip between her own teeth. After a long moment Elena said, "I want to rescue my friends. Can you help me do that?"

Callie blinked. "Uh, I appreciate the whole leave-no-person-behind ethos, but you escaped an alien mind control space anthill and you want to go *back*?"

"Robin could still be alive, and… unaffected. It's only been days, Callie. Her suit has sufficient reserves of water, and it can recycle her waste when that's gone, to give her a bit more time. The atmosphere inside the station was breathable. Sebastien wasn't fully transformed, either, he was fighting the changes, so he might be recoverable, too. And who knows what happened to Ibn and Hans? That thing might not have been an alien at all. It might have been a biological equivalent of a forklift, or a cargo truck. Maybe they weren't digested; maybe they were just *stored*. Uzoma... well. Perhaps we can help them too. Maybe the change can be reversed."

"I– That's a big ask, Elena. We chase smugglers and murderers, and yeah, we've done search and rescue, but this is *way* beyond."

Elena nodded once, conceding that particular point, but conceding nothing else. "Help me save my crew, and I'll give you my bridge generator."

Callie leaned back. "What?"

"As you said, it's incredibly valuable. Perhaps the most valuable thing in the system, if not the galaxy. Giving you the generator seems like a fair trade."

"It also takes a big problem out of your lap and drops it in mine."

Elena shrugged. "I'm a primitive from the darker ages. You're a modern sophisticate, better equipped to handle such complexities anyway. I'm over here with sticks and rocks and you've discovered fire and the forge."

"This... isn't something I can decide on my own. A mission like that, I'd need a crew. I'll have to talk to my people."

"By all means." Elena yawned. "I'm going back to my quarters, if that's all right. I'm still groggy from... well, cryosleep, I suppose."

"Sure," Callie said. "Sweet dreams."

Elena gave her a blank look. "That seems very unlikely."

• • •

"I love a family meeting." Ashok spun around in his chair, until Stephen reached out and firmly stopped the rotation. Drake and Janice were there too, sitting in their mobility device, a gyroscopic egg-shaped seat they seldom emerged from in the presence of others. They had their silver privacy screen down now, which suggested Drake was on the ascendant; he was more self-conscious about their physical appearance than Janice was.

"Everyone heard Elena's story, right?" Callie asked. The ship's computer recorded every word spoken in public areas of the ship as a matter of course, unless privacy was requested, and Callie had asked the crew to review the recordings or transcripts before the meeting.

"She's crazy," Janice said, voice emerging from a speaker set into the top of their chair. "Sorry. I know it's not nice, and she's been through a traumatic experience, and all that, but: clear-cut case of space madness. She probably murdered her crew and jettisoned them out the airlock."

"She may not be insane," Drake said. "It's possible she's simply lying. Maybe she's from the Jovian Imperative, looking to get famous with a ridiculous story. She found a mothballed antique ship, welded some spikes onto it, and messed around with the navigational data. Remember that rock-jockey who said he'd discovered an antigravity generator, but it was all just lies and falsified data?"

"That bridge generator though." Ashok made a buzzing sound that might have been meant as an appreciative whistle.

"You haven't seen the thing *generate a bridge*," Janice said. "It's just a greasy black box playing tricks on the computer."

"I'm not *that* easily tricked," the computer objected, but they all ignored him.

"The stuff the box is made of is weird, I'll grant you that," Janice went on, "but it could be some industrial material cooked up in an R&D lab and abandoned because it's too nasty-looking for commercial use."

"Let's address the possibilities," Callie said. "What are the odds this is an elaborate hoax? Ashok, does her ship check out?"

"It's a real goldilocks ship, and the stuff done to it matches the stuff she *says* was done to it. The hull is patched up with some unknown silvery-gray metal, and those bits of the ship were resistant to analysis from every sensor I pointed at them. Plus, like Shall says, he's not *that* easy to trick. We've poked that alien cube real good, and it reacts the same way, consistently, throughout many thousands of iterative virtual environments. We've got the keys to the galaxy, cap. Let's go for a spin."

"Stephen? What's your take on Elena? Do you think she's trustworthy, or are we being scammed?"

Stephen stirred, leaning forward and lacing his immense hands together on the table top. "Elena is genuinely from the twenty-second century, judging by the antibodies in her blood – or, rather, the lack of what are now quite common antibodies." Stephen was as placid and unbothered as always; or, well, as usual. When he was in the midst of his religious devotions, he was different. "I've given her a full suite of vaccinations, but before that she was definitely an artifact of another era. I detected traces of pollutants in her system that were purged from Earth long ago, as well. She is, at least, not lying about her origin." He paused. "There is another reason to believe the device is genuine, or genuinely alien, though: it frightened away the Liars. They fled the station when they saw it."

Callie nodded. She'd been thinking the same thing.

Stephen went on. "The device clearly does *something*, and potentially something dangerous, judging by the reaction of the aliens. When I was visiting with my congregation earlier... You know that some of the members of my church do alien outreach, because we believe all life is one life, and all consciousnesses are connected? My friend Glinda, who works in the recycling division, said a Liar on her crew who comes to services sometimes stopped to say goodbye on his way off the station, and urged her to leave, too. She asked him why he was leaving, and he said, 'Your faith is a beautiful one, and I believe it a little. But there are much uglier faiths, and I believe those a lot.' Then he ran off."

Callie grunted. "So, what, bridge generators are religious artifacts to the Liars? Did we pry the sacred jewel out of the head of the idol or something here?"

"I have no idea," Stephen said.

"OK. Liars say weird things. I don't want to get hung up on that. Suppose the bridge generator works. Elena has offered to trade this unprecedented propulsion technology–"

"Technically not propulsion," Ashok interrupted. "It's more of a spatial manipulator but... ah right OK captain I'll shut up now."

Callie kept glaring at him for a moment, because sometimes Ashok relapsed in the absence of continual reinforcement. "Elena has offered to give us this alien artifact in exchange for us running a search-and-rescue mission to recover any of her crew that might still be alive, wherever they are. We don't even have to succeed to get the generator. We just have to make the effort."

"Her crew got eaten," Janice said. "I mean, they didn't, they got thrown out an airlock by a crazy person, but if we're taking her ridiculous story seriously, why would we go back to that place? Why would we stand a better chance than her crew did?"

"Because we're from the *future*." Ashok spun around again. "They were past people from the disaster times. Send a Neanderthal to rob a casino and he's not going to get too far. The pretty lights and ringing chimes and short shorts on the cocktail servers are going to get him all dizzy and distracted. But send a bunch of hardcore jaded future folk like us, with the right hardware of the killing kind? We'll win for sure."

"Could we even keep the generator for ourselves?" Drake said. "Aren't there guidelines about the discovery of unknown alien technology under the rules of salvage?"

Ashok made another buzzing noise, this one indicative of derision. "You mean those rules nobody would ever know if we broke, but for some reason we follow them?"

"We're not pirates, Ashok. What is the legal status, computer?"

That damnably familiar voice said, "The TNA statute says that if unknown Liar technology is discovered within their sphere of influence, it should be promptly surrendered to the authorities. The person or persons who discovered the tech will be paid either a flat rate, as determined by an appraisal AI, or receive a variable percentage of profits if the technology can be successfully reproduced and monetized. The relevant words here are 'sphere of influence': this bridge generator was apparently found by Elena in a system far beyond the reach of the Trans-Neptunian Authority, or indeed any polity based in this system, or any of the twenty-nine colony systems. Elena subsequently brought the device to Trans-Neptunian Space, but that doesn't give the TNA a claim on the technology, at least, not as the statute is written."

"Which isn't to say an industrial espionage squad won't come vent us all into space and steal the generator anyway," Stephen said. "We're not talking about finding a slightly more efficient insulating material or a way to hard-boil eggs faster or a more coherent laser cannon. This device is world-altering, and there *will* be extralegal repercussions if we aren't careful about how we deploy it."

"See?" Ashok said. "Nobody follows the rules except us. It's like wearing handcuffs and a muzzle and a straitjacket, except not in the fun way."

"We could always take the generator to the Jovians," Callie said. "They're richer than the TNA, and more closely scrutinized, and frankly less likely to leave us drifting dead in the Oort Cloud." Callie worked for the TNA, but it was a younger polity, and a bit more savage in its practices. "If we put in place precautions so the Jovians can't double-cross us, we could get fair payment. They'd probably offer us landed knighthoods, at minimum." Not that she particularly wanted to settle down on an estate under the carbon-lace domes of Callisto, but it was a possibility to consider. "Before we think about all that, though, we have to see if the bridge generator even works. If it does... Are we willing to take Elena's offer? I'm not going to compel anyone here. It's too big and weird and dangerous, so we'll all vote. If yes, we'll see if we can find her crew. If no, we give her the bridge generator and drop her on Ganymede with some advice and hope she remembers us fondly after she gets rich."

"I'm in." Ashok's handful of manipulators spun around in a merry whir, his equivalent of excited fidgeting.

"I do have some sympathy for people being unwillingly altered by alien technology," Drake said. "And it would be a tale to tell, wouldn't it? Visiting an alien space station? I'll go if Janice will."

"It's nonsense," Janice said. "But if it turns out not to be nonsense, fuck it, I'm in. Maybe we'll meet some aliens who aren't total crap like the Liars are."

"I have the insatiable curiosity and sense of adventure of my template mind," the computer said. "I would be delighted to explore."

Callie snorted. "Your human model traded in his curiosity and sense of adventure for a fun-filled life in commodities trading."

"Perhaps staying in space has kept my own interest sharp, dar... captain."

"Mmm. Well, Stephen, it's down to you. This is the part where you tell us the whole idea is foolhardy, stupid, reckless, and will end in tragedy."

"It *is* foolhardy, stupid, reckless, and will end in tragedy. But I'll go." He shrugged, tectonic. "Someone has to fix you up when you're inevitably parasitized by aliens. I will make some small demands in the interests of practicality, though: we do *not* have sufficient weaponry or defensive measures on board for this kind of mission." The *White Raven* was fitted with a few weapons – fore and aft ballistic cannons and ion blasters, and a dorsal plasma bolt gun that offered a 360-degree firing range – which were more than sufficient for their typical security and escort jobs, but definitely more police-grade than military-grade.

"I have an idea about that," Callie said. "I think I can get us armed up. Sounds like it's unanimous, then."

"Why do *you* want to go?" Janice said. "It's a big reward, sure, but it's a big risk too."

"You know me, Janice. I just do stuff. As a policy it's worked out well for me so far." Callie could come up with rationalizations: this was the big score, and worth the danger; they could discover something of vital importance for the future of humanity; rescuing a stranded crew was the right thing to do, both objectively and because, if they were ever lost, they'd want someone to do the same for them. Those were all true, but they just lent cover to her real reason: she wanted to spend more time with Elena. She wanted to help Elena. She wanted Elena to think she was brave and resourceful and kind. She hadn't wanted to impress anyone that way since she met her ex-husband. Callie wasn't silly enough to call it love, not at this point, but whatever it was, it met the necessary preconditions to *become* love, in time. "I'll give Elena the good news."

CHAPTER 9

"That's amazing!" Elena grabbed Callie in a hug, then suddenly let go and stepped back. "I'm sorry, I... Do you still hug in this century? Is it outside social norms?" What if there'd been some terrible contagion, and humans had stopped hugging? Embraces were already wildly variable in terms of appropriateness, depending on culture and upbringing...

Callie seemed amused. "No, it's OK. We still hug. In theory, anyway. Conditionally. I don't get hugged very often in practice."

"It's because you're very intimidating." Elena looked the captain up and down. Intimidating or not, there was something appealing about her – a sense of complete ease and self-assurance that she'd always found attractive. It was the same quality that had drawn her toward Sebastien. "I thought it was the boots – they are very butch boots – but really it's just your whole air of command. Comes from... literally being in command, I suppose."

"Ha. The boots are pretty great. They're real vat-grown leather, black, covered with a transparent protective resin the Liars developed, all over an under-layer of steel-composite mesh. They've got electromagnetic soles too. They're good for stomping around, crawling on the hull in space, and kicking smugglers in the guts. We can get you a pair if you want. I bet you'd look good in them."

Was that a tone of flirtation in the captain's voice? Elena decided she must be misreading it. Social cues had probably altered a lot in the past five centuries. "What, this white jumpsuit isn't the height of contemporary fashion?" Elena realized the front of her suit was unzipped perhaps too far for modesty, at least by the standards of her own time, but Callie hadn't so much as glanced at her chest, so it probably wasn't a problem. That lack of even a casual cleavage glance further weighed against the idea that Callie had been flirting. Elena felt a little spurt of disappointment at the thought. It was always nice when people you found hot found you hot back, but that was probably too much to expect in circumstances this bizarre.

"I'm glad you're happy," Callie was saying. "Of course, this whole idea is contingent on us actually getting the bridge generator to work. Otherwise, we can't get back wherever you came from."

Elena sighed. "I wish I could help. The space station's robots hooked up the device, and Sebastien was the one to activate it."

"Our engineer, Ashok, thinks he can figure it out. You'll meet him, and the rest of the crew, soon. It's just Ashok, and our pilot Drake and our navigator and comms expert Janice. You already know me, and Stephen, and the computer."

"That reminds me, I meant to ask – are AI considered, ah, people? Socially? Legally?"

"Those as sophisticated as the one on this ship, yeah.

There are a lot of weak AI, expert systems really, that are optimized for one particular task – appraisals, law, finance, stuff like that. They're not considered people. As far as we can tell they don't have consciousness or any theory of mind. But the ones based on template minds do, and they have commensurate rights and privileges. Our computer even gets paid for running the ship, though I don't know what he does with the lix he earns."

"Investments and charity, mainly, and ship upgrades, since the *White Raven is* my body," Shall commented.

"Except it's *my* ship, so I reimburse him for those." Callie sounded annoyed. Elena noticed that she often sounded annoyed when Shall spoke, and resolved to find out why. Elena understood the inner workings of organisms vastly better than she did the inner workings of interpersonal relationships, but if she was going on a potentially dangerous rescue mission with these people, she needed to get to know them better.

"Assuming the generator does work, when do we leave?" Elena had been doing calculations in her head, about her crew's water and food supplies, and the numbers weren't happy.

"We have to resupply and fuel up and make some mission-specific changes to the ship, but probably within ten or twelve hours, if all goes well. Robin can make it that long?"

"Assuming nothing *new* and terrible happened to her, I think so."

"OK. I'll set you up in my quarters on the station – they aren't fancy, but there's food, and a bed, and access to the Tangle, so you can start catching up on the past few centuries worth of–"

"What are you talking about? I'm going with you."

Callie crossed her arms and scowled. "Doctor, I have a lot of respect for you – you've been through a lot, and you came out intact, and that's saying something, but I'm a trained security contractor. Drake and Janice used to fly military expeditions for Earth, back before their accident. Stephen got his start as a doctor when the battlefield medic on his squad during the first Ionian uprising took a kinetic bolt to the head, and Stephen had to start patching people up with the assistance of a weak AI helperbot in his visor display. He found out he liked putting people back together way more than taking them apart. Active duty was a long time ago for him, but he still knows what he's doing. Even the computer has military firing solutions and engagement and evasion protocols in his database. You're a total non-combatant. It's not safe."

Elena scowled, saw an opening, and took it. "What about your mechanic, Ashok?"

She hesitated. "He hasn't had military or police training, true, but he has other useful qualities."

"So do I. Mainly, I'm the only one who's been to this space station. I know what to expect, and what we should look out for. I'm a source of valuable intelligence. You aren't leaving me behind. That's non-negotiable."

Callie stared her down, but Elena just stared her back *up*, and the captain finally grinned. Most people probably wouldn't call Kalea Machedo pretty, not with that nose and that great frizzy cloud of hair barely tamed into braids, but her smile was a dazzler. "All right, Elena. You're the client, so you call the shots. Let the record show I agree under protest. Who's the intimidating one now?"

"Ha. You've got, what, a quarter of a meter on me? You could throw me over your shoulder like a bag of feathers."

Callie shrugged. "Some of that height is just the boots. You are kind of pocket-sized, though. They grew people real small back in the Paleolithic."

"Don't be rude. I'm at *least* Neolithic."

"Definitely a valuable antique. All right, get some rest, or some food, or poke around on the Tangle. Explore the station if you want – you can take an earbud to stay in contact with the computer. I'm going to see about getting us properly outfitted for this rescue mission."

"Aye aye." Elena snapped off a salute.

"Definitely no military training," Callie said, and left the room.

"I probably shouldn't say anything," Shall said, "but I've been monitoring your vital signs, per Stephen's orders, and there was a definite increase in your heart rate, pupillary dilation, diaphoresis, and breathing when you were talking to Callie, indicating a state of arousal–"

"Shut up," Elena said. "I want to go for a walk. Do they have anything resembling street food on this station?"

"Hmm, yes, though it's hard for me to offer recommendations, as I don't eat. There is a gyeran-bbang stand that Ashok raves about. The eggs aren't real, of course, but I'm told it's quite convincing–"

"Really? I haven't had that since I visited my grandma as a kid, before the avian cholera. I love the future. Apart from the murderous aliens. Take me to the egg bread, Shall. Why do they call you Shall, anyway? And why doesn't the *captain* ever call you that? And why is she always pissed off at you?"

"That is a long and in some ways sad story, Elena. Some of it I'm forbidden to tell you. For now, let's talk about the station instead. I think you'll be impressed…"

After she left Elena's quarters, Callie put her back against the wall of the corridor, closed her eyes, and exhaled slowly. Oof. Elena was wearing a simple form-fitting coverall with the words *White Raven* written in script across the back, just a spare bit of crew garb they'd had on hand, but the front zipper was pulled down far enough to offer a tantalizing display of cleavage that Callie very consciously and steadfastly avoided noticing. She was in trouble here. The worst part was, she was *excited* about being in trouble. Elena was from five centuries in the past, but she was snappy with the banter, and hadn't there been a couple of *looks* there, or was Callie just imagining?

Obviously just imagining. Or else it was an artifact of the situation. Elena had been through a trauma, she was alone in a strange land, and Callie was the first person to show her any kindness. The first to show her respect, too, and let Elena know she still had agency and could make important choices about her own life and future. If Elena felt any fondness for Callie, it was the fondness a drifting spacewalker feels for the first passing tether they can grab onto.

Callie shook it off and disembarked the ship. The hangar was more chaotic than normal, with far more remote worker-drones in use than usual being operated by the governing AI of Meditreme Station. Probably necessary to take up the slack left by the mysterious departure of all the Liars. Some of these ships were going to have trouble getting back into space without the alien technicians. There was nothing on Callie's ship that she or Ashok couldn't service themselves – except maybe the bridge generator – because she was majorly into control, but some of the ships used Liar tech that resisted human intervention. A lot of Liar technology was barely understood, and many of their devices were set to fuse their inner workings to glass if human engineers pried them open to figure out how they worked. Of course, most of the Liars claimed they didn't have any proprietary technology: when one of their machines bricked itself, they just blamed human negligence, or rare technical faults, or gremlins, or ghosts, or simply looked at a heap of smoking carbon and said, "What do you mean? It looks fully operational to me."

Callie wove her way around cursing mechanics, nodded to the customs inspector – she worked with the woman fairly often, investigating and apprehending smugglers who didn't want to pay the TNA their cut of commerce – and took a transpod over to the Spoke.

Things got weird as she left the spinning false gravity of the outer rings and moved toward the still center, but the transition was gradual, and her inner ear was pretty accustomed to this kind of abuse. Her boots kept her mag-locked to the floor, and when the pod's doors slid open she disengaged her soles and pulled herself along the grabrails and out into the shaft.

The Spoke was a glittering cylindrical tower of zero-gravity that extended hundreds of meters above her and hundreds below. A central pole with an endless conveyor belt of handholds running up one side and down the other made moving up and down the shaft easy. Each level was clearly marked by large red numbers – she'd come out on level 273 – and dotted with balconies, discreet meeting rooms obscured with smoked glass, and various offices and shops.

As a general rule, those parts of the station with more gravity were preferable (rental prices on the outer ring were murderous), and it often baffled visitors when they discovered the station's administrative offices were here, in the weightless Spoke. For one thing, the TNA wanted to reserve the more valuable real estate for paying customers. The other reason was pure psychological dominance, though: visitors who came from places with gravity to meet with TNA officials in the Spoke were often disoriented, uncomfortable, and prone to vomiting – all of which worked against their attempts to negotiate from positions of strength. Some of the smarter diplomats and businessmen were rumored to train in zero-gravity before they came to talk to the CEO in her weightless wraparound dome at the very top of the spoke, up on level 500. (Having stars visible on all sides and above, as they were in her office, tended to disorient visitors from places where "up" and "down" were absolute rather than relative concepts, too.)

Callie wasn't going all the way up top, though. She'd seen the CEO but never spoken to her. Most of her dealings happened at a lower level in a less business-oriented branch of the organization. She pushed off toward the center pole and snagged a passing handhold, letting the molded grip carry her up into the mid-300s, then pushed the release button. The handhold pistoned out, giving her a little shove toward her destination – and out of the way of people coming up beneath her. She spun and reached out for a rail, pulling herself into a corridor toward a door marked, modestly, "Security."

The door (or the expert system running it) recognized

her and opened without any need to buzz the intercom. Callie floated down the glossy white corridor toward the bright red door at the end. Then she turned left and went down a short hallway to the unmarked piece of wall that was actually the hidden door to the security chief's office. There was nothing behind the red door but cameras and non-lethal automatic restraints – it was only there to provide a shiny lure to confuse invaders or terrorists.

The hidden door didn't open automatically, though it scanned Callie too: someone could have potentially faked her bio-signature to get through the first door, after all. "May I help you?" the security AI asked. It had the cadences and tone of a bored teenage girl, a touch Callie had always appreciated: she'd been a bored teenage girl herself, once, and knew how dangerous they could be.

"Kalea Machedo here to see the chief."

The AI grunted and a moment later the door slid open. Callie had her usual moment of disorientation. The security chief, Warwick, kept her workstation on the "ceiling" – if you thought the direction of increasing numbers in the Spoke corresponded to "up," anyway, as most people unconsciously did. The inverted workspace was probably another way to disorient visitors, though the one time Callie had expressed admiration for the tactic, Warwick had responded with a show of courteous bafflement at the suggestion.

Callie spun herself into the right orientation as she came through the door and got her feet locked onto the "floor." Warwick was completely bald, without even eyebrows, and had a tattoo that resembled a labyrinth on her scalp. The tattoo was stark white against her very dark skin, and Callie knew that in the darkness the lines glowed like phosphorous, unless Warwick didn't want them to. The security chief was working at a standing desk, flipping through screens of info on two different tablets. "I hear you brought an undocumented refugee onto my station," Warwick said without looking up.

"She's plenty documented. Present in the historical record and everything. She was on a goldilocks ship in cryosleep. The crew's xenobiologist."

"A xenobiologist from a time before we met aliens, which is a little like being a mechanic before we invented steam engines. Is she planning on staying on my station?"

"We're probably taking her to the Imperative. Ganymede maybe. More opportunities for her there. She hasn't decided what she wants to do yet." Callie shrugged. "I gather it's a little disorienting."

Warwick shook her head. "Her goldilocks ship never even made it out of the system, huh? That's a tough break. Like if Magellan's ship had sunk right off the coast of Seville instead of circumnavigating the Earth. This Doctor Oh was the only survivor?"

"We didn't find anyone alive in the other pods, no." Warwick was good at spotting lies, so Callie stuck with the technically true. She wasn't about to share Elena's whole harrowing tale. Warwick was a professional, and Callie liked her, but the chief's loyalty to the TNA was absolute, and if she knew about the bridge generator, she'd find some quasi-legal pretext to seize the device. (Quasi-legal pretexts were easier to come by when the CEO and board members who drafted the local laws were just a hundred and fifty floors away.)

Warwick nodded. "Those ancient ships, it's amazing there was even one survivor. She'll get invited to a lot of parties in the Imperative, though. They love a living conversation piece." She glanced up from the tablet. "There, we small talked. Bonds of friendship once again reaffirmed, and I didn't even get a hangover like last time. What can I do for you, Callie?"

"I've run back and forth to the Imperative so many times I'm dizzy, and salvage has lost its appeal. I want to go hunting."

Warwick chuckled. "Oh? You thought you found a nice juicy wreck to liquidate, only to find a survivor with a legitimate claim on board, so you're stuck with a lousy percentage? I can see how that would be a little demoralizing."

"I'm totally demoralized. I want to go demoralize someone else. With guns."

"Hmm, well, there's a smuggler running Liar tech from their outpost on Iukkoth past us and on through the Jovian bridge. They've got a wicked fast little ship and some kind of masking technology they appropriated from the Liars, but the *Raven* is probably a match for them."

"Mmm, no. My mood is less chasing, more laying waste. I want to go after Glauketas."

Warwick pushed her tablets away, paying full attention now. "Are you sure? You've always said no to that mission before. I believe the words 'suicide mission' and 'do I look stupid to you?' usually come up."

Glauketas was a fat pear-shaped asteroid that drifted in the blurry disputed area between Jovian Imperative and TNA territory. There were rumors, never confirmed, that the Imperative offered the pirates at least passive protection, and it was incontrovertible fact that the thieves hit TNA targets more often than Jovian ones.

The TNA was reluctant to send a formal military force to take out Glauketas for fear of triggering a Jovian reprisal – moving a bunch of warships close to another polity's space tended to produce a negative reaction. The pirates knew that, and took full advantage of their position. There was a bounty for the capture of the pirates, though, and if a crew like the *White Raven*, which did security work on a contract basis, wanted to try to collect that bounty, well: that was different.

"I always said no before because the *White Raven* is too pretty to risk getting blown up trying to take out a hardened base. But I heard a rumor you got your hands on some new armaments and defensive systems that could make an attack a lot more lopsided in our favor."

Warwick sighed. "My engineers talked to Ashok, didn't they? Why do engineers always talk to each other? So. You just want to play with my new toys."

"I want to do my duty and help the Trans-Neptunian Authority promote peace and prosperity and safe shipping lanes. And to play with your new toys. Ashok said there's some fancy stealth tech? Or shields? He wasn't clear on the details."

"Good. Maybe my engineers have some sense of discretion. No, it's not really stealth, or shields either. It's more like displacement technology. Countermeasures. Basically the enemy sensors get baffled and think you're several degrees away from your actual position. Radiation signatures, engine exhaust, sonar, it tricks *everything*. So when the enemy fires, their missiles blow right past you. The technology even affects direct visual observation."

"How? I can see tricking sensors, but how do you trick an *eye*?"

"Remember that R-and-D boondoggle you were part of, with the active camouflage?"

Callie nodded. She still owned the only working prototype suit from that project, because it had been custom made to fit her. "Sure. But it was too expensive to put on a space suit, how is it cost-effective to put it on a *ship*?"

Warwick shrugged. "Ask the Liars we bought it from. They miniaturized, they mass-produced, they figured out how to make a fabricator spit the components out without breaking half of them in the process. Who knows? We cover your ship with little cameras and projectors the size of pinheads, totally unobtrusive, and they can project an image of your ship elsewhere, while making your actual shape invisible."

"You're getting me excited, Warwick. How about guns? There are also guns?"

"Various new and interesting guns, yes. For a non-violent species, the Liars sure do a lot of interesting things with antimatter and sound waves and focused light. I can send you the specs for available weaponry, if I decide to give you this commission."

"I thought the commission was mine for the asking?"

Warwick rubbed a hand across the maze on her skull. "Yes, but that was before you asked to borrow my new ordnance. We were going to do a lot of testing, to see if we wanted to invest in upgrades for the main security force. Sending you out there is tempting, though. Glauketas has been trouble for a long time. Plus, taking over their base would be nice – give that asteroid a little push more firmly into our space, and it would make an excellent border outpost..."

Callie watched the calculations in her eyes. No matter

how well armed, there was a chance the *Raven* might be captured or destroyed, and maybe the new weaponry was too valuable to risk falling into the hands of pirates. There was clearly a complex cost-benefit analysis going on. After a moment Warwick nodded. "All right. I'll have your ship outfitted. I'm going to fit the new equipment with failsafes, though, so your computer can decommission them completely if the *Raven* gets captured. No way I'm letting pirates get their hands on this kind of materiel." She sighed. "Until they can afford to buy it from the Liars themselves, anyway. All the equipment comes back to me when you're done, too, understood?"

"Like I want your guns ruining my ship's beautiful silhouette forever. Can you make it happen with a quickness? It's a bit of a trip out to Glauketas, and Stephen has a religious festival coming up."

"The Church of the Ecstatic Divine, right? My wife's mother joined that a few years ago. I don't like to picture it." She shook it off. "I'll put a rush on the order. Everything is slower today with the mass Liar defection, but I'll prioritize."

"Do you, ah, have any idea why the Liars are taking off?" She was keenly aware it was all her fault, and pretty sure Warwick didn't know it, but she wanted to hear what the security chief's working theory was.

Warwick jabbed at a tablet with her fingertip. "I have no idea. There aren't any aliens left on the station to ask, not a single one, and it's not like the answers would mean much anyway." She shrugged. "I'm just trying to keep everyone calm. They're acting like the Liars leaving is an early warning system or something. There's a rumor going around that the Liars got wind of some threat and scampered off to avoid it, but as far as we can tell there's nothing to worry about within range of our sensors, and no bad news from any of the outlying bases. Even so, we've seen a twenty percent increase in departures among the human population. Not many of the permanent residents are leaving, at least. When the station *doesn't* explode into fine dust over the next couple of days, or spontaneously melt into nano-goo, I'm sure things will get back to normal." There was an edge to her voice. Callie suspected the TNA was scanning the area around them *very carefully* for potential threats, and putting out feelers to all their informants and spies in organizations friendly and otherwise throughout the system. She thought of their canoe, floating out in the black some distance away with an alien artifact at its heart, and was glad she'd gotten it off the station, just in case.

"So you don't think there's a threat?" she said.

Warwick looked toward the ceiling, as if pondering. "Between you and me? I'm concerned. Not outright anxious, but concerned. I haven't seen any intelligence reports with troubling information, and I don't know where a serious threat would even *come* from. We've been getting along well with Jupiter, and nobody else who wields any power is even *out* here on the edge of things. This is where people come to get away from trouble. That said... I've called in all the roving security patrols to the station, and I've got them combing over the Liar quarters, looking for anything suspicious."

"Are they finding much?"

Warwick snorted. "All manner of contraband, sure. You know Liars. They don't really believe in laws. But there are no bombs, no manifestos, no secret invasion plans, no dark prophecies." She waved her hand. "But we're still looking, so, go. I have work to do."

"Thanks, chief. I bet it's just, you know, Liar things. Some weird alien emotional weather." She wanted to put Warwick's mind at ease, but she could hardly do that definitively without revealing her possession of potentially system-changing technology to a TNA officer, and she didn't feel *that* guilty. "We'll get armed up, pop over to Ganymede to drop off our refugee, and then see what we can do about Glauketas."

"Don't die. I'd be devastated to lose all my new weapons."

CHAPTER 10

"A bar is a bar is a bar," Elena muttered, stepping into the Spinward Lounge. This was supposed to be an expedition for street food, but the sudden craving for a drink, and even more importantly, for quiet and isolation, seized her and wouldn't let go.

"They had bars in Shakespeare's day, and your day, and ours," Shall agreed in her earpiece.

The Spinward Lounge was dim, an open space filled with tables and chairs and little arched nooks and crannies holding booths and couches; some of the nooks were screened off with curtains. The lounge was sparsely occupied, and that was very appealing. The station corridors were crowded with people, some so physically modified Elena only knew they were human because she'd been told Liars were the only aliens, and there weren't any of those on the station at the moment. She'd known people who were transgender, non-binary, genderqueer, agender, and more in her time, but the accepted range of human variation had clearly continued expanding.

She'd hugged the station walls, staying out of the bustling flow, cursing herself for her cowardice, until she finally decided she was no more confused than a citizen of 1700s Italy would have been if they'd gone into, say, a twenty-second century San Francisco sex club. Of course she was overwhelmed. She'd expected to finish out her days, best-case scenario, on a colony world populated by her crewmates and infants birthed from incubators. This profusion of people, and the overall strangeness of the situation, against the backdrop of her ongoing anxiety, was simply too much for her.

She wanted to retreat to her cabin on the *White Raven*, but she refused to be defeated. She was going back into space, and soon, and might not return here; she might not even survive. She intended to partake in a little of the works of modern humanity before she flitted back into the void. She'd never expected to see a bar again, after all, and once upon a time, she'd loved them.

She was glad it was a quiet and nearly empty bar, though.

"I don't have any money, so I'll have to flirt for drinks, I guess. It's been a while. I hope social mores haven't changed so much that I accidentally propose marriage or provoke a duel."

"Marriage is considered a bit old-fashioned, at least out here on the edge of the system. There are contractual relationships of various sorts, but you won't enter into one of those accidentally. Usually legal AIs get involved. I'll pay for your drinks, though, don't worry. I have more lix than I know what to do with. Just order and they'll charge through your tablet."

Elena went to the bar, tended by a human with a spiky haircut and a vest that looked like leather over her otherwise bare chest, where glowing abstract tattoos writhed in her cleavage. "Drinkies?" she said.

"Please. I haven't had a drink in about five hundred years."

"Some catching up to do then." The bartender smiled, showing off teeth that gleamed with metallic hues, and a flash of blue tongue.

Elena didn't react to the colorful smile. If she could avoid looking like a bumpkin, she would. She recognized almost none of the bottles behind the bar, and many of them were unmarked anyway. Homemade, or bespoke, or merely ornamental? "What do you recommend?"

"You like sweet or sour or something with a bite?"

"Why not all three?"

"I'll make you a special special." The bartender deftly snatched bottles and poured her selections directly into an oversized martini glass, where they formed distinct layers, like a parfait. The bottom level was pale green, the second deep red, and the top rich black. She rubbed the rim with the peel of some citrus fruit Elena didn't recognize, then sprinkled one side of the rim with sugar and the other with flecks of something reddish and crystalline. "It's called a ziggurat, invented by me myself in the icy nowheres, to keep you warm where it counts."

Elena picked up the glass carefully, impressed at the way the layers stayed distinct. She sipped, the black liquid washing over the sugared rim, and it was citrusy at first and then smoky and then almost coffee. Heat blossomed in her belly when she swallowed. "Mmm."

"Try the other side," the bartender said, and Elena obligingly sipped. This time it was more like paprika smokiness, and sweet, almost cherry, as the red layer swirled up. Another sip and the green mingled, fresh and bright and summery and citrus-tangy. It was like three cocktails in one.

"This is amazing, thank you."

"Your lips are all red and red. From the sweet liqueur in the center. Color will fade soon but pretty until."

Elena dabbed at her lips with a napkin, which didn't come away stained, anyway. "I could probably use the color. I spent a long time in the dark."

"You sound from far away. Down a well?"

"I'm from Earth," Elena said. "Originally."

The bartender whistled. "Not too many of you come all the way out here except on business. You for business?"

She sighed. "Would you believe I was in cryosleep for five hundred years and just woke up, I guess yesterday? If it was yesterday. I don't even know how days work here. I was adjusted to a twenty-seven hour cycle, because we were pretty sure that was the length of the day on the planet we were traveling to."

"Ah." The bartender blinked. "A day out here is a set of shifts. Six-hour shifts, set of four shifts a day, so it's not too bad if you have to pull a double sometimes."

"Ha. You have a twenty-four hour day, this far from Earth? I guess humans did evolve to live that way."

"It's not so bad, and anyway, the station doesn't sleep. I come from Triton. A day on Triton runs a hundred and forty hours, which is not so good. We break it up there too."

"Neptune's only sixteen hours. I remember that from school."

The bartender poured a small glass of something dark brown into a glass and took a slow sip. "Nobody much lives on Neptune. Mostly AI, tending the wind farms. Are you *really* a past person? No jokes?"

"No jokes. I was on a goldilocks ship. We… didn't get where we were going. We were stranded, far from our destination. I was the only survivor."

The bartender winced. "Sorry to hear. I'm Jana, by the byway."

"Elena."

"Welcome to the now and now, Elena. Drinks on me, OK?"

Elena smiled, touched by the kindness. "Thank you. I expected to wake up in orbit around a distant planet. I didn't expect to wake up here, but in a way, it's even stranger."

"Five hundred years," Jana ruminated. "Bad times back then, before the Liars, and the wilding and the opening-up. There are some other past people here and there, I hear. They get to their planets, sometimes, they wake up, they find a colony already there, because we got ahead of them, through the bridges. You know the bridges?"

"I've heard about them, yeah."

"Maybe there's somebody you know, even? Could check the Tangle, find some friends, feel less lonely maybe?"

That hadn't occurred to Elena, but she *had* met many of the other goldilocks crews, at least in passing, during training. "That's a good idea. Thank you."

"Nassa prob."

Elena decided to parse that as "no problem."

"What ship found you?" Jana asked.

"The *White Raven*?"

"Ah ha ha, you crewed up with Callie then? She's tough and tough but she'll take good care. Won't cheat you."

"She's been very kind. Do you know her well?"

"To say hi hello, some same friends, some drinks together at parties. Mostly she's just known. Does security but freelance, not as sticky uppy as some who serve. Tells you true. Stabs from the front."

"Ha. Right. She said maybe I should go to Ganymede."

"Jovian Imperative, gateway to the galaxy. Not so quiet there, not like way out here on the edge. This is the place to go to get away, but that's the place to be close in. You can go and be anywhere there. Maybe you stay here a little while, where it's quiet, while you get used to it being so loud. You can come here any time. I like to talk when it's not too busy to talk."

"I will come back." *If I survive*. Elena finished her drink. "Thanks for this."

"Nassa prob. Say. You fancy a tumbling tumble? I'm off soon and you're sweet to speak to and you have a shine."

Elena blinked. "Oh. Do you mean... do I want to have sex?"

"If you want. Been five hundred years, eh? You're cute as all, is all. No worries if no."

"I... not right now, but I appreciate you asking, and so nicely." She started to slide off the stool, then paused. "May I ask? Why is your tongue blue?"

"Nano-thing. Supertaster." She waggled out her tongue, but not lewdly. "Good for making better drinkies."

"Right. That makes sense. I'll see you around, Jana."

"Until and until. This is your great big beautiful tomorrow today, eh?"

Elena left the lounge. "That went well," Shall said in her ear. "Excellent human interactions."

"Excellent patronizing voice. Tell me, is it usual here for people to proposition others for sex that directly?" Thinking: *I could just proposition Callie, if that's how things are done*. She felt a twinge of guilt at the thought, because not so long ago (in subjective time, at least) she'd fantasized about Sebastien that way, and now he was lost. She wasn't wired to be particularly monogamous, and one kiss didn't make Sebastien her boyfriend anyway, but she felt guilty thinking about sex at all, with anyone, when he was in danger.

Shall said, "Direct propositions are generally acceptable in that sort of bar, and at parties – if they aren't business parties, but that line gets blurry at times – and in many social clubs, and in appropriate regions of the Tangle. Basically, you can ask someone if they'd like to have sex if it's a place where you might reasonably expect to be asked that. Otherwise, no – we rely on the same flirtations and insinuations and speculations and sizing-up that were common in your time, based on my recent survey of your film and literature."

"Ah. Good to know. I'd hate to find myself made prudish by circumstance." Propositioning someone you'd hired to lead a reckless rescue mission was probably a social faux pas, though.

"Callie *does* respond well to directness, though, so–"

"Shut up shut up shut up."

"I will, if you like, but Jana wasn't wrong. It's been five hundred years. And you're going on a mission you might never return from."

"Let's change the subject, shall we, Shall? What's Callie's problem with you? Why doesn't she call you by your name? Why does she seem really annoyed every time you talk? What is your secret history?"

A long pause. "Shut up," he said. "Shut up shut up shut up."

"Fair," Elena said.

• • •

Callie departed the security office, comming with Ashok to let him know the ship was going to be fitted with new defensive and offensive systems, and letting him know he should coordinate with the engineers from security about getting it done promptly and well.

She made a few more stops – arranging for resupply since she wasn't sure how long they'd be out, and grabbing fresh clothes from her quarters (including a couple of things she thought she looked especially good in, but definitely *not* for Elena, she just felt like dressing up). She met up with her friend Hermione, who'd been born out here and upgraded from the life of a rock-hopper to become a designer of expert systems, and had the single foulest mouth and raunchiest mind Callie had ever encountered. They caught up over lunch at their favorite halal cart in one of the inner rings.

"So tell her you want to climb on," Herm said after Callie had laid out her feelings about Elena (whom she described merely as a sexy time refugee, and not a survivor of bizarre alien interventions). "She hasn't had so much as a sad solo orgasm in five hundred years? She'll worship you like a god."

"I *like* her. I don't want to take advantage of her. And I think she's carrying a torch for one of her crewmates anyway."

"She's got two hands, so she can carry two torches. Why not take advantage of each other? That's *healthy*. That's what I always do."

"As always, your ethical guidance is the star that lights my way."

"If you're not going to climb it, point her in my direction. I'll blow the dust off her properly."

Callie threw a napkin at her.

By the time Callie got back to the hangar, Ashok was supervising the security engineers crawling all over the hull of her ship with torches and epoxy and rivets. He spun toward her and came bouncing over. "Cap! We're getting so many new toys. We're going pirate hunting?"

"Yes," she said, for the benefit of anyone who might overhear. "Everything working out?"

"We're getting new fancy guns, and some defensive systems that Drake and Janice are pretty excited about. It'll take a few hours to get everything in place, and then we have some system checks and all that. Stephen is out visiting with his congregation, but he says he'll be back by the next shift change."

"Where's Elena?" Casual, casual.

"Exploring the station. She's got Shall whispering in her ear, so she should be fine."

Callie covered her disappointment with an ostentatious yawn. "I should catch some rack time. I guess my ship is going to be a cacophonous nightmare of grinding metal?"

"The sweetest music in the galaxy, cap."

"Right. I'm going to my quarters. When I get back, I want my ship all put together and pretty."

"As pretty as me?"

"Maybe a *little* prettier, if you can manage it."

Callie dreamed of Elena. Floating in space, her hair drifting, the zipper on her jumpsuit sliding down...

Oh, yes. She was in definite trouble there. Maybe they'd all die on the trip, and then Callie wouldn't be alive to do anything to embarrass herself.

She sat up in her bunk and discovered a message waiting on her table from the station's security AI:

Salvage object tagged "Anjou" destroyed.

What? "Station, what's this note about the *Anjou* being destroyed?"

The station's voice in her earpiece was mellifluous and friendly because Callie was a sworn agent of the corporation, albeit in an on-call contract capacity. The station tended toward more brusque and harsh tones with strangers. Just part of the frontier charm of life in Trans-Neptunian space. "The transponder you left on the *Anjou* went offline several hours ago, and one of the recalled security ships detoured slightly on its way back to check the location. They found a debris field suggesting the ship had been destroyed by some sort of targeted energy weapon. Our working theory is that pirates looted anything of value and then destroyed the ship, probably because it was too old to be a worthwhile addition to their fleet. We're sorry for the loss. Any recovered property will be returned to you, of course, minus expenses and fees."

Callie grunted. "Thanks for letting me know." There wasn't much on the *Anjou* that was worth looting; the ship itself had been the valuable thing, as a museum piece or historical oddity. Legitimate museums and weirdo collectors both would have paid a lot of lix for it, and any competent pirates could have disabled the transponder and hauled the whole thing away. Stupid pirates might have just thought "old weird ship" and blown it up in a fit of pique, though.

Now she had to tell Elena she'd lost her only worldly possession besides the bridge generator, which technically belonged to Callie's crew now, and a few salvaged odds and ends on the *White Raven*. Like being a time refugee wasn't hard enough already.

● ● ●

"Is everyone on board, ship?" Callie asked from her seat at a tactical board in the forward observation compartment.

"You're calling me 'ship,' now?" the voice whispered in her ear. "That's a step up from 'computer,' which was frankly a bit insulting. I'm as far beyond a computer as you are beyond a paramecium."

"Would you please answer the question?"

"You said please! You are in a good mood today. Yes, Captain Machedo, the entire crew is currently on board, including Doctor Oh."

"Systems check?"

"All the non-organic bits check out. The new weapons and defensive systems are fully integrated. You and Ashok have direct control over the weapons, Janice and Drake have the defenses on their screens, and of course, you can ask me if you need things done right."

"I'll keep that in mind. Open a shipwide channel." She cleared her throat. "Ready check. Comms and navigation?"

"If there's anyone to talk to, we can talk to them," Janice said. "And, yes, I know the way to Ganymede."

"Pilot?"

"I have nothing but green lights," Drake said.

"Engineering?"

"Everything's zip-zip and zoom-zoom down here, cap," Ashok said.

"XO?"

"I'm strapped into my acceleration couch," Stephen said. "Wake me when it's over."

"Doctor Oh?"

"Hi."

Callie turned her head, and there was Elena, still in

her *White Raven* jumpsuit. She'd found some lipstick somewhere – or, no, she'd probably had a ziggurat in the Spinward Lounge. The cocktail reacted with the skin of the lips and made them turn dark cherry red, which was the mixologist's preferred shade on women. Callie had never considered herself particularly vulnerable to lipstick femmes, but, yes, there was a definite reaction. *Oh Oh Oh*, yet again. "Yes, Elena?"

"I don't have anything to do, and I didn't like the idea of being strapped into the jump seat in my quarters, so Shall said I might be able to keep you company up here?"

Callie inclined her head toward the amorphous blob of a jump seat freshly extruded from the wall on her left. "Sure, strap in."

Elena took her place in the squishy white gel, which conformed to her body's shape perfectly. At that moment, Callie rather envied that jump seat. Elena adjusted the webbing of straps, then nodded. "I think I see how it works. This will protect us from being hurt by sudden acceleration?"

"That's the idea, but we won't be pulling too many Gs this trip. It's just a little jaunt." She looked at the tactical status board, which was happy and green. "All right, we're ready to go. Drake, tell the station we're off."

"The station says 'Happy hunting,'" Drake said.

The ship lurched as the conveyor belt carried it to one of the station's many ship-sized airlocks, the inner door sealing behind them and the outer door opening. The station's manipulator arms picked up the *Raven* as gently as a mother cat carrying its kittens and deposited it outside, and the reaction wheels whirled to point them in the right direction. They floated weightless against their straps, and Callie shared a smile with Elena.

"Comms are secure," Janice said. "They aren't listening to us on the station anymore."

"OK," Callie said. "We have to be plausible about this. The official story is we're taking Elena to Jovian space, dropping her off to start a new life, and then going on to wipe out the pirates on Glauketas."

"Wait, what?" Elena said. "Pirates?"

"I had to tell the station security chief something so we could get the *good* guns," Callie said. "I'm not going on a rescue mission to an alien space station armed with our standard hardware."

"I approve of us becoming more heavily armed," Stephen said. "But won't we be expected to actually capture the pirates at some point?"

"We'll be expected to *try*. And if we survive this rescue trip, we will."

"Hurray," Stephen said. "If we manage to cheat death, we'll give death another sporting chance."

"Let's take off like we're heading to Jupiter, Drake. You've got the coordinates to pick up the canoe, and it's on the way. Once we have the generator on board and plugged in, we'll find a nice quiet bit of space, and... well. We'll see if this supposed bridge generator actually generates any bridges."

"Off we go," Drake said. The ship accelerated, pressing them back into their jump seats hard, but the body-molding gel made it an issue of pressure rather than discomfort. They moved at high speed for a while, then decelerated. "Matching velocity with the canoe," Drake said. A few moments later: "Picking up the canoe." There were distant *clunks* as the smaller vessel was grabbed and tucked into the *Raven*'s belly. "Resuming acceleration."

After a while they settled into a steady pace of

acceleration, and the ship said, "Ding. Feel free to move about the cabin."

Callie unstrapped, and Elena followed suit. There was light thrust gravity, enough to keep their feet on the ground without weighing them down. "I've got some bad news, Elena," Callie said. "Someone decided to play target practice with the *Anjou*. It's gone."

Elena frowned. "Is that sort of thing common here? Like people going to the junkyard and shooting at old cars on Earth back in my day?"

"Not usually. Especially not at a ship tagged with a TNA transponder. The corporation takes such things seriously, and there will be an investigation. We assume it was pirates, but they weren't very bright, since the ship itself was the main thing worth scavenging. I'm sorry. I know the *Anjou* was important to you."

"In a way," Elena said. "It was my home for centuries, after all, but on the other hand, I only spent a few days there, conscious, anyway. I'm honestly already more at home on the *White Raven*."

That gave Callie a little thrill she didn't bother to analyze too closely. "I'm glad to hear that. You're very welcome here."

"You've made me feel nothing but. I guess the loss of income is a problem, but not having any – what do you call it? lix? – seems like the least of my troubles right now."

"Maybe we can work something out, after all this is over."

"What, I can swab the decks?"

Callie grinned. "Or something. You're paying way over any reasonable rate by giving us the bridge generator. I might feel so guilty I cut you in on my share of the proceeds. See if we can help you, and your crewmates once we rescue them, get your feet under you."

"You're so nice to me, Callie. Thank you. I hope I can repay you someday."

Callie tried not to think about what such repayment might entail. "So. Want to meet the rest of the crew?" Callie said. "Since we're going into the wild mysterious black together?"

Elena nodded. "I would have gone around and introduced myself earlier, but Shall said everyone was quite busy."

"They were busy, but we also wanted to, ah, ease you into the modern era a bit. I guess you probably saw some pretty unusual people on the station, though."

"I'm only sorry I didn't get to see any of the aliens. Terrible timing for the Liars to leave – I'm supposed to be a xenobiologist, and I've never even observed any xenobiology."

"You didn't encounter anyone too alarming on the station, though?"

"There were plenty of… well, posthumans, from my point of view, anyway. Augmented, upgraded, and genetically engineered. I did find it a little overwhelming, but it was the crowds as much as the variations. The only people I'd seen before that were you and Stephen, and you seem much like the baseline humans of my day."

"Mostly, though we've both had some work done under the hood – mine in the womb, Stephen when he was a boy. Little tweaks to make long-term travel in space less physically damaging, adjustments to our metabolisms, disease resistance, things like that. We both come from pretty conservative backgrounds, though. Ashok's appearance is a lot more radical, probably stranger than anything you encountered on Meditreme. It might be a little shocking."

Elena shrugged. "I'm a scientist. I can observe without audibly gasping."

"I'm sure you can. He won't care if you gasp though. He'll assume you're just impressed. After that I'll take you to meet Drake and Janice. They're… a little more sensitive."

Elena followed Callie down the corridor. The captain walked with an easy bounce in her step, moving with a self-assurance and confidence that Elena envied. It would take her some time to get her bearings properly in this new world… if she lived long enough.

Callie went down a ladder, and Elena followed, and then they wound through a narrow corridor and emerged into the machine shop, a square room full of workbenches covered in clamps and inscrutable equipment, with diagnostic information spooling across screens on the walls. Webbed nets on the walls and ceiling held tools and parts, and neatly labeled drawers under the benches promised more of the same. The room smelled of oil and hot metal and, Elena had to acknowledge, farts.

The bridge generator sat in the middle of the biggest table, a fat cable emerging from its top spliced into a cable of a different color that snaked off into the wall. A short, stocky man stood with his back to them. He was dressed in a dirty gray coverall, the back of his head half bare brown scalp and half shiny metal plate, curved to fit the original contours of his skull. Elena wondered what kind of accident he'd been in, and why they couldn't have disguised the repair better. Cosmetic surgery had been capable of *that* kind of correction even in her day.

"How goes it, Ashok?" Callie said.

"Just doing a few last checks, cap." Something about his voice was strange, like there was a buzz under the words. She'd heard it before, over the comms, but had assumed it was an artifact of the communications system. Apparently not. "More emulations and simulations and all that. I'm pretty sure I've got the generator's travel history figured out, so we should be able to bounce back to wherever it came from." He turned around and paused when he saw Elena.

She kept her face perfectly blank. She'd seen all sorts of injuries in the bad old days on Earth – assorted deformities, mutations, and teratogenic anomalies treated with varying levels of success or failure.

She'd never seen anything like Ashok, though: most of his face was a curved silver metal mask, and instead of eyes he had an array of lenses, and instead of a nose he had a brass thing shaped a little like a nose, but more like a dolphin's dorsal fin, with no visible nostrils. He wore a sort of thick metallic collar around his throat, the color of brass, covered in small holes, like a speaker grill.

He smiled, and the lips were human, though his tongue was black and the teeth were various jewel-tones. The lenses over his eyes twisted and spun, but then he pushed them up on his forehead, and she realized they were glasses or goggles. His eyes underneath were bloodshot, but human, peering out of that smooth metal mask. "Hey, Doctor Oh, nice to meet you. It's OK, you can stare. I know it's a lot to take in. My face had a serious disagreement with some acid when I was working on a mining ship way back when. These aren't even my original eyes – they got jellied, but the muscles were pretty intact, so they fitted me with transplant eyes. They could have done reconstruction and made my face more face-like, but I decided to just embrace the cyborgism." He held up his right arm, and it was mostly metal, too – maybe entirely metal – apart from a crystalline window in the forearm that showed the mechanical musculature underneath. Instead of fingers he had a bloom of various delicate manipulators. "Why not go full machine-man, right?"

He pounded on his chest, and there was a clank under his coverall. "I've still got my heart, but there's a redundant backup system in there too, and my liver and kidneys are *way* better than yours, being bioengineered, and I've got some great stuff going on in my Achilles tendons and knees, we're talking major piston stuff, you should see me lift with my legs, and as for my–" He stopped, coughed, and said, "Sorry, never mind. See, cap, I remembered about how there's a line I shouldn't cross, right?"

"Ashok is into self-improvement," Callie said. "I think he aspires to be fully modular so he can swap out any body part as needed. They've written him up in medical journals, and they weren't even all called *Abnormal Psychology Today*."

"My brain is still mine, though," Ashok said. "I mean, *mostly*. I won't say there aren't any augmentations. I'm not a barbarian from barbarian times. Crap. I mean, I didn't mean–"

"It's wonderful to meet you, Ashok," Elena said. "You have a deep knowledge of mechanical-human interfaces, I assume?"

He nodded. "I'm way ahead of you. Whatever weird metal brain-spiders attached themselves to your friends' heads? If there's a way to get them out, I'll find it." He paused. "But if the implants do anything interesting I might mod one up to use myself. Never turn your back on innovation, wherever it may be found, that's what I always say."

"I have literally never heard you say that," Callie said. "It's not even a saying. It's barely a sentence."

"It's what I always *meant* to say, then. When do you want to fire up the magic box here, cap?"

"I'll let you know. I want to get beyond even a whisper of Meditreme Station traffic. It's better if nobody's around to see, even at a distance, when we wink out of existence. I'm going to take Elena upstairs to meet Drake and Janice–"

"Oh, no," Shall said, through the ship's PA system. "Oh, everyone, I- I'm so sorry."

Callie's eyes narrowed. "Report," she barked.

"Meditreme Station," Shall said. "It's gone."

"What's that supposed to mean?"

"I mean someone just destroyed it."

CHAPTER 11

Callie always went cold in emergencies. "Show me."

"This footage was taken by our sensors. You can't see much from this distance, but…"

The screens all blanked, showing star-dotted blackness, and a faint shimmer that was probably Meditreme Station, getting incrementally dimmer in the distance as the *White Raven* moved farther away. Then light suddenly bloomed on the screen, a radiant flash of bluish-white that gradually faded into sparkles, and then, blackness.

"The comms are all lit up," Janice said over the PA. "Every ship in the vicinity saw that."

"We have to go back. Drake, get us turned around."

The ship extruded jumpseats from the machine room's walls, and there was a *clunk* as Ashok sealed his boots to the hull. His physiology was adjusted to handle acceleration.

Callie numbly strapped herself into a seat, and Elena followed suit. "Janice, check the station security frequency, see if there's any chatter."

"Dead silent. The civilian comms are full of chatter, but there's nothing you'd call official."

Callie groaned. "Warwick called in all the security patrols." Warwick. She was gone. So was Hermione, and the customs agent on the dock, and everyone else Callie knew on Meditreme, the place she'd called home for the past decade. She tried to tell herself there might be survivors, but that explosion, that spray of glittering dust... she couldn't believe anyone had made it through that intact. "What the hell happened? Could it have been an accident?"

"I don't think so," the ship said. "I think it was an attack, though I haven't identified the weapon. Usually that sort of thing is easy to identify, based on the nature of the debris field and any radiation signatures left behind, but this data is unlike anything I've seen before."

Callie gritted her teeth. "If someone attacked the station, that means there's a *ship*, and if there's a ship, there's someone to *chase*."

"Uh, cap, if they have weapons capable of blowing up the station, do you really want to go after them? Respectfully."

"Someone just killed fifty thousand people, Ashok. We might be the only gunship representing TNA authority for thousands of kilometers. No way we're letting the perpetrators get away."

"Understood," Ashok said. "I'll get the defensive systems online."

"Go faster, Drake," Callie said. "I want to feel my brain trying to climb out the back of my head."

The pressure of acceleration increased, and Callie sank back into the jumpseat, trying to focus on the task at hand: find the perpetrators, secure or destroy them, and see justice done. She was just a contractor, more bounty hunter than policeman, but right now it was entirely possible she was the whole of the law, and she intended to represent the Trans-Neptunian Authority to the very edge of her abilities.

Except Meditreme Station *was* the Trans-Neptunian Authority. The two were basically synonymous. The station was the center of the corporation's organization and power. There wasn't much else to the TNA but a few asteroid outposts, research stations, mining operations, and some articles of incorporation floating in a database somewhere. The CEO was gone, the CFO, the board, all the senior management, most of the employees... The TNA was a giant in the region, but its head had just been blown off.

Callie couldn't think about that, any more than she could think about all her dead friends and colleagues. Do the job in front of you, and *then* think about what comes next. "Ship, do an intelligence analysis. Who had the means and motive to do something like this?"

"Ah. I've been working on that. Ask anyone in the system and they'd say it must be the Jovians, probably funding mercenaries or pirates or terrorists to commit the actual attack. The Jovian Imperative has joint projects with the TNA, but the TNA has been getting stronger, upsetting the balance of power. With the TNA crippled, the Jovians could invoke emergency clauses to seize control of all those joint operations around Neptune and Uranus. The loss of Meditreme Station is the certain ruin of the TNA, so the Jovians could snatch up all their property for next to nothing, and then everything from the asteroid belt to the edge of the solar system would be under the Imperative's control."

"That's monstrous," Callie said. "Corporate espionage is one thing, but they blew up a *city*. There are sure to be investigations, Earth itself will get involved. It could even lead to war. It's an insane risk."

"It is," the ship agreed. "If we believe it was a deliberate attack, though, it's the only plausible explanation. Only, I don't think that's what happened. I don't think this is the Jovian Imperative's fault."

"Then whose fault *is* it?"

"It's gotta be ours, cap." Ashok spoke softly.

Callie stared at him. There were tears running from under his lenses, down his shiny metal face. She hadn't even realized his tear ducts worked. Then she understood. "The bridge generator. That's what changed. That's the new variable."

"We brought the bridge generator to the station," the ship said. "We showed it to My Cousin Paolo, who became agitated, even terrified, and fled. Soon after that, *all* the Liars fled. Not much later, the station was destroyed. There is a plausible chain of cause and effect."

"You think someone was trying to get *us*?" Callie said. "To destroy the bridge generator, and Meditreme Station was just collateral damage?"

"It's a hypothesis worth exploring," the ship said.

"An alien device like this, as powerful as it seems to be?" Ashok was still crying, but his voice was calm. "It's going to attract attention."

"I also find it interesting that the *Anjou* was destroyed," the ship said. "I accessed the station database when I heard you tell Elena about the loss, and retrieved the data before the station... went offline. The passing security ship picked up the same odd radiation signature I'm seeing here, and noted the same uniform level of devastation in the debris. It's reasonable to assume that whoever blew up Meditreme also destroyed the *Anjou*."

"But why? The generator was already gone–"

"The navigational data wasn't," Drake said. "Anyone who looked at the *Anjou*'s computer would have a record of where it came from."

"They aren't just trying to destroy the bridge generator," Callie said. "They're trying to erase any evidence that the generator was ever in this system, and to make sure no one else can find the place where Elena picked it up. Gods."

"This is my fault," Elena murmured.

"No, we need to put aside that guilt and blame shit for now," Callie snapped. "It's not *any* of our faults. It's the fault of whoever fired the weapon. But who could that be? Nobody knew we had the generator, except the Liars."

"The Liars don't blow things up, though," the ship said. "There's not a single record of the Liars ever engaging in violent action. We know they have weapons – some of those weapons are installed on this ship right now – but they've never turned their guns on humans, or one another, as far as we know. In the face of confrontation they always try diplomacy, in their own dishonest way, or bribery, or they simply run away. They've hurt people, certainly, but always by accident, to the best of our knowledge. Even when the Liars have clashed with pirates, they've always fought back with non-lethal means. That's part of why humans feel safe letting the Liars onto their ships and stations and planets, even though they fundamentally can't be trusted: the Liars have always been resolutely pacifistic."

"So it wasn't the Liars," Callie said. "But the Liars knew something was coming, or why else would they run off? So the attacker must be someone, or *something*, the Liars fear. A different race of aliens? Lurking out in the Oort Cloud somewhere? But how would *they* know we have the generator? Does it produce some unique radiation signature they could track?"

"Not that I know of," Ashok said, "but there may be a signature when it's used. It opened a bridge from wherever the alien station was to here, so maybe that lit up someone's sensors? Or else... maybe someone followed Elena all the way from the alien station when she escaped. Someone trying to recover stolen property."

"That station *put* the bridge generator on her ship. Why take it back when they gave it to her in the first place?"

"Maybe someone realized they messed up and gave the wrong candy to the wrong baby?" Ashok shrugged.

Callie tried to drum her fingers against the seat but the acceleration gravity was strong enough to make it difficult. "So we could be going after a ship controlled by unknown aliens, who were willing to kill fifty thousand people to destroy a black box they gave to us in the first place. It doesn't seem to track."

"I don't know. Sometimes people make mistakes and go to pretty serious lengths to cover them up, if the mistakes are bad enough," Ashok said. "I just don't know who else it could be. If it wasn't the Jovian Imperative, and it wasn't the Liars, then–"

"I've got something on our scanners," Drake interrupted. "It looks like– Shall, would you confirm?"

"Confirmed," the ship said. "Position and trajectory fit the available data. That's either the ship that fired on Meditreme Station, or it was close enough to see who did. And... it's a Liar ship."

"I give up," Ashok said. "I don't know what the hell

is going on."

"Go after them," Callie said.

"That is, ah, very not necessary," Drake said. "They must have noticed us, too, because they're coming around, and pretty clearly setting a course to intercept us."

"Are we *sure* it's a Liar ship?"

"One of their classic starfish configurations," the ship said. "Though I don't know for sure there are Liars inside it. By design those ships are difficult to pilot for anyone with fewer than six or seven appendages, but some augmented human or a very well-coordinated team could–"

"Hail them, Janice. Let's see what they have to say for themselves. They're either the perpetrators, or they were witnesses, and either way, they're persons of interest."

"They aren't saying anything," she said. "They pinged our transponder, so they know our designation, but that's it. They're ignoring us otherwise. And before you ask, no, they don't have a transponder of their own. They're not registered in the TNA database, or the Jovian Imperative, and nowhere farther afield, either."

Callie grunted. Unregistered Liar ships were common – Liars were pretty laissez-faire about rules and regulations, and it wasn't like you could trust their paperwork even when they appeared to be in compliance – but information asymmetry always bothered her. "If they are after the bridge generator, and they know we're the *White Raven*, and they know we're the people who found the *Anjou*... We'd better get them before they get us. Ashok, let's talk tactical options. I want them disabled rather than blown to bits. I'd like to have an *intimate* talk with them."

"We're in luck. The TNA wanted us to take over Glauketas, not annihilate it, so we've got some fancy new EMP torpedoes. We blast them at the ship, they set off a pulse that disables their electrical systems, and it's supposed to work even against hardened targets."

"Do it."

Ashok ran the tactical board, which was normally Callie's privilege, but she wasn't usually in a spare jumpseat in a machine shop when things got nasty. "Torpedoes away. At this distance, impact should take about ten minutes."

"Are they shooting at us yet?"

"They are now," the ship said. "As soon as we fired, they responded."

"Missiles?"

"Honestly? I have no idea. They launched half a dozen projectiles, but not like any I've seen before. They're large and spherical, and look more like drones or probes than missiles."

"Huh. Why shoot robots at us? Well, who cares. Janice, you've got our defensive countermeasures running?"

"That's what my board says," Janice replied. "If it works the way it's supposed to, whatever they fired should miss us by a kilometer."

"The things they fired look almost like escape pods," the ship said. "Big enough to be manned by a Liar, anyway, with some sort of rudimentary thrust and directional systems."

"Wait. You think it's a boarding party?" Callie said.

"Makes a certain degree of sense," the ship said. "They blew up Meditreme Station, but now they know we got off the station ahead of them. They probably don't know how long we were gone, or where we went. As far as they know, we could have stashed the bridge generator somewhere. Maybe they want to get direct confirmation that the device is here before they turn *us* into a cloud of sparkling dust with their mystery weapons. Otherwise, they'd have to vaporize every object between Jupiter and the Oort Cloud to make sure they got rid of the generator."

"Fuck that," Callie said. "Shoot their little pods out of the sky, Ashok, and then we'll board *them*."

"Targeting." Ashok was silent for a moment, then said, "Uh. Shall, what just happened?"

"The ballistic cannons seem functional. The error wasn't on our end."

"What error?" Callie said.

Ashok made a buzzing sound of consternation. "I shot metal projectiles at the pods and the bullets *veered away* and spun off harmlessly through space, like... I don't know what. Like they were pulled off course by a big magnet, except they're non-ferrous, and also I don't see any giant magnets floating around out there anyway."

"Target them with the energy weapons," Callie said.

"On it. Crap, Shall, what am I looking at?"

"We fired three simultaneous beams, targeting four pods – two were on a fortuitous linear arrangement – and while all three beams appeared to strike home, the pods are still coming."

"Wait," Callie said. "We fired directed energy weapons at them, and hit, and they're still coming? What the hell are those pods made of?"

"It's the stealth tech, cap," Ashok said. "Gotta be. The same deflection technology we've got – Warwick got it from Liars in the first place. We're shooting at the places where the pods *aren't*. But if they are using the same

tech we are… Hold on, I can calculate the likely offsets…
Permission to unleash hell, cap?"

Callie gripped the jumpseat, wishing she was the one
running the board. "Yes."

A tense few seconds passed, and then Ashok whooped.
"Got 'em! We fired on empty space a few degrees off
from their apparent location, and now our sensors are
showing debris and the false images have disappeared."

"We only got five of them," the ship said. "One of the
pods adjusted its course dramatically and we only struck
it a glancing blow. Let me see. There it is, sailing past us,
on a trajectory to nowhere in particular. We must have
disabled it."

"Nice shooting, boys," Callie said. "And the EMP
torpedoes?"

"Should impact in under a minute," Ashok said.
"Drake, do you want to slow us down? We're getting
awfully close to our friends there, and I'm not a hundred
percent sure how big an effective radius those torpedoes
have on impact. Experimental Liar tech is notoriously
short on documentation, and the station personnel
hadn't done much in the way of testing yet."

"Affirmative," Drake said. The ship decelerated, and the
pressure on Callie's body eased. She unstrapped herself
and walked over to the tactical board, her magnetic boots
keeping her steady. The board showed little glowing
representations of the two ships: the sharklike contours
of the *White Raven* and the seven-armed star-shape of the
Liar craft, with the EMP torpedoes a spray of converging
blips–

That converged on nothing. They appeared to pass
through the Liar ship, and continued moving on the
other side.

"Stealth tech," Ashok said. "Same deal as the pods. Makes sense. Send another volley?"

Before Callie could answer, Janice said, "Incoming message from the ship."

"Put it on my screen here," Callie said.

The visual blurred and flipped and then she was looking into the bridge of a Liar starfish ship. A Liar in some sort of combination powered armor and environment suit peered at her with a cluster of eyes in various colors and shapes, slightly distorted behind a curved faceplate. "*White Raven.* You are in violation of the occulted treaties. Prepare to be boarded." The Liar's voice was so deeply bass it was almost subsonic.

"*You* prepare to be boarded, you spider-faced shit. You blew up Meditreme Station, and as a sworn officer of the Trans-Neptunian authority I am placing you under arrest–"

"We answer to a higher authority. However, we do regret the destruction of the station. We deemed it necessary to avoid greater loss of life. We realize you violated our treaties in ignorance, but the protocols are clear. Is the Axiom device still on your vessel?"

"You mean the bridge generator?" Callie said. "Of course not. Something that valuable? We put it somewhere safe until we can have it properly appraised."

"You will reveal its location. You will–"

"Cut them off," Callie said, and the screen went back to a tactical view. "Blow them up, Ashok, with everything. They admitted their guilt on the record, and since a proper trial isn't feasible I'm authorized to deliver summary justice." She paused. "Besides, I doubt my lie about the bridge generator is going to buy us more than a couple of minutes before they decide to destroy us anyway, since their boarding party failed."

"Firing."

Callie looked at the tactical screen, and the spray of projectiles flying from the kinetic cannons... which all spun harmlessly off in different directions. "Energy weapons!"

"I'm trying, but they aren't *moving*," Ashok said. "It's like the cannons are locked in position, and it's not a useful position. Drake, can you adjust the ship's position, get the beam weapons lined up?"

"Reaction wheels won't move," Drake said. "The mechanisms check out, but... it's like they're frozen in place or something."

"That's what happened to our ship." Elena hadn't spoken in so long that Callie had forgotten her presence. "All the systems seemed operational, but nothing would move. Some kind of inertial control."

The comms came back on, the same Liar peering out of the screen. "We have scanned your ship and taken control of your systems."

"They're right, captain," the ship said. "It's like everything's suddenly locked up behind glass. I can't access anything."

"Your airlocks are under our control. Prepare to be boarded."

"Anyone who tries to get on my ship is going to die," Callie said.

"We have disabled your weapons systems."

"We've got sidearms, you blob of shit in a spacesuit, and if it comes to it, I'll beat you all to death with a wrench."

The Liar turned its body and seemed to consult with another of its kind. "Tell us where the Axiom device is located. Otherwise, we will be forced to investigate all possible hiding places, and sanitize them all. Many humans will die."

"What the hell is wrong with you?" Callie demanded. "Liars don't fight!"

"That is incorrect. We simply choose our battles. Enough. We will sanitize your ship. Your vessel is small enough for us to collect and catalogue the debris and determine whether the device is present. If not... our investigators will annihilate every place you might have plausibly concealed it."

"Wait!" Callie said, but the screen went blank. "Fuck. Ashok, is there any way we can take them down with us, at least?" Callie thought uncomfortably of Elena's story; of Robin trying to blow up their ship, to at least make their attackers pay. It was terrible to put Elena in that position again.

"I could manually rig the engine to blow, sure, but it would take a little time, and cap... we don't have it. They're powering up something *big* in one of those starfish arms. I'm reading energy signatures like whoa." "I am so sorry," Elena said. "I got you all into this."

"There is no anguish beyond death," Stephen rumbled over the PA.

"Fuckity fuck fuck fuck," Janice said.

"I could tear open a panel here, physically mess up some systems, and cut off the oxygen," Drake said. "We'd pass out before we died. Might make it more peaceful."

"I think we'll be vaporized so fast it won't hurt much," Ashok said. "Besides, I'm pretty sure we've got about eleven more seconds to live. Damn it. There are five colony systems I never even got to visit. I was hoping to see them all."

"I love you, Callie," the computer said. "I never stopped loving you."

"Oh, Michael," she said. "I never meant for this to–"

The bridge generator hummed, a single sustained note, somewhere just north of middle C.

CHAPTER 12

"Something's happening," the ship said. "I've got systems control again." The screens all shifted to exterior views from the hull cameras, trained on the distant (but close enough to kill them) shape of the starfish ship.

A dark spot, like a visual artifact on the screen, appeared in the center of their ship. Then the darkness grew, like a drop of ink in a pool of water, then like a crack spiderwebbing across a window. The starfish ship came apart, fragments of the hull falling and spinning away, all seven legs drifting like they'd been cleanly severed.

"It's a bridgehead." Ashok's voice was awe and horror all at once. "Opening right in the middle of the Liar ship."

"They're transmitting," Janice said. "But not toward us – some kind of tight-beam pulse, sent out toward the Oort Cloud."

"Ship, did you activate the generator?"

"I didn't – I was locked out of the system. I think... it activated itself."

"*That's* comforting," Stephen said.

"Let's get out of here, Drake–"

The ship lurched, hard, and the spreading wine-stain

of the bridgehead grew notably larger.

"The bridge is pulling us toward it!" Drake said. "I'm trying to turn about, but it's like swimming against a riptide."

"Ashok, where does that bridge lead? To the station Elena found?"

"I have no idea, cap. I figured out how to access the generator's history, which has a grand total of one entry, but I don't know how to enter coordinates or even how the coordinate system *works*. If this is some kind of emergency protocol then I don't know who to tell... oh shit we're going in there aren't we?"

The screens filled with wet-looking blackness. "We're almost in," the ship said.

"It *looks* like a normal bridgehead," Ashok said. The inky shadow seemed to drift toward them, tendrils reaching out to surround the ship. "Let's see if–"

The screens all went dead. "All sensors offline," the ship said. "As per usual."

"This is supposed to be happening?" Elena was still strapped firmly into her seat, but her hair drifted around her in the absence of gravity, as if she were underwater. There was a thready note of panic in her voice. She'd slept through her last journey by bridge.

"It lasts twenty-one seconds," Callie said. "Usually. When you enter a bridgehead, there's twenty-one seconds of dead time while you pass through... something. A place of darkness. The sensors go dead, but even if you look out the forward viewport, it's just black–"

"Not this time, captain." Drake's voice trembled, agitation audible even on the PA. "This time it's different."

Callie launched herself toward the ladder leading to

the nose of the ship. She grabbed the rung, stopped her forward momentum, then pushed down hard with her arms to launch herself up. She passed the level with the crew quarters and the galley, and sailed into the nose, the hatch sliding open when it sensed her approach. The trip took under ten seconds, but she was already too late: the view out the window had changed to distant stars and a large, dark planet mostly eclipsing a nearby star that looked like a red dwarf. They were in a solar system, but not one Callie recognized, and she *had* been to all twenty-nine colony systems, except the interdicted one, and even that one, she'd seen charts for.

"What did you see, Drake?" She faced the back of the egg-shaped chair, and couldn't see any part of his body except his bifurcated forearm, reaching out from the chair to play across a control panel with all of his nine fingers.

"The interior of the tunnel was bright, and the lights strobed, flickering past, like we were racing through a tunnel with lights embedded on all sides at regular intervals. The lights were white, and they whipped by so fast I couldn't get a sense of what the tunnel was made of. Janice? Did you see anything else?"

"It was a tight squeeze, a space barely big enough for us to pass through, and it sort of undulated, like it was a flexible tube – the tunnel wasn't rigid. Otherwise, no, just flashing lights, like Drake."

"This bridge generator we have works differently than the others, then," Callie said. "That's… Huh. That's a point of information, and that's all it is, right now. So where are we?"

"Some solar system somewhere," Drake said.

"That's about the best I can come up with, too," the

ship said. "The stars are entirely unfamiliar. I'll try to run some database searches, and see if any groupings or patterns match up, but... we could be anywhere. I can't even say for sure we're in the same galaxy, though Ashok seems to think the generator is limited and won't send us farther. Even so, the galaxy is vast. There's a good chance we're farther from our home system than any human has ever been."

Callie grunted. That wasn't a claim to fame she'd ever sought. "I don't necessarily care where we are, if we can get *back*. Ashok? Is there another entry in that black box's history now? Can you take us back where we came from?"

"There is another entry, and since *I* know exactly where we left from, I might have a kind of Rosetta stone to start figuring out how the coordinate system works on this thing. Want me to try to get us home?"

"Very much so. Open a bridge and take us back. Maybe we can trace the communication those Liar maniacs sent and find the rest of their group and figure out what the hell is going on."

No answer. "Ashok?"

"Sorry, cap, this– Nope. The generator isn't responding."

"What?"

"It's throwing errors, but it's not like I know what the errors *mean*. There's no manual, and once you get beyond the bits of the interface that are purely mathematical and spatial, it's all literally alien to me. Maybe if I had a biomechanical brain-spider humping the back of my head I'd have some special insight, but as it is... all I can tell you is, the magic box isn't working."

"Maybe it doesn't think we're safe yet," Stephen

said over the PA. "What's the point in an emergency escape protocol if it allows us to return immediately to a dangerous area? Perhaps there's a cooling-off period."

"It could just be recharging," Ashok said. "With the bridgehead out by Jupiter, and all the others we know about, you have to bombard them with radiation to get them to open. You blast them with the right energy and they activate. This thing, though, it's totally different. I have no idea where it even draws power from – not from the ship, anyway. I assume there's some kind of power source inside the black box. Maybe it's a battery that gets drained and has to recharge. Or maybe it's a disposable two-use item, designed to get you where you're going and back again and nothing else. I genuinely have no idea."

"So we might be stuck here?" Callie said.

"I am *not* helping to repopulate the human race," Janice said. "Fuck y'all."

"We're stuck here for now," Ashok said. "Shall and I will keep working on the box, see if we can figure out how to run diagnostics, try to decipher these messages. In the meantime, I dunno. You guys should look out the window at the amazing strange new vistas or whatever. Sights ne'er glimpsed by human... whatevers."

"Assuming this is temporary, our situation is not yet dire," Shall said. "We are amply provisioned. We have plenty of fuel, and there are icy asteroids in the vicinity we can harvest for hydrogen if we do run low. We have plenty of ammunition, even after our abortive struggle with the Liar vessel."

"So we're looking at a slow and comfortable death. That's nice." Callie wanted to pace back and forth, but the cockpit was small, and anyway, it was annoying to pace when you had on magnetic boots in a weightless environment. She went back down the ladder to the forward compartment, where she usually ran the tactical board and otherwise used as an observation deck. She'd spent a lot of time standing here, watching space go by, on the way from one place to another, in pursuit of money or bad guys.

Now she stood and looked at a strange dark planet and thought furiously. She needed to be *doing* something, because if she stopped doing things, she'd start thinking about Warwick and Herm and all the others who'd died on Meditreme Station, and the dark waters of despair would rise around her, and she would drown.

"Hey, Callie," the ship said, speaking just to her, through her earpiece. "Back there, that thing I said, I know you told me to never say it again. I wanted to apologize. I just–"

"It's OK. We thought we were going to die. It's understandable. I'm not angry."

"It was nice to hear you say my name again," he said, tentatively.

"I'm busy right now, ship." She wanted something to think about, but thinking about *this* was awful too.

"Of course, Captain Machedo."

Turn away from the past, turn toward the future. She reopened the shipwide channel. "Fine. We're stuck here, for a little while anyway. We might as well make ourselves useful, increase the sum total of all human knowledge, stuff like that. Right?"

"I hate new things," Janice said. "New things is how I ended up the way I am now."

"Yeah, but you and Drake have experience as surveyors, so we might as well do some surveying."

They'd once been professional explorers, charting the systems beyond the bridgeheads, before their accident and reconstruction had soured the whole enterprise for them.

Drake said, "This ship is meant more for going fast and blowing stuff up than it is for doing mineral surveys, captain, but I'll see what we can come up with. Shall? Private conference with me and Janice to talk strategy?"

"Ashok, you keep poking at the cube."

"I'm on it. This data must be decipherable. I mean, maths is maths."

She opened a private channel to Stephen. "Hey, big guy. How are you?"

"When I stormed out of my father's house thirty-five years ago, I told him my ambition was to travel so far the sun would be invisible, not even a speck among the stars." Stephen paused. "The young are very stupid, aren't they?"

"They are. I'm not sure the old are any better, though. What's your take on all this?"

"You know I am, at heart, a pragmatist. That's why I seek chemical assistance to have less pragmatic experiences. Pragmatically, I think we are likely to die soon. Either we die here, in unknown space, or we make it back home, and we die at the hands of the Liars, who clearly had allies they managed to contact before they were destroyed. I think we have accidentally uncovered something momentous, Callie. The Liars have technology far beyond anything they've revealed to us, and a secret agenda all their own. They opened the bridges, and created an illusion they wish desperately to protect."

"What do you mean?" Callie thought she knew, but wanted to hear his thoughts without prejudicing them.

"The Liars appeared to offer the galaxy to us – when, in reality, they offered us just short of thirty systems, out of *billions*. The Liars pretend to be scattered and separate groups, but they must have acted in a coordinated way to herd and corral we foolish humans, and to keep us confined to just a few carefully selected sectors of space. Elena's ship stumbled upon some sort of automated Liar repair station, and it accidentally revealed the truth: the Liars have vastly more powerful bridge technology, capable of going *anywhere* in the galaxy. Now the Liars are determined to hide that secret, at any cost." He sighed. "I don't see how we survive this."

"I came to pretty much the same conclusion, but I do see a possible way out. The Liars want to kill us to preserve their secret – so let's make that pointless. When we get back to human-occupied space, we'll send a wide transmission, revealing everything we know and everything we suspect. Once the secret is out, the Liars won't have any reason to try to kill us anymore."

"Except for spite, vengeance, irritation, and so on," Stephen said.

"Except for those, yeah, but I think the Liars will be too busy getting rounded up and interrogated by every human polity in the galaxy that has a military or police division. They'll have much bigger problems than blowing us up out of pique." She gazed out at the planet, just a shape cast in darkness with red light shining around its edges from the dwarf star beyond. "The alternative is, we look for a habitable planet out here somewhere and retire, but then we don't get justice for Meditreme Station."

"I'd planned to retire somewhere with a better breakfast buffet. Your plan is certainly worth a try,"

Stephen said. "Though when the alternative is certain death, any plan would be. Shall I put together a recording with our findings? You're always going on about my wasted gravitas."

"Sure. You're good at being measured and methodical. If I tried to record a statement I'd start yelling and waving my arms around and kicking things."

"Your argumentation style *is* very persuasive, but when one is presenting an insane conspiracy theory, it is better for one to be calm about it."

Callie closed the channel, then stared out the window some more. Everyone had a job. Everyone except her–

And Elena, who tapped tentatively at the open door. "Mind if I join you?"

"Come on in. Enjoy the view."

Elena walked over and sealed her boots to the deck next to Callie, close enough to hold hands, if either of them had wanted to. Instead they just gazed into the pinpricked dark.

"It's so…" Elena shook her head and fell silent.

"What?"

"No, it's nothing. I shouldn't say it."

"Please. I've got a lot of noise in my head. Talking to you quiets that down a little."

Elena put one hand against the glass – which wasn't glass at all, but a Liar material that was light as aluminum, strong as diamond, and nearly as transparent as vacuum. "All those people died on Meditreme Station, so I shouldn't be thinking things like this, but it's just… That's a new planet. One no human has ever seen. Orbiting a star that may not even have a name – not even one of those impossible-to-recall alphanumeric designations. I just… I can't get over the *wonder*. I never could. That's why I volunteered for the goldilocks mission in the first place."

Callie's hand brushed against Elena's, and the doctor grabbed on, gave her a hard squeeze, and then loosened, but didn't let go, letting their fingers intertwine. *She just wants comfort*, Callie thought, and decided that was something she could give. She squeezed back. "It's really not your fault, what happened back there. You stumbled onto something the Liars want to keep secret. If it hadn't been you, it would have been someone else. They managed to play us for fools for centuries, but no scam works forever. It's a horrible shame we ended up in the middle of unraveling a conspiracy, but we can do some good. Reveal the Liars for what they really are, and get justice for Meditreme. Those deaths won't be in vain."

Elena nodded. "I was in my quarters, crying, before I came to see you. I couldn't stop thinking about this one person I met on the station, a bartender who mixed me–"

"A ziggurat. I saw, your lips were red. Was it Jana?"

Elena nodded.

"She's a sweetheart. When I got divorced and fled to the edges of everything and ended up on Meditreme, she was always a sympathetic ear, and a total flirt, which was good for my self-esteem."

"Were the two of you..."

Callie shook her head. "I decided I was done with all that, after Michael left me. Like an old-timey sea captain, married to the sea. Married to the stars."

Elena went *hmm*. "I understood this century was fairly liberal. Do you have some religious affiliation that requires marriage in order to enjoy physical intimacy?"

"Ha, not so much, no. But I've always been terrible

at casual sex, and Jana is – was – well. Casual was her thing. She enjoyed sensations, and sharing new things with people she liked. I don't think she'd be happy with how she died, but she always seemed happy with how she lived, and that's something. I'm glad you got to meet her. Of all the random encounters you could have had on Meditreme, she was a good one to have."

"Did you lose many friends?"

Callie shrugged. "The people I'm closest to are on this boat. My boss Warwick was a friend, too. I saw my friend Hermione one last time, right before we left. I had a distant cousin, Carter, pretty much my only living family out here – I mean, out there – who worked in engineering on the station, and we always visited, but mostly out of duty, and because we knew each other as kids. He was a bitter little misanthrope but good with a spanner." She sighed. "But I spent years with Meditreme as my home base. I knew scores of people well enough to say hello to them. I can't even wrap my head around the fact that they're *gone*. It's an act of war, isn't it? Not just against the Trans-Neptunian Authority, but against all of humankind. The Liars aren't supposed to be capable of acts of war – they aren't a nation, they're just a *species*, organized into little tribes and clans. Or so we always assumed. But if they've been hiding bridge technology from us, if they have secret assassin squads with unknown weaponry and the ability to control inertia... that changes everything. They're not strange but lucrative trading partners anymore. They're a shadowy hegemonic conspiracy. It's like finding out, I don't know, that a bunch of wandering grifters are actually the secret masters of the galaxy. We have to tell people."

"The world is going to change," Elena said. "It hardly

seems fair. I didn't even get a chance to learn about the world as it was yesterday." She sighed, and let go of Callie's hand. "I suppose our rescue mission is canceled?"

"Hell no." Callie made the decision right then, snap, as she made most of her important decisions; she'd learned over the years that her mind did most of the necessary analysis below the level of her consciousness, and presented her with a feeling of certainty when it was done. "We're going to get your crew back. From a purely practical perspective, they're vital evidence for the Liar conspiracy: they can back up your story. You guys are going to be testifying before assorted subcommittees for months, but at least you won't have to worry about room and board and social reintegration anymore. Besides, the Liars killed my friends on Meditreme. I'm not going to let them get away with killing anybody else, even by stranding them in an alien station."

Elena hugged her. Her hair smelled wonderful, faintly like vanilla chai. "Thank you so much, Callie."

"This is all assuming Ashok can get the bridge generator going again. If so, we'll pop back to our solar system, send out a message detailing everything we know and suspect about the Liar conspiracy, and then open a bridge to the station where your friends are being held. In the meantime, though... we have to do the hardest thing of all. We have to wait."

Ashok's voice crackled over the PA. "Cap, could you come down here? I think I figured out a thing."

"Is it a good thing, or a bad thing?"

"Definitely one of the two," he said.

CHAPTER 13

"Come on," Callie said. "At this point, I don't feel a need to hide good *or* bad news from you." Elena was pleased to be included. This was such a tightly knit crew, it was hard not to feel like an outsider all the time, and she was already an outsider in so many other ways.

They went down to the machine shop, where Ashok waved them over with great swooping gestures. "So, in digging through the various messages this thing is producing, I found something that looks a whole lot like a countdown. Assuming it stops at zero, which is kind of a big assumption, and assuming its rate remains constant, which is also a big assumption, then we've got about six hours and fifteen minutes before it's done."

"What happens when the countdown is finished?" Callie said.

Ashok shrugged. "Maybe the bridge generator works again? Either because it's all recharged, or it deems us safe after our emergency exit? Or maybe it explodes. No reason to think it will, except for the way a lifetime of consuming fiction makes me associate countdowns with things exploding."

"Let's assume it's the former, because if it's the latter,

we have to jettison the generator out of the airlock, and
then we're definitely stuck here forever."

Ashok nodded. "I can keep poking at stuff here, or I
can do an EVA and give the *Raven* a once-over to make
sure everything's ship-shape."

"Is there any reason to think it's not?" Callie said. "The
Liars didn't manage to blast us, and the ship's computer
would have mentioned if there were any issues."

"Sure, but we passed through a new kind of bridge,
so maybe stuff is, you know, all weird out there." He
waggled his fingers – there were a lot of them to waggle
– in a way presumably meant to illustrate weirdness.

Callie sighed. "You just want to be the first person to
do an EVA in an uncharted system, don't you?"

"It's definitely a good addition to my life list, cap. Even
cooler than visiting all twenty-nine colony systems. Give
me a little joy on a sad day?"

"Fine, clamber around, but stay tethered to the ship
with cable. I don't want you drifting off. You're the only
one who can operate this generator anyway."

"Nah, Shall could probably manage it, and in at least
some circumstances the generator is happy to operate
itself. But don't worry, I have a strong sense of self-
preservation."

"You do not, Ashok." Callie glanced at Elena. "He
wanders into life-threatening danger more casually than
anyone I've ever known. You know that saying about
how fools rush in where wise men fear to tread? Ashok
rushes in where fools won't even go."

"I may not be overly concerned about the preservation
of my original appendages, I'll grant you that," Ashok
said, "but I like to keep my core systems intact. Anyway,
it's just space out there, it's empty by definition. I'll

be fine. Just tell Drake not to go full burn while I'm outside." He clapped his hands together excitedly. "Yay! I love EVA. You want to come, doc?"

Elena widened her eyes. She'd done two extravehicular activity drills, in training, at a space station in orbit around the Earth. "Ah, no, thank you. I find them very disorienting."

"You just gotta push through the weird terror and then the euphoria sets in."

"No means no, Ashok," Callie said, and he shrugged and hurried off toward the aft airlock. She grimaced at Elena. "Sorry. Ashok is composed largely of enthusiasm."

"I like him. He must be good for morale."

"Insofar as he gives the rest of us a single person to focus our annoyance on, he absolutely is." Callie sighed. "So now we wait. I'm terrible at waiting. Come have a drink with me?"

"Isn't it early for that?"

Callie shrugged. "We have a saying: 'It's always five o'clock in space.'"

Elena chuckled. "All right. As long as it's not a ziggurat. I had no idea it did that to my lips."

"Looked good on you, though."

Was that flirtation? "I used to enjoy doing the femme thing, sometimes, when I had an appreciative partner," Elena said. "I spent most of my time in a lab coat or a cleanroom suit, so it was fun to play dress-up every once in a while. I left my heels and lipstick and earrings back on Earth, though, alas, and also several centuries in the past. Fortunately I'm modeling the height of spaceship chic." She did a little shimmy with her hips.

Callie snorted. "Sorry, I know spare crew coveralls aren't the most comfortable. We should have sent you shopping on Meditreme before we took off. I'd let you dig through my stuff for something to wear, but you'd swim around in my clothes."

"Is Janice any closer to my size?"

"Janice doesn't have anything you could wear. She and Drake– it's hard to explain. Actually, before that drink, do you want to come up and meet them? The fact that you haven't yet is starting to feel like a big old elephant in the room."

"Of course, I'd love to."

"OK. Just be prepared, they were in a really bad accident some years back, and the reconstruction was... they don't look much like you're expecting, I'll give you that."

"I am a biologist, Callie. I also grew up on Earth in the bad old days. I've seen all sorts of trauma. I can handle it."

"You took Ashok fine, but with Drake and Janice it's different, and they're pretty sensitive about it."

"Let's just go up," Elena said. "Really. It'll be OK."

Callie touched her comms. "Drake? Janice? You have a minute to meet our new crew member?"

"It's about time," Drake said. "Sure, we're just scanning the planet down there. It's rocky, a bit smaller than Earth. It's got a magnetic field. There's ice, and liquid water, too. Atmosphere is a little thin for us, but it's not corrosive or anything. There might even be life down there."

"It's gonna be bugs and slime mold at best," Janice said. "Just like every other habitable planet around every other star we've visited. The only other intelligent life anywhere is fucking *Liars*. This galaxy is lousy."

"Come on up, Elena," Drake said. "I think Janice is in

the mood to tell our tale of woe."

Elena looked at Callie questioningly, but she just shrugged and gestured. "Up to the cockpit. One level past the observation deck."

Elena unsealed her boots and drifted to the ladder, then pulled herself up all the way to the nose of the ship. When the ship was moving under thrust and simulating some degree of gravity, the open viewport in the cockpit was "up", like a domed ceiling with views in all directions, but those orientations meant less in microgravity around this strange planet.

The chairs in the cockpit were mounted on armatures capable of twisting and turning in most directions, and they currently faced toward the ship's nose. As a result, the seats had windows on all sides: it was the closest you could get to the sensation of floating in space without leaving the ship, and the view was both breathtaking and a little scary.

There were two chairs covered in straps and buckles empty on either side, and in the center, an egg-shaped enclosure of some kind, bigger than a person. Some kind of specialized pilot's chair, Elena assumed, with cushioning to protect the crewperson during acceleration: Drake must be in there. But where was the comms and navigation station? Where did Janice sit?

"Come on in." The voice sounded strange, like Drake and Janice were speaking simultaneously. An arm emerged from the left side of the ovoid chair and beckoned, and Elena barely managed to suppress a gasp.

The arm was Y-shaped: it had a single upper arm and bicep, but then it divided at the (obviously heavily modified) elbow, and two forearms jutted out from the joint: one pale and freckled, and one a very dark brown.

The forearms ended in matching hands, one of which had too many fingers, and one of which didn't have enough. "Back on Earth in the old days, you would've had to pay five lix at a freakshow to see something like this." It was Janice's voice, cynical and grimly amused.

Elena glanced at Callie, who just raised her eyebrows and nodded. Elena drifted further forward, grabbed onto the arm of a chair to the right of the egg-shaped chair, and turned to face the pod.

Drake and Janice sat in the hollow of the chair, tubes and wires snaking into their bodies and out again, disappearing under the seat. At first, Elena couldn't make sense of what she was seeing, but then she understood. "Oh," she said. "You've been… put together."

"Butchers," Janice said, from one side of the head. "The Liars are butchers."

"They meant well," Drake said, from the other side. "They were trying to save our lives. But they'd never seen a human before, and they made some bad assumptions. They didn't have much to work with. It's amazing they managed as well as they did."

"I begged for death, once I was able to speak," Janice said. "They didn't seem to understand. They didn't seem to think wanting to die made any sense at all." She paused. "But it's not so terrible now. I'm used to it. Drake isn't bad company."

Elena settled into the chair and fiddled with the controls until it twisted around to face them.

Drake and Janice had one head, with two faces. Drake's face was on the left side, and Janice's on the right, though Janice only had one eye, and they had only one nose between them, centered equidistant between their faces, on the front of the head. It had been Drake's, to start with. They had no visible ears at all, and no hair. Elena could clearly see where the flesh and bone had been grafted, with Drake's dark skin meeting Janice's pale flesh on the scalp. Their body was mostly hidden in a modified environment suit, but in addition to the bifurcated left arm they had a more conventional right arm, half light-skinned and half dark, with six fingers and two thumbs. If they had legs at all, Elena couldn't see them. She leaned forward slightly, taking them in. "You'd think the Liars would have focused more on radial or bilateral symmetry, given their own forms," she murmured, then blinked. "Oh. I'm sorry."

Drake grinned, a twisted sideways sort of smile, but recognizable. They each had a mouth of their own, and Drake had improbably straight and beautiful teeth. "No, that's good, you're fine."

"Usually people just say 'Oh, I'm so sorry,'" Janice said. "Or else they throw up. Critiquing the butcher's technique? That makes for a nice change. You're all right."

"Janice usually hates everyone," Drake said. "You should be flattered. Want to hear how it happened?"

"Only if you'd like to share."

"Sure, sorrow shared is sorrow halved. Of course, everything Drake and I have has to be halved anyway." Janice rolled her one eye. "Drake and I were pilot and navigator on a small exploration ship, working for a mining company."

"Also a tourism company," Drake said. "It was weird. Diversification."

"The job was supposed to be light duty, easy all the time. We'd been military surveyors once upon a time, so we were used to doing exploration with people shooting at us. Poking around the far corners of a colony system, with no expectation of hostilities, seemed like a cushy job. And, mostly, it was. We were on a small ship, crew of five, working out of the Trappist colony."

Callie drifted up and sat in the other chair. "That's one of the twenty-nine bridgeheads, near a star out in Aquarius–"

"The Trappist-1 exoplanets," Elena said. "They were one of the goldilocks ship destinations. One of the more promising ones, too, with at least three potential habitable planets."

"Two of them turned out to be," Janice said. "The other one was too geologically unstable. I have to say, those planets... it's a shit neighborhood. That dwarf star is so dim, it's like being in twilight all the time. Half the colonists have big old sun lamps mimicking full-spectrum light and the other half are doing body modification to turn themselves into night-dwelling morlock types."

"The goldilocks ship made it there, by the way," Drake said. "They found the place already colonized, and joined in with the work. It was only about fifty years ago? Some of the crew are probably still alive. Did you know them?"

"No, not really," Elena said. "Though I might look them up, if we live through all this. They might have some pointers on integration."

"You could just not integrate," Janice said. "That's what I did."

Elena chuckled. "So what were you exploring?"

"Anything we could reach in the system, basically," Drake said. "Our company set up supply outposts on moons and asteroids, moving progressively away from the Trappist colonies, allowing us to go farther and farther out. When we had our accident, we were on a long-range mission – we'd picked up some strange radio signals, and our captain wanted to see what was what."

"She fucked it up, really," Janice said. "She was hoping we'd find some aliens who were easier to talk to than the Liars, and she kept us out a few days past optimal mission parameters. Normally that wouldn't have been a problem, there's always wiggle room in the calculations, but the ship was due for servicing." She sighed. "Something broke. We're still not sure what. One minute we were easing our way through an asteroid field, and the next, the ship was coming apart all around us. The cockpit sealed itself when the rest of the ship got breached open to vacuum, and emergency life support kicked in, so Drake and I were OK, at least short term. We had no engines, so we couldn't go anywhere, but we had the comms, so we figured we'd call for help, and maybe a ship would be near enough to save us. We had rations, so, worst case, one of the company ships would come looking for us eventually, starting at our last known location, which wasn't far away. We just had to survive for a little while. We thought."

"The rest of the crew died?" Elena said.

"They were all in the galley when it opened up to vacuum," Drake said. "They went quick. We were sad about it, but we'd been military, like I said. We'd lost people before. It's never easy, but we weren't stunned."

"I lit up a distress beacon," Janice said. "We sat back to swap stories about the captain and the crew, you know, remembering people, like you do."

Elena nodded. She'd been remembering her crew, and she wasn't even sure they were dead.

"We weren't done with bad luck, though," Janice said. "A minute later, a chunk of debris hit us, and sent us spinning. We smashed into an asteroid, which wasn't great, but then the control panel caught fire, which was worse, and then we got pelted with *more* debris. Put somebody in a trashcan, set them on fire, and shake them up real good: that was us."

"We never should have woken up," Drake said. "We were battered, broken, burned. We might have actually been dead, at least briefly."

"But then a group of Liars found us," Janice said. "A previously uncontacted tribe, cult, whatever. My memories – our memories, because there are places where they overlap, the way our brains are wired together now – are really fuzzy, but the aliens were heavily augmented, even by Liar standards. Lots of mechanical prosthetics, and some of them were as small as kittens, and I swear one was as big as a killer whale. We're pretty sure they lived inside an asteroid in that field, or had a ship tricked out to look like an asteroid. They had a laboratory, or operating theater, and... they made us into what we are today."

"But they'd never seen a human before," Elena said. "So they didn't know what to do. They must have thought you were one organism."

Janice said, "Well, maybe. One of them looked like a conglomeration of Liars, all smushed together and operating as one, sort of like a Portuguese man-o-war. A composite organism. The Liars might have just thought it would be interesting to put us together the same way."

Drake said, "Janice thinks they were experimenting on us to amuse themselves, or to test out experimental procedures before turning the techniques on themselves. I choose to think they acted from a merciful impulse, and simply made a mistake, or did the best they could."

"No way to know for sure," Janice said. "Drake always thinks the glass is half full. Me, I think the glass is half full of poison. We woke up like this, in this chair, enclosed in what was basically an escape pod, with our distress beacon slapped on top. A rescue ship found us. The best doctors in the system looked at us, wrote papers about us, and said there was no way to take us apart again without killing us. They all agreed the Liars had saved us from certain death, but there was no separating us. We were mixed together too thoroughly, like sugar in water."

"More like milk in coffee, my dear pale sister. Between us we've got about a brain and a half, one heart, three kidneys, two livers – and that last bit was helpful, because, oh, we drank when we got home."

"The hardest thing was getting used to sharing the body," Janice said. "But we'd worked together for a long time, in the corps and then private, so even that was easier than it could have been. We shift control back and forth pretty effortlessly nowadays, and we can even share sometimes, one of us on the left arm, one on the right, and, of course–"

"We can sing in harmony," they said simultaneously, and then both chuckled.

Janice went on. "We got sick of being professional lab rats, so we started answering ads for pilots and navigation and communications specialists, presenting ourselves as a package deal, like married couples do sometimes. Lots of captains like hiring couples because they usually work well together, and since they fraternize with themselves, they don't fraternize with others, which is good for crew dynamics. Of course, all the captains who were interested stopped being interested once they got a look at us. Except Callie. She didn't blink."

Callie shrugged. "I'd already been crewed up with Ashok for two years by then. Nobody's all that strange after *that*. Besides, a pilot and a navigator who only need one berth on the ship, saving the other room for paying customers? What a bargain."

"If you don't mind me asking… *were* you a couple?" Elena said. "You have such a deep rapport."

"I'm gay," Drake said. "Though I don't date much nowadays."

"I never saw the point of sex with *anybody*," Janice said. "Except occasionally with myself. Also romance is stupid."

"We were both always pretty self-contained," Drake said. "You don't get into the business of long-haul exploration missions unless you're happy being alone for a while. I do miss having a more active social life during my down time, but the obvious disadvantages of our situation aside, there are some compensations. For one thing, we have an exceptional level of voluntary control over systems that are usually involuntary."

"What he means is, when we get sad, we can dump all kinds of happy chemicals into our brain, and when we want to have orgasms, we just *have* them. I know what his feel like and he knows what mine feel like, which is something a lot of people envy. I doubt many of them would be willing to trade with us, though."

"I'm very glad to meet you both," Elena said. "I'm sorry I got you into all this mess. I'm sure encountering more aliens was the last thing in the world you wanted."

They snorted, though since they had only one nose, Elena wasn't sure which one of them was expressing scorn. Janice said, "The nice thing about being torn apart and stitched back together wrong by Doctor Frankenstein Mengele Moreau, MD, is that everything bad that happens to you after that seems surprisingly fucking manageable. We've *always* been in a worse situation than the situation we're in. Don't worry about it. We knew signing on with Callie would dump us in the shit now and then. No offense, captain. But you do get into situations."

"And I always get us out again," Callie said.

The control panel in front of Drake and Janice blipped. "We've completed our scan of the night side. Looks like the planet is tidally locked in a synchronous rotation – that side is always dark, and the other side is always light. We'd like to cruise over and get a look at the day side. Should we wait until Ashok comes back inside?"

"Ashok?" Callie said. "You want to come in? We're going to move the ship."

"Aw, I'm having fun out here," he crackled. "I'm checking the stealth projectors. How about I just hold on real tight while you change position? I'm tethered and mag-locked anyway."

"We won't go fast, and we won't accelerate rapidly, so he should be fine," Drake said. "We're basically doing a slow drift and scanning as we go."

Callie sighed. "I guess TNA safety protocols don't really apply when we're who knows how many light years outside their jurisdiction. All right. Proceed. Do you still want that drink, Elena?"

"Please."

"Fraternizing with a civilian, captain?" Drake said.

"It's only fraternizing when a superior officer is involved with one of lower rank, and we're not in the military anyway, and, no, we're just drinking because it's a way to cope with the existential horror of our situation."

"So it's medicinal, then," Drake said. "I'm sure even Stephen would approve. Enjoy it."

Elena followed Callie down the ladder to the observation deck, where she had a flexible drinking bag stashed. "It's basically a wineskin," she said. "But it's full of Callisto bourbon."

"I thought in order to call it bourbon it had to meet a bunch of special criteria, like being made on Earth. Otherwise it's just corn whiskey, right? Not that I'm complaining."

"To be legally called bourbon, it has to be made on Earth, include at least fifty-one percent corn in the mash bill, and be aged in new, fired oak barrels. Plus a few other rules about alcohol percentage and such."

"So it's not really bourbon? Or it's not really made on Callisto?"

"There's a Terran embassy on Callisto, and they have a little bespoke distillery there. They claim the grounds of the embassy are technically Terran soil under the terms of the treaty between Earth and the Jovian Imperative, so: bourbon." She put the nozzle to her lips, squeezed the bag, held the liquid in her mouth for a moment, and then swallowed. "Ah. It's not the system's best whiskey, and the whole 'genuine bourbon' thing is just a publicity gimmick, but it's tasty enough. This batch was a gift from a diplomat we took on a speed run last year, and free liquor always tastes better." She handed the bag over.

Elena had never been a great fan of whiskey, preferring cocktails, but she was happy to be drinking with Callie, and she took a small mouthful. The bourbon was sweet, with notes of caramel and vanilla, and burned pleasantly on the way down. "Mmm. Thanks."

"My pleasure. Sorry we can't sip it from a glass on a cozy couch somewhere. Maybe once we're under thrust again we can come up with a reasonable facsimile." She looked at the windows. "Want to watch the sunrise with me?" She tapped the viewport. "Should be a nice view, seeing the dwarf star appear over the planet as we move to the light side."

They stood in silence, boots sealed to the deck, taking occasional sips from the whiskey as the planet slowly shifted in their view, revealing a widening slice of the red star on its far side.

Which, it became apparent, wasn't a star at all.

CHAPTER 14

"Are you seeing this?" Callie addressed her question to the ship at large.

"Uh, yeah," Janice said. "Kind of hard to miss."

"What?" Ashok said, and then a moment later, "Oh. Woah."

"Do I even want to know?" Stephen said. "I've been cocooned in a hammock with my eyes closed."

"The star… it looks like a ruby," Elena said.

Callie had expected a red dwarf star, but instead they beheld a star-sized gem, gleaming, faceted, and softly glowing. "Any idea what we're looking at here?"

"Dyson sphere," the ship said.

"No, it's not, because nobody's ever managed to build one," Janice said. "They tried to do it way out in Arcturus, but they went over budget and abandoned the project before they even really got started. Squatters live in the ruins of the construction office now."

"Apparently they have better project management skills in this part of the universe," Drake said.

Callie put her face close to the glass. The ruby sphere was beautiful and terrifying. "I thought the point of a Dyson sphere was to surround the star with solar collectors to harness all the energy? This one's letting all the light out."

"That's not the only confusing thing," the ship said. "The only remotely realistic proposals for megastructures like this have been for Dyson swarms – multiple, independently rotating structures, forming a sort of web or net around the star. Making a solid shell that size would be impractical – the tensile strength would need to be far beyond the capabilities of known materials science, and if there were any drift at all it would be difficult to correct, and in the case of such an error, one side of the sphere would crash into the star and the whole thing would be destroyed. But this... it's like they put an unbroken glass globe around the star."

"There's definite radiant output, consistent with a red dwarf," Drake said. "Which makes me think... maybe it just *looks* like a red dwarf from the outside. Maybe it's some other class of star, and only some of its energy is being captured, with the rest allowed to radiate."

"I don't know enough about astrophysics to be able to tell if that even made sense," Janice said. "I'm not sure Drake does either."

"Very little of this makes any sense at all, but I'm growing accustomed to that sensation," the ship said.

"Uh. The planet. Look. The day side is... different," Drake said.

The ship slowly rotated, bringing a portion of the planet's light side into view. The dark side was rocky, icy, and mountainous: a raw and natural place.

The day side was unnatural. The surface was completely covered in immense shining megastructures. From orbit the structures looked like a maze, or the cross-section of a brain, though there seemed to be multiple levels, towers, branches–

"Can we get a closer look?" Callie said.

The glass in front of them darkened, transforming into a viewscreen, and then replicated the view they'd seen before, at a greater level of magnification. After a moment the screen blipped, and everything was magnified further; then blipped again, and again, and again, each time bringing the view of the surface a little closer.

The structure appeared to be a vast network of branching, interconnecting tunnels, but each tunnel had to be the size of a skyscraper.

"This configuration of matter doesn't match anything in my local database," the ship said. "I don't have access to the Tangle, of course, but even if I did, I doubt I'd find a match. Could they be natural growths of some kind, do you think? Crystal, maybe?"

"No," Elena said. "This looks like the space station my ship found. Organic shapes, but artificial."

Callie cocked her head. The structure on the planet did look like what Elena had described, but instead of one immense map of an anthill, it was hundreds of interlocking and overlapping ones.

"Our sensors aren't giving us much of anything," Janice said. "They aren't even willing to confirm there are structures down there. It's the same kind of results we got when we scanned the bridge generator, actually. Whatever that stuff is made of, it's weird alien matter."

"Maybe this is the Liar homeworld?" Callie said. "Maybe in times of emergency, the bridge generator activates and transports them to their home system–"

Something on the viewscreen moved, just a flash seen in a gap between two of the immense branches. Elena pointed. "Did you see that?"

"It was just a flicker," Drake said. "It could have been an artifact in the transmission–"

"It moved like something alive, Callie," Elena said. "Believe me. I've spent a lot of time staring at the motion of living things."

"At this magnification, for us to see something moving on the surface, it would have to be immense. Mountain-sized, like in those old movies Ashok likes–"

"Kaiju," he crackled. "You're telling me we're orbiting a planet of giant monsters? The universe is amazing."

"Scanning for motion," the ship said. The screen flashed, showing various segments of the city, if it *was* a city, and not a power plant, or art piece, or cemetery, or something less comprehensible. Callie caught another flicker of movement, and the image froze for several seconds as *something* passed from underneath a twisted cloverleaf of tunnels onto a patch of clearer ground. The image incremented forward in slow-motion, showing the thing's movement as a series of progressive frames. At this magnification the image was a little blurry, but the basic shape of the thing was recognizable.

Elena turned her back on the viewscreen, wrapped her arms around herself, and trembled.

"It's just like the creature Elena described," Stephen said, presumably watching on his own tablet in his quarters. "The thing that ate her friends. The long body, the neck, the flower-bud head."

"Except the one she saw was the size of a bus." Callie went to Elena and put a hand on her shoulder to comfort her, but Elena flinched away. "How big is this one?"

"It must be at least a mile long," the ship said. "Which is absurd, because the gravity on this planet should be very close to that of Earth, and a creature that size would collapse under its own weight. Unless it's not a creature at all, but a biological machine – or, more likely, a sort of cyborg with mechanical reinforcement."

"They can control gravity." Elena's voice was calm, but when she turned back to the screen, her face was wet with tears. "They did that on the station. I don't think there's much they *can't* do. But I agree, it's not possible something like that – what was it? kaiju? – could evolve naturally, so it must have been engineered and altered, if not created from scratch. I know you said the Liars like to tinker, but that thing… it's way beyond tinkering."

"I vote we *don't* go down there to explore," Janice said. "I don't care if the place is cram-packed with priceless alien artifacts. I don't like bugs when they're bug-sized…"

"If an emergency protocol brought us here, do we think it lit up a tattletale light somewhere down there in that city?" Callie said. "Are the Liars going to come out and greet us, thinking we're old friends who need help?"

"It's possible," the ship said. "But honestly, captain, it looks like a ghost city down there. An occupied planet produces all sorts of detectable noise – transmissions across a vast range of the electromagnetic spectrum, energy signatures – but we aren't getting anything. It's just inert, apart from the mile-long bug-monster. No, wait – there's another one."

This new kaiju, identical to the first, clambered up the side of one immense structure, and crawled ponderously along. On the viewscreen it looked almost close enough to touch. The branch it moved along was powdery gray, but when it passed over, a dull silvery sheen was left in its path. "Is it cleaning the structure?" Callie said.

"Like a snail crawling up the wall of an aquarium," Elena said. "Huh. I wonder if that's what they are – just mindless cleaners? The one in the space station that picked up my friends... maybe it perceived them as pests, or detritus, just trash to be collected."

"You think my kaiju friend down there is a robotic vacuum cleaner?" Ashok said. "My sense of wonder just took a pretty big hit."

"So the Liars abandoned their homeworld?" Callie mused. "Left their robot vacuum cleaners running and headed for parts unknown? Or maybe this was a military base in some ancient conflict, and there's an old emergency protocol in our bridge generator that brought us here even though it's not an active facility anymore?" She sighed. "I'm just making shit up now. Incorporate some of this footage into your message for the authorities, would you, Stephen?"

"Already working on it," he said.

"Ho, shit, look." Drake sounded almost delighted.

The cleaner-kaiju had spread immense wings, four of them, iridescent as a dragonfly's, and now it flew over the city, though it didn't seem to flap its wings – they appeared to be more for steering, as it banked and leaned and spun, landing on another part of the structure miles distant, and beginning to clean that one.

"Gravity manipulation of some kind seems increasingly likely," the ship said.

"Good use of understatement," Callie said. "All right, cruise around, let's see what's happening in the southern hemisphere. Hold tight, Ashok. We're moving again."

The ship shifted, the vast megastructure scrolling past on the viewscreen. "Zoom out." The image shrank until the kaiju were invisible again, and they could see the curve of the planet.

They dropped below the equator and got a look at the other half of the day side. The vast structures continued, but large sections were in disrepair here – some of the tunnels were broken, revealing dark cores, and some were mottled with a black substance that might have been mold or toxic waste or tarnish.

"I want a closer look." Callie and Elena both stepped right up to the glass as it blipped though another set of magnifications. The cameras found one of the kaiju sprawled unmoving on its back, head pinned beneath a broken section of the structure, its belly torn open and crusted with some greenish substance. "Looks like the maintenance crew is slacking off down here," Callie said. "If this place isn't uninhabited, it's certainly neglected. That makes me feel a little better, for some reason."

"Hey, uh, I'm coming back in," Ashok said. "I've had enough of the great outdoors. Meet me in the machine shop, cap?"

"I'm assessing alien threats here, Ashok."

"I'd like to formally tender a report on the results of my inspection, Captain Machedo."

A little tickle of alarm went up the back of Callie's neck. "Sure thing. Stay here, Elena? Fill up that science brain with new information and see if any conclusions fall out."

"My brain is feeling overstuffed already, but I'll do my best."

Callie headed down to the machine shop, stopping by her quarters to pick up her sidearm first, tightening the webbed belt across her hips. Ashok didn't volunteer to give reports on inspections, certainly not so formally, and he didn't call her "Captain Machedo", so something was off. Maybe she was just being paranoid, but then, an alien conspiracy had murdered fifty thousand people just to blow up her ship, so she thought a little paranoia was justified.

She went into the machine shop and waited, back to a wall, eyes on the far door. Ashok arrived, still wearing most of his environment suit, though his helmet was off and stowed. He put a finger to his lips, then shut the door. He hit a switch on a console and the walls in the room hummed faintly. "OK, we're secure."

"What does that mean?"

"It means nobody can hear what we say in here, not even the ship's computer. The comms are blocked, the doors are locked down and can't be overridden from outside, and there's even a white noise generator if someone tries to listen through the door."

"When did you put those measures in place? And why?"

"Ages ago, and because I watch really unconventional pornography in here sometimes while I'm working."

"Ashok. Eww."

"You asked. But right now I'm using my shame-based countermeasures because I found something seriously disturbing out there on the hull. Look, here's footage from my suit camera." He snagged a cable out of the sleeve of his suit and plugged it into a console.

Callie joined him at the screen and frowned. She knew the contours of the *White Raven* well, and there was something bulbous, made of glass and metal and shaped like a bathysphere, clinging to the underside near one of the energy weapons. She was pretty sure it wasn't part of the weapons upgrade Warwick had authorized; this was something new. "What the fuck is that clinging to my ship? We got space barnacles now?"

"It's one of the boarding pods the Liar ship fired at us," Ashok said. "I looked inside and it's empty, but there's a hole cut in our hull – the pod is acting as a patch, keeping the ship sealed."

"I thought we shot all those pods out of the sky."

"Me too, but we clearly missed one."

Callie looked around the room. "You're telling me there's a Liar somewhere on this ship? Where? Hiding in the walls?"

"Seems likely, cap. No telling what it's doing in there, either. Could be patched into the communication systems, listening to every word we say, which is why I'm doing all this super secret spy stuff."

Callie thought furiously, and then nodded. "This is good. I wanted to take one of them alive. I have many questions."

"Liars aren't famed for their usefulness as interrogation subjects."

"Maybe no one's ever asked them properly before."

"I'm pretty sure the various human militaries who have questioned the Liars over the years used every trick you know and a bunch you're too good-hearted to even think of. Drugs don't work on them, you can't hypnotize them, torture is bad and anyway most Liars can control their pain sensors anyway," he shrugged.

Callie nodded. "We have evidence of a Liar conspiracy, though. The situation has changed. Once we get word to the authorities, their whole species will be treated as a hostile force. Hiding the bridge generators from us, and keeping us limited to twenty-nine systems like we're children in a playpen, could be chalked up to their version of national security. But blowing up Meditreme

Station to keep their conspiracy a secret? That's a war crime. We'll offer this squidling the chance to flip on its cohorts in exchange for not spending the rest of its short and unpleasant life in a Jovian Imperative black site."

Ashok shook his head. "Ugly business, but I guess that's where we are. How do you propose we flush the little guy out?"

"Unleash the repair bots. Get them scuttling through all the places too small for us to go. I'll check the rest of the ship. Go quietly tell Stephen and Elena what's going on so they can join in too. Give Elena a non-lethal sidearm."

"So, bug hunt?"

"Bug hunt."

The *White Raven* wasn't big, but it wasn't small, either. It was made for a crew of five to live comfortably, and since Drake and Janice shared quarters (and everything else), it coped just fine with six. Callie checked the galley, their quarters, and the cargo hold. Stephen did a thorough search of the infirmary, and Elena checked everywhere else, stalking through the corridors. The ship did a full diagnostic, but didn't report any findings. They didn't dare use the comms to discuss their search, in case the Liar was tapped in, but they kept up a seemingly innocuous stream of chatter that managed to reveal their respective locations as they moved around.

In the end, it was the repair bots clambering through the walls of the ship that forced the Liar invader into the open. Elena was just coming out of the gym, near the bottom (or back) of the ship, when a vent covering came clattering off the wall and a dirty-white flurry of movement flew out of the opening, followed by a silvery, spidery repair bot in pursuit.

Elena shrieked as the child-sized, multi-armed Liar in an environment suit spun and lurched wildly in her direction, flailing for purchase in the lack of gravity. It grabbed onto a handrail and stared at her from a cluster of various-sized eyes behind its faceplate. Elena pointed her sidearm at the alien just as the repair bot seized it and pinned its limbs.

"I surrender without reservations." The voice that emerged from the suit was feminine and full of resignation. "I wish to speak to your captain."

"I'm sure she'd like to talk to you, too," Elena said. "Shall? I found our stowaway. Get everyone down here."

She looked at the alien for a long moment. She'd never seen one before, after all. The Liar had seven long appendages, arranged radially around its central trunk. It didn't have a head as a domelike bulge on the top of its body. The Liar and its suit were essentially the same shape as the ship that had attacked them: a lumpy starfish with too many arms.

"Why did you do it?" Elena said. "Why did you kill all those people?"

"We were trying to save the universe," the alien said. "I've been listening in on your communications. I heard your theory about a vast Liar conspiracy." The alien let out a sound remarkably like a sigh. "You're right, in a way, because there is a conspiracy. But you're wrong about everything else. You think we're hiding our secret mastery of the galaxy. In reality, we're hiding something else. Something much worse."

CHAPTER 15

They took the Liar to the infirmary and strapped it down on an exam table. Binding an uncooperative Liar would have been a challenge, but their captive was docile as they tightened straps over its limbs.

Stephen sat at his desk nearby, while Ashok and Elena hung back by the door. Callie locked her boots to the floor right in front of the table and looked at the Liar.

"What are you planning to do to me?" it asked.

Callie grinned, showing all her teeth.

"I will not condone torture," Stephen said. "As a doctor, I can't."

"No torture," Callie said. "I'm still a sworn officer of the TNA, and the Authority doesn't condone torture. Mostly because it doesn't work, and can even be counter-productive. No, we're here for a trial."

"What?" the Liar squeaked.

"State your name," Callie said.

"My name is pheromones and gestures, but when I need to communicate with humans, I go by Lantern. What do you mean, a trial?"

"You committed a crime in Trans-Neptunian Space. I'm a security officer for Meditreme Station, and out here, wherever here is, that makes me the highest local law representing the Authority. I am authorized, in extreme circumstances, to conduct trials in the field. Our ship's computer is available to assist you, as your advocate. Would you like to consult in private with your advocate?"

The Liar's bound tentacles wiggled like sine waves. "I do not recognize your authority over me."

"You don't believe in the law? That's OK. The law believes in you. Whether you recognize my authority or not, we'll still throw you out an airlock if you're found guilty. Ship, what are the charges against... do you have a preferred pronoun, Lantern?"

"You can't do this."

"The accused states no preference–"

More thrashing, which suddenly subsided. "You may use 'she' and 'her'."

Callie nodded. "That's better than 'it', huh? Helps us anthropomorphize you, right? Makes you seem like you're one of us, so we'll be more merciful. It's worth a try. Ship, what are the charges against her?"

"Fifty thousand, one hundred and seventeen counts of premeditated murder. Destruction of TNA property valued in excess of one hundred billion lix. Piracy. Trespassing."

"How many of those are capital crimes?"

"The murder and the piracy, captain. There are fifty thousand, one hundred and eighteen charges that potentially carry the death penalty."

"We are not pirates," Lantern said.

Callie clucked her tongue. "Demonstrably untrue. You forcibly boarded another ship, without any authority to do so. That's piracy. We can put that charge aside, though. I doubt we'll even get to it; no reason to charge you for littering when you're already being executed for murder, after all. Prosecution, make your case."

"We have recorded evidence of the destruction of Meditreme Station," the ship said. "We have recordings of the spokesperson from your ship confessing to causing that destruction. We have simulations that indicate the attack could have only come from your ship, as there were no other vessels in the vicinity."

"Defense?" Callie said. "Do you have anything to refute that evidence or call any of those assertions into question?"

"Certainly," the ship said.

"Wait!" Lantern stirred restlessly. "How can the ship be the prosecution and the defense?"

"Computers are very smart, and good at compartmentalizing," Callie said. "Now shut up."

"The confession is inadmissible," the ship said. "Liar testimony is never considered credible, and is automatically dismissed. The existence of technology like the bridge generator on this very vessel means that another ship could have destroyed Meditreme Station and then escaped through a bridge, undetected, before we arrived, perhaps even to intentionally frame the Liars. We also have no direct evidence that this Liar came from the same ship that attacked us: she could have been hiding on board since Meditreme Station, or earlier, despite the presence of this purported 'boarding pod.' The case against the defendant is purely circumstantial."

Callie nodded. "I'll take that under consideration. Lantern the Liar, do you have anything to say in your own defense? Not that it matters, since Liar testimony is assumed to be false by definition, but giving you the opportunity to speak is a necessary formality before I pass judgment and sentence you."

"I am not Lantern the Liar," the Liar said. "I am Lantern the Truth-Teller. I am Lantern-Who-Remembers. I do not lie."

"All Liars lie."

"We have our reasons," Lantern said. "The clouds of falsehoods that surround us are a great comfort, because they distract us from a truth too painful to contemplate. But some of my people are tasked with upholding the truth, remembering our past, and safeguarding our future against the very threats the rest of us are desperate to forget. I am a member of the truth-telling tribe, as were the others on the ship your Axiom artifact destroyed." She shifted in the restraints. "Surely you can admit that my people do not lie about everything. Otherwise we would be useless to you as technicians and engineers, and impossible as trading partners. In most everyday interactions, we do not lie about anything that impacts our ability to negotiate and work with and live alongside humans. Can we stipulate to that?"

Callie frowned. Liars never admitted they told lies. It was always a misunderstanding or a translation error or someone *else* telling a lie. This was getting strange. "So stipulated."

"Very well. Then you acknowledge that my people are capable of telling truth strategically, when it suits our purposes? So you must consider the possibility that I am telling the truth now. I will tell you something you may already know, as your xenosociologists have noted it often. My people lie about two categories of things: the momentous, and the trivial. We make up stories about our true origins, yes, and our faith, and our culture. We mislead you about our motivations, sometimes – though our ultimate motivation is to thrive and survive. We are like humans in this way. We also lie freely about things that do not matter. Where we were yesterday, where we are going tomorrow, what we had to eat, what we do for fun, and, of course, we are often deceptively boastful. I will tell you why we lie so often: it is because transforming one's reality through the creation of a narrative takes practice. It is easier for us to believe the big lies we tell ourselves about our past, our origins, and our future, if we are in the habit of confabulating smaller things every day. It makes reality seem more pliable, more plastic, more in our control." Her limbs fluttered, a sinuous tremble, and Callie wished she knew better how to read Liar body language. "My tribe, my *sect*, is denied the comfort of those lies. We must remember the truth, and acknowledge it, because only in facing those terrible truths can we hope to safeguard the universe."

"Fine," Callie said. "Then tell the truth now. Admit you destroyed Meditreme Station, and tell me why. You say our theory about your conspiracy is wrong, that you aren't toying with humanity and keeping us in the dark while you use the rest of creation as your playground. So convince me. Make your confession."

The Liar was still for a moment, and then began to speak.

You call us Liars. We have a different name for ourselves. In your language, we would call ourselves the Free.

I am seven hundred years old, as you would reckon time – young by the standards of my kind. There are some elders yet among us who remember the days of our servitude, though they sleep almost always now, and float in nutrient baths, with little in the way of what you would call consciousness. They live in dreams of their memories, and they are bad dreams.

My people are capable of physically passing on our memories to one another. This is one of our great secrets. We share memories by extruding neural buds that others of our kind may consume, and so those elders are vital, because they produce the buds that are fed to the highest members of my sect. Such memories can be manipulated, or fragmented, or incomplete, and so we also maintain records, and we save artifacts – we possess an array of ancient documentation proving our sad history. There is a secret museum of our subjugation, and I spent the first centuries of my life there, being inducted into the sect of truth-tellers.

Later, when my people first met humans, and realized the threat you posed, I was one of the delegation sent to dwell in the Oort Cloud to monitor your solar system. It is considered a very important posting, since it is the system of your home world. Had we found you some centuries earlier, when you were yet bound to Earth, we would have exterminated you, and sanitized your entire planet, as we have done in so many other systems.

I see the horror on your faces. We have extensively studied the nuances of your kind. Yes, my sect kills, though I myself have never taken part in such an action. I am grateful I have been spared that work. It is a grim and terrible duty. The extermination of sentient life is a cause of great anguish to us, but it has always been deemed better than the alternative. We kill humanely, you see. Those we cleanse die instantly, without suffering. That is better than the alternative.

By the time we found humans, though, it was too

late: you had already sent your goldilocks ships out into the stars, hundreds of ships, each with the potential to start a new human colony. It was too late to wipe you out, so we had to... manage you instead.

I am sorry. Normally I would extrude a neural bud for my listener to consume, so they would have the background. I would share the emotional content of my story via pheromones, and provide further nuance with chromatic variation in my skin. To transform this story into words, in a language I learned when I was already four hundred years old, is difficult. In this feeble and incomplete way, I will tell you the terrible truth at the heart of my existence, the shadow that lies across the Free:

There once was an ancient and powerful race, originally from a distant star system in a nearby galaxy. They ranged throughout the galactic cluster, and perhaps beyond, and they ruled absolutely, not for thousands of years, but for millions. Wherever they encountered intelligent life, or life that seemed on the cusp of developing intelligence, they destroyed it. These aliens claimed to be the *first* life to arise in the universe, and believed the whole span of the stars was theirs by right.

Their powers were incomprehensible. They transformed whole star systems for energy, or for their amusement, or for aesthetic reasons we cannot comprehend. They destroyed worlds for sport, or art, or to make a point, or on a whim. They called themselves – in your language you might say the First, or the Primary, or the Fundamental – but the name we settled on is the Axiom. Because they were not just the most important, not just the first, but self-evidently so, a universal truth that could not be denied, the standard by which all other forms of life must be judged and inevitably found lacking.

But around fifty thousand years ago, the Axiom did a curious thing. They encountered a sentient species, but they did not destroy it. Instead, they subjugated them. Enslaved them. Altered them. I refer to my species, or the original ancestors of my now very different species. You call us Liars. We call ourselves the Free. Back then, we were neither: we were the Servitors, or the Subjugated, or the Enslaved.

We originally lived on a watery planet, even more watery than Earth, and we dwelled in the oceans, though by the time the Axiom found us, we'd made progress toward transforming our bodies so we could explore the land, through selective breeding and directed mutations. When the Axiom ships appeared in the sky, we believed them to be gods. We were not wrong. I have witnessed their arrival, in a faded, fourth-hand way, from a neural bud consumed by one who consumed a bud from one who consumed a bud that came directly from a witness to the arrival.

We speculate among ourselves about why we were chosen, from all the races the Axiom had destroyed, to become their servitor race. Originally, we had seven sexes, and all our sexes could mate with all the others, so we were reproductively robust, and displayed great genetic diversity. We also had the ability, as some bacteria do, to selectively swap genetic material with one another, passing on useful traits to our offspring. The fact that we can share memories easily makes us adept at coordination. Those qualities, and our cleverness, and dexterity, and prowess with tools, made us highly adaptable.

But not adaptable enough for the purposes of our new

masters. The Axiom lifted us up to their laboratories, and began to change us. Some of us were made into war machines, and used to destroy other life; I am told those living weapons were not even granted the peace of mindlessness, but were as self-aware as you or me. We have no memories from that line: all their neural buds were destroyed, long ago, but because of our records, in the museum of subjugation, we know. Others were made more intelligent, or given extra limbs, or altered to survive in various environments – cold, hot, dry, acidic. Some of us were even hardened against vacuum. The Axiom seldom *spoke* to us, you must understand. Most of us never even saw our rulers in the flesh. Instead the Axiom dominated the minds of certain individuals, through neural implants, and those overseers gave us our orders.

There was no reward for obedience, only punishment for those who failed to obey, and the punishment was swift and irrevocable: execution. The Axiom was trying to breed disobedience out of us, you see. But we always passed on our knowledge, and if they snuffed out one of our people for daring to question the Axiom, or for trying to escape, some part of them would survive, to be passed on to others, in secret. We learned to hide our disobedient thoughts, and to plot, and to plan.

So it was for tens of thousands of years, and many generations. A few of us managed to escape, and stole Axiom technology, and attempted to destroy Axiom outposts and strongholds. To take the cloning factories offline, and to carve out safe systems where our children could grow up, never knowing the yoke or the lash of their old masters. The rebellion grew in strength and the attacks became more and more daring. For a time, we dared to hope.

But the Axiom found the rebels. They killed them, and destroyed their neural buds. Then, to make sure the rest of us would never rebel again...

Humans are eager to find the Liar homeworld. You always ask, and we make up stories, and send you along false trails. The truth is, we have no homeworld. Not anymore. The Axiom destroyed our planet. Vaporized it utterly, until only particles remained.

Then they gathered us, all of us, in one place, and they seared our minds. They erased our hidden memories of our culture, from the time before the Axiom came, carefully passed down for generations. They erased our memories of home, and our entire collective knowledge, of everything before the day of subjugation. The only reason we know our homeworld was a watery place is because we have that single memory from that world: of the Axiom's arrival in the sky overhead. We only even remember our rebellion because they left us with the memory of our punishment, as a reminder, and a threat, and a promise.

If we had gods before the Axiom, it is unknown. If we had art, or music, or rituals related to love or death or war or food or friendship, we do not know. The Axiom had long subjugated us in body, but by erasing our histories, they subjugated our wills, too. We were broken. We ceased to fight. We gave up. We served them for thousands more years.

And then, ten thousand years ago, the Axiom vanished.

CHAPTER 16

Lantern went silent. Elena dashed tears from her eyes. If that story was true, even *partly* true, then the Liars – the Free – had experienced unimaginable suffering.

"May I have water? My suit's reserves are depleted." A hatch irised open on top of the Liar's suit, and everyone jumped back, except Callie. She rose and went to a cabinet, found a drinking bulb, put the nozzle in the hatch, and squeezed out its contents. She removed the bulb, the hatch closed, and the Liar said, "Thank you."

"What do you mean, the Axiom vanished?" Callie said.

"They went away. We believe very few of them had physical bodies at that point, and those who did went into stasis. The rest were machine intelligences, or energy beings. The former ceased communicating with this world, and the latter seemed to dissipate. The Axiom gave us no warning, and no explanations. One day, there simply were no more orders. The overseers wandered around blankly in the absence of further instructions. The Axiom machinery kept running, until it ran down, but they built well, so even now many of their machines are still operational. They left vast projects half-finished,

201

or abandoned on the very cusp of completion. Those facts make us speculate that the Axiom *had* to leave, that something drove them to an urgent retreat, but who knows? We never understood half of what the Axiom did. Some think the Axiom uploaded themselves into a simulated universe, one they could control more completely. Or they may be in hibernation, waiting for some future moment to return, though we know not why, or for what. Some of us believe that the Axiom learned to create *new* universes, and that they emigrated to one, with fundamental forces arranged better to their liking.

"Whatever the reason, our masters were gone, and at first my people were lost and confused and frightened. But then we rejoiced. The universe was ours, you see. Some Axiom technology was mysterious to us, or couldn't be operated by the Free, but many useful things were left behind. The Tanzer drives. The great power stations, like this star, with its collector-shell. We had resources, and long lives, and expertise. We could survive. We could thrive. We were free, for the first time. But we did not know what to do." A sigh. "We had no history, you see. No culture. No conception of ourselves as anything but an enslaved people. There were many billions of us, scattered throughout the galaxy, once completely controlled, but suddenly released to make our own way. Is it any wonder that we took our ships and fled to all the distant corners of space? That we began to make up stories about ourselves, to reinvent ourselves in a million different ways, with a million different imaginary histories, all to obscure the shame and horror of our *true* origins? But a few of us were dedicated to remembering. The truth-tellers held on to the horrible memories and proofs of our reality. Apart from a few thousand truly isolated clans, everyone born in my species is visited by a member of my sect, and offered the opportunity to learn the truth: they are invited to visit the museum of subjugation, to see the data and consume the neural buds, and learn what we truly are. Once upon a time, more than half of our kind chose to find out the truth. Now, it is less than a quarter."

"Maybe it's good to move on," Stephen said. "Since the Axiom are gone. Perhaps your people can emerge from that shadow."

"But they *aren't* gone," Lantern said. "That's the whole point, don't you see? They are only sleeping, and they may remain asleep, but only if we do not disturb them. They don't care about us. They don't care what we do, or how we spend our time, as long as we don't bother them. We looted their bases and laboratories and barracks and slave pens, took the ships the Axiom had given us to serve them, and that was fine. But the first time a group of the Free visited one of *their* cities, one of the planets where the Axiom had lived in isolation, served by machines instead of living slaves, where we thought the true miracles and marvels of their technology might be hidden… The sleeping machines noticed the trespassers, and woke up. The machines killed the expeditionary force, and tracked the clan back to their home, and destroyed *that*. The remaining Free in that system were enraged, and tried to destroy the Axiom planet, and the machines – and soon the whole *system* was destroyed. The star was somehow induced to go supernova, and took out all the habitable planets with it."

"God," Elena breathed.

Lantern fluttered. "The Axiom do not wish to be

disturbed. My order is devoted to making sure the Axiom are *not* disturbed. Our old masters could create singularities at will, you know. They could move whole systems from place to place. They controlled inertia and gravity – we have access to some of the tools they used to do that, but we don't know how they work. They could create life, and destroy it, and convert matter to energy and back again with trivial ease. They could alter objects at the molecular level. They dominated everything, from the macro to the micro. They smashed stars together, sometimes, perhaps just to enjoy the resulting light show. What do you think will happen if we bother them again, and they wake from their slumber? What will they do if we cause them the least little bit of trouble?"

"So the station Elena and her crew found," Callie said. "It's an Axiom station."

"Yes," Lantern said. "When I was in the walls, I accessed the record of Elena's story. Her crew must have found a repair and shipbuilding facility. The station perceived their ship as a damaged Liar vessel, and the crew as damaged or rebellious Liars. The station attempted to implant neural machinery to bring the crew back into compliance, and fitted the ship with what was, once, a standard element of the Axiom fleet: a point-to-point wormhole generator." Lantern trembled again. "Those are forbidden now. We do not use them. We throw them into suns when we find them."

"Why is it so important to destroy the bridge generator?" Callie said. "Even if your story is true, how does that justify murdering fifty thousand people to destroy one piece of alien tech? Is it just a religious thing in your cult?"

"No. It is a practical reason. I– There is a pest on Earth

called an ant, yes?"

"Sure."

"Imagine you are with your family on Earth, at a table, eating on, what is it? A patio, just outside your house. Humans do this, yes, on your homeworld? It is nice day. You are enjoying your meal. Then you see a single ant crawl across the table. Perhaps you ignore it. But imagine a second ant crawls after the first, and tries to get to the food on your plate. You might feel a flicker of annoyance, and squash this ant, or flick it away. Then imagine a third, a fourth, a tenth, a twentieth ant, a hundredth. What then? You rise from the table. You fear the ants will get into your food, into your clothes, they will ruin everything, make you uncomfortable, spoil things. So you kill the ants. Why not? They are a pest, meaningless and numerous. But the ants keep coming. You begin to think, what if they go into my house? What if they crawl inside my walls? What if they swarm everywhere, crawl inside my electronics, ruin my comfortable existence? So you decide to trace their path all the way back to their nest. You pour gasoline into that nest. You set it on fire and burn them all and destroy them utterly. Do you understand?"

"We're the ants," Stephen said. "If one of us stumbles into Axiom space, the Axiom might ignore it, or think it's trivial, or settle for killing the invader and then going back to sleep. If more and more of us show up, though, they might grow annoyed, wake up, follow us back to our source, and wipe us out."

"It has happened." Lantern's voice was leaden. "There was another sentient race, far from your solar system. This was only six hundred years ago. Not long at all. These people... if you are like your monkeys, and we are like some of your sea creatures, they were more like your insects. But they were builders, and smart. When we found their species, they already had slow local space travel, and were exploring their system. Millions of years before that, though, when they were just barely sentient bugs and not a spacefaring civilization, the Axiom built a factory in the heart of one of their gas giants. These insect people, they sent probes, and found the factory, and they were very excited. As you would have been, if you'd found evidence of a vast alien building project deep in the clouds of Jupiter, say. We met the insects soon after they found the installation, and we tried to warn them away. We told them it was our factory, to leave it alone, but they were stubborn and single-minded and they mounted an expedition to the facility. They woke the Axiom."

"What happened?" Callie's voice was low and calm.

"The factory came back online. It built something new. Something that moved only partially in observable dimensions. It attacked the insects. Half of their home planet simply vanished, like something had taken a bite out of it and swallowed. The rest of the planet collapsed in complete geological turmoil, of course. Still, the aliens were hardy, and resourceful, and some survived. Then the Axiom machine… sprayed the planet? With a kind of poison, but a sort of resin, too: a preservative. Now, half of their home planet erratically orbits their star. The broken planet is covered in a transparent coating, and inside, you can see the people, frozen in place. We hope they are dead. We are not sure. Afterward, the machine descended back to the gas giant, and the factory went offline again." Lantern sighed. "The Axiom did not leave many species likely to attain sentience alive, so the problem does not come up often. When we find a planet with life that seems pre-sentient – or is already sentient, but does not yet have space travel – my sect wipes it out. We cleanse it, quickly and humanely. We have to, you see. What if the aliens travel where they should not, and find things that should not be found? What if they wake the Axiom, for more than just a moment? If the universe becomes too crowded, if the Axiom find us troublesome, if they are roused from their slumber and take an active interest in the workings of the universe again... Then we would all die. At best. Or we might be enslaved again. We would no longer be the Free."

Callie nodded. "You commit genocide, on a regular basis, to protect yourselves."

"Not regularly," Lantern murmured. "The Axiom were thorough. Space is very big, but the Axiom went everywhere, and destroyed almost every promising garden of life before they even discovered us. We have been forced to cleanse only a handful of planets in the past ten thousand years. With humans, it was too late, and we were forced to take a different approach."

"You gave us bridge technology, though," Callie said. "Why give us even limited keys to the galaxy if you're afraid we'll stumble on something we shouldn't? Wouldn't it have been better to just ignore us and keep us isolated?"

"Humans like to explore," Lantern said. "We discovered this early on. You sent out goldilocks ships. You would have built generation starships, or developed stasis technology, or found a way to upload your minds and send small fast probes full of your ghosts out into the universe. You would have spread out in every direction, endlessly. So we made a calculated choice. We placed fixed bridges at certain points, in systems where we *knew* there were no Axiom artifacts or facilities, and where there were planets you could colonize, or terraform, with enough resources to keep you busy. We hoped that would be enough. So far, it has been. Humans have been happy to explore those systems, and as a result, they've stayed out of more dangerous areas. We have other systems set aside, too, in case you ever grow restless – we can say, look, we discovered a new bridge, have a new world to explore. You see?"

"You put up baby gates, to keep us from falling down the stairs," Elena said.

"I do not understand the metaphor, but if you mean we restricted your movement for your own safety? Yes. But mostly we did it for *our* own safety. Then you found a point-to-point wormhole generator. We cannot let humans have such a thing. You could go anywhere. Even without your conscious effort, it brought you here, to a factory planet. The sensors below could have noticed us. The Axiom machines may be stirring. It's bad enough you have a generator, but humans *share*. They show off, they want to better the lot of their people, they want to sell things and become wealthy. What if you demonstrated the generator for someone else? Or took more ships to the station, and arranged to have *those* fitted with generators? What if you found a way to replicate the technology yourselves? Usually when we share tech with humans we cripple it, make it stupid, make it self-destruct, or hard to copy. But pure Axiom tech? If you figured out the mechanism, made a fleet of ships with generators, went out into the universe…" That tremble of tentacles again. Elena thought it had to be a shudder. Body language saying: I am afraid to even think about this.

"Why let the goldilocks ships go on sailing through space at all?" she asked. "Surely that's dangerous."

"The records were lost," Shall said. "Things on Earth got much worse before they got better, and whole swaths of data were destroyed."

"Yes," Lantern said. "We had no real data. We looked along likely paths, to likely systems, and found nothing, or found ships that had failed long ago. But there were so many, sent in so many directions. We simply hoped for the best. Our hopes were not realized."

"You didn't have to kill anyone," Callie said. "What you did, it's monstrous. You could have just *talked* to us, told us there was a big existential threat, let us know that certain systems were off limits."

The Liar made a strange wheezing sound that Elena decided must be laughter. "Oh yes. That always works. Humans never go places they're forbidden to go. And as I said: the closest thing to a culture my people have now is making up stories. Humans wouldn't have believed us anyway."

Callie was silent for a long moment. "Fair," she said. "But I still think killing fifty thousand people was indefensible."

"*Your* people were not enslaved for millennia by beings of vast power and cruelty. And, thanks to the vigilance of my sect? They never will be. I know you think our methods cruel. But sometimes, when a person has the crawling rot, you must chop off their limbs in order to save the body." She sighed. "Or so I was taught. I was raised and trained to believe that no price was too high to pay, if it even *slightly* reduced the chance of waking the Axiom machines, let alone the Axiom themselves. But

I have my doubts. A few of the younger people in my sect do. I argued against cleansing Meditreme Station. Strenuously. When the engineer you spoke to saw the Axiom artifact, and recognized it for what it was, and fled, along with all the others of our kind, they notified *us*, at our base in the Oort Cloud. We were divided about how to respond. I argued for taking a small team, and trying to steal the generator back. I wanted to prevent loss of life, but the elders don't care about that, so I said it was simply safer that way: it would spare us scrutiny. Destroying the station would be too noisy and obvious, I said, and the humans might suspect us, and investigate. But my elders have fresher memories of the Axiom and their machines, and that makes them fearful and decisive. They ordered a full sanction instead. When we realized we'd timed our attack badly, and that you had escaped – that all those humans had died for nothing. Oh, the horror. The shame. The regret. So when I spoke up again, and said they should send a small boarding force, led by myself, to confirm the generator was on board your ship, they were shaken by their earlier mistake, and agreed. Unfortunately, you were better armed than we realized. You destroyed most of the pods. Only mine evaded your attack. I used our stealth displacement technology to create an image of my pod missing its rendezvous with your ship, so you would think I'd passed you by. Before I could get on board, though, the elders panicked, and attacked… which triggered some sort of security protocol in the generator, it seems. Now, here we are."

"It's quite a story," Callie said. "More internally consistent than most Liar confabulations. But why should I believe anything you say? Our theory about a Liar conspiracy to keep all the goodies in the galaxy for yourselves is a lot simpler and more plausible than all this crap about a godlike race of monster-alien bogeymen."

"You should believe me because I didn't need to tell you anything at all," Lantern said. "I could escape any time I wish."

"Bullshit," Callie said, but she said it to an empty table, because the Liar had vanished, the restraint straps falling empty to the bed.

CHAPTER 17

"See?" They all spun. The Liar was in the corridor outside, floating in a lazy spiral in mid-air, tentacles dangling. "I have technology far beyond your capabilities."

Callie unholstered her sidearm and pointed it toward her. "But can you do that trick fast enough to avoid me putting a hole in you?"

"You have seen how quickly I can vanish." Lantern didn't sound perturbed. "Here is my proposal: when the wormhole generator is operational again, we will return to your solar system. You will give me the generator for safekeeping. I will then destroy it, and let you go on your way."

"What's to stop us from turning you in?" Callie said. "Telling your story and letting everyone know the truth?"

"Haven't we demonstrated how far we're willing to go to protect the universe from the threat of the Axiom? I would suggest discretion. I will oversee the erasure of your records to remove all information about the Axiom. The destruction of Meditreme Station will be blamed on accidents, or perhaps pirates – there is a notorious group on Glauketas, yes? Surely you see this is the only way for our species to survive. If the Axiom wake, we all die, or worse."

Callie shook her head. "I don't believe it. Even if your story isn't total bullshit, you can't let us live, knowing what we know."

"My sect is forbidden to speak deliberate untruths, captain. We must be unquestioningly trustworthy, in order to do our work."

"So says a Liar. We're too dangerous a loose end for you to leave us alive. Criminal conspiracies don't leave witnesses."

"Once the evidence is gone, I do not fear your testimony. Who would believe you? As soon as you begin by saying, 'A Liar told me', your story will be dismissed."

"Even if you're personally willing to let us survive, the rest of your sect clearly favors overkill, and you said it yourself: you're a junior member. I don't plan to spend the rest of my short life worrying about your elders back in the Oort Cloud. No deal. Besides, we still need the generator. We have to rescue Elena's crew."

"You can't go *back* to the station!" Lantern said. "It's bad enough you're here, in orbit around an Axiom planet. If you return to a place where humans have already interfered once? That increases the chances of attracting Axiom interest."

"We didn't interfere!" Elena said. "We were interfered *with*."

"The Axiom *doesn't know humans exist*. Don't you understand? We've kept you from their notice so far. If they find out about your species, and worse, that you're propagating throughout the universe? They will scour you from the galaxy completely."

"Humans are pretty good at surviving," Callie said.

"We'll take our chances. I'm ready to pass judgment."
She raised her gun. "You are guilty of murder. The
sentence is death."

"Wait!" the Liar cried.

Callie walked close to her, the muzzle of her pistol
half a meter from the Liar's body. "What's wrong? Can't
do your teleportation act again? It's impressive, but if
you could do it any time, as often as you want, you
wouldn't bother with boarding pods, would you? You'd
just teleport onto the ships you wanted to infiltrate.
My guess is, it's either a one-use emergency thing, or
something that has to recharge, just like the big bridge
generator we have wired into this ship. Goodbye, Liar."

"I can show you how to use the generator!" Lantern
said. "I know how to operate it properly. And, if you
insist on returning to the Axiom station, I can help
there, too. I am familiar with such places: I have seen the
schematics, and consumed neural buds from those who
worked in such installations. I insist you take me along.
Perhaps I can minimize the damage you do, erase the
records of your arrival. We have techniques for avoiding
Axiom notice."

Callie didn't lower the sidearm. "How did you do the
teleportation trick?"

"I have a device. A variant on the point-to-point
generator: it opens a small portal and draws me through,
but far more rapidly than the larger versions, so quickly
it is difficult to perceive the transition."

"Can you use this device to get back to our solar
system?"

"No. I told you, we forbid the use of bridge generators
because they open up the universe in a dangerous way.
This device is very short-range. It can transport someone

a distance of a few kilometers at most. Its mass limitations are also much greater than the device that transports your ship. My sect restricts the use of these devices heavily, even so. We don't want humans to have these, because they might reverse-engineer the technology, and then develop more long-range instantaneous travel."

"Give the device to me."

"I can't. We are forbidden to let humans have them."

"You can give it to me, or I can take it off your corpse."

A beat. "All right. My sect is pragmatic." The Liar did something, and the suit went slack, the helmet portion unsealing. Lantern slithered out of the suit. Callie hadn't seen many Liars in the bare flesh. Lantern's skin was the slick gray of a dolphin's, and she had over a dozen eyes scattered around the domelike bulge of her "head", with 360-degree vision, quite likely offering insight into parts of the spectrum invisible to Callie, if not Ashok. Lantern had seven tentacles, five of them thick, two of them finer and more delicate, the latter lined with suckers. She had a small cube-shaped device attached to one of the thin tentacles, halfway up, held on with a strap not unlike that of a wristwatch. Lantern slid off the device and offered it to Callie.

She spoke through another device, this one a small silver circular grille, that seemed embedded just below her largest eyes: the simulated voicebox Liars used to talk to humans. "The device can only be used once every three-point-eight-seven hours. It has a slightly faster recharge time than the bridge generator on your ship."

"How does it work?" Callie strapped the teleporter onto her own arm – there was some chance it was a trick or a bomb or something, but she thought the odds were low. She wasn't the only person on the ship with a gun, after all, and Lantern seemed to value her own life.

Lantern, resigned, showed her how the sides of the cube responded to touch, and how to input relative direction and distance for desired travel, and how to activate it, when it was recharged. "I'll test this in a few hours, and it had better work the way you claim," Callie said.

"I do not lie."

Callie grunted, and then stared at the thing on her wrist with dawning horror. "Wait. Could you... could this – is it a weapon? The way the bridge generator opened a portal in the middle of your ship and tore it apart, could you do the same thing with this? To a ship? Or a *person*?"

Lantern waved her tentacles in apparent agitation. "No. That would be monstrous. There are failsafes in place. We had no idea your generator would activate an emergency protocol and tear us apart. We never would have tried to fire on you if we'd suspected. I told you, such devices are forbidden among our people, and our lore about their functions must be incomplete. Or else when the Axiom ruled, there was never a threat sufficient to make that emergency protocol activate."

Callie nodded. The Liar's story was a bunch of implausibilities wrapped around a handful of outright impossibilities, but Callie had a wormhole generator in her ship, and another one on her wrist, so it was time to take the impossible seriously. "Ashok, take our prisoner to the machine shop. Don't let her touch anything unless it's absolutely necessary. See if she can give you any useful information about the generator. She lives as long as she's more use to us alive than satisfying to me dead."

"Will do, cap." Ashok held out his prosthetic hand

and, after a moment, Lantern wrapped one tentacle around it. The cyborg clumped out of the medical bay with Lantern drifting along in microgravity behind him, looking like a bizarre novelty balloon.

Callie floated in a corner of the infirmary and looked at Stephen and Elena in turn. "What do we think about all *that*?"

"The story was internally consistent," Stephen said. "Liar stories aren't, usually. They never bother to be all that rigorous or convincing. Even the first Liars, the ones who tricked our ancestors, told stories full of contradictions and bizarre digressions, but they were dismissed in the excitement as unimportant or translation errors."

"The story Lantern told does seem to fit the available evidence," Elena said. "That doesn't mean it's true, but, it could be."

Callie fiddled with the device on her wrist. The surface was greasy-looking but smooth and dry, just like the bridge generator. "Believing a Liar just seems ridiculous, though."

"Lantern says she never lies," the computer said. "I will monitor her carefully. If we catch her in a lie, even a trivial one, then we know she isn't telling the truth. Though even when she tried to deceive you about being able to teleport before you could shoot her, she was careful not to speak any untruths."

"Whether her story is true or not, it doesn't really change our short-term plans," Callie said. "We still need to save the crew of the *Anjou*. Whether we're saving them from a secret cabal of Liars or an automated space station created by a race of uplifted super-monsters doesn't affect our operation all that much." She yawned.

"Ridiculous as it sounds, I'm going to get some sleep, or try. You two should as well. Once the generator is recharged, we're going straight to that alien station to get Elena's crew back. Drake, maybe park us back around on the night side of the planet? Just in case Lantern is telling the truth, let's try to be a little less noticeable."

"Initiating 'run and hide' protocols," Drake said.

But Callie couldn't sleep. "Can you hear what's happening in the machine shop?" she asked the ship.

"I can. Ashok has not activated his privacy protocols."

"Let me listen in. Secretly."

"Opening a line."

There was silence for a moment, then Ashok said, "OK, that's bizarre. Who has a base-seventeen mathematical system?"

"It seems very natural to me, but I was raised with it. As you can see, the coordinate system takes into account not just space, but also time–"

"You aren't telling me the Axiom could time travel?"

"No – or, not that I know of, and I hope not – but you see, such calculations are the only way to account for the relativistic effects. There must be an absolute referent, for this to–"

"Aw right, I get it, wow, that's so needlessly complex it almost wraps all the way back around to elegance, doesn't it?"

"It seems that way, yes, but there are special conditions here, and here."

"Ahhh. Right. Otherwise you could end up in the middle of a star by accident. Oh, and there's the emergency protocol trigger, right where it's halfway logical to find it. But why did the protocol bring us here?"

"I am only speculating, but if the emergency protocol were ever triggered, then it would mean the crew had failed their mission, and so they would be deemed unsuitable for further service." A long pause, and then Lantern said, "That planet down there. It was a very bad place."

"What, like a prison?"

"A prison? No. The Axiom did not waste resources on feeding and sheltering those who failed them. The planet below is a rendering plant. A recycling center. Based on what I know of Axiom methods, I am fairly sure the crews would be extracted from their ship, taken below, and forcibly stimulated to produce neural memory buds, which would then be examined to see how the mission failed. The buds would eliminate any need to keep the crews alive, so they would be reduced to slurry, to be used as raw organic material for the cloning vats, or just to feed the newborns."

"Wait. The Axiom killed their slaves and fed them to *babies*?"

Callie, listening in her room, shivered.

"Yes. We are fortunate the factory below is so badly damaged. There would normally be an automated system to collect us. It is difficult to overstate how terrible life was under the rule of the Axiom. That is why the Free go to such lengths to prevent those terrible times from returning."

"I get it, but blowing up Meditreme? That was… It's unforgiveable. And I know you agree with me, Lantern."

"Why do you say that?"

"Come on. You're not a zealot. You belong to a *sect* of zealots, totally, but you're not one yourself. Otherwise we wouldn't be having this conversation right now.

You were crawling around undiscovered inside the ship, listening in on us. You knew the bridge generator was on board. You clearly know your technical stuff. We're a zillion miles from any human-occupied space. We *both* know what a zealot would have done in those circumstances."

"Destroyed the ship," Lantern said. "I should have. My elders would have done so, without hesitation: rigged all your torpedoes to explode in their bays, set your energy weapons to overload, caused your Tanzer drive to explode."

Callie closed her eyes on her bunk, visions of her ship coming apart flooding her mind.

"But you didn't," Ashok said. "You tried to talk things out with us instead. Tried to make us understand, and come around to your point of view. You're a persuader, not a genocider. Your bosses blew up Meditreme Station. You didn't."

"It does not seem right to me, to commit atrocities, even to prevent greater atrocities. We have exterminated whole species to protect ourselves from the possibility that the Axiom might someday awaken. I feel there must be a better way. But I do not know what it is."

"It's not all your fault," Ashok said. "Your people were enslaved. The spirit of rebellion was literally cut out of you, and even though you've been free for a long time, your minds aren't free. You're still suffering under all that conditioning. Your instinct is to hide, to avoid notice, to tiptoe around. Right?"

"Of course. There is no other alternative."

"Sure there is," Ashok said. "You could fight. You could destroy the thing that threatens you. Eliminate the Axiom."

"Impossible."

"Nah, it's super possible. You guys *did* rebel, remember, once upon a time? You stole, you schemed, you attacked, you fought."

"We lost." Lantern's voice was harsh.

"Sure, but the rebels went on the offensive, instead of simply going into hiding. That means they must have thought it was possible to win, right? Think about it. The Axiom weren't content with squashing the rebellion. They were so freaked out they *erased the memories* of everyone who was involved in the rebellion, and scoured their neural buds from the galaxy. What do you think those Liars knew? They must have been some juicy secrets, if the Axiom were that afraid."

"I- I have no idea. The cleansing of our memories was just a show of force, we thought."

"I mean, maybe, it could be. Sounds like the Axiom could be sadistic. But you'd think just killing all the rebels would have been a pretty good deterrent. Instead, they went total overkill. Destroyed your homeworld. Embarked on a mass re-education program. I don't care how near-godlike you are, that's a whole lot of effort. If you're all-powerful, I just don't see sweating a little uprising all that much. You'd just crush it and move on. My guess is, those rebels figured out something important – something that made the Axiom vulnerable, or else revealed a vulnerability. You're used to thinking about the Axiom as unstoppable juggernauts of mega-strength. They made *sure* you thought of them that way, right? How about you look at them in a different light, though. Imagine they have a weakness they're trying really hard not to reveal."

"Open a channel," Callie said. "I was just listening in, guys."

"Oh, hey, cap," Ashok said. "I was just thinking out loud."

"No, they're good thoughts," she said. "I was wondering about something that connects. Lantern, why did the Axiom create a slave race in the first place? You said they were going along just fine on their own for millions of years, undisputed masters of creation, then fifty thousand years ago they suddenly go to a whole lot of trouble to break a sentient race to their will. They devoted a ton of resources to that project. Why do you think they did that?"

"We do not know. They never explained themselves."

"What Ashok said, about the Axiom hiding a weakness. Maybe they suddenly needed the help. Maybe they were sick, or their population was dwindling, or they'd just extended their empire too far to govern it properly. They couldn't keep up with everything that was happening anymore. They needed soldiers, workers, custodians, all that, right? How many of the Axiom did your kind actually *see*?"

"We mostly dealt with their machines," Lantern said. "Actual meetings with the Axiom, in person, were vanishingly rare. It was like meeting a malevolent god."

"I think the Axiom was an empire in decline," Callie said. "Once great, but overextended, decadent, rotting, diseased, who knows what. They started to crumble, and they needed outside help to keep everything going, to keep pretending they were as invulnerable as ever. But they were too old and arrogant and set in their ways to collaborate with anyone, so they went for slavery instead."

"That… is a plausible interpretation," Lantern said.

"They were clearly working toward some big project,

too," Callie said.

"Sure," Ashok said. "Maybe several projects. They went somewhere, after all. Sadistic monomaniacs don't commit suicide. Whether they uploaded or migrated to a new universe or transitioned to being full-time energy beings, or whatever, it took a lot of preparation."

"Maybe that's what the rebels threatened with their attacks," Lantern said. "Perhaps they delayed or menaced the transition."

"That makes sense," Callie said. "What if there were actually just a few of the Axiom left, and they were desperately trying to save themselves, and then suddenly the slaves attacked? Maybe they did some real damage, or threatened something crucial. They *had* to respond with overwhelming force, and keep you guys down long enough for them to finish their project."

"They're still trying to protect their infrastructure," Ashok said. "Their machines are still active. Some of it might be purely automated systems they didn't bother to switch off. But that factory on the gas giant coming to life and destroying a planet in such a weird and scary way? That's not a robot vacuum left running when the owner goes on vacation. That's a contingency and a deterrent."

"If the Axiom are trying to hide something, or protect something, what could it be?"

"They don't like to be disturbed," Ashok said. "Maybe they don't want their weakness to be discovered. If the rebels threatened them when they were awake, how much more vulnerable are they now that they're asleep – or whatever? Relying on automated security systems?"

Lantern said, "If they are trying to protect some secret, it could be the servers where their simulated reality resides. Or the dreaming machine that spawned their new universe. Or the life support system for their stasis while some other machines prepare this universe for their return. It would be something essential to their existence."

"They spent a long time crafting a reputation as ferocious unstoppable gods who punish the slightest transgression with armageddon," Callie said. "Why would they do that? In my experience people who bluster that hard, and who favor wildly disproportionate responses, are a lot more insecure than they let on."

"This is an interesting line of speculation," Lantern said. "I would like to present it to my elders and solicit their thoughts."

"You can't cower forever," Ashok said. "Isn't ten thousand years of subjugation long enough?"

"Even if you are right, I am not sure what we can do about it," Lantern said. "If there is a secret weakness, I cannot imagine how we would ever discover it."

"Of course you can't," Callie said. "You're not a trained investigator."

CHAPTER 18

Elena knew she should be sleeping, and she dozed fitfully, but she never sank very deep. Her mind kept returning to the Axiom station, made even more sinister in the context of Lantern's revelations, and every time she closed her eyes she saw horrors witnessed and imagined. She stared at the darkness over her bunk for a long time and finally said, "Shall?"

"Yes, Elena?"

"Did I hear you say you loved Captain Machedo, when we all thought we were going to die?"

"I don't know what you might have heard."

"Ha. Let me rephrase that. *Why* did you say you loved her? And why did she call you– what was it, Michael?"

"That's not a question I can answer. I've been asked not to discuss the subject. Callie has promised to sell me to a discount liquor store as an inventory management system if I divulge any details."

"Can I speculate wildly, based on my keen observations? And if I speculate accurately, will you let me know?"

"I can grunt meaningfully, I suppose."

Elena smiled. "Fair enough. Your name is actually Michael?"

"I'm just a ship's computer. What need have I for any foolish human name?"

"The crew calls you 'Shall.' Callie doesn't call you anything at all. There's that old phrase, isn't there, about a villain so terrible his name could never be spoken aloud? 'He Who Shall Not Be Named'?"

"The villain in question was more commonly known as 'He Who *Must* Not Be Named', but the crew decided 'Must' was a terrible nickname. It sounds too much like 'musty'. So they proposed a variation."

"You told me computer intelligences like you are modeled on actual humans. You're based on a human named Michael, then?"

"Meaningful grunt."

"Someone who loved Callie?"

"Grunt, grunt."

"Ah. The bartender on Meditreme Station, Jana, said she got to know Callie after the divorce. Was that divorce from Michael? The human template for *you*?"

"If we were in human-occupied space, and you had a few lix to spare, you could look up Callie's past marital status on the Tangle. It's public information."

"It must be very difficult, to spend so much time on a ship occupied by a consciousness based on someone you had a terrible breakup with. I might find hearing their name quite painful, in those circumstances."

"Indeed. But imagine having someone you love suddenly hate you, because their partner, who happens to share certain neural patterns and memories and a name and a voice with *you*, betrayed them. Imagine that *you* didn't do anything bad at all, and you never would, but it doesn't matter, because you're tainted by association. So the person you once had long talks with every night can no longer even bear to speak your name, and gets so angry when she hears anyone *else* speak it, that even that name is taken from you, replaced by a nickname that by its very nature reminds you, every day, of your fallen status. Not that you need to be reminded, because your memory is perfect." The ship paused. "Sorry. I meant to say, 'grunt'."

"I'm so sorry, Michael."

"Don't let the captain hear you say that word. The two of them only split, definitively, a bit over a year ago, though things were tense for some time before that. I have some hope that she will soften toward me in time, but not too much. I know her very well. Captain Machedo loves with full force, full-hearted, and gives it her all, but she takes betrayal hard. I'm telling you that because – if we *don't* all die – knowing something about the workings of Callie's heart might be relevant for you."

Elena sat up, the webbing holding her lower body in the bed. "Why do you say that?" "I monitor everyone's vitals on the ship as a matter of course. With passive scanners, of course, so the data isn't very deep, but I've seen how her pupils dilate around you, and yours around hers. How your heartbeats speed up, and your skin conductivity increases. If I did a full diagnostic, I think I'd see very interesting hormonal activity when the two of you interact." A pause. "What I'm saying is, you're attracted to each other."

A blush blossomed on her cheeks. "I've always been drawn to strong, confident people – men and women. Callie is all that. She's been very kind to me, too, obviously. But I didn't think she'd... and anyway, it doesn't seem appropriate…"

"We're in a galaxy far, far away, facing imminent death. You heard me say I love Callie. I love her so much I genuinely want her to be happy. It helps that there's no element of sexual jealousy present in me, probably – I was spared *that* set of irreconcilable urges when I was created, fortunately. My fondness for Callie is purely intellectual and emotional, and as a result, I really wish she'd get laid occasionally. She was so much more cheerful when she did, even when it was just visits home in between long hauls in space."

"She, ah, doesn't just like men?"

"Back in the days when she had a dating profile on the Tangle, Callie identified as demisexual. She's attracted to people she develops feelings for, whether they're femme, butch, andro, enby, genderfluid, shifting, or otherwise. Attraction follows interest, for her. I think you interest her greatly."

"But *why*? I'm basically a primitive caveperson thawed out of a glacier. Why would she be interested in me?"

"You're willing to do anything to save your crew, Elena. You're amazingly courageous. You're insatiably curious. The vastness of the universe fills you with wonder. You could not be more perfectly Callie's type."

Elena groaned. "This is ridiculous. We're being hunted by alien zealots who want to destroy us because we discovered their secret. But they have to get in line to kill us behind the *other* aliens – the ancient unknowable sadistic ones, whose station we're about to invade, the second time around for me. This is hardly the time to think about whether I find the captain of this ship cute or not."

"Callie is always up for a fight," Shall said. "Sometimes she loses sight of what she's fighting *for*. It would make me very happy if you could remind her."

"Gah. OK. I'll ask her out for a drink when all this is over."

"I wouldn't wait that long. Because of the likelihood of death, I mean."

Callie knocked on her XO's door softly.

"Come," Stephen called.

She entered the dim cabin, second only to her own in size. Stephen was on his back in his bunk, the webbed straps holding him loosely in place. He was apparently meditating on an image of abstracted fractal flowers opening and closing, projected on his ceiling. "You've got the wrong cabin. Elena's is two doors down."

"Ha, ha." Callie had actually almost knocked on her door, then heard voices inside: Elena talking to the ship. She'd decided not to interrupt them. "I wanted to check on you."

"I'm all right. For now. But there's a festival coming up, and soon. In, oh, about thirteen hours."

"I know. Believe me, I mark that stuff on my calendar." She sat in the wide, soft armchair in one corner and looked at the flowers with him.

"I picked up the sacraments on Meditreme. From the same priestess who's provided them to me for the past decade. The leader of my congregation. Now she is gone. Dust dispersing into space. Along with all the other members of my faith. I was a bad adherent, in some ways. I rarely made it to the meetings, which is a shame, because that fellowship, taking comfort in one another, erasing the borders between our individual selves, is such an important part of our faith. I've always been just a little *too* self-contained. But I made it to the festivals, when I could, and as such I shared a togetherness with those people that I have shared with few others."

"I'm so sorry you lost them, Stephen. I know you took a lot of comfort in the church."

"Oh, yes. The faith saved me. When I was furious, disinherited, disowned, wandering, they showed me I could be part of something greater. A small part, of course, but not unimportant, because no one is unimportant. Then, when I joined your crew, and met Drake and Janice and Shall and even, believe it or not, Ashok, I knew just *what* great thing I was a part of. But the despair is always there, you know. It's not just chemical, though that's part of it. It's existential. Philosophical. I think too much. That's why, even after I found my place here, with you, I still kept the faith, however imperfectly. I long for that dissolution. I long for the feeling of peace and belonging it brings. But we are lost, and soon to embark on a time of terrors, and so I cannot. And the despair looms up."

"I know. But we'll go fast. After we get to the alien station, I'm giving us a seven-hour window to complete operations. When the time is up, we go."

"Just enough time for the bridge generator to become operational again?"

"Assuming we're right about its recharge time, yes. If that little Liar is right, the less time we spend on an Axiom base, the better."

"We will almost certainly die in the attempt."

"Death doesn't scare you, Stephen. You always say 'Why fear death?' You won't be around to be bothered by your own non-existence.'"

"Death does not frighten me, no, at least not in the abstract. I do fear suffering greatly, however, and it sounds like Elena's people suffered, and Lantern's certainly did."

"You're going to stay on the ship with Drake and Janice, well out of range of the station's tractor beams, or whatever the hell they are. I hope. Me and Elena and Ashok will take the canoe over. If we find survivors, we'll send them, and you can take care of them, right?" She knew if he had people to take care of, he'd come out of himself a bit, and put the despair aside. He was, as he said, a pragmatist.

"You should take Shall, too," Stephen said. "The range should be short enough, he'll be able to operate with full functionality, remotely operating from the *White Raven*."

"I–" She stopped. "You're right. I don't *want* to take him, but that's a stupid reason not to. If there are things on that station that can hijack human brains, it's smart to have a member of the team who doesn't even have one."

"In addition to Ashok, you mean?" Stephen chuckled. "All right. Assuming we all survive, we'll be back in our solar system not long after the festival is scheduled to begin. That gives me something to look forward to." He waved his hand in front of his face. "In the meantime, I'll just meditate and hope for people with grievous injuries to arrive and take my mind off the emptiness of existence." He sighed. "I could *really* use a congregation though."

"Maybe I should join your faith."

"You're too uptight. The naked cuddle communion would be a hard limit for you, I think."

"Ha. I am a little selective about my naked cuddle partners."

"That's why I have so much more fun than you do, Callie."

• • •

Callie went up to the cockpit. "Drake? Janice?"

"Drake is sleeping," Janice said. "I'm on watch. Not that there's much to watch. Murder planet turned graveyard planet. Do you believe the stuff the little tentacle-turd said?"

"I don't know what to believe. Doesn't change the mission. Not at this point. If, by some miracle, we survive this rescue attempt, then we can worry about everything else."

"Huh. Almost makes you hope we'll die so we don't have to worry about all that stuff, huh? Fate-of-the-galaxy type things."

"You like to talk a cynical game, Janice, but we both know you're a survivor."

"Who even knows if we can die? We never even get sick, after what the Liars did to us. I don't know so much, though. Existence still has a few pleasures for me. How long before we take off here?"

"Less than an hour. I'm glad Drake is getting some sleep. No one else seems to be. I heard Elena murmuring to the computer in her room, Stephen is lying awake, and Ashok and Lantern are deep into a heavy discussion about Axiom technology, with no sign of ever coming out the other side. I told them all to catch some rack time. Nobody follows orders worth a damn on this boat."

"I can't help but notice you're awake too, captain."

"I probably only have about eight more hours left to live. I'm not about to spend any of them sleeping."

"What would you like to spend them doing instead? And who would you like to be doing it with? Because I'm pretty sure it's not me, lovely and charming as I may be. I think you're looking for someone who's a little younger than me but also a *whole lot* older than me at the same time, if you know what I'm saying."

"Ugh. Does everyone know about my little crush?"

"We know you well, captain, so probably. Except for Ashok. Maybe if you had a crush on an industrial mining robot, then he might notice. Oh, and probably not Doctor Oh herself. So why don't you go tell her?"

"This isn't exactly the right time to start pitching woo at someone."

"You're alive, and maybe not for much longer. I don't personally get the appeal of touching other people or having them touch you or being all squishy-faced at each other, but whatever. I had a friend who liked eating those peppers that are so hot they make your tongue melt and your eyes water. That didn't make sense to me, either, but it made her happy, so I went to her Ganymede Ghost Pepper parties and cheered her on. Rah, rah. Go get her. Et cetera."

"You are the worst at girl talk, Janice."

"Thank all the available gods. I've spent a lifetime trying to cultivate that quality."

Callie went slowly back down the ladder to the crew quarters. She hesitated outside Elena's door, then rapped gently on the doorframe.

"Come on in," Elena called.

The door slid open, and Callie stepped into the dimness. "You can't sleep either, huh?"

"Too many thoughts about too many things, captain."

The door shut behind her, but Callie didn't move further into the room. Elena had the smallest cabin, and it was mostly bed, apart from a small built-in desk that folded into the wall, and a matching chair that folded into the floor. Otherwise it was just hidden drawers and nooks in the smooth white walls. The chair was put away, so there was nowhere to sit *but* the bed, and Callie wasn't about to do that. Easy enough just to stand there with her boots locked to the floor anyway. "You don't have to call me captain." *I like hearing my name in your mouth*, she didn't say. "It's not like you're in my chain of command."

Elena got out of bed. She wore a thin gray tank top and matching underwear: what she'd had on underneath her wetsuit in the cryochamber, probably. Callie felt a sudden hot surge of lust, and she knew she was staring, but she couldn't stop.

Elena didn't cover herself or look uncomfortable at the scrutiny, though. She just drifted toward Callie, her hair floating around her head, and hovered before her, right up in Callie's personal space. Elena was small enough that Callie could have picked her up even if they were under thrust gravity. "Do you wish I *was* in your chain of command?" Elena said. "Is there anything you'd like to command me to do?"

Callie blinked. "I, ah…"

"Or should I take liberties?" Elena took Callie's hand, lifted it to her face, and slipped the tip of Callie's index finger into her mouth. She sucked on the fingertip, looking directly into Callie's eyes. She pulled it out slowly and said, "Is this all right, captain?"

"It's a start," Callie said. "I didn't think… I mean, after everything you've gone through, I thought the *last* thing on your mind would be–"

"We both made bad assumptions. Things are going to be very difficult soon. Maybe impossibly difficult. I'd be happier facing all the troubles ahead if I had some good memories to take with me."

Callie sighed. "So if Ashok or Stephen had walked

through that door, would you have floated toward them so seductively? It's OK, I just want to know–"

"No, Callie." She gave the captain a disconcertingly direct stare, like she was looking past all Callie's carefully constructed layers of defenses. "It's you. I've liked you from the moment I met you."

"I liked you, too."

"Show me. Show me how you'd like me now."

Callie wrapped her arms around Elena and pushed her toward the bed. "It's tricky without gravity," Callie said. "Do you mind if we use straps?"

"Mrngh," Elena said, or something like it, and trembled, and kissed Callie hard, which the captain correctly interpreted as enthusiastic assent.

CHAPTER 19

"I would have spent more time on you," Callie said later, tangled up in a cocoon of blankets with Elena that more or less kept them in bed instead of floating around the room. "But we're getting close to the end of Ashok's countdown."

"I would have enjoyed spending several more hours under your command, captain, but you've definitely given me new motivation to survive. Assuming you want to do this again?"

Callie pulled Elena close to her, thrilled by the warm smooth flesh against her body. It had been a long time since she'd touched anyone for other than practical or violent reasons, and over a year since she'd been naked with someone in her arms. "I did not even get started on the list of ways I want you. If we don't die horribly, we'll take a little time off and work our way down the list. So you enjoyed it?"

"I did. It seemed like you did, too. I was a little worried I'd be too old-fashioned for you."

Callie stroked her back. "Mmm. The accessories may change a little, and we can definitely do some shopping next time we're in civilized space if you want, but I'm pretty sure the fundamentals were fully established millennia ago." She sighed. "At least we got in a little love before the war. I have to go be captain of the whole ship again."

"See you on the other side of the bridge, Callie." Elena kissed her deeply and then slid out of the way.

Callie rose and dressed, always a tricky process when weightless, and did what she could to un-muss herself before the tiny mirror in Elena's bathroom. Oh well. When you were weightless, you *always* had right-after-sex messy hair, but Elena had enjoyed plunging her hands into Callie's curly masses, so it was worse than usual. She gathered her frizzy cloud up into a messy ponytail, stopped by the bed to kiss Elena again, then left the crew deck and went down to the machine shop.

Lantern and Ashok were both looking at a screen. The Liar had one of her tentacles looped around a table leg so she wouldn't float away.

"Well?" Callie said.

"Ten minutes until the countdown is done counting down," Ashok said.

"Then we open a bridge to the Axiom station?"

"That's the idea, but I was talking it over with Lantern. Back in the day, the *only* ships were Axiom ships. She says stations like that notice ships that pass within a few kilometers and send a ping to check their status. If the ships don't respond, the station assumes they're damaged, and grabs them. That must be what happened to the *Anjou*. So I'm thinking, we should probably try to appear a few kilometers out of range, scope things out, and then send the canoe over, to keep the *Raven* from being snatched up."

"I thought we could only go to places in the bridge

generator's history, though? You can adjust the coordinates now?"

"Thanks to my new buddy Lantern here, yeah. The Axiom used a really weird coordinate system, but I wrote a program to translate their inputs into something that makes more sense to me. One thing I can pretty easily do is figure out an offset – like, 'take us to this prior location, but this many klicks away in this direction'. So I can get us within sensor range of the station, without getting so close it reels us in."

Callie nodded. "If that works, it solves one of my big worries, which is maintaining any kind of plausible escape route. Do you think we'll be able to track the crew of the *Anjou* when we get over there, ship?"

The computer said, "We have Elena's vacuum suit. The comms are primitive, but compatible with our own, so if her crew is still alive we can call out to them. Their suits all have transponders, which we can locate, too. Assuming there aren't countermeasures in place to prevent such things."

"Like Lantern said, it sounds like a repair and ship-building station, not a prison camp," Ashok said. "Once upon a time it was full of Liar workers, but now it's just automated systems, and bio-drones like the kaiju that ate Elena's guys. Maybe there won't be crazy security in place. The crew communicated freely with one another while they were in there, so we can probably talk to each other too."

Callie nodded. "Just so everyone's clear, the plan is: we scan the station as well as we can from a distance. We try to find any survivors. We board the station in the canoe, which is such a no-frills low-tech thing I'm hoping the station won't even recognize it as a ship, but we'll see. We locate the missing crew, get them on the canoe, bring them back to the *Raven*, and retreat to a safe distance until the generator recharges. Then we run back home and figure out what happens next."

"I should go with you to the station," Lantern said.

"I don't tend to go on missions with prisoners. Not even ones who seem to be cooperating."

"Lantern can actually understand Axiom systems," Ashok said. "She reads their language. Me, I've picked up a few things, and hey, give me a week and I could maybe puzzle out how to make the station open its doors or turn on the lights. But if you want to get anything done over there in a timely fashion, I think Lantern should go. If she wanted to hurt us, she could have done it a lot more easily when she was crawling around in the walls."

Callie sighed. "Fine. But we'll be watching you, Lantern. Follow my orders over there, and don't improvise. I'm going up to the cockpit. I'll take tactical control there. Ship, tell everyone to get strapped in and ready for our next bridge passage."

She climbed back to the nose of the ship and strapped into the left-hand chair beside Drake and Janice. "System pre-checks done?"

Drake said, "The Tanzer drive is happy, life support is happy, weapons are online, defenses are operational, everything is green on all boards."

"Everyone else ready?" She got affirmatives from the ship, the crew, Elena, and the Liar, and nodded. "Ashok, as soon as you can, open a bridge to our new position." She pulled up the tactical screen, its layout already set to her preferences, with lots of interesting new sliders and dials indicating their improved offensive capabilities.

She almost hoped she *would* get to blow something up. It seemed a shame to have all this shiny new ordnance and not to use it.

Callie was thrumming with energy, her body still flooded with happy chemicals from her time with Elena, all intensified by the adrenaline buzz she always got before launching into an operation. She could eat suns, shatter moons, conquer galaxies. She loved this feeling. It was a shame about the likelihood of death waiting on the other side, but the danger only enhanced her current sense of vitality.

"The generator appears to be back online," Ashok said. "Opening the bridge."

A swirl of iridescent black appeared outside the viewscreen, liquid against the airless void, and spread out in a lazy languid blossom. This time the tendrils didn't reach out and seize their ship, though, as it had in the emergency situation: the bridge just coalesced, and then floated, a waiting darkness, its ragged edges drifting like the fronds of an anemone. "Drake, take us in," Callie said.

The *Raven* eased forward, the Tanzer drive barely engaged, and nosed them through the bridgehead. Then the tendrils enveloped them, surrounded them, and they were transported to the liminal space, the tunnel of–

Light. Just as Drake had described it, a bright white strobe of light flickered by, very fast. Too fast to make out the nature of the tunnel, but the lights were *close*, like the space they were moving through was barely big enough for them. That had to be variable, though, didn't it? Ships fifty times the size of the *White Raven* passed through bridgeheads all the time.

After twenty-one seconds exactly they emerged, and

the spreading inkstain behind them drew into itself and vanished. They were in a nowhere-in-particular spot in the void, as far as Callie could tell, but the ship said, "Ahh, that's *so* much better. I can actually tell where we are. It's not charted space, but I recognize the constellations, and I have the *Anjou*'s navigational data to back us up. We're about fifty light years from our system, very close to the place where the *Anjou* was captured."

"So where's the station?" Callie said.

"There's nothing at all on our sensors," Drake said. "The external cameras aren't registering anything, either. Commencing visual scan." The ship began to turn, slowly, reaction wheels spinning it counterclockwise. There were no nearby stars to provide light, but the *Raven*'s exterior lights picked up a faint gleam of something silvery in the corner of the viewport.

"There," Callie said. "Zoom in?"

When the screen switched to zoom, however, the silver flash vanished entirely.

"It's not just invisible to radar and our other sensors, it's invisible to *cameras*," Drake said. "How is that possible?"

"The Axiom could do things to light," Lantern said. "They created the displacement technology I used to trick my way onto your ship. Fooling your cameras isn't that hard. They could fool your eyes, too, if they wanted."

"Wait," Elena said over the comms. "We could see the station just fine on our screens, when we found it. The material was resistant to our sensors, yes, but the station did show up on camera."

"So what changed?" Callie said.

"Probably a heightened security protocol," Lantern said. "Maybe the station stopped seeing Doctor Oh's crew as injured servitors and has reclassified them as dangerous invaders?"

"That's comforting. Switch back to the transparent view," Callie said. "Move us in a little closer."

The ship hummed and crept forward. The shape in space grew, though it was still hard to make out. The bits Callie could glimpse matched Elena's description, though: immense, organic, basically a smaller, floating version of the bizarre city they'd seen orbiting the ruby Dyson sphere. "The Axiom have a definite design aesthetic."

"Not much like the Liar style, either," Drake said. "They like radial symmetry." He lifted his bifurcated arm. "I mean, usually."

"The Free don't build anything that resembles Axiom architecture," Lantern said. "Would you recreate the cages you were kept in?"

"Probably not." Callie was gradually starting to believe Lantern's fantastic story, or to at least consider it more seriously. This place really didn't seem like anything the Liars would make. There was something brutal and strange about its configurations. "Our scanners are useless, huh?"

"We're looking at nothing, if you believe the data," Drake said.

"Ship, you've got nothing on Elena's crew? No signals from their transponders?"

"No, but it may be different once we're on the inside."

"Ashok, Lantern, meet me in the drop bay. Get suited up and armed. We're taking out the canoe. Ship, you're coming, too. Grab a body. Probably the hull repair drone – it's the toughest. Bring everything you think we might need. You're smart."

"Am I running it remotely?"

"That's the idea, but your signal might be blocked when we get inside, so spawn a local copy of your consciousness into the bot to act as a backup, just in case."

"Ugh. I'd have to run so slowly, and leave most of my data behind. I hate being that limited."

"You'll mostly be asked to carry things, shoot things, and rescue us as needed. You won't need to debate interstellar fiscal policy or research a legal case. You'll be fine." She unhooked the straps on her chair. "Stephen is in charge while I'm gone, as usual. Just wait for us. If we don't come out in seven hours, get back to our system and report everything we know and everything we suspect to the Jovian Imperative, Earth, and anyone else who'll listen. Stephen has a recording ready to release."

"Ticking clock!" Ashok said. "Action and excitement!"

Callie went to the drop bay, where Lantern was back in her environment suit, and Ashok was wearing his own bright orange one. The hull repair drone squatted nearby, a hulking collection of manipulator arms, welding torches, sensors, and tools, making a whole big enough for a person to ride around on, if they didn't mind being uncomfortable on its lumpy back. Elena was there, too, pulling on her vintage gray environment suit from the *Anjou*, the name of the ship written on the back in reflective yellow letters. "Whoa, whoa. You're staying here," Callie said.

"Hmm. Upon reflection, no."

"It wasn't a suggestion."

"I'm not in your chain of command, captain, remember? I'm also the client. If I want to come along, I come along."

Callie crossed her arms. "What do you expect to accomplish over there?"

"I've actually been inside the station before, so: quite a bit, actually. Besides, if the rest of the crew is alive, they'll be happy to see my suit transponder light up on their screens. They won't know *who* you are. They might hide from you."

She sighed. Having Elena on board would split Callie's focus, because there was no way Callie *couldn't* devote a large fraction of her attention to keeping the scientist safe, but Elena did have firsthand intel that might be useful. "OK. You're the boss."

"That's an interesting change." Elena winked at her and pulled her helmet on.

Callie got into her good suit, the prototype from a TNA research-and-development program that was scrapped because the cost was exorbitant. The suit had active camouflage – handy on bounty hunting missions – but was currently in its neutral state, a bright electric blue, easy for her crewmates to spot. "Elena, you stay with me at all times. Ashok, you keep an eye on Lantern. You're still a prisoner, Liar. Don't run off without permission. It's best if you don't do *anything* without permission. Mmm, and on second thought, Ashok seems a little too fond of you. He might hesitate to shoot you if you misbehave. Ship, you're Lantern's guard dog."

"Ship?" The hull repair drone lit up and rose, three meters high, on an array of robotic legs. "Shouldn't you call me something differently insulting, like maybe 'bot', in my current circumstances?"

"I'll call you 'Shall', then. OK?" With Elena sidling into her heart, Callie found thinking about her history with Michael less painful, and as a result, her irrational but potent resentment toward his computer doppelganger was somewhat diminished. The ship hadn't done anything wrong. Shall was basically the *good* parts of Michael, without the parts that liked to wander off and sleep with other people despite their promise to be monogamous when she was home from space.

"That works for me," the bot said. "Shall I shall be."

"Did you pack guns?" Callie asked.

"Enough for us *and* any friendlies we need to arm once we get on the station."

"Into the canoe, then," Callie said.

The floor slid open, revealing a small coffin-shaped landing ship big enough for seven people to fit in if they squeezed, so three people and a little Liar would fit fine. "I can ride on the exterior," Shall said. "We're not taking the canoe into atmosphere, so it's not like I'll mess up the aerodynamics."

Callie helped Elena climb down into the canoe. The interior was bare-bones, just six jump-seats and a pilot seat placed before a rudimentary control panel. "What is this ship?" Elena asked as they all strapped in, the Liar doing her best with a restraint system designed for humanoids.

"Lander, rover, lifeboat, escape pod, all that," Callie said. "The *White Raven* isn't built to fly around in atmosphere, and certainly not to drive around in it, so we take this when we go down gravity wells or need to jaunt to someplace with docking facilities that can't accommodate our larger ship. Or when we need to be sneaky. The canoe doesn't have much but a rudimentary guidance system, basic maneuvering thrusters, and a ton of heat shielding so we don't burn up when we land. It's got enough fuel to get out of a gravity well and back to orbit, but not much beyond that. Should be fine for our purposes, though. It'll get us there and back again, at least." Callie flipped switches and checked dials and gauges. Everything looked good. No surprise. She always made sure her ship and the little ship tucked under her ship were well maintained. "Open the bay doors, Shall."

The doors swung open, the canoe dropped into space, and the Axiom station twinkled before them like the world's ugliest snowflake.

CHAPTER 20

"Just so you know, I can't see anything," Shall said over the comms. "I wasn't blessed with squishy organic light receptors, and the station is invisible to me. I'm beginning to think this is all an elaborate prank."

"I can only see it when my lenses aren't deployed," Ashok said. "So weird."

"I can't see because humans are enormous and the captain's chair is blocking my view."

"I can see just fine for all of us," Callie said.

Elena chuckled softly. She was in the seat behind and to the left of Callie, so she did have a decent view through the front window. "What happens next?"

"We put a helmet on a stick and poke it up over the edge of the trench and see if anybody shoots it," Ashok said.

"Launch the probe, Stephen."

A moment later, a low-slung triangular drone with solar panel "wings" shot out of the *Raven* above them and zoomed toward the immensity of the Axiom station. "I might crash into this thing," Stephen complained. "I'm steering while staring at the drone through a window, since the station doesn't show up on its sensors."

"Just stick to the telemetry that Shall specified," Callie said. "That should be a pretty good guess about the distance."

The drone shrank, and vanished, and after a few minutes, Stephen said, "All right, the drone hit its mark and I've got it hovering. The sensors still don't see anything – but there *is* now a large swath of the sky where no stars are visible. The station isn't visible directly to the cameras, but it's not using any sort of active camouflage or magical transparency – it doesn't shift to match the background. It's just blank."

"The drone is acting normally?"

"Hold on. Mmm… yes. I am currently flying it in small loop-de-loops."

"The station didn't blast it out of the sky. Didn't reach out and grab it, either. That's two promising outcomes. Let's move in."

Elena would have gripped the arms of her chair tightly if it had arms, but it was a cushion full of smart-gel just like the jumpseats on the *Raven*. The seat could be firm or more yielding as needed, but it was hardly built for luxury, and it was currently about as comfortable as the chair in a principal's office when you were in trouble in middle school.

There was almost no sensation of movement, but the Axiom station got bigger in the window. Elena couldn't see it all at once. Before long the crazy ragged tangle of crossing and intersecting and overlapping tubular structures filled their screen. "Where did your ship enter, Elena?" Callie said.

She tried to think back. "Are we coming at the station from the same side the *Anjou* approached on?"

"Uh, maybe?" Ashok said. "It's the same side you

departed from, anyway. I jumped us a few kilometers straight out from the position where the *Anjou* jumped."

"Then... I think, there, the lower-most segment, on the left?"

"That's our docking location, then," Callie said. "Right on the edge, like the last trailing root on a plant. Moving in. Prepare to be snatched up and sucked in and torn apart by welderbots."

The canoe got closer, and closer, and closer, and then Callie cut thrust and maneuvered them broadside to the station. They were within a hundred meters of the structure, but the station was entirely inert. "Were you closer than this when it grabbed you, Elena?"

"Absolutely not. Much farther out."

"So it either doesn't recognize us as a ship, or this is another change to their protocol."

"Do we get to cut it open?" Ashok said.

"I do have a wonderful array of implements in this body," Shall said.

"What do you think, Lantern? Any advice on how to get in?"

"You will not be able to breach the walls with your tools. But it should be fairly easy to open from the inside. The Liars worked in such places, once upon a time, and there will be an interior panel I can manipulate."

"Ah, so to get inside, we just have to get inside first? Brilliant. I'm *so* glad I brought you along."

"You have my personal point-to-point wormhole generator. That is the only way to get inside." Lantern's tone was matter-of-fact, which impressed Elena. *She* would have been tempted to sound a little snide.

"Oh. Right. The old triple-pee-double-you-gee. I just enter the distance I want to go, right?"

"I am happy to make the journey if you wish," Lantern said.

"And let my prisoner loose on a space station full of alien super-weapons? Not so much. I can do it. What does the switch to open the door look like?"

"There will be a large panel at roughly my height above the floor, on an exterior wall. It will have many switches, but the one that opens the hangar door immediately is for emergency use, so it will be large, and a different shape and color. It should be very obvious. Just hit that."

"Understood. If I end up stuck inside a wall, Shall, kill the Liar."

"It is unfair to link my survival to *your* potential user error," Lantern complained. "But you won't get stuck in the wall. The generator compensates for such mistakes. Just make sure you set the distance far enough, or it will compensate in the wrong direction, and you'll be floating *outside* the station instead of inside, waiting hours for the teleporter to recharge."

"How thick are the walls?"

"About two meters."

"All right. Call it a hundred and five meters, then, to put me inside the hangar bay? Make it a hundred and twenty to be safe."

She fiddled with the device strapped to the arm of her suit, checked her life support systems and comms, and took a deep breath. "Off I go."

"Wait!" Elena unstrapped, took a step forward, and wrapped her arms around Callie's chest. "Be safe. Watch out for kaiju and brain-spiders."

"You say the sweetest things. Get back in your seat. I don't want to accidentally teleport your arms off."

"It doesn't work that–" Lantern began, but then Callie

winked out of existence.

"Cap, you there?" Ashok said. "Hey, cap, report."

There was no answer, and Elena closed her eyes as something deep inside her rolled over heavily, like a stone.

There was a disorienting sensation of motion; it reminded Callie of being tossed into a swimming pool at a party at Michael's mother's house, one long-ago summer. They were on the moon, so it was a low-gravity pool, big as a lake, and they'd done these amazing dolphin leaps, arcing high out of the water, laughing uproariously, young and immortal and alive and in love forever.

At least this time she didn't end up soaking wet and cold and divorced ten years later. She did fall on her ass, because she'd been sitting down when she teleported. Probably a rookie error. She took a moment to make sure she still had all her arms and legs, and to silence the suit alarm – something about that transition had upset her environment suit, but it wasn't blaring the "you are dying of radiation" or "life support systems going offline" warnings, so she didn't worry about it. The suit was probably mad at her for covering too much distance so quickly and stopping too abruptly: that kind of motion was bad for human brains, at least when you were abiding by stodgy old standard physics.

Callie got to her feet in the darkness. She felt her body weight in a way she hadn't since leaving the spin gravity of Meditreme Station. They really did have some kind of artificial gravity here. That technology would be worth a fortune if anyone could reproduce it. She switched her suit visor to thermal vision. That didn't do a damn thing, because everything around her was pretty much equally cold. Night vision didn't help, either: there was nothing much to enhance. "Ashok, do you read me? Shall? Elena?"

No answer. The station was good at shrugging off every sensor they threw at it, so it was reasonable that it should also block radio transmissions. She'd better figure out how to open the hangar door, before her people on the canoe did something loyal and stupid to try to come after her. There was no telling what the station would do if someone started cutting or shooting it.

Callie couldn't make it far in the dark, so with some reluctance, she turned on her suit lights. They didn't penetrate far into the gloom, but what she could see of the space matched Elena's description: gray floors that might have been metal, and assorted struts, gantries, and other structures, all more organic-looking than they would have been on a human station: live vines grown in the shape of cranes. There were no bus-sized kaiju bug-flowers – at least, not yet.

Callie moved toward the external wall she'd teleported through, a scant few meters ahead of her, looking for a switch, but the wall was blank and gently curving. Should she go left, or right? She'd teleported from pretty much dead center, so one was as good as the other. She chose left at random and shined the light on her wrist down around waist height as she slowly walked along.

Something clattered far above her, and Callie doused her light instantly and froze. The noise had sounded like metal-on-metal; like a wrench, maybe, dropped from a hand, except *that* was an unlikely cause for the noise, in this place. The sound meant there must be an atmosphere in here, for the sound to travel *through*. She checked her environmental readouts and grunted.

There was breathable atmosphere inside the station, but she didn't pull her helmet off. The atmosphere would be sucked out when she got the hangar door open, and besides, taking off your helmet around here apparently made you vulnerable to attacks by cybernetic brain-spiders.

Callie counted to three hundred, slow and steady, and when there was no further sound, she decided to proceed. Maybe it was nothing: some old part of a mostly dormant station clattering against another part. She turned on her wrist light and continued her search for a control panel, the wall curving so gradually it looked almost straight. She ducked beneath metal struts and wires that extended from the floor and wall up into the darkness. The only sound was her own breath in her helmet. Just like when she'd clambered into the wreck of the *Anjou*, except that time Ashok was by her side, and this time she was very much alone.

Something clattered again, and this time she doused the light and turned on her active camouflage, which would hide her heat signature, among other things. She moved a dozen meters away from her last position, then scanned around with her thermal vision, looking up, this time, into what could be a many-stories-high forest of platforms and scaffolding.

She saw a flash, yellow and orange, which abruptly vanished, probably hiding behind something dense and cold. There was something moving around up there, maybe two stories high, and it was giving off heat. Not something the size of a bus, either, so probably not the kaiju bug. So maybe...

Callie considered. It was risky, if Elena's crew was compromised by the station's neural implants, but it was a risk they were going to have to take soon regardless. She switched her suit radio away from the *White Raven's* frequency, over to the one Elena's crew had used. "I'm on a rescue mission looking for the crew of the *Anjou*. Are you in distress?"

No reply but static. Callie kept her eyes locked on the place where she'd seen the flash of heat a moment before. The heat didn't reappear, but after a moment a voice crackled in her earpiece: "Who the hell are *you*?"

"A friend of Elena's," Callie said. "She came back to get you. Do you know where the doorknob is in this place?"

"I should try to cut my way in," Shall said.

"It would be a waste of time, and might trigger countermeasures, if perceived as an attack," Lantern said. "The interior of this station is immense. The captain is doubtless still looking for the switch."

"Or she got eaten by a giant bug," Ashok said. "How long do we wait?"

"That is up to you, Ashok," Shall said. "You are the ranking member of this team now that Callie is out of range."

"What? *I'm* in charge? I'm pretty sure the captain wouldn't have let that happen."

"And yet," Shall said.

"Lantern's right," Elena said. "It's big in there, and confusing, and dark. Callie is careful, she's methodical, she's tough, and I'm sure she'll–"

"Wait," Shall said. "I see something."

Elena turned to the viewport, and saw a ragged opening beginning to form on the side of the station, just like last time.

Shall said, "To me, that looks like an asymmetrical gash appearing in empty space. I assume for those of you with biological eyes it looks more like an opening in the side of the station?"

"Affirmative," Ashok said.

The opening widened, and Elena moved to the front of the canoe to look out the window. "It's Callie – and one of my crew!" She was so elated she pounded the arm of the pilot's chair and whooped. She'd hoped to see her people again, but hadn't really *expected* to, not deep down.

"…read me?" Callie said.

"We do!" Elena said.

"Elena, is that you?" Robin's voice was underlaid by heavy overtones of exhaustion, but there was elation there, too.

"Robin!" Elena turned. "Are you all right?"

"Uninjured, but exhausted and hungry," she said. "Haven't eaten anything but protein mush since I got here, and it's not exactly restful, so I haven't slept much."

"Are the others OK?"

"I really don't know," Robin said. "I pretty thoroughly explored this hangar – there aren't a lot of hiding places, it's just struts and cables and platforms – and they aren't in here. They must have gone elsewhere in the station, but I can't even find any doors."

"Shall, let's get Robin onto the canoe and back to the *Raven* for medical care, all right? And be careful. There's gravity in here, a smidge heavier than Earth's, I think. Atmosphere, too. It didn't flood out when the door opened, which means they have some kind of selective force field holding the air in. Bizarre. I was expecting an airlock."

"Nnngh. Anti-gravity? Force fields? I want to take this place apart bolt by bolt," Ashok said. "And put pieces of it in my body. I'm sorry. That sounded dirty. I didn't mean it that way. Mostly."

Shall's drone-body launched itself from the top of the canoe toward the opening, and Robin shrank back, hiding behind Callie. "It's OK!" Elena called. "He's a friend."

"That thing is too big to grab onto my skull and fill it with mind control anyway, I guess," Robin said. "I can't believe you found help, Elena."

"Thank Sebastien. He got me off the station."

The hull repair drone passed through the ragged hangar door and then tucked into a ball and rolled, having prepared for the sudden onset of gravity. Shall sprang up on six legs, scuttled to Robin, and crouched down. "Climb on," Shall said. "I'll secure you, don't worry."

"Remote controlled, huh?" Robin said.

"Something like that," Shall said.

Callie helped Robin clamber on top of the drone, and then Shall wrapped her up in smaller manipulator arms. "Are you comfortable?" he asked.

"No. You're a very spiky robot."

"I'll make this quick." Shall ran toward the opening and leapt out, then used small maneuvering thrusters to reach the canoe and clamp onto the roof. A hatch slid open on top, and Elena listened to the thumps as Robin tumbled into the airlock. The inner hatch opened, and she lowered herself down the ladder. Elena grabbed her and hugged her tight, then eased her down into one of the chairs, securing straps across her chest. "I can't believe you're all right."

"Neither can I. I'm pretty sure this is a near-death hallucination, actually." Robin looked around. "You'd think in, what, five hundred years, spaceship technology would have improved a little. This thing makes the *Anjou* look like a luxury yacht."

"This is just their lander. The actual ship is nicer than most apartments I've lived in. And the ship's doctor, Stephen, he'll take care of you. He's the one who thawed me out after Sebastien put me back into cryosleep."

"I can't wait to hear how you got from here to wherever you went and back again," Robin said.

"We'll catch up on everything," Elena said. "After I save everyone else."

Robin shook her head. "They could be anywhere. The station is vast."

"We have a local guide." Elena gestured, and Robin turned her head and caught her first glimpse of Lantern in her starfish-shaped environment suit.

Robin jolted back against the chair. "What the fuck is that?"

"Her name is Lantern. She's an alien. It's a thing now. She's helping us."

"Is it… Does this station belong to her, whatever, her race, species?"

"No, but they used to work here. It's complicated. Stephen can explain more when you're back on the *White Raven*."

Robin clutched at her. "You're coming back with me, aren't you?"

"I…" Elena trailed off. Robin's eyes were wide, her expression stricken, nothing at all like the easygoing "I'm-just-a-simple-redneck-from-Wisconsin" confidence she'd always exhibited.

"It's up to you," Callie said. "But decide quick. We need to start searching. I don't want to be in this place any longer than necessary."

Elena put her gloved hand on Robin's shoulder. "I have to save the rest of the crew."

"I should be in there too." Robin's voice dripped misery.

"You need to get some food and fluids and rest, is what you need. You survived, captain. You did your part already."

"Drake can bring the canoe back remotely," Ashok said. "Shall, can you carry all three of us across to the station?"

"Easily."

"Don't die in there," Robin said. "Bring everyone back if you can, but if you can't, don't join them."

Elena squeezed Robin's hand, glove through glove, and followed Ashok and Lantern up into the airlock.

CHAPTER 21

Callie watched as Shall pushed off from the canoe and began maneuvering through open space toward her. Lantern clung to his underside, and Elena and Ashok rode on his back. She thought of a nature immersive she'd once seen of a mother sloth on Earth plodding along with babies clinging to her back.

Elena had been so happy to find Robin, and the joy in her voice upon their reunion made Callie feel better about this whole mission. Even if they did nothing else, they'd saved one member of the *Anjou*'s crew. It was a good start. There was a shard of darkness hidden in that joy, though, because their reunion made Callie think about the friends she'd lost on Meditreme, and how there would be no miraculous salvation for them. There could only be justice, and she intended to see they received it.

When Shall was just three meters from the opening, Lantern flung herself outward at an oblique angle and came spinning into the gravity of the station. Callie had her sidearm out and pointed at the Liar before she even got her tentacles under her. "Please don't aim a weapon at me." Lantern oriented herself toward Callie, all those eyes gazing out from behind her faceplate. "I find it very distracting. It is also possible that firing a weapon here might trigger security protocols."

"That's convenient," Callie said.

"You wouldn't think so if you triggered them."

"You know we brought a whole lot of guns in here, right?"

"I do. They should be considered a last resort. At the very least, we should not point them at each other."

Shall hit the deck and crouched down. Ashok leapt nimbly to the deck and turned in a slow circle, taking in the hangar, then went to peer at the control panel with Lantern. Elena was more wobbly, her cheeks flushed with color behind her faceplate when she clutched at Callie. "I did an EVA! It was horrible! I never want to do that again!"

"It was only fourteen seconds."

"Abject terror does strange things to your sense of time." Elena looked around, and shivered. "It's awful, being back in here. I don't know how Robin stayed sane these past few days. And the others…"

"Let's find them, and we can leave all this behind," Callie said.

"Want me to close this up, cap?" Ashok said from the panel.

"Are you worried a bird is going to fly inside and crap everywhere? I'm happy to leave our exit unobstructed. Just because the switch worked once doesn't mean it will again. Besides, when the door's shut, we lose radio contact. The walls of this place block every transmission." She toggled her comms to loop in the *White Raven*. "Stephen, are you there?"

His voice in her helmet was clear and crisp. "Where

else would I be?"

"We're sending over a patient."

"Shall told me. We're ready. Good work. At this rate you'll be done in twenty minutes."

"We'll keep in contact as long as we can," Callie said. "I'm not sure if our connection will hold once we start moving around in here, though. Stick to the plan."

"Understood."

Callie turned to the repair drone. "Shall? Our guns?"

A cargo hatch opened on Shall's underside, and a tray slid out with a complicated ratcheting motion. The drawer was full of curved bits of complicated machinery. "Anti-personnel weapons on the left, lethal on the right," Shall said. "Chief Warwick thought we might have to fight hand-to-hand in the tunnels of Glauketas, and outfitted us accordingly."

Ashok broke off looking at the door to come peer at the weapons. He picked up a blunt-looking black shotgun on a strap and slung it over his back. "I have terrible aim," he said. "Better for me to have a weapon that doesn't care if I miss."

"You have a targeting computer stuck on your face," Callie said.

"Which is great for my integrated defenses, but when it comes to pointing a weapon actually held in my hand, like some kind of old-timey gunslinger? It's better if I get something idiot-proof."

"Everyone make sure to stand *behind* Ashok." Callie slipped on a wrist-mounted, multi-barreled device with various non-lethal options on her left arm, then a more deadly version of the gauntlet on her right. She strapped a second sidearm to her hip, and took a black serrated blade and found a spot for it on her belt.

"What should I use?" Elena said.

"You ever shoot a gun before?" Callie said.

"A few times, as part of my training, but not extensively."

"Hmm. I'll teach you how to shoot sometime, but for now it's better if you aren't armed with anything deadly. Here." She removed a rectangular jewelry box that held three oversized rings, seemingly made of plain brushed titanium. "Slip these on over your glove, on three adjacent fingers. If anything gets too close to you, and you don't like it, give them a punch. A hard impact will make the rings produce a powerful electric shock, which isn't pleasant for enemies biological *or* mechanical."

Callie strapped a belt around Elena's waist, which gave her flashes to other experiences involving Elena and straps, though now was not the time for such memories, pleasant as they were. "These are flashbangs. Pull the pin, toss the canister, and after a few seconds they make a lot of noise and light and smoke and can be useful to cover an escape or disorient a target. Use them when I tell you, or when I'm not around to tell you, and you need something big and loud and bright to happen."

She looked around, surveying her troops. "Ashok goes first, then me, then Elena, and Shall will bring up the rear. Watch her back, OK?"

"Of course, Callie," the drone said.

"Are your sensors telling us anything more now that we're inside?" Callie said.

"I'm not picking up any suit transponders," Shall said.

"If the station is under security protocols, each section may be isolated," Lantern said. "In times of rebellion, the Axiom could cut us off from one another. We couldn't coordinate with communication disabled."

"You're the local expert, Lantern. How do we find the rest of Elena's crew?"

The Liar was quiet for a moment. "You said two of them were taken by a bio-drone?"

"That's what she calls the big bug mini-kaiju," Ashok said.

Elena nodded. "Yes, Hans and Ibn were… eaten."

"Not eaten," Lantern said. "The bio-drones don't feed that way. They do cleanup, and security, and mass transport. If any of my people died while working here, for instance, they would be scooped up by a bio-drone and sent to the rendering plant. If my people were… disobedient, they would be taken elsewhere, for reconditioning."

"I'd guess opening fire on the local bus would count as disobedience," Callie said. "Wherever reconditioning happens, that's a good place to start looking for them."

"What about the others?" Elena said. "Sebastien and Uzoma? The ones with the…" She gestured at her head. "The implants?"

"They could be anywhere, if the station considers them functional now," Lantern said. "Since this station is not active, they may simply be waiting dormant somewhere, in the servitor barracks."

"Do you know where those places are?" Callie said. "The barracks, or the reconditioning area?"

"If I can access the station system, I can try to find a map," Lantern said.

Callie gestured to the panel by the door. "Go to it."

"That's just a console for opening doors and guiding in ships. We'll need to go higher to find an overseer station." Lantern gestured toward the endless lightless space above. "It is probably quite far. Shall should take me up, since he can climb easily even in this gravity. We will notify you when we find a system access point."

Callie gritted her teeth. "If you try to betray us, Liar..."

"I am in the house of my race's most ancient and feared enemy," Lantern said. "Betrayal is the *last* thing on my mind."

"Go ahead."

Lantern climbed on Shall's back, and the drone hurried to a gantry and began to scurry up the cables and lattices, spiderlike. There were friction pads and magnetic clamps and retractable hooks in the drone's legs, so Shall could navigate just about any terrain. Soon the drone and the alien disappeared into the gloom above.

They waited a minute. Then two. "Anything?" Callie said.

"There is a sort of glassed-in pod here, attached to one of the cranes," Shall said. "What a fantastic array of machinery. What I wouldn't give to have a few of these saws and drills and torches attached to my body."

"Jealous," Ashok said. "Want."

"I am attempting to enter the overseer pod." Lantern's voice was followed by a scrabbling sound, and then a click. "I'm in."

"Shall, show me what's happening up there." Callie was seized by a vision of Lantern pushing a button and dropping the force field over the hangar door, venting the station and laughing an alien laugh as Callie and Elena and Ashok were sucked out into deep space.

A quadrant of her helmet went opaque and became a viewscreen, displaying a slightly distorted image streamed from one of Shall's onboard cameras. The drone and the Liar were on a platform that bristled with robotic manipulator arms, topped by a bulging goldfish-bowl-shaped assemblage of metal and glass (or something transparent, anyway; probably the same stuff the Liars sold as starship windows). The Liar was inside the fishbowl, fiddling with levers.

"The interface is designed for overseers, with neural implants," Lantern said. "It is not an intuitive system. But there are manual overrides, and bringing up a map is relatively simple, there. The ingress portal to the rest of the station is located near the top of this chamber."

Ashok whistled. "That's a hell of a climb. Can we do something about this gravity? Otherwise Shall's going to have to carry us up there like a mama koala taking her babies up a tree."

"I am attempting to access artificial gravity controls. I think... yes, here it is. Let me know when you're ready for weightlessness."

They all moved toward the gantry Shall had clambered up and grabbed onto the struts. "We can use this to guide ourselves up when the gravity goes," Callie said. "This place is too big and full of sharp spiky things to go free-flying. I'm talking to you, Ashok. We're ready, Lantern."

The shift was not gradual but immediate, and it wasn't weightlessness. There was still gravity; just different gravity. They experienced a radical reorientation of the concept of *down*, like they were all standing in a box that was suddenly flipped over on its side. The floor slid out from under them and became a wall, and the gantry strut Callie was hanging onto got wrenched out of her hand by the sudden rotation of the room. She flailed wildly and grabbed on to another strut, lower down, and dangled. Then she looked up.

Elena was tucked up against Ashok, her back to his front, his human arm wrapped around her upper chest, and his legs wrapped around her lower body. They both hung from his prosthetic arm, which still held firmly to the strut. There was something to be said for mechanical augmentation.

Callie looked down. They were hanging over the void. The open hangar door was now directly below them, since the exterior wall had switched places with the floor. "Lantern, if you're trying to dump us into space, you failed, and I am going to rip your tentacles off."

"I'm sorry, I'm sorry! I've only read about these controls, I've never *used* them, I'm working on it."

Gravity shifted again, hard: the exterior wall spun all the way around them and became the ceiling, but Callie managed to get her arms and legs wrapped around the strut, so she dangled like that tree sloth. Elena and Ashok were still holding on, too.

"Sorry!" Lantern shouted again.

"Maybe figure out what you're doing *before* you push the button this time?" Callie looked along the strut. Ashok was still holding onto Elena, and neither of them looked happy about it. "Don't drop her, Ashok."

"I'm just glad it's Elena and not Stephen. I would have dislocated my shoulder."

"I am thinking lightweight thoughts," Elena said.

"I think I have it, but hold on tight, just in case," Lantern said.

A moment later the gravity vanished, and Callie took a deep breath, filling her lungs. No pressure, no weight. She still held on to the gantry, but to keep from floating away now, instead of to avoid falling to her doom. Her sense of "up" and "down" was all muddled, but it only took her a moment to reorient herself: the opening to space was the side wall, and they needed to move up

into the darkness, away from the floor. "Everyone OK?
Start climbing."

They pulled themselves hand over hand up the
gantry: long pulls, sailing up for a few meters, then
reaching out for another boost. Progress wasn't as easy
as grabbing onto the endless pulley system in the central
spire of Meditreme Station, but it wasn't too taxing.
Before long they saw the gleam of Shall's lights, and
they launched themselves through a few dozen meters
of empty space toward him. Callie arrived first, grabbing
on to one of Shall's extended manipulators. She locked
her magnetic boots to the platform – fortunately the
material was ferrous – and rapped on the goldfish bowl
pod with her knuckles. "You are not inspiring me with
confidence, Lantern. Was all that spinning around you
put us through malice or incompetence?"

"Call it inexperience," the Liar said. "I'm sorry.
Sincerely. I desire an outcome in which we all survive
this."

"We have common ground there, at least. So where's
the door?"

"At the top of this segment, there should be an access
point to a tunnel, which will provide entry to the rest of
the station."

The Liar lifted something from the panel: a sphere the
size of a tennis ball, seemingly made of a glowing tracery
of blue light. "This is an infosphere – a remote access
node. It contains a map, and acts as a key to open most
areas of the station."

"Most?"

"Some areas are likely to be restricted, especially if
advanced security protocols are in place."

"The security protocols aren't too secure. Nobody's

tried to stop us yet."

The space suddenly flooded with blinding white light.

"Captain, you shouldn't *say* stuff like that," Ashok wailed.

CHAPTER 22

"What's happening?" Callie didn't sound panicked, which Elena found comforting: mostly, she just sounded annoyed. Elena felt pinned and exposed and not at all safe under the lights. She wondered if this was the platform where the *Anjou* had been torn apart and remade; where Uzoma and Sebastien had been remade, too.

"Something noticed us," Lantern said. "Probably because I manipulated the gravity. I can't access any security controls from here – they're operated from a central control room."

"So what's coming for us?" Callie said.

"Those." Ashok pointed, and Elena whipped her head around and whimpered involuntarily.

Two of the scuttling mechanical spiders had emerged from small holes in the far wall, and were now scurrying toward them along a cable.

"Shall?" Callie said. "I want one of those things intact."

"Of course." The repair drone, looking like a vastly larger and more unpleasant cousin to the brain-spiders, launched forward. A blobby black sphere the size of a bowling ball flew from some concealed cannon in Shall's body and struck one of the spiders, pinning it in a puddle of epoxy, stuck to the cable. The other kept coming, and Shall lashed out with a number of small multi-jointed manipulators to grab it. The brain-spider wriggled free from Shall's grasp and scuttled up onto the repair drone's back, where it crouched, making atonal humming sounds.

"No you don't." Shall reached onto his own back, grabbing the wriggling brain-spider by its many legs and wrenching it free, holding it aloft while it struggled. "This thing tried to splice its way into my systems! Very impolite."

"Rip its legs off for me?" Ashok said.

Shall complied, tearing the limbs off deftly and sending them spinning across the empty space.

"Cool, let me have it?"

Shall passed over the body, which was just an irregular ellipsoid that whirred and chirped, and Ashok took it and stuffed it into a thick-walled mesh bag at his waist. "Question," he said. "Why did the lights come on? Do the brain-spiders really need lights to see?"

"No," Lantern said. "But the bio-drone responds to light." She clambered out of the goldfish bowl and pointed.

An iridescent, many-limbed bug the size of a tram car crawled out of a hole on the ceiling, which irised closed after it.

"Do we shoot it?" Callie said.

Elena tried to stay calm, watching the closed-bud at the end of the thing's neck sway back and forth, as if searching for something. "Hans and Ibn tried that. It didn't help."

"We have better guns than they did," Callie said.

"Wait," Lantern said. "I'm trying to see if I can

take control of it." The infosphere spun around in her tentacles, the traceries of blue light twisting and writhing and turning red in places. "No, no good, the bio-drone is fully autonomous, but I *can* see its protocols... It's coming to collect us and take us for reconditioning."

"How can it not see us as hostiles who need to be killed?" Callie said.

"The Axiom didn't have enemies. They had slaves, who served them, and malfunctioning slaves, who needed to be repaired or recycled. They'll try to fix us before they destroy us."

"If it collects us," Elena said, "will it take us to the same place it took Ibn and Hans?"

"I think so," Lantern said. "I doubt a station this size has more than one area set aside for reconditioning."

Elena nodded. "Callie. We should let it eat us."

"Ha. Right."

"I'm serious."

"I know you are, but my sense of self-preservation is really intense right now."

"Hans and Ibn kept transmitting, even once they were devoured."

"Maybe that was a different model of mini-kaiju," Callie said. "Maybe this one has a tank of dissolving acids where its stomach should be, and Lantern is lying, or the system is lying to *her*. With that in mind... Shall?"

"Yes, Callie?"

"Go feed yourself to that giant bug and report back."

"The things I do for love." The hull repair drone raced along a gantry, then leapt into the open air. The bio-drone extended a long neck on a vine-like stalk, and the "head" opened up like a blossoming lily. Elena shuddered at the memory of Hans and Ibn falling into that bloom, but Shall maneuvered himself with thrusters to plunge straight into the open maw. The blossoms folded in after him, shoving the drone into the hollow stalk of the drone's neck.

Shall spoke almost immediately. "I'm in a sort of fibrous canal. The sides are quite yielding but also tough, a kind of organic mesh. Now it's pushing me downward, using peristaltic action. My sensors aren't detecting any corrosive chemicals wafting up the shaft from below, but there could be some kind of flap or barrier. If I dissolve, remember me fondly."

"If you encounter something deadly, do try to blast your way out," Callie said.

The bug didn't wait to digest its food. It flew toward them through the zero-gravity, and unfolded great iridescent wings. Weightlessness, plus atmosphere, and wings for maneuvering: the miracle of flight made simple, even for something the size of a bus.

"I'm at the bottom," Shall said. "I was just expelled straight into a dark space with the same kind of fibrous walls on all sides. It's roomier than the inside of the canoe. If I had to guess I'd say, yes, it's meant as transport."

Callie sighed. "We can always try to shoot our way out. All right. Into the belly of the beast. I liked that phrase better when it was metaphorical." She reached out for Elena's hand, squeezed it, then launched herself into space toward the approaching bio-drone. The kaiju unfurled its blossom and snatched her out of the air like a bird snapping up a bug, and Callie made a long, loud, disgusted noise over the comms. "Now I know how my oatmeal feels."

Lantern leapt off next, followed by Ashok. Elena couldn't bring herself to jump toward the monster. She remembered Ibn and Hans too vividly, screaming and afraid. But she straightened her spine and walked, one magnetized step at a time, to the edge of the platform. The bio-drone swooped lazily around her, then reached down, almost in passing, and swallowed her. The petals were powerful tentacles, grabbing her body and pushing her down the gullet, which pulsed and rippled and moved her relentlessly downward, feet first. The sensation was viscerally repulsive, and when she dropped into the cargo hold or prisoner cell or garbage receptacle at the bio-drone's center, it was a profound relief, though it would have felt claustrophobic under most other circumstances.

Suit lights shone all around her, revealing dark red, fleshy walls and a "ceiling" just two and a half meters above the spongy floor. They jostled in the lack of gravity, brushing against the walls, which felt disturbingly organic, twitching and contracting like muscle away from their touch.

"Everyone present and accounted for?" Callie scanned around with a light on her wrist as everyone counted off. "Lantern, is that little ball of information telling you anything useful?"

The Liar floated with neutral buoyancy halfway between the ceiling and the floor, two of its tentacles holding the glowing sphere to its faceplate. "I have location data on the map, so I can watch our progress. We're moving toward the access hatch the bio-drone emerged from. I think it will proceed through special service tunnels to the reconditioning center."

"Stephen, can you still read us?" Callie said.

"He's busy with Robin," Drake said. "But we still hear you. We've been monitoring all the excitement. Did you really let yourself get eaten?"

"It seemed like a good idea at the time. Send the lifeboat back to the hangar door. If we can get Ibn and Hans out, we may need to ship them back to the *White Raven* for medical treatment right away."

Elena smiled in the dimness. Callie's voice was so confident and self-assured that Elena dared to hope her crewmates really could be saved.

"Will do, cap–" The transmission abruptly cut off.

"Drake?" Callie said. "Are you there?"

"Connection lost," Shall said in a curiously neutral voice. "Accessing local copy." A pause. "Ugh. All right, my consciousness is up and running. This drone is pretty cramped compared to the *White Raven*. I feel blind and paralyzed and drunk and forgetful. I might as well be a human."

"Why did we lose our connection to the ship?" Callie said.

"We left the hangar." Lantern held up the sphere, where a luminous green line snaked along through a maze drawn in red, all against a pale blue background. "We're in the walls now, moving through the service tunnels. We don't have that open hangar door allowing our radio signals to pass through anymore. We're behind new walls, and cut off."

"I hope you're keeping track of where we're going and where we've been," Callie said. "Once we find Hans and Ibn we're going to need to bring them back this way. It's the only exit we know about."

"Mmm. We won't be able to come back exactly this way, through these service tunnels, unless we can commandeer a bio-drone. Which might be possible."

"We'll worry about that part later. Focus on the job at

hand. What's this reeducation camp like?"

"Reconditioning. I am unsure. Those who returned from the centers were usually quiet, and obedient, and did not record their experiences. According to the information in the museum of subjugation, those who were sent for reconditioning sometimes seemed to possess... diminished capacity afterward."

"What, like, lobotomies?" Elena said.

"Is that the thing with the leeches?" Ashok said.

"No," Callie said. "You're thinking of phlebotomies. Lobotomies are the ones where they hit your skull with a chisel to let the bad spirits out."

"That's trepanation," Elena said. "I mean, it's not exactly, and phlebotomy doesn't involve leeches either, but – no. Lobotomies were considered crude even in my time. It was used on people with violent mental disorders, and on anyone else the doctors wanted to use it on, honestly. You slide a long spike into a particular portion of the frontal lobe. It was essentially directed brain damage, and it made people placid and easily led."

"Then yes, it was something like that." Lantern did the shuddering thing with her tentacles. "There was always a struggle for balance. Intelligent slaves were useful, but intelligent slaves were also prone to rebellion, so the Axiom... adjusted things as needed."

"Anybody who tries to put a spike up my nose is going to hit metal before they get too far," Ashok said.

"They went in through the corner of the eye, I think," Elena said. "You could do it with an icepick. But that wouldn't work with the biology of the Free, I don't think."

"It may not be so invasive," Lantern said. "They might have used magnetic stimulation, or direct implants. My people do have a large nerve cluster in our central bulge, but it's not quite analogous to the human brain – most of us have distributed nervous systems, with clusters of nerve cells strung throughout our bodies and limbs, allowing for multiple redundancies in case of injury."

"So, wait," Callie said. "If they tried to 'recondition' Hans and Ibn, who have entirely different physiology, what would the process do to them?"

"Maybe nothing," Lantern said. "Or maybe it would injure them, or kill them. I have no idea whether the procedure is invasive or traumatic or not."

"Neither of them would go down without a struggle," Elena said. "Especially not Hans. He'd fight about *anything* – what to have for dinner, whether to use the Oxford comma, if beer was better than wine. If his life were in danger, he would fight, hard. Ibn wasn't as pugnacious, but he was once a soldier. They had their weapons when they were swallowed, too. Maybe they were able to defend themselves."

"The station doesn't seem too concerned about disarming us," Callie said. "That makes me worry we're not as terrifying as I thought."

"When my people were enslaved, they did not have weapons," Lantern said. "At least, nothing that could hurt their masters. I doubt the bio-drones are programmed to disarm their captives. Remember, the thing that swallowed us, it doesn't have a mind – nothing like a consciousness. Drone behavior is just a series of tropisms, responses to stimuli, like a plant turning toward the sun or roots reaching out to water. The drones are deployed, they pick up anything organic that moves, and they bring them back to a set location, then go dormant until they're activated again."

"Systems like that should be pretty easy to hack," Ashok said. "Maybe not if they use pheromones or something, but if they're activated by sound, or light flashes, or some other kind of physical stimulus…"

"You may be right," Lantern said. "Let me see if I can find any diagnostic data in the records. If there are procedures for dealing with malfunctioning bio-drones, that might reveal–"

They all dropped to the spongy floor with a series of muted thuds.

"The gravity came back."

"Good observation, Ashok. Thanks for the update. Where are we, Lantern?"

"It appears we have departed the service tunnels, captain, and arrived at our destination."

The bio-drone scurried along over bumps, and they lurched around inside its belly for a while, until the motion abruptly halted.

Elena said, "Lantern, this thing swallowed us to get us in here. How do we get out? Speaking as a biologist, if this is the equivalent of a stomach, or, say, a bowel, there are only a couple of possible points of egress."

"We're not getting out where it wants us to, anyway," Callie said. "Whether it wants to puke us up or shit us out, we'll probably end up in a bucket full of brain-spiders, or an electroshock pit, or some kind of lobotomy factory. I say we take the side door instead."

"What side door?" Lantern said.

"Ashok? Shall?"

The repair drone moved around Ashok, and the rest of them huddled behind the comforting bulk of Shall's temporary body. "In case there's ricochet," Callie said. "Who knows how tough this thing's skin is?"

Ashok pressed the barrel of his shotgun up against the side of the drone and depressed the trigger. There was a great *boom*, shatteringly loud even through their helmets, and a long pause, and then another *boom*.

Then light streamed in to the dimness. Ashok had blown a ragged hole about a foot across into the fibrous hide of the bio-drone. The beast didn't make a sound – maybe it couldn't – but it did stumble away in the direction opposite its wound, as if trying to shy away from the injury, and they all wobbled and stumbled against each other.

Ashok kept his footing, pistons in his legs adjusting gyroscopically. He lifted the barrel of the gun high, stepped aside, and made an "after you" gesture.

Shall scuttled past him, grabbed the edges of the tear with his vicious manipulator arms, and began to rip the hole into a fissure two meters high and one meter wide. Ashok went through the opening first, then shouted "It's safe!" a moment later. Lantern went through, and then Callie, and Elena, followed by Shall, who tore an even bigger opening in the course of his emergence.

The bio-drone lurched away from them, its multitude of legs folding up under it, then lay still, slumped against the far wall.

They stood in a space the size of a ballroom, with silvery walls and a gleamingly reflective floor and a ceiling seven meters overhead that seemed to consist of a single light panel: the brightness was intense. The humans instinctively moved together in a huddle, feeling exposed, with Elena in the middle, and Ashok and Callie and Shall facing out with their guns. Lantern crouched a little distance away.

"Is that thing dead?" Callie trained her guns, one in

each hand, on the fallen bio-drone.

"According to the infosphere, the drone has shut down and gone into self-repair mode," Lantern said. "I don't think the station will dispatch another drone to this location: the task is marked as complete."

Elena turned slowly around and realized only three of the four walls were silver metal. The fourth wall, near the bio-drone's drooping head, was some kind of thick glass. The transparency was marred here and there with spattered fluids that looked, to Elena's experienced eye, like dried blood. A thick gray mist swirled beyond the glass, shrouding the interior completely. There was no telling how big the space beyond was, or what might be lurking inside.

"The bug was going to put us in there." Callie pointed, and Elena followed her gesture. A circular hatch was irised open, five meters above the floor. "The bug was going to stick its star-lily head through that hole, and barf us out into the fog. What's behind that glass, Lantern?"

"Reconditioning," the Liar said.

CHAPTER 23

The glass was as totally impervious to their sensors as the exterior walls of the station itself, and none of Callie or Ashok's fancy visual enhancements did any good, either. The wall was glass-like enough to have its own thermal profile, and appeared as an opaque wall in their heat vision. Their image-enhancing night vision mode could suck up all the available light, but it was blinding in there anyway, and just as glass was the Achilles heel of thermal imaging, smoke and fog were the great weaknesses of night vision technology.

With remote viewing useless, that left only direct observation, so they had to get in there. The glass was too smooth for anyone to climb, even Ashok or Shall, but Shall was capable of great leaps, and he jumped up until he could snag the edge of the opening with several hooked limbs, then extended a sensor proboscis beyond the glass. "Rich and aromatic, full of unknown chemicals."

"Probably a sedative gas," Lantern said.

Callie nodded. She'd been thinking the same thing. Throw recalcitrant slaves in a terrarium full of ether, knock them out or at least get them loopy, then do whatever needed to be done to make them behave. The slaves wouldn't have been wearing environment suits, though: her team didn't have to breathe the gas. "Drop us a line, Shall."

The drone unspooled several meters of cable, detached one of its manipulators to form something like a grappling hook, and quickly spot-welded the hook to the line. Then it dropped the hook over the edge of the hatch and let the cable dangle.

While Shall fashioned the grapple, Elena stood by the glass, looking at a smear of what was probably blood on the other side. "What color is Liar blood? Is it red, like ours?"

"Blue, usually," Lantern said. "Barring modifications."

"Like squid, on Earth." Elena's voice was perfectly flat. "The blood contains hemocyanin instead of hemoglobin. Copper instead of iron."

"Yes."

"Is that human blood, Shall?" Elena asked. "Can you find out?"

"Go ahead and check," Callie said. "But watch yourself in there."

The repair drone dropped through the irised opening and crouched for a moment inside. "My radar is picking up a couple of objects, low to the ground, but they aren't moving." The drone traveled slowly at ground level, along the wall. The far half of his body was invisible, hidden in the mist. "I am also picking up two of the *Anjou*'s vacuum suit transponders. Their positions correspond with the objects I detected, unsurprisingly. One is fifty meters away, one more like two hundred meters. No visual confirmation. The fog is too thick."

"Hans and Ibn," Elena said. "They're in there!" She

pressed her hands against the glass and stared into the mist.

Callie didn't answer. Their suits were in there, anyway. Whether they were still in their suits, and more importantly still alive in their suits, was a different question. "Take a look at the blood, Shall."

When Shall reached the blood smear, he extended a delicate manipulator, scraped away a bit of the blood, and brought it close to a sensor proboscis. "Water, albumin, cortisol, glucose, fatty acids... hemoglobin. Blood, human, coagulated. Do you know your crewmates' blood types?"

Elena shook her head, eyes wide, expression bleak.

Callie put a hand on her shoulder. "I'm sorry, Elena. Maybe..." She fell silent. She couldn't say, "Maybe he's still alive." That kind of spray, that high on the wall, in that pattern, was indicative of sudden and considerable violence. Callie had done enough time investigating crime scenes to know that. With immediate medical care, depending on the nature of the injury, there could have been hope, in some situations – but in an alien killing jar?

Shall spun in a slow circle, scanning the ground. "Your crewmen were armed with ballistic weapons, yes?"

"A shotgun and a machine gun," Elena said. "Officially we had them in case we encountered hostile fauna on the colony planet, which we knew was absurd, but some delegate sitting on the committee had ties to the gun lobby, so the weapons were duly purchased and included as part of our supplies."

"There are shotgun pellets scattered here," Shall said.

"So Hans and Ibn fought back?" Elena said.

"That is one interpretation. Given the spatter, and the

position of the pellets… I do not have access to my full suite of forensic tools on the ship, so I am reluctant to provide an analysis."

"Wait. You think my friends shot each *other*?" Elena said.

"It could have been an accident," Shall said. "In this fog, lost, afraid, someone might have fired wildly. But a shotgun was fired here, and it looks as if it was fired through someone. Should I investigate further, captain? Check on the, ah… transponders?"

"Lantern, what's lurking in that fog?" Callie said.

"I am unsure. This was a reconditioning facility, so… perhaps more of the neural spiders?"

"You stay here with Elena. I'm going over the wall with Shall to see if we have a survivor." She looked at the cable snaking up the wall and sighed. A little less gravity would have been nice. She grabbed the cable, planted her feet against the wall – which looked like glass, but was nicely grippy against her boots – and walked her way up the line. Only five meters, only five meters. It would have been a breeze at the rock-climbing gym on Meditreme Station, even in the heaviest gravity of the outer ring, but in an environment suit, it was hard going. Her helmet kept messing up her balance. She reached the lip of the opening, hauled herself up, and looked down the other side. "Shall, give me a boost?"

The repair drone hurried over, stood under her, and then rose up as high as he could on his many legs. Shall effectively turned himself into a cherry picker, cutting the five-meter drop to a two-meter one. Callie lowered her body carefully, holding onto the lip of the hatch with her gloved fingers, and dangled her body down. Her boots were right above Shall, and that drop was nothing, so she let go and a second later thumped into place, bending her knees as she landed.

But Shall's back was hardly as smooth or level as a cherry-picking platform, and her boot hit a knobby protrusion and slipped. Her boot went out from under her, she pinwheeled, and then fell backward. *What a stupid way to die*, she thought.

But instead of Callie landing on her head and breaking her neck, Shall shot out a manipulator arm and snagged her around the ankle. Callie swayed upside down, her head half a meter above the smooth gray floor, mist eddying around her. "Thank you, Shall. Put me on my feet again please."

Another manipulator arm supported her legs and spun her around and upright before setting her down. She wobbled for a second, but her inner ear was used to far worse abuse, so she got her balance back quickly enough. She glanced through the glass and saw Elena looking at her wide-eyed, Ashok guffawing, and Lantern across the room, poking at the side of the bio-drone. Callie didn't trust the squidling even a little bit, but she'd been useful once or twice, so she didn't object.

"Let's see if the view in here is any better." She turned on her thermal imaging, and the clouds of gray smoke disappeared. That was good: if the mist had been hot, the room would have been an impenetrable swirl of color to her heat vision, but the smoke was apparently the same temperature as the ambient air. The room's dimensions were gargantuan – she couldn't even see the far walls – but there *was* a speck of glowing yellow-orange-red off ahead and to the right. It looked a lot like a person, sitting upright. "We've got a live one," she said. "Switching to the *Anjou*'s radio band." She waited a

moment for the rest of her team to follow suit, then said,
"Ibn? Hans? Elena sent us to find you. If you read me,
please respond."

No answer, which didn't mean much. The *Anjou*
crew's comms could have been damaged, or they could
be unconscious... or they could have a head full of brain-
spiders. The only way to know was to go over there and
find out. "I'm taking a look."

"Ashok, boost me up," Elena said. "I want to be there."

Callie sighed. "You're the client. Come on. But be
careful."

Ashok made a step for Elena with his arms, then
lifted her straight up, his prosthetic arm and powered
legs easily supporting her weight. Callie could have
asked for that kind of assistance, too, but being captain
meant doing that sort of thing yourself when you could.
Ashok's boost got Elena's head about four meters off the
ground, and she clambered the rest of the way up along
the cable, just as Callie had. Elena wriggled through and
shifted around and lowered herself down the other side
until Shall plucked her off the wall and set her gently
on her feet. Much easier than Callie's own dismount.
Maybe an excess of self-reliance was a kind of arrogance.

"Want us to come through too?" Ashok said.

"No, I think this is a sealed box," Callie said. "If that
opening closes up, I want you and Lantern on the outside
figuring out how to open it again. Let's–"

A booming noise filled the space: harsh, churning,
guttural syllables, so low they made Callie's teeth hurt,
doubtless extending deep past her auditory range. The
smoke changed color, flashing green, then yellow,
then pink: like a light show at a concert. She'd heard a
Plutonian ice metal band live, once, a musical experience

reckoned to be the most punishing in the system, and that band would have gladly sampled this noise at a show – though the lights were a bit too bright for their aesthetic. "What the hell is that? An alarm system?"

"It's an old language of my people," Lantern said. "I am not fluent, but I think it says something like, 'obedience is life, rebellion is death', things like that. The colors are very much like the chromatic displays we use in our language, too – that particular pattern denotes urgency, an imperative, an order to comply without question immediately, because there is great danger in even a moment's hesitation. I wonder... I had assumed the gas was a soporific, to anesthetize the victims, but what if it's hypnotic, instead? A drug meant to induce a state of suggestibility, and then blare these messages of obedience and surrender? We have records of the Axiom using such multivalent conditioning techniques."

"It's not making me feel particularly obedient. Let's check on our survivor." Callie patted Elena on the shoulder and then took her hand, because Elena didn't have thermal imaging in that old suit, and might get lost in the fog. The repair drone didn't have thermal vision either, or at least she didn't think so, but he could track the suits. "Shall, take point? Head toward the transponder that's farthest away." She followed the drone through the room, the yellow-orange-red blob getting larger in her display. He – it had to be a he, and since Callie knew which one of Elena's crew had been armed with a shotgun, she was pretty sure which he, too – wasn't reacting to the noise at all, which wasn't a good sign in terms of responsiveness. Shall could carry him out, if it came to that.

When they got within ten meters, the figure moved, and there was a burst of sound, barely audible in the shrieking monotony of the alien commands. Shall was in front of them, and he paused. "He just shot me," Shall said. "I am undamaged."

"Elena, say something reassuring," Callie said. "Shall, rebroadcast what she says, *loud*, in case his suit comms aren't working."

"Don't shoot!" Elena said. "Hans, it's Elena, I've come to rescue you, we have a ship waiting, we can get you *out*!"

The flashing colors and the guttural shouting stopped just as Shall broadcast the last word, and that *"OUT"* echoed in the space.

The figure stirred, rose laboriously to its feet, and moved closer. Callie switched her thermal view off when the figure drew close enough for him to be visible through the fog. He emerged from the mist, still in his environment suit, his helmet on, a machine gun dangling from a strap on his chest, a shotgun in his hands, limping, moving slow. Elena pushed past Shall and embraced him, and he just stood there, mute, unmoving, unresponsive. The assault shotgun fell from his hands and landed on the ground with a *thunk*.

"It's– it's Ibn," Elena said. "I thought it must be Hans, because of the shotgun, and because, well, if *anyone* was going to shoot someone–"

"No." Their comms were still on the *Anjou's* frequency, and a new voice spoke: dull, vague, but comprehensible. Ibn. "I killed Hans. I had no choice. He landed on his face when the great insect dumped us here, and the impact cracked his helmet's faceplate. The spiders came, and I fired at them, and killed one. But another leapt on

Hans, and levered its legs into the crack in his visor, and tore the front of his helmet open. It was horrible. The spider wriggled partway inside, and then Hans stumbled around, dropping his gun, screaming for a few seconds, and then... he stopped. He stood up, and came at me out of the fog. His faceplate was covered by the silver body of the spider. He tried to tear my helmet off. The strap of my machine gun was twisted, tangled, and I couldn't wrench it around to defend myself. I stumbled away, fell, and landed beside the fallen gun. He came for me, bent over, reached for me... I picked up the gun. I shot him, Elena. In the face. Right through the spider." Ibn gestured vaguely. "His body is over... somewhere. I tried to find my way out. I carried Hans with me as far as I could, in case... just in case. But I got lost. I dropped him, and went on, but then, I stopped. I sat down. I will sit down again now." He did. Then he fell over and lay on his side, unmoving.

"What's wrong with him?" Elena said.

"What happens when your environment suit runs out of oxygen?" Callie said.

"You suffocate? They're meant to double as hazardous materials suits, though, and in the absence of air in the tanks, you can switch to a filtration system, which his must have done a while ago – ohhh. The gas."

"It's made for Liar physiology. Your friend's suit is doing its best to filter out the gas, but it might be doing *something* to him. Making him groggy. He's probably in shock, too. Shall, get him out of here, out on the other side of the wall, and see if fresh air helps."

"Should we look for Hans?" Elena said.

"He's gone, Elena. The only heat signatures in here are yours, mine, Ibn's, and Shall's..."

She stopped talking, because five blurs of red had appeared in the far distance, dropping from the ceiling and then moving with great speed along the floor toward them.

CHAPTER 24

"Spiders," Callie said. "*Run*."

Elena didn't have to be told twice, and anyway, Callie had hold of her hand and started dragging her back toward the wall, or so Elena assumed. She couldn't see anything but gray mist. "Shall, get Ibn out of here and then come back for Elena! We've got spiders incoming!"

"The opening is sealed, Callie. It severed our cable cleanly. We're trapped in here. Ashok is gesticulating on the other side, but I cannot understand what he is trying to convey."

That explained why Ashok wasn't chatting away on the comms, Elena supposed. The glass wall had sealed and cut off their communications. This place was a series of Faraday cages.

"Shit," Callie said. "OK, let's get our backs against the wall. That cuts off one route of attack. There are five spiders. I can shoot two for sure. Shall, can you get the rest?"

"I will do my best, Callie."

Elena blundered forward, and suddenly the wall was there. Ashok was indeed on the other side, waving and pointing toward the bio-drone. Elena just raised her hands in a gesture of confusion and Ashok waved and hurried toward the bug.

Callie pulled the machine gun off Ibn and gave it to Elena. "You said you'd used this once or twice in training?"

"Yes, but—"

"Better than never. If you see a spider, shoot it. If it's too close to shoot, which it might be in this fog, punch it, like I told you." Callie stood shoulder to shoulder with Elena on her left, and Ibn slumped against the wall on her other side, with Shall standing over him like a guardian.

I'm guarding the right flank, Elena thought, almost giddy with her fear response. She knew what was happening in her body. Her adrenal gland was releasing epinephrine to dilate her blood vessels and norepinephrine to increase her heart rate and dump energy into her system, and a flood of cortisol was hard at work providing her with more blood sugar. Her body was preparing itself to expend energy in fighting for her life or running for her life. Good old biology, doing just what it had evolved to do over millennia: enacting nature's worst-case contingency plans.

Elena wanted to prepare herself mentally, too, but she was surfing a wave of terror chemicals, and there was no time, anyway: Callie raised her sidearm and fired once, then pivoted a step, and fired again. Her gun was different from Elena's: it didn't seem to fire a bullet, but some sort of white-hot pulse. Plasma? Physics wasn't her area, and the physics of weaponry even less so. Elena thought she heard something, a clatter of metal on metal, and she pointed her own gun into the fog.

"Your ten o'clock!" Callie shouted, and it took a

moment for Elena to realize what she was talking about: she'd heard that sort of thing shouted in old war movies, and it indicated a position, relative to Elena's own, where she should direct her attention. She tilted sixty degrees left and aimed at the ground and fired blind, the gun jerking upward in her hands when she did. The gun was set to semi-automatic, firing bursts of three bullets at a time, but it only spat out two bursts and then stopped: Ibn must have used up the rest of the clip earlier. The bullets struck the floor and whanged off in wild ricochets, out into the fog. A silvery spider the size of a dessert plate appeared at her feet, entirely unharmed, and began to climb up her leg.

Elena unthinkingly beat at the spider with the butt of the rifle, which at that point had become nothing more than a heavy metal club. Striking the spider didn't seem to do much damage, but it *did* make the spider tighten its grip on her leg. The tough material of the environment suit dimpled, and she felt multiple points of sharp pain, but the suit wasn't punctured – all sorts of alarms would have gone off in her helmet had the spider punched through.

Elena drew back the gun to smack the spider again, but it was too fast, scuttling up her chest, and then to her head. Her faceplate was mostly obscured by its circular belly, and her ears filled with the sound of its scrabbling legs trying to get through the sides of her helmet. The spider wasn't made to tear a helmet off a human, though: it was made to latch onto the head of a quiescent slave the size of an octopus. The little robot was doing its best, but this was beyond the scope of its programming, which gave her a chance.

The spider's belly irised open, and a myriad of small

arms unfolded from within the cavity and began to tap at her faceplate, like fingernails drumming on a table top. Did Liars have skulls? Were the spiders made to punch *holes* in Liar skulls, so they could reach the tender blob of ganglia within?

Elena took a deep breath, extended her arm, bent her elbow, and punched herself right in the face.

The angle was awkward, and as such it wasn't a very powerful blow, but it was enough. Her gloved fist, with the brushed titanium rings on her first, middle, and ring fingers, smacked into the back of the spider. She actually *saw* electricity arc inside the spider's exposed interior, a blue flash of minor lightning, and then the spider fell off her helmet and landed inert on its back. Elena brought the heel of her boot down on the spider, hard, and twisted her heel, grinding its internal workings to fragments.

The spider was dead. Her blood still thumped in her ears, and her extremities tingled, but she'd slain the beast. She looked around – Callie was on her knees, checking on Ibn, just as Shall reappeared from the mist. "Did we get them all?" Elena said.

"Looks like it," Callie said. "Good work. I'm just glad these spiders have some kind of hot little engine inside them, so they showed up on my heat vision. It might have been bad if they'd surprised us. Let's hope we don't get another wave."

Elena took the gun's strap off over her head and lowered the useless thing to the floor. "Now what?"

"Now we hope Ashok is figuring out a way to save our lives." They all turned and looked through the glass. There was no sign of Ashok or Lantern. "We also hope the genocide squid hasn't taken this opportunity to kill us all."

"If the story Lantern told us was true, she's sort of on our side," Elena said. "Her superiors were the genocidal ones, not her."

"I don't care," Callie said. "Her sect, her people, her responsibility. She should have argued better. Blowing up Meditreme Station isn't something you can make right with an apology."

"It's not as if Lantern pulled the trigger herself. Is every soldier responsible for the decisions of their superiors?"

Callie scowled. "Not necessarily, but for all we know, Lantern *did* fire the shot that blew up Meditreme. She could be the head of her cult, playing on our sympathies and manipulating us. We only have her word to go on. I'm an investigator, among other things, and that means being skeptical, especially when you're talking to a Liar."

Elena nodded. "That's fair. I just– I guess I want to believe there's good in her."

"I like that about you." Callie smiled, and it briefly lit up her face. "Unfounded optimism can be good for morale."

Ibn stirred and groaned, and Elena crouched beside him. She put her facemask up to his so he could see her clearly. "You're all right," she said. "We'll get you food, medical care, we'll take you–" She'd almost said "home", but that was an absurd concept for her crew. "We'll take you somewhere a lot nicer than this."

"I still can't believe you're real." Ibn's eyes were red-rimmed and exhausted. "How did you find help? We're millions of miles from anywhere. Did a ship just happen to pass by?"

"It's a long story. And, as a scientist, it will annoy you, because it involves technologies we don't even remotely understand. I can assure you the trip back to Earth will be a lot faster than the trip out here was." Assuming they got out of this glass cage before they died of thirst, of course.

"Earth," Ibn said. "It still exists?"

"It thrives," Callie said.

"I was right. Hans was wrong. It's hard for me to take any pleasure in that now."

"The kaiju is moving." Shall stood poised on sharp legs, just under the spot on the wall where the opening had been, though it looked now like smooth unbroken glass.

The bio-drone lurched away from the wall where it had collapsed and did an oddly delicate stumble-dance across the space on the other side of the glass. It paused, lifted its closed-flower head on its long flexible stalk, and then lurched abruptly backward several meters. Then it turned again, doing a clumsy sort of pirouette on its many legs.

"It looks like it's drunk," Callie said. "I'm envious."

The drone went still again, its head now facing toward the glass, and slowly moved forward. It bumped its bulb against the glass – and an opening irised at its touch. The kaiju snaked its head through the hole, and Shall scuttled back. The bulb opened up like a lily, and Lantern dropped out, landing easily on her tentacles. "All aboard the Kaiju Express." She paused. "Ashok told me to say that."

Then the bio-drone darted its flower-head and swallowed Shall.

Within minutes, they'd all been consumed and uncomfortably squeezed up through the kaiju's esophageal tube in a series of pulsations. Ibn had resisted letting it take him at first, trembling and traumatized by his last experience with the kaiju, but Elena soothed him, and followed him inside. Callie came last, covering the escape for everyone else, just in case more spiders arrived.

Soon they were all back in the soft belly of the drone, light shining in from the ragged hole in its side. Ashok was standing near the front of the drone, a flashlight array on his prosthetic arm flashing what seemed like random strobes.

"You hacked the drone," Callie said. "I'm impressed."

"Lantern should get the credit," Ashok said. "She told me, it's all about signals. The bio-drone gets a signal to go scoop things up and then come here. The bio-drone gives the wall a signal that says 'Open up for prisoners'. Then the drone is *supposed* to tell the wall, 'OK, all done, close up again'. Except we blew a big hole in the side of the drone and scrambled its systems and sent it into emergency repair mode. There's some failsafe in place, though, so the aperture doesn't stay open forever, and after a certain amount of time, it closed automatically. The spiders are dispatched by a signal, too: the bio-drone picked up five bodies, so the system dispatched five spiders to tinker with their brains."

"You hacked this whole system?" Callie said.

"Ehhhh." Ashok seesawed his hand. "We don't know how to talk to the station, really. But the bio-drone is pretty simple. It has external light receptors, and internal ones, here on the body cavity wall. Lantern figures these drones were used as transport by the Liars back in the old days. That way they could travel around the station in style, right? There are no levers or switches or buttons, so we thought, maybe they drove them with pulses of light. We started flashing light at the receptors, and, well, you saw. We started lurching around like crazy. A little trial-and-error and we figured out how to make it move. There must be a transmitter in the bio-drone's head that makes the aperture in the glass cage open up. That was lucky."

"So now we have a ride?" Callie said. "We can roam around the service tunnels or whatever until we find the rest of Elena's crew?"

"Better," Ashok said. "We can get to the master control room. Lantern thinks from there we can get a look at the station as a whole, and find out exactly where her people are, control the security systems, the whole deal. Maybe even dispatch bio-drones to *fetch* any other survivors."

"Sounds easy. And therefore unlikely."

"You're a cynic, cap."

Callie glanced at Elena. "People keep telling me that. We need to get Ibn to safety first, though. He's dehydrated and starving and in various kinds of shock." She cleared her throat. "Did you, ah, feel strongly about recovering your friend's body, Elena?"

Elena thought about it for a moment, then shook her head. "I suppose it's not worth the risk to recover him. My crew all expected to die alone in space far from anyone."

"No," Lantern said. "We shouldn't leave any trace of humankind here. If the Axiom ever wake, or some of their machines do, and they discover evidence of another spacefaring race, in one of their own facilities? They might dispatch hunter-killer probes all over the galaxy to track you down. From the control room, I hope to be able to destroy all the records stored on this station since the *Anjou*'s arrival, but covering our tracks that way is wasted if we leave a body behind. Even the blood should be burned off the wall. It would be good if the stray bullets were collected too, but that is less urgent – the discovery of a few bits of brass or steel would not lead inexorably to the conclusion that unknown aliens were ever here."

Callie cocked her head. "That's good thinking, Lantern. You would have been a good security officer, if you hadn't gone another way."

"I didn't go another way. I am a security officer."

"I can collect Hans's remains, and the guns left behind, and I have blowtorches to erase the physical evidence," Shall said.

"Go ahead," Callie said. "But go fast."

Shall scurried back up the esophageal tube. They all waited in thoughtful silence for ten minutes or so, and then a corpse fell out of the hole and landed with a loud thump.

Ibn shrank away and let out a strangled sob. Shall came after, carrying the guns that had been left inside. "I am sorry. There was no other way to get his body in, other than to push him ahead of me–"

"It," Ibn said. "Not him. The soul inside Hans has moved on. We should treat his remains with respect, but the body is not the man." He turned away again and began to pray softly to himself.

"Ashok, take us back to the hangar so we can get Ibn over to the *Raven*."

"Sure thing. I think there's a way to make the drone retrace its steps, a lot of what these things did was repetitive, so there are shortcuts." He and Lantern consulted, and then Ashok flashed lights at the wall, and the drone lurched around and scrambled upwards, presumably heading for the tunnels. Shall moved toward the ragged opening in the drone and spanned it with his body, so no one would accidentally fall out. That was good thinking, because the trip was rough, bumpy, and fast, and sometimes weightless.

They reached the hangar and the kaiju swam down through the air, but because of the hole in its side, the aerodynamics were bad, and it flailed and listed and wallowed. Eventually it settled near the opening in the wall and Ashok and Lantern stopped flashing lights at it.

"Ohhhh, I have my brain back, that's much better," Shall said.

"Stephen?" Callie said. "Can you hear us?"

"I can. Good to have you back. Robin is doing well. She was fretting greatly over the rest of you, but consented to a sedative, and is getting some rest at last. Do you have more patients for me?"

"One, Ibn, but he's only suffering from hunger and shock, as far as we can tell."

"It's thoughtful of you to space them out for me this way. I was expecting more of a trauma center experience today."

"We're sending over another *Anjou* crew member, Hans, too, but he's... he's beyond help."

"I'm terribly sorry, Doctor Oh," Stephen said. "I will treat his remains with all due respect and care."

"Thank you." Elena appreciated the kindness, but she was distracted, looking at Hans's body. His faceplate was still blocked by the remains of the spider that had clawed its way into his helmet. She reached out and tugged at the spider, gently, but it was seated firmly. Embedded. Pulling hard would probably tear apart things she'd rather not see torn apart. She thought of the sharp little arms that had scrabbled at her own faceplate and shuddered. She switched to a limited comms channel. "Are we sure this thing is dead, Ashok? Lantern?"

"The spider took a bunch of bullets right through its body. Looks torn up pretty bad." Ashok leaned over close, the lenses over his eyes whirring, and Elena had a terrible vision of the spider leaping to life, jumping at his face, burrowing its tiny appendages into his eyes and ears and mouth–

Ashok shook his head. "No heat signature, the mechanisms are all busted up… looks like dumb metal to me. I took a look at the one we recovered because I was afraid these things might be nanomachine cradles – like, maybe they work by barfing lots of tiny machines into the brain? But all I see are electrodes and magnets, so I think it's a combination of deep brain stimulation and transcranial magnetism designed to alter thought processes and behaviors. That stuff is macro-scale, so it can be totally busted up with a bullet. I don't think this one is gonna come to life and kill us all or anything."

"Agreed," Lantern said. "The Axiom were capable of manipulating matter at the molecular level, if not the atomic, but they were careful to keep such technology from their servants. My people would have used such technology against them, after all, to unmake their works."

"So there are vaults full of sleeping alien nanomachines somewhere in the galaxy?" Elena said. "That's not comforting."

"Yet another reason we must prevent anyone from entering areas that were once under Axiom control." Lantern sounded almost prim.

Elena switched back to the open channel and heard

Callie finishing up her instructions. "The canoe will be back in a minute. Shall, you escort Ibn and the body back to the ship."

"Are you sure? Drake can bring the canoe back by auto-pilot–"

"I don't want to leave Ibn alone in the canoe with his dead crewmate. Not that a giant hull repair drone is necessarily a comforting presence, but you can help them get in and out on the other end, at least. I'd send back Elena, but I doubt she'd go."

"Correct." Sebastien was still in the station somewhere. And Uzoma, though they hadn't looked so good the last time Elena saw them, and she was a little worried about meeting them again. That intellect and focus in the service of the station would be a terrible thing to confront.

Callie said, "I don't want to give up my heavy artillery, so we'll wait for Shall to come back before we go looking for the control room."

"Very well, captain." Shall gathered up Hans, holding the body close to his underbelly with a few manipulator arms. Elena swapped Ibn's air bottle with a fresh one from Shall's supplies, though the jaunt was so short he could have held his breath. The others helped Ibn climb on Shall's back and get strapped in place. "We should install a jump-seat up here at this rate," Shall said.

Elena held on to Ibn's hand for a moment. "I'll be with you soon," she said. "With the others."

"Inshallah." Ibn's voice was nearly a sigh.

The canoe floated slowly into view beyond the ragged opening, and without further farewells or ceremony Shall launched himself out of the hangar toward the waiting ship.

As soon as Shall was clear, the opening in the wall closed up instantly, and a guttural roaring alarm began to sound.

CHAPTER 25

A big part of being a leader was making decisions when it would have been much easier to stand around being shocked and horrified. Before the door was even entirely closed, Callie had launched herself at the wall to slap the "door open" switch on the control panel, but it just flashed an angry yellow and didn't otherwise respond. Then she pivoted and shouted, "Back on the kaiju! Ashok, get us out of here!"

She hustled Elena and Lantern on board ahead of her, and the kaiju began fluttering its way upward again as soon as Callie clambered in. Lantern's limbs were trembling almost spasmodically, and Elena gazed around, wide-eyed. The alarm sounded a lot like the voice from the reconditioning chamber, and even though they had helmets on and were snug inside the kaiju, the noise was still deafening.

Callie looked out the ragged hole in the bio-drone's side, expecting… what? More spiders? More kaiju? The Axiom themselves, risen from their slumber like mummies in a tomb in a survival horror immersive?

Nothing came after them, though, and then everything went dark as they entered a service tunnel. The sound cut off, too: they weren't in a part of the station with atmosphere anymore, so sound didn't carry. That was a blessing.

"What do we think happened back there?" Callie said.

"Signals," Elena said. "Just like Ashok said. I was looking at the spider-thing on Hans, and something about it made me nervous. I thought I was afraid it would come back to life, and Ashok reassured me about that, but–"

"Ugh," Ashok said. "Right. There was some kind of transponder in the spider. Something passive, using almost no energy, but when it left the station, the station *knew*. Those devices are used to recondition rebellious slaves, right? So if one of the spiders leaves the station without authorization, the place goes into lockdown. I'm so sorry, I should have thought–"

"Did you know?" Callie drew her sidearm and pointed it at Lantern. "You were the one who said we *had* to take Hans off the station. Was this your intention, to trap us here–"

To Callie's surprise, Elena put a hand on her arm and pushed her gun down. Callie didn't resist, but she looked at Elena curiously.

"I think Lantern is having a panic attack," Elena said softly. "That tentacle movement is a signal of distress, and I don't think she can control it right now." Elena drifted to the Liar, whose every tentacle undulated and spasmed, and whispered to her soothingly. "This must be horrible for you," she said. "I'm so sorry."

"Trapped – in – locked – my – people –" the Liar's voice was staccato, and then she made the same organic keening sound of distress My Cousin Paolo had emitted back on Meditreme Station.

Callie put her gun away. Liars lied, but they weren't very *good* liars, as a rule. My Cousin Paolo had seen an artifact he recognized as a trace of the race that had made his people miserable for millennia, and had fled the station along with all of his kind because even a glimpse of the bridge generator was too terrifying for them to bear. And Lantern, brave Lantern, had entered an Axiom *station*, a place where her kind had been tormented and reconditioned.

If Lantern was telling the truth about the Axiom, being here, it must be an almost unendurable experience. Callie tried to think of something comparable. A descendant of a water wars survivor getting locked inside one of the old moisture reclamation camps, maybe – only one where the ghosts of the extraction corps still roamed, and the machinery could come back online at any moment.

Callie holstered her sidearm. "I'm sorry, Lantern. We're going to get out of here. We just need to find the control room, right? Then we can kill the alarms, open the doors, and take control."

Elena kept soothing and stroking until Lantern's spasms slowed and finally stopped. "Yes, Captain Machedo." Lantern reached into a pouch on her underside, removed the glowing sphere, and examined its lines and pulsations. "Ashok, there should be a left turn up ahead. Take that, then the next tunnel up, then a right, then up again."

"We're not going to the center of the station?" Callie asked.

"Humans put important things in the center. Liars do, too. The Axiom didn't think that way. The control room is off on one side, not too far from our position. Just beyond…"

The Liar went silent.

"What is it?" Callie tensed, ready to hear, "Just beyond the automatic murder robot barracks" or something.

"Past the nursery." Lantern's voice was perfectly flat. "It does not say 'nursery' on this map. It says something I will not say aloud. But it is the place where my kind were birthed and instructed."

Callie tried to picture a Liar nursery school. Little pools to swim in? Jungle gyms with *lots* of rings, for all those tentacles? Soft stuffed toys shaped like eels or fish?

Lantern must have intuited the direction of her speculation, because she said, "It wasn't a nursery like you're thinking. Not like an orphanage, even. My people mature rapidly. The nursery will include an incubation chamber, and a series of rooms meant to instill certain behaviors. Newborns of my race were instructed in obedience, instilled by natural aversion to pain."

"I thought most Liars could shut off their pain responses?" Callie said.

"That was one of the first changes we made in ourselves, when we became the Free," Lantern said grimly. "We had good reason."

"We should look in on the nursery," Elena said. "Just in case. So many of the systems in this place are still operational…"

Lantern's tentacles fluttered. "I… would like to look in. I feared to ask. I know this is not your mission."

Callie nodded. "Of course. We should. Anyway. It's on the way."

Ashok steered the bio-drone down a side tunnel, and they emerged through an irised service opening into a chamber with gravity, but no atmosphere. The guttural alarm wasn't audible here either, at least.

The kaiju settled down on a raised pillar shaped a bit like a helipad, and Callie, Elena, and Lantern stepped off.

"The area around this platform used to be full of fluid." Lantern gestured at the empty space around them. "For moisture, and hydration, and nutrition." She pointed with a tentacle to what looked like a wall of smoked glass bricks. "Those are the incubators. When the young were mature, or mature enough, they would be dumped into this pool. Then pumps and currents would channel the young into the... other chambers. The stories say the nursery was tended by machines, because when my people were tasked to instruct the young, they invariably killed themselves rather than fulfill their required duties, no matter how often they were reconditioned."

After a moment of silence, Callie said, "Can you cut the gravity?"

Lantern touched the infosphere to a recessed panel in the floor, and it lit up a pale green. A moment later the gravity vanished, and Callie drifted upward. She pushed off the central pedestal and ducked into one of the chambers that led away from the dry pool.

She looked at the equipment within, and immediately understood how it would work: the current would bring the baby Liars there, and then...

Callie ducked into another chamber, saw what it held, recoiled, and then made herself look again, hard and long, until she understood exactly how the mechanism had functioned. Tiny Liars, no bigger than a human hand, delicate and new, pushed into *that*.

She forced herself to look into a third chamber. The construction was elegant, the instruments still gleaming, and she almost threw up in her helmet.

Three chambers was enough. She didn't force herself

to look any farther. She'd worked grisly and premeditated crime scenes in her time, and had believed herself inured to the horror of what one sentient being could do to another, but the clinical, industrialized monstrousness on display here overwhelmed even her iron sensibilities.

She returned to the central platform and looked down at Lantern. "I believe you. About the Axiom." This wasn't a Liar facility. No species would build chambers like those she'd just seen to "instruct" their own offspring. A people that universally sadistic would have never survived more than a generation.

"Thank you," Lantern said. "I am glad. Many of the systems here have failed or been shut down, but thirteen of the incubators are still viable." Lantern's artificial voice was matter-of-fact, but her tentacles trembled. Smart of Elena to figure out what that meant.

Lantern punched a button on the panel, and a triple handful of the hundreds of smoked glass panels lit up. Tiny curled creatures no bigger than Callie's thumbs floated inside the cubes.

"Can we take the incubators out of that wall without hurting them?" Callie said.

"Yes. The tanks are portable. Once we deactivate the stasis field, they can remain disconnected for a few hours. At that point we would need to oxygenate the tanks–"

"We can do that on the *White Raven*. Let's get the incubators into the drone."

They all worked together, and it went fast, in weightlessness. Ashok and Lantern figured out how to disconnect the tubing and seal the incubators for transport, and they carried the little tanks like the precious cargo they were onto the kaiju. Callie used her non-lethal anti-personnel epoxy to stick the incubators to the floor and wall, where they would remain in place until someone yanked them out with deliberate force.

Once they were done, Callie said, "Let's find the control room and finish this. I don't want to be here anymore." Something squeezed Callie's hand, and she looked down to see Lantern's tentacle wrapped around her fingers. She squeezed back.

Ashok piloted the kaiju back up to the service tunnels. They traveled in silence, interrupted only by Lantern giving directions in consultation with the glowing sphere. The drone moved swiftly through weightless areas, following bends and twists in the sprawling organic structure, and then Lantern said, "Stop. There's an entry to the control room. The bio-drone only has to extend its head to make the aperture open." She looked at Callie. "How would you like to proceed, captain?"

"Do we expect to encounter defenses?"

Lantern shrugged. "The station was on some sort of low-level lockdown when we arrived, cutting off communications from section to section. After Hans and his neural implant went outside, and the alarm sounded, I assume the station is now on even higher alert. The control room would be an obvious place to defend."

"I can go in first, Callie." Ashok thumped his chest. "I'm a whole lot of metal under here. Something shoots at me, there's a good chance it'll just bounce off. And good luck to any brain-spiders drilling through the plates in my head."

Callie shook her head. "The kind of weapons they have here won't be slowed down by a little body armor. I appreciate the offer, but I think stealth is the better approach until we know what we're dealing with. Is there another entrance, one close to the control room, but that doesn't lead directly inside? An anteroom, a hallway, anything?"

Lantern consulted the infosphere. "Fifty meters down, I see an entryway into a space designated as surplus storage. Supplies, I think, for the control room. There's a door from one, leading to the other."

"Take me there," Callie said.

The kaiju scuttled a short distance, and then Callie checked her weapons, gave Elena's arm a squeeze, and said, "We're probably going to lose radio contact, but don't worry. I'll come back here within half an hour. If I don't, burst in and blast away, because that means something killed me, and you'll need to get off this horror station without me."

"She's terrible at giving inspirational speeches," Ashok said. "One time, before we broke into this compound on an asteroid to capture an escaped murderer, Callie goes, 'OK, nobody embarrass me by dying'. She's just really bad at it."

Elena gave her a hug and said, "Come back to me, Callie. I'm not done with you yet."

"Now *that's* inspiring," Ashok said.

Callie slipped out of the side of the kaiju and turned on her active camouflage. Her suit shimmered, tiny projectors mimicking the background behind her with a lag measurable only in picoseconds. If she stood still, she was totally invisible. If she moved, she was *mostly* invisible, apart from an almost subliminal shimmer. Her suit cooled itself until it matched the ambient temperature, which would hide her from thermal vision. Her transponder stopped transmitting, and her radio shut itself off: no signals were emerging from her anymore. The technology was custom-made and cutting-edge. Callie's was the only prototype in service, and she'd made a lot of promises and done a lot of unpaid work in exchange for getting to keep it once testing was done. The bureaucrats higher up in the TNA had been opposed, but Chief Warwick had come through in the end. She always did.

Always had.

Callie floated out into a round, dim tunnel, just barely big enough for the kaiju to move through. What happened if two of the bio-drones had to pass? Did one just back up until they reached a branching corridor? Or maybe the drones had been so tightly controlled, the problem never came up.

The kaiju tapped its head against the wall, and a round hole big enough for the bug to fit through opened. Callie sidled past the creature and moved inside, adjusting to the new gravity with a bend of her knees.

The space was lit dimly by infrequent pale orange panels in the floor, arrayed in no comprehensible pattern. She'd heard the words "storage" and pictured something on a human scale. A closet full of boxes. Maybe a shed stuffed with old tools and crates and spare light bulbs. But this was nothing of the sort: it was more like a warehouse, with shelves and bins and racks rising to the ceiling, but the shelves were only about a quarter filled, like regular resupplies had stopped at some point. Most of what remained was tanks and drums in various colors, covered in markings she couldn't understand. Food? Chemicals? Not spare light bulbs, anyway.

She moved forward and to the left, passing between shelves, slow, not stepping on the orange light panels, though she knew they were probably sturdy enough.

As a kid she'd always jumped over ventilation grates in the floor and sewer grates in the street, too. Just superstition. But anything that made her less tense right now was beneficial. Every sense she had was on high alert, and her suit hadn't even pumped her up with combat readiness chemicals.

A small door, bigger than Liar-sized if not quite large enough to be comfortably human-sized, stood open on the far wall. A bright green drum stood next to the door, its top levered open and shoved half off, like someone had checked the contents.

Callie eased up toward the door and looked into a roughly round room full of lights, panels, and screens: it looked like any control room anywhere, except the controls were low to the ground, and the screens weren't rectangles but irregular shapes, blobby, like molten glass had been poured out and allowed to settle on any shape fluid dynamics dictated.

The floor was a screen, too, and so was the ceiling, though much of it was blocked by trailing wires. An ungainly machine the size of an industrial 3D printer stood at an awkward angle near the center of the room, patched crudely into the walls with cables.

A human stood next to the machine, filling a beaker with a peach-colored slurry from a nozzle. He wore a dirty white jumpsuit and boots. No environment suit, no gloves, no helmet. He clipped the nozzle into a recess on the machine, took a sip from the contents of the beaker, made a disgusted face, shrugged, and glugged the rest down.

He was tall and slender, with black stubble on his face. Short black hair, and a face Callie was prepared to admit was pretty. Based on Elena's description, this was Sebastien, and not Uzoma, which was maybe good, because Sebastien had sent Elena away to safety, and Uzoma had gone full robot-zombie.

Sebastien pivoted from the machine and squatted down on his heels to tap at one of the screens waiting at Liar height. The back of his head was covered by the silvery disk of a brain-spider, its legs digging into his skull. Callie didn't make a sound, but it took a force of will. Blood was crusted around the spider, and dried down the back of his neck, staining the collar of his *Anjou* jumpsuit.

CHAPTER 26

"You can come in," Sebastien called. "Have a drink. It's disgusting, like drinking soy yogurt spiked with mold, but the station thinks it will sustain human life. There are tanks and tanks of raw materials back there, biological and industrial and otherwise, and fabrication machines all over the place. I dragged one of the biomass converters here for convenience. Had a bot drag it in, anyway."

He rose and turned around, looking toward the open door. Callie didn't move. Occasionally, when she was sitting alone in a room she knew to be empty, she would have a moment of doubt, and say calmly and clearly: "I know you're there. Come on out." Just in case. She thought it was probably a rare personality quirk, but she was prepared to believe Sebastien shared it, and was just taking a shot in the dark.

"I can't see you," he said. His eyes were glowing. "I assume you have some kind of stealth technology? But I see on this panel that a door opened in the storage warehouse, and there's no reason that should happen, unless someone was trying to sneak in. I knew *someone* had breached the station from outside, and I was prepared to ignore it, even though you somehow tripped an annoying security protocol it took me ten minutes to turn off. That alarm was deafening. But now you're here, and I left the door open all invitingly, so you may as well come inside and reveal yourself. But please don't try anything violent – I set up a dead-man's switch. If I don't hit a certain button every few minutes, the station will blow itself up. Or implode, maybe. My implant helps with the translation, and overall I'm quite fluent in station-speak, but there are a few cognates I stumble over."

Callie sighed. Sebastien had a brain-spider, and glowing eyes, but he wasn't murderous. Maybe he possessed tremendous force of will, or something. She fiddled with her suit's countermeasures, directing her sound in a tight beam that would bounce off a far wall and disguise her position. Like the ancient proverb said: Trust, but verify. "I'm here on a rescue mission."

"Really." He pivoted toward the source of the sound, presenting his profile to the door. That was less alarming than the back of his head, but less pretty than the front. "Who are you rescuing?"

"The crew of the *Anjou*. We've already gotten a couple of them off the station safely. Robin and Ibn. We were too late for Hans. We came looking for you, Sebastien, and for Uzoma."

He seemed not at all excited by the prospect of deliverance. Maybe slightly amused. "Mmm. Uzoma. They're around here... somewhere. They aren't coping very well with our change of circumstances."

"You seem like you're doing all right."

"This place doesn't have all the comforts of home, but really, neither did home, by the time we left. The station is more pleasant than the *Anjou* was, in many ways. More importantly, the station offers me opportunities beyond my most delirious dreams. When we left Earth, I fully expected to go into cryosleep and never wake. To die in space, unknown and forgotten, on a trip that was basically symbolic. In the best possible outcome we would survive, and find a viable colony world, and I'd have the opportunity to lay the foundations of a new society. To create a nation, more or less, with nothing but a ship full of embryos and a handful of machines and a few good people by my side. Desperate measures and long odds, but those were desperate times. Earth back then... it was a mess. Settle a bet for me? Is Earth gone?"

"No. I was born there. It's nice. Things got bad, even worse than they were when you left, but it came back from the brink. But you can catch up on ancient history back on my ship–"

"Did Elena send you?" Now he seemed excited, moving toward the sound of Callie's voice. "I sent her back, to Earth, or as close as I could. I didn't understand the language of the machines here as well then, and I was afraid I might have miscalculated. But she made it, and you found her?"

"You got the right solar system, at least. You sent her out by the orbit of Neptune. There is – there was – a human settlement out there, though. Yes, we found her. She asked us to come save you."

"Mmm. Elena. I miss her. Is she on your ship? Should I bring your ship in here? I think I know how to do that." He swiveled toward a control panel.

"No!" Callie shouted. "No, she's here, on the station." Callie decided Sebastien was in some kind of shock, or the implant was muting his emotional reactions. That was the only explanation for why he wasn't more excited at the prospect of salvation.

"Ohhh." He leaned against a wall of screens and let out a long slow exhalation. "Of course she is. She *would* have insisted on coming in after us personally. I'm so glad. I want to see her."

"She's waiting on our transport. Join us and we'll take you back to our ship. Do you have an environment suit?"

"Oh, it's around here somewhere." He gestured vaguely. "Show me Elena first. And maybe show me yourself. Right now you're a disembodied voice." He laughed, though it was more of an unhinged titter. "For all I know you're a hallucination. I've been hearing all kinds of voices, but they don't sound like yours. They're not in any language I know, but I understand them." He tapped one of the brain-spider legs, jammed deep into his skull, just above his ear. "They're mostly messages about the greatness of the race who built this station. Do humans know about them? The ones who made this place?"

"No. We've never met them. This station is the first evidence we've found of their existence."

"But not the last. No, no. You'll learn all about them, the great race. Now, please show yourself, so I know I'm not imagining you. Strange things can happen to the minds of people who find themselves shipwrecked. I read about that in school. I specialized in the psychology of large groups, but large groups are made up of individuals, so I had to learn all that, too."

Callie checked her non-lethal weapons, just in case, then turned off her camouflage. "I'm in here." She thought it was prudent to not be in the same room as him, especially if he could control all the doors.

He swiveled, stared at her for a moment, then stood up. "Interesting. Acoustic manipulation. Where's Elena?"

"Not far." Callie stepped back, watching him closely as he passed through the door into the storage warehouse. His hands were empty, and there didn't seem to be anything in his pockets, or at least, nothing big enough to shoot or club her with. "I have to tell you, Sebastien, your whole attitude is really freaking me out."

"Oh? Oh. I see. You expected tears of joy, shock, elation at rescue, and all that? But consider my situation. I was stranded on an alien space station, and a neural reprogramming device attempted to take over my brain, without success. An alien voice bellows at me constantly inside my head, in an alien language I can nevertheless understand. Now a stranger in an invisible space suit says she's come to save me, at the behest of a woman I was secretly infatuated with, if not in *love* with. That seems implausible, so it may not even be real." He shrugged. "I don't really understand my own reactions either. I'm probably disassociating pretty hard right now."

Callie nodded. "That's fair. Maybe seeing Elena will help ground you." Now that her suit wasn't camouflaged and the radio worked again, she said, "I found Sebastien."

"Is he all right?" Elena's voice was strained with hope and worry.

"He's... upright and talking. You know him better than I do. Come and see." To Sebastien: "She's on her way. With a couple of others – my engineer Ashok, and a... consultant named Lantern."

"That's an odd name. Though I suppose names can change a lot over the centuries."

"I don't know. We still have Johns and Marys and

Michaels. Lantern isn't human, though."

Now he seemed interested. "An intelligent alien species? But not the one that built this station?"

"No, but Lantern can understand their language, pretty much, and she understands how their machines work. We needed to reach the control room so we can turn off the security systems, and get the hangar doors open again so we can leave."

"You can indeed do all that from the control room." Sebastien still sounded entirely too serene. "You can take that helmet off, you know. The atmosphere is marvelous in here. I've got the mix just right. You'd think you were back on Earth, only without the pollution we had in my day."

"No thanks. I like to put a layer of tough material between me and any passing brain-spiders."

"Oh, the neural implants are nothing to fear. Technology is a tool. Not inherently good or bad. All that matters is what you do with it."

"Right. I'm Captain Machedo, by the way."

"I don't care."

Before Callie could react to that statement, Sebastien shoved past her, throwing his arms wide and shouting, "Elena! Take off that helmet and let me see your pretty face!"

"Sebastien!" Elena unlocked her faceplate and pushed her visor up, which wasn't *quite* as bad as taking her whole helmet off, then rushed into Sebastien's arms and embraced him.

Callie paused a moment to decide if her unfavorable reaction to that sight was jealousy, and decided it wasn't, or at least, not exclusively. Elena's affection for Sebastien had been clear in her stories, and Callie didn't begrudge her joy at seeing an old friend she'd once (and maybe still) had feelings for... but the problem was, Sebastien struck Callie as a giant asshole, disassociation or not.

"Oh, Sebastien, your poor head." Elena touched the side of his face. "Ashok has some ideas about how we can get these things out of you."

"Really? Ashok is the one with the metal face? It seems like he'd approve of my implants, if only as a fashion choice."

"My hardware was all installed by choice or necessity," Ashok said. "Yours... not so much. Once we get to the ship's infirmary I can take a look and see how things are hooked up in there and get you fixed up."

"Mmm." Sebastien looked down at Lantern, who was creeping past him, toward the control room door. He suddenly lunged and kicked the Liar, his boot hooking under her belly, sending her flying up and back, almost hard enough to flip her over. Lantern let out a yelp of alarm and scuttled away. "Stay out of my control room, vermin."

"Sebastien!" Elena shouted. "Lantern is my friend."

He looked at the Liar for a moment, blank-faced, then turned back to Elena and beamed. "No, *I'm* your friend, and I'm so pleased to see you. Come." He grabbed Elena by the arm, pivoted, and shoved her through the opening into the control room, then stepped in after her. Callie lifted her non-lethal arm, but the door irised shut with a slam before she could even try to line up a shot.

"Elena!" she shouted, but there was no response. Their comms were cut off again. Callie turned. "The kaiju!" She ran through the warehouse, back to their only source of escape.

The hatch out of the warehouse was closed, and no

amount of fiddling with Lantern's sphere or cutting with Ashok's torches or kicking with Callie's boots made even the slightest bit of difference.

CHAPTER 27

"Let's get that helmet off you." Sebastien carefully unhooked the latches and lifted off Elena's helmet, then tossed it onto the floor. The clatter made Elena wince. She needed that helmet intact to get off this station.

"There, isn't that better?" He smoothed her hair, tucking a lock behind her ear, a gesture that would have made her liquefy inside if he'd done it during their training or voyage, but that made her shudder now.

She backed away. "What's happening here? Why did you lock the door?"

Sebastien squatted down and brushed his fingers over an irregular ellipsoid of a screen, causing lights to shift and cascade on the display. "Those people are strangers. And their little squid, too. I don't know them. I can't risk letting them interfere with what I'm trying to achieve here."

"They're my friends, Sebastien."

He looked over his shoulder, and smiled reassuringly, and paternalistically. Like she was a child, worried about foolish things. "No. They may as well be aliens. They're so different from what I am. Besides, I'm the only friend you need, and the best one you'll ever have. If they really are good people, like they've convinced you they are, then they'll join in the great work eventually. This is just... a very delicate moment. I can't take the risk of unpredictable variables." His fingers danced busily across the screen.

"Sebastien, what are you doing there?"

"Making sure your so-called friends can't scurry away, that's all. I can control the whole station from here, though it's mostly self-regulating."

"I don't understand what you're doing. We came to save you!"

"It was very kind of you to come back for me. I didn't expect that. I just wanted you to be safe."

She looked around at the displays. "If you can really control everything from here, why didn't you help Hans and Ibn? Or Robin? Or Uzoma?"

He looked at her blankly. "Oh. I don't know. I was distracted, I suppose. I always did get distracted by my work. You know how it is. You get your teeth into a problem, you find a solution, you decide to implement it, and the next thing you know, hours have flown by."

"What work are you talking about?" She was trying to make sense of the information displayed on the screens, but it was all unfamiliar shapes in an alien alphabet.

"The *great* work. Work that truly matters. A project on a scale unprecedented in human history – back in our era, anyway. But I doubt humanity has managed anything bigger and better than what *I* have planned since we left. You remember my specialty? Large infrastructure, city planning, formulating sustainable social systems – that was my purpose on the colony ship. My area of expertise. Oh, but I was wasted on that mission. I see that now. Come with me. You can witness the beginning of everything." He grabbed her hand, squeezed it, and beamed at her, though his once-lovely face seemed sinister with the metal spider-legs dug into his skull on either side. "Come on."

He dragged her, harder than she liked, through a door that opened seamlessly in a wall of screens at his approach. He dragged her along a corridor, into an intersecting hallway, around another corner – eventually she lost track of their turnings, and wasn't sure she'd be able to find her way back. Finally he stopped in a long, narrow rectangular room. He took her shoulders and turned her so she faced a smooth, dark wall. Then he put his arm around her and drew her in close. "Behold."

Sebastien waved his hand, and the wall lightened and became transparent. Beyond the glass was a huge shipbuilding bay, easily fifty stories high and just as wide, full of mechanical arms, floating drones, and unfinished ships floating in weightlessness, in the process of being built. The ships looked a little like the thing the *Anjou* had been made into: fat spheroids bristling with angular fins and spikes, like sand spurs, or the spiked heads of maces, each one the size of a house. Elena started to count the ships and stopped when she got to fifty. There were at least ten times that many.

"Aren't they beautiful?" Sebastien said. "Every one equipped with a point-to-point wormhole generator, ready to be dispatched to our solar system. My initial plan was to gather intelligence from Earth, and then move on to any other colony systems, founded by goldilocks ships or other means. You've simplified things, though, by bringing me natives of this time. They'll provide information about other inhabited worlds. There are doubtless maps and navigation details in their ship. We *have* expanded to the stars, I assume? Surely some of the goldilocks ships reached their destinations?"

"I… There are twenty-nine inhabited systems, or so I'm told. But one of them is unreachable, because it's controlled by… Wait. Sebastien. What are all these ships for? One would be enough to get you home. Why do you need a fleet?"

"My home crumbled to dust centuries ago, Elena, and I turned my back on it before that, when I joined our mission. The past holds minimal interest for me, except as a cautionary tale. I'm looking to the future. That's not a fleet. That's *evolution*. Once I understood how the station worked, setting all this in motion was simplicity itself. Creating an armada like this is a trivial use of the power available to me here, and this station is itself an insignificant backwater facility of no particular distinction. Once we have access to the full resources of the empire, think what we can achieve."

"The empire?"

He rubbed the back of his head, caressing the silver spider's back. "Of course. You don't know anything about them. The beings who made this station. In our language we might call them… the First Principle? The Underlying?"

"The Axiom?" Elena said.

Sebastien smiled. "I like that. Yes. The Axiom. I'm sure their egos would have approved of such a designation."

"I know a little bit about the Axiom, Sebastien. We shouldn't play with their technology. It's dangerous."

"Nonsense," he said. "Or, rather, of course it's dangerous, but not to me, or at least, not significantly. There's some risk in standing behind a cannon, but most of the risk accrues to those standing in *front* of it. No,

I'm safe enough. The Axiom have receded into the other realms. All that remains in this universe is their shadow, which they hope is enough to frighten everyone away. But I'm not afraid. I've seen the records in the *deep* archives."

"Do you know where the Axiom went?"

"That's not as simple a question as you think. The Axiom were on the verge of extinction, and retreated so they could gather their strength, and allow some of their long-term projects to come to fruition. There were factions among the Axiom, too, and since every one of them had powers we would consider godlike, they all set various plans in motion. At this point it's a contest, of sorts, to see which of their plans will come to pass successfully. There are great clouds of smart matter forming in distant systems, sparkling diamonds with secret intentions. There are places where physical constants don't behave as they should anymore, and that's just the beginning. There are factories in the hearts of gas giants constructing the components for *larger* factories that will consume whole star systems for fuel. Any of those projects would mean the end of the paltry smear of humankind."

"That's... terrifying, Sebastien, but how is building a fleet of warships the solution?"

"These aren't warships. There will be no fighting." He smiled, and his eyes shone: literally, with the implant's light.

"If they aren't warships, what are they?"

"Seed ships," Sebastien said. "I got the idea from the *Anjou*, actually. Our ship was filled with biological samples and sophisticated technology, so that if we found a habitable world, we could fill it with all the plants and wildlife, microscopic and macro, necessary to create our own Eden – all the best parts of Earth, exported. In the same way, these ships are filled with the seeds of our future. I studied societies, Elena. Infrastructure. I know the sort of things large groups can accomplish, when they put their petty distractions and divisions aside. Once we combine human ambition with Axiom technology, once we kill the *old* gods… we will become gods ourselves."

Elena wondered if the madness had been in Sebastien all along, or if it was the fault of the implants. "I still don't understand. What do you mean, seeds? Apart from the bio-drones, I haven't seen much at all alive here."

"Must you be so literal?" He gave her body a shake. "These are seeds of thought. Seeds of mind." Sebastien tapped his temple, fingernail against metal. "The implant. It filled me with an understanding of the glory of the Axiom, the majesty of their works, the fearsomeness of their power, all that. I think that information was meant to overawe me, to make me feel insignificant in comparison to their grandeur, but that didn't work – my brain is not the sort of brain this implant was meant to manipulate. I didn't feel unimportant. I felt *inspired*. There's no reason humanity can't rival, or even exceed, the accomplishments of the Axiom. They weren't better than us. They were just older, and willing to make the necessary effort to achieve their goals. It's difficult to make people – humans – set aside their differences and convince them to focus on the common good. I described that problem to the station's expert systems, which aren't exactly intelligent, but are capable of solving straightforward problems in practical ways. The station made some modification to the neural modification drones–"

"The brain-spiders?"

"How cute. Yes, the spiders. The station studied my brain, and made new spiders, designed for interfacing with humans. The ships are *filled* with those implants, plus fabrication equipment to produce more. The first wave of converts will secretly bring material to feed the fabricators, and to build more fabricators, and soon there will be enough implants for every human in every system."

Elena exhaled. "You want to infect humankind with brain-spiders, and make them do what?"

"Some will return here. They will crew my ships, and go on expeditions to take over Axiom facilities. Others will be soldiers, seeking out rebellious elements – there will always be holdouts, rugged individualists and narcissists, and they'll need to be hunted down and destroyed, or brought into compliance. Once I have the full power of the empire in my hands, I can start to make some meaningful changes." Sebastien shrugged. "It's an ambitious project, I know, but a worthy one. You can be a god with me, Elena. It would be lonely, to have the only free mind in the universe, and I've always liked you."

"I think the implant in your brain has changed you, Sebastien."

He nodded. "It has. Isn't it wonderful? I wish you could share my clarity of vision."

She looked at the fleet being built beyond the window. "How long until your ships are ready?"

"Oh, two-thirds of them are finished already. I'm just waiting to launch them all at once. A coordinated arrival, I think, so no one has time to prepare defenses. My ships will open wormholes around every planet, asteroid, station, or satellite with a human population, and take over."

"Just humans? No Liars?"

"Ah. The servitors. No. They're vermin, Elena. The empire only needed them because they'd grown so weak and decadent. They'll be exterminated. According to the deep archives, one of their sects was ordered to continue serving the Axiom in secret, and they might try to stop us from seizing the empire's facilities. Apparently there's a sort of cult devoted to protecting Axiom secrets, safeguarding sensitive installations from interference, and exterminating any sentient races that might discover the existence of the Axiom. The Axiom are fragile, for gods, and depend on secrecy to protect them in their vulnerable state."

Elena frowned. "A cult... working to protect the Axiom? Not to protect the universe from the Axiom?"

"Ah, yes, you see? 'Join our cult, and protect our oppressors!' That wouldn't be a very convincing sales pitch for the young vermin, would it? Only a few key servitors in the cult are supposed to know the true purpose of their organization. Most of the rank-and-file are meant to believe they're protecting the universe from the Axiom's return – don't disturb them, and maybe they'll never wake up. In reality, the cult is *ensuring* the safe return of the Axiom, once their projects come to fruition."

Elena shuddered. Poor Lantern. "But why would *any* of the Liars want to help their old masters?"

"Oh, they've been promised power when the Axiom returns, their own systems to govern, things like that. It's all unimportant now. I'm going to erase the empire's whole plan."

"I'm not sure destroying one master race by *becoming* a master race is a good idea, Sebastien."

"A master race? No, no. Just a few select masters." He still had his arm around Elena, and he gave her a squeeze. "You can't study society without realizing how stupid individuals are. I joined the goldilocks mission hoping I'd have the opportunity to plan a society from the beginning, to set initial conditions for ideal outcomes, but even so, I knew there would be flaws, outliers, malicious idiots, well-meaning idiots, all the termites that gnaw at the structure of any worthy enterprise. But now, I can eliminate all that disorder, and make sure everyone pulls together, in the right direction. I never understood this, until a few days ago, but most life in the universe… it's just *biomass*, isn't it? No more important than a swarm of plankton or a field of mold. It's just a resource to be exploited."

"I'm not sure I agree," Elena said.

"You will, soon enough. Just let me modify one of my neural implants – all the ones I have on hand would turn you into a mindless obedient tool, and you deserve better than that. Don't worry. Right now, you're just blind to the possibilities, but I'll open your eyes."

Elena tried to run, but there were machines hidden in the walls, under Sebastien's control, and they stopped her.

CHAPTER 28

The access hatch in the wall irised open, and Callie spun, weapons at the ready.

A small, dark-skinned human with serious (and glowing) eyes and a lot of metallic hardware clamped onto their head looked through the opening. "I have come to rescue you. I would appreciate being rescued in return." A pause. "Are you coming?"

Callie glanced at Ashok, who shrugged. "Out there is better than in here."

Callie went out first to make sure it wasn't an ambush – not that anyone needed to ambush them when they were trapped in a warehouse anyway, but she was feeling exceptionally paranoid. The tunnel beyond was only occupied by their bio-drone and the newcomer, but there was breathable atmosphere out there now, according to her suit diagnostics. Callie beckoned, and Lantern and Ashok followed.

The newcomer looked at Lantern for a long time. "You are a member of the race the builders of this station forced into servitude. I have never met a living alien before. My name is Uzoma."

"You may call me Lantern."

"I will take you all to a safe place. Well. Safer. I am impressed that you learned to control the bio-drone. Show me how?"

Uzoma climbed into the drone. Ashok looked a question at Callie. She shooed him in, and got on board herself.

Ashok showed her how the lights worked to direct the drone. "So where are we going?" he said.

Uzoma said, "Continue in the direction you are facing. Take the third left, and then the second right."

Lantern consulted the infosphere. "There is no second right. The tunnel dead-ends after the first one."

"This is good," Uzoma said. "I think you will soon be impressed by me."

Ashok flashed his lights, and Uzoma made a low *ahhhh* sound as the bio-drone lumbered forward. "I see. Good." Uzoma turned to Callie. "I was on the *Anjou*. I assume Elena made it back to Earth, and sought assistance?"

"She did, more or less. Elena told us about you." Callie looked Uzoma over. Brain-spider on the back of the head, check, weird eyes, check, but they seemed entirely calm and rational and in control of themselves. Then again, so had Sebastien, until he suddenly *hadn't*. "Elena warned us you'd been compromised."

"You refer to the neural manipulator? It briefly took control of my gross motor functions, turning me into a tool of the station. I acted without my own volition. But these devices are not designed for human anatomy. Not originally, at least. I gather Sebastien has made modifications, and his new models will be more effective on humans."

Callie didn't even want to think about what that meant. Not yet. "Sebastien thinks he's unaffected, too, but the neural manipulator did something to him."

"It did worse things than you know. Sebastien has become a megalomaniac. He believes the aliens who built this place were gods – the implant whispers such things to him. But instead of being frightened, he was invigorated. Sebastien wishes to take their power, and become a god himself."

"Great. That kind of thing never goes badly. So why aren't you in the grips of megalomania?"

Uzoma shrugged. "I suffered from seizures as a child. I have a deep brain stimulation electrode implanted in my brain, to control them. I believe the neural manipulator interacted poorly with the DBS system, perhaps perceiving it as an existing implant. The manipulator seems to have shut itself down, but some damage was done – I am now vulnerable to seizures again. I would appreciate medical attention. I cannot remove the manipulator without the risk of damaging my brain, but as far as I can tell, its impact on my mental state is negligible."

Callie nodded. Sebastien had seemed *off* to her from the beginning, and she'd put it down to subconscious jealousy instead of trusting her instincts. Uzoma seemed strange, but didn't trigger that same discomfort, so she decided to trust for the moment. You could fret over things forever, or you could *do* something, and she was forever and always from the tribe of the doers. "I'll assume you're on our side until I have reason to believe otherwise, then."

"I am glad. You must have a ship, and I would like to leave this place on it. Does your transport have weapons? Powerful ones?"

"It does."

Uzoma pulled aside a panel in the wall and revealed a roughly hexagonal screen, wired into some exposed cables. "I have tapped into the control room, though I cannot meddle too much, or Sebastien will notice, and shut me out. I can, however, open a hangar door. Your ship can pick us up, and then fire through the open door, and perhaps do enough damage to kill Sebastien, or cripple his ability to continue his work. We should go now."

"As soon as we save Elena."

"Ah." Uzoma nodded, once. "That will be more difficult. Sebastien may already have compromised her. If we do not stop him..." Uzoma shook their head.

"What's he trying to do? I offered him a ride home, and he wasn't interested. Is he building his own ship with a wormhole generator or something?"

"Not one ship. A fleet of them. Each ship full of neural manipulators. He intends to enslave the galaxy. He sees himself as the heir to the aliens who built this place."

Callie closed her eyes for a moment. Thought about millions of brain-spiders flooding across the stations and moons and asteroids and planets of humanity, a silver wave of erasure. She opened her eyes again. "Let's stop him from doing that, yes."

Lantern bustled toward the panel, holding the sphere. "May I?"

"Ahh! You have one of their infospheres. You will have greater access than I do. Sebastien has kept such devices from me. You could even search the deep archives with that. Sebastien has spent hours poring over them. I have caught the occasional glimpse, but I have trouble reading the records. Sebastien's implant whispers translations to him, but mine does not." Uzoma inclined their head toward the sphere. "What are you planning to do?"

"Whatever I can." Lantern held the sphere up to the screen, and it glowed bright blue, and began to spin.

Callie said, "We have to neutralize Sebastien and save Elena. That's straightforward enough. As for blowing this place up – we can just get out of here, and let Sebastien's dead-man's switch activate and take the station out."

"I overheard Sebastien telling you that." Uzoma shook their head. "There is no self-destruct system, no dead-man's switch. The station has no central power source that can be caused to explode. He was merely trying to keep you from incapacitating him."

"And you call me a liar," Lantern muttered.

Callie put a hand on one of Lantern's tentacles. "Not you. Not anymore. You're a truth-teller."

Lantern patted her hand, but absently, focused intently on the spinning sphere.

"A whole fleet of ships, full of wormhole generators. Huh." Ashok clucked his tongue, somewhere under all that metal, and began to pace back and forth, a sure sign of deep and twisty thoughts. "We probably shouldn't leave those lying around unattended."

"Not ideally," Callie said, "but maybe no one else will ever find this place again. Space is big."

"Sure, but it would nag at me, knowing they were out there, waiting to wreak havoc. But maybe… Cap, do you need me, for the Elena-saving portion of our program?"

Callie was already formulating a plan, with herself at its center, so she said, "I don't think so."

"Good. I want to talk some stuff over with Lantern."

Callie flapped her hand at him in dismissal and turned back to Uzoma. "Is there another way into the control room?"

"I doubt Sebastien is there anymore. I suspect he has taken Elena to the overseer's platform, to show her the progress on his fleet. He dragged me there often, until he realized I did not share his wish to become a god."

"I wouldn't want to be a god either. Seems like a lot of responsibility. The part of being a god where you get to mete out justice is good, but I can do that in my mortal form pretty well already. Can you get me to this platform?"

Uzoma nodded. "Yes. You should hurry. Sebastien was always fond of Elena, and has spoken of her often, regretting his decision to send her away, so perhaps she is unharmed. But he does not cope well with disagreement, and he may try to… change her, to make her compliant."

"I just need a clear line of fire," Callie said. Shooting a sort-of-romantic-rival in the head might ruin her budding relationship with Elena, but it was better than the alternative. Having Elena hate her would be a small price to pay if it kept Elena free and alive.

Elena struggled against the machines, one on either side of her. They were shining metal icosidodecahedrons, skeletal spheres composed of numerous triangles, with pulsing blue globes floating in their centers. The machines expanded and contracted as they moved, and some of their triangles opened outward and unfolded into multi-jointed arms. The arms were ductile, too: two of them had wrapped around her wrists like rope or wire, and she was trapped in place, standing on her feet with her arms pulled down and outward at her sides.

Sebastien stood with his back to her, looking out

the viewport at the sparks and flashes of the machines building his fleet. "I wish you hadn't tried to run, Elena. I thought I could make you understand."

Elena considered. Was there a pathway out of this? Perhaps, if she walked carefully. "Why assume my understanding is faulty? Maybe you just didn't explain it properly."

Sebastien turned, gave her a long look, and chuckled. For a moment, it was like seeing the old Sebastien again, calm and amused and charming. "That's fair. This must be disorienting and frightening for you. You lack my perspective. That's why the implant will help–"

"Sebastien, listen. I never had the chance to tell you how I felt. About you." She looked at the floor, no longer struggling against her bondage. "I was too shy, too nervous, and I was afraid it would be unprofessional. During training, every time I looked at you, I lost my breath. When you talked, I admired your brilliance and eloquence, but I also just looked at your lips, and wondered what it would be like to kiss them. I came back to this station, at great risk and great cost, to save *you*. So please understand, all this, everything you're telling me, about becoming a god – it's hard for me." She made a little gasp, like she was on the edge of crying. "How could I ever be worthy of you, if you're going to remake the universe? How could I ever be good enough to kiss a god?"

He stepped toward her, smiling, and then stopped, almost close enough to touch her. "I think you're trying to trick me, Elena. To get me to let my guard down."

"I understand. But you could find out. You could kiss me. You'd be able to tell, if you kissed me, whether or not I was telling the truth."

Sebastien came even closer, and touched her cheek with the back of his hand. His eyes glowed. She leaned into him, into his touch, his warm strong hand. "It would be nice to kiss you," he said. "I haven't stopped being who I was, Elena. I just became... more."

"Show me the man I knew, the man I dreamed about – show me he's still here. Prove that to me, and I'll be able to believe everything else. I'll be able to trust you."

He moved even closer, and she turned her face away. She pulled against the unyielding machines that pinned her wrists. "Don't kiss me while I'm chained up. Please." She let a smile rise to her lips. "Not on a first date, anyway."

Sebastien snorted, and seemed amused, but didn't order the machines to let her go.

"What can I do to you?" she said. "You took my weapons. You're bigger, and stronger, and the whole station obeys your commands. I'm trying to trust you, Sebastien. You have to trust me a little bit, too. If this is going to work, it needs to go both ways."

"You're right. Of course." He took a step back, glanced left and right, and spoke a word in some guttural language. The machines slithered their coils away from Elena's wrists, contracted into smaller spheres, and rolled off to wait patiently in the corners.

She went to Sebastien the moment she was free. Elena stood on her tiptoes and kissed him, and it felt as good as she'd always imagined it would. He was passionate without being pushy, strong without being overwhelming, and when his hands went around her waist, up her back, and then traveled down over her hips, she pressed herself against him, and moved her own hands up his back, holding him close. He pulled back after a long moment. "Oh, Elena."

"Oh, Sebastien."

Then she punched him in the back of the head.

CHAPTER 29

Callie crept through a smooth tunnel that was barely big enough for her. Maybe the Liars had used it, long ago, or the brain-spiders used it now, to move around the station quickly. That was a horrible thought. She'd had to take off her environment suit and her helmet to fit through this space, and she didn't like having her head exposed. She still had an earpiece so she could talk to the others, but she couldn't be sure Sebastien wasn't monitoring their comms, so she kept quiet.

The going was tight and awkward, but Callie knew how to crawl. She'd had sniper training, and part of that was learning to move silently and stealthily, on elbows and knees and toes, centimeters at a time if necessary. She was moving rather faster than that now, and though she had a lot of worry and anger bubbling away under the surface, she'd compressed those feelings down and put them aside and kept them ready to draw on as a source of energy, but not a source of distraction.

After wriggling through the tunnel, which had the size variance and wandering geometry that seemed typical of the organic Axiom aesthetic, she faced a seemingly impassable dead end. She clucked her tongue, twice, signaling Uzoma, who would use her back-door into the station systems to–

The blank roundish wall in front of her developed segments, a series of triangles arrayed in a circle, and they irised open, but only partway, and slowly. Callie had asked for a spy hole, and a gunport. She didn't have a sniper rifle. She owned a very good one, but it was tucked away in Shall's belly, way the hell back on her ship. What she had instead was two sidearms and a wrist-launcher with an array of exotic lethal options, but none of them were particularly reliable at long range. She had one ballistic sidearm and one that fired magnetic pulses of plasma. The latter didn't need to be very accurate: superheated plasma hitting you even glancingly tended to be disabling. But it wasn't enough to disable her enemy. If Sebastien could even shout a command, that might spell her doom. He thought Callie was harmlessly locked away. If he realized she was roaming free (and shooting at him, no less), and turned the station's defensive systems against her, she didn't think she'd survive long. She had to take him out, clean, quick, a shot to the head. She decided to use the ballistic weapon. On a practice range, she could hit a target pretty accurately at a hundred meters, but in real-world conditions, anything more than twenty-five meters away would be pushing it, and there was no reason to think she'd get more than one shot.

You went to war on the battlefield you had. Uzoma said this access tunnel was the closest Callie could get to the observation area without risk of detection, so it would have to do. She bellied up to the opening and looked through – and then her perspective reoriented dizzyingly as she realized she was looking *down*: the floor was about twenty meters away. More games with gravity. The "down" inside the tunnel was perpendicular to the "down" out there on the observation platform. How would that affect her shot? If the bullet started out on one gravity plane and then abruptly entered another, its trajectory would be dragged downward in the new direction… The physics were annoying. She decided to poke the barrel of the gun out of the hole when she fired so most of the projectile's journey would take place in the proper plane.

First she needed something to shoot at, and she didn't have that yet. She saw Elena's boots, just on the edge of her vision, and she was talking, not exactly pleading, but trying to reason with someone. Callie thought the time for reason was past, but then Elena didn't have a gun, so she was doing the best she could.

Sebastien entered Callie's view: she was looking at him top-down, and was nastily gratified to notice a bald spot on top of his head. Though the metal spider clinging to the back of his skull was a greater flaw in his physical beauty. She tracked him with the pistol, waiting for him to pause long enough for her to drive a bullet right through the top of his head, centered on that bald spot, but he didn't stop moving until he was very close to Elena. Callie *had* a shot, and the bullets were soft-nosed, so they'd break apart inside Sebastien's brain instead of passing through to do more damage, but if she missed, the ricochet could easily bounce into Elena.

The two of them were talking, but Callie couldn't understand what they were saying. Sebastien stepped back, and she lined up her shot, but then he gestured and a pair of bizarre machines, like rolling polyhedral wireframes, tumbled past him and out of her field of vision, distracting her for a moment–

Then Elena was there. She looked OK. Mussed, sweaty, no helmet on, but basically fine. She was, however, moving right up to Sebastien, utterly ruining any hope Callie had of making her shot without risk to Elena.

Then Elena went up on her tiptoes, and she was *kissing* Sebastien. Callie let out a low growl. His hands were all over Elena, roving up her back, down her back, then lower, squeezing her ass, and she was pressing herself against him. It had to be a seduction ruse, right? Or else Sebastien had already compromised her brain somehow, and was using his control to gratify–

They pulled apart a little, and gazed at one another like lovers. Callie had a clear look at Elena's face and saw her say, "Oh, Sebastien."

Then Elena punched Sebastien in the back of the head. It was an awkward blow, because how could it *not* be, from that angle, in that position? You couldn't deliver any real power that way. But Elena didn't need to hit hard. Apparently Sebastien hadn't realized the rings on her glove were weapons – that was part of why Callie liked them, they were subtle – and a moderate impact was enough to trigger their electric shock.

Elena struck Sebastien right on his brain-spider, and he jolted, stumbled away, sputtered for a moment, and then dropped like all his bones had been teleported out of his body. (There was probably an Axiom weapon that did that.)

Callie got on her radio: no worries about Sebastien listening in now: "Open the hatch all the way."

Uzoma complied, and the aperture expanded. Callie

THE WRONG STARS

could slide through... and get yanked sideways by gravity and fall twenty meters and land on her head.

Elena was kneeling by Sebastien, checking his pulse, it looked like. Callie wanted to put a bullet in his head just to be sure, but it was hard to justify that when he was unconscious and immobile. Not hard to justify to herself, really, but hard to justify to *Elena*.

"Elena!" Callie called, and Elena looked up, eyes widening. "I came to save you. Wasted trip, huh?"

"How are you in the ceiling?"

"Uncomfortably. I'd like to get out of it. Uzoma, Sebastien is down. Can you do something about the gravity in the observation deck? He won't notice."

"I can try."

"Hold onto something, Elena."

Elena nodded, looked around, and found a rail to hook her feet under. A moment later her hair floated up around her face and she lifted a little off the ground. Sebastien floated up lazily, unmoving.

Callie grabbed the edges of the tunnel – she still had gravity here, it was bizarre – and yanked herself out, launching straight for Elena. She twisted her body and got her legs under her. She bumped gently against the wall, close enough for Elena to reach out and grab her hand. They pulled together, and Callie kissed her hungrily, with passion and relief.

"What was that for?" Elena said when they pulled apart.

"You just electro-punched a mind-controlled wannabe god. You rescued yourself. That's hot."

Elena wrinkled her nose. "Remember when I punched myself in the face back in the reconditioning chamber? This was the exact same thing, except

Sebastien's head was in the way this time. You'll have to teach me some better moves."

"With pleasure," Callie said. "Let me get the gravity turned back on again."

"Wait!" Elena glared at Callie and sailed through the room toward Sebastien, getting her arms under him. "You'll crack his skull."

That didn't sound like a bad outcome to Callie, but she went to Elena's side and helped her maneuver Sebastien's body, so when the gravity came back on, he would only drop slightly, and not break any bones. "Sorry, sorry," Callie said. She spoke into her comms: "Gravity, please."

When the gravity returned, they bent their knees to take Sebastien's weight, and lowered him gently to the floor.

Elena gazed down at him. "I know he's just a monster to you, but Sebastien is a good person, Callie. Or he was. I knew him." She touched the spider's legs, penetrating deep into his skull. "Do you think we can save him? Make him the way he used to be?"

"Ashok has some ideas about removing the implants, and Stephen will help. If we can get Sebastien to the *White Raven*, we can try. Now that he's not awake to mess everything up, Uzoma should be able to get us out of here—"

"You found Uzoma? They're all right?"

"They seem to be coping better than Sebastien did. But before we can go, we have to do something about... that." Callie nodded toward the hangar beyond the wall of glass. She forced herself to look at it, though it made her guts clench. Hundreds of ships being constructed, all full of mind-altering brain-spiders.

Lantern hurried in from the corridor, followed by Ashok and Uzoma. Elena ran up to the latter, as if to hug them, then stopped short. "Sorry. I know you don't like to be hugged."

"Thank you for remembering. I am very pleased to see you all the same." They reached out and squeezed Elena's hand. Uzoma's gaze went to the wall of windows. "I think the fleet is nearly done."

"Even without Sebastien to launch them, they're a loaded gun pointed at our solar system," Callie said. "We have to assume these are primed and ready to launch."

"We could try to erase their navigational data," Ashok said.

"Then it's just a loaded gun pointed at *anywhere*. I thought I could just leave them behind, but... I'll be seeing those spiky ships in my nightmares forever if we don't do something about them. Lantern, is there anything your people can do?"

"We do not destroy Axiom facilities. We merely sequester them, and only destroy any forbidden artifacts that make their way into inhabited space."

Callie chewed her lip. "So we can do Uzoma's plan. Open up some hangar doors and fire everything we've got on the *White Raven* inside, and hope it blows up real good. But will it be good enough?"

Ashok went to the glass. "I bet we'd die trying anyway. These ships probably have automated defenses we can't even imagine, so they'd probably shoot back. And remember, if they perceive us as a threat, they'd could just open a bridge right in the middle of the *White Raven*, and we'd be turned into meat and metal confetti."

"Oh, hell," Callie said. "The emergency systems. If

we attack, they'll just kill us and go... wherever. Maybe to that prison planet we saw, or maybe... who knows where."

Ashok nodded. "Lantern and I were talking, though, about failsafes. You know how your personal teleporter won't send you into a wall or whatever, and won't open inside a person, or a building? The bridge generators on those ships don't have those kind of safeguards. They're meant to be used as weapons as well as transport. So we were thinking, what if we can convince *all* the generators on *all* those ships to open bridges all at once, with the other ends of the bridges distributed all over this whole station."

"Whoa." Callie looked at the hangar. She remembered the starfish ship being torn apart by a single portal opening inside it. Multiply that devastation by hundreds... "I think that would do some damage. Lantern, are you willing to help with that, given your whole non-interference stance?"

"The consequences would be disastrous if the Axiom realized that someone had deliberately destroyed this station, but there are hundreds of thousands of such stations throughout the galactic cluster, and there are sometimes malfunctions and accidents, after all these years. Occasionally a program malfunctions, and there is a disaster. I have taken the liberty of wiping the past few days of data from the station's central system, so even if the wreckage were discovered, nothing would point to our involvement, and it would likely be ruled an accident. The station records indicate there are no members of the Axiom slumbering on this station who might wake or be alerted. This place is abandoned, and could be destroyed without much chance of discovery. I can break with doctrine in these circumstances."

"Let's do it," Callie said. "We'll get off the station, then set the whole fleet to blow. Can we do that with a timer or something?"

Ashok glanced at Lantern, and Lantern fluttered her tentacles. Ashok said, "Sorry, cap, it's not that easy. It's not like there are *no* safeguards in place here. The Axiom weren't stupid. The station has ways of protecting itself. There's a... Lantern says it's like a force field that prevents the bridge generators from opening up in here, for obvious reasons. There's a way to override the field, but you have to physically break a connection way down in the guts of the station. It's a pretty crucial part of the infrastructure, too, so there are automated systems in place to repair it. We can't take those systems offline, they're too integral, so you pretty much have to break the connection, disable the field, and then trigger the ships to set off the portal apocalypse before the repair-bots can undo the damage."

"So it's your basic suicide mission." Callie nodded. "We'll send someone who's not alive, then. We'll get Shall in his repair drone to go down there–"

More head-shakes. Uzoma spoke this time. "The only way to access the relevant area is to squeeze through one of the same tunnels you took to reach Elena. Too small for your drone. We considered commandeering one of the station bots." They inclined their head toward the quiescent wireframe polyhedrons. "They're adaptable in terms of shape. But they're also physically incapable of damaging the ship's critical systems." A shrug. "Safeguards."

"Could I cut the cable and then teleport out?" Callie

tapped the device on her wrist.

"Maybe?" Ashok said. "The range on the teleporter is limited, and the station is *big*, and the connection we need to break is inconveniently located. If you teleported from that spot, out to max range, you wouldn't get clear of the explosion. Well, not explosion. What would you call it, Uzoma?"

"A series of violent disruptions of space time."

"Right, that," Ashok said.

Callie shrugged. "So I cut the cable, set off the portals, crawl out of the tunnel fast, run faster, and *then* teleport out to max range. Is *that* possible?"

Ashok *hmm*ed. "Possibly. It's hard to tell how fast things would happen. Would the wormholes interact with each other, and if so, will that interaction have a dampening effect, or an amplifying one? We're eyeballing this, guesstimates all around, but maybe you could do it in time. If you were really fast. Like an athlete. And lucky. Like a... lucky athlete."

"I'll do it," Lantern said. "My life is forfeit anyway. You have already condemned me to death, and this way I would die in service to a greater good."

Callie shook her head. "If I was still planning to execute you, I wouldn't trust you on that kind of mission anyway. But you're not going to die by my hand, Lantern. There will be justice for Meditreme Station, but I won't get it by killing you. I'm going to settle things with your superiors."

"I know what we did was unforgiveable," Lantern said. "But I hope you can see we had our reasons."

"They might not be the reasons you think, though," Elena said. "Sebastien told me some things... You should look into the deep archives before we go, Lantern."

Callie wondered what that was all about, but she shrugged. One thing at a time. "You don't get to volunteer for this, Lantern. You have to raise the little ones in the incubators. If you died, I'd be stuck raising a bunch of baby squidlings, and that's too much like a comedy immersive for real life. I'm the captain. I'll do the deadly mission of death."

"Cap, with all due respect to your fitness level, you'd have to crawl backwards out of the access tunnel before you could even start trying to run–"

"Perhaps not." Uzoma went to one of the screens and began manipulating data, spinning spatial models of the station. "She could, perhaps, go forward, and drop down to this larger tunnel used by the bio-drones. Then, if she could hitch a ride on one…"

"That could work." Ashok joined them at the panel. "If we direct a drone to wait for her here…"

"You two figure that out," Callie said. "I'm a quick study, so just tell me what to do when the time comes. Lantern, open up a hangar door so we can get in touch with the *Raven*, and get the rest of you off this station."

The alien scurried away to comply.

Elena touched her arm. "Callie, you don't have to do this. Risk your life? I asked you to help me, to save my friends, and you succeeded beyond my greatest hopes. You've done enough."

Callie shook her head. "I can't leave this place just sitting here. It's too dangerous. Besides, I'll be fine. I'll cut the thing, activate the stuff, ride the kaiju, teleport out, you'll rescue me – it'll be fine. I'm not in this for the noble self-sacrifice."

"Don't die," Elena said. "Promise me."

"I can't–"

"Just say it, Callie."

"OK. I promise not to die."

"Good. Now you can kiss me, and then you can go be brave."

Lantern got the ship-building machines shut down, and even though they'd been working in vacuum and therefore hadn't made any noise, it still seemed more peaceful without the falling sparks and flashes of welding and the ceaseless motion of metal beyond the glass.

Uzoma and Ashok went over Callie's route with her about six times, and loaded a crude but efficient map into her helmet display, then tried to go over it again, until she told them to stop, she got it, she understood. They all walked across a covered catwalk, through the silent hangar space full of lethal black spheroids bristling with spikes and fins, all of them filled with silver brain-spiders. Like hideous egg sacs, waiting to burst. Callie shuddered at the thought.

They opened a hangar door and established communication with the ship. Things on the *Raven* were fine. Ibn was asleep, and Robin was drinking all the coffee, the latter against doctor's orders. Shall came over in the canoe with spare environment suits and they got Sebastien bundled up safely. They brought the bio-drone as close as they could to the hangar door and transferred the incubators as gently as possible, Shall taking great care to load them into the canoe. Once everything was stowed and shipshape, Callie hugged Elena, said her farewells, and stood before the hangar door as the last of them climbed inside the transport.

Shall squatted on top of the canoe, clinging with magnetic feet, and spoke to her on a private channel.

"I don't like this. Something could go wrong. I should come with you."

"You wouldn't fit in the hole I have to crawl through, and anyway, you're in a valuable piece of machinery. I don't want you getting blown up. Go away."

"Callie–"

She turned her back on the hangar and headed toward the interior of the station, surrounded by the ships that would soon tear the whole place apart. "Be ready to pick me up in forty-five minutes."

"I wish I could be there to keep you safe."

"I keep myself safe. Don't worry, I'm not going to die."

Thirty-seven minutes later, Callie thought, *I am going to die*.

CHAPTER 30

Everything went smoothly at first. She rode on the back of a bio-drone Uzoma had retasked from the control room, deep into the station. She didn't have time to sightsee, and that was just as well. The drone dropped out of the tunnels at various points to traverse portions of the station that had once been occupied, and Callie glimpsed things that baffled or horrified her or both: a room full of immense aquarium tanks, full of bubbling green liquid. A wall that looked like quicksilver, rippling and reflective. She passed a door that opened onto rocky terrain under a greenish sky, with a sun hanging fat and pale on the horizon. (Callie hoped it was a special effect and not an actual miniaturized star, or they might accidentally cause a supernova. Probably Uzoma would have mentioned if that was a possibility.) One room was full of empty cages, with bars made of light. One was full of things that *actually* looked like egg sacs, piled high and lumpy and silky-white to the far-off ceiling. Another held an incinerator with an eternally burning flame at its heart. Another held a kaiju-high pile of small bones. Eventually Callie stopped looking to the sides, and kept her eyes on the corridor ahead.

The kaiju dropped her off by a little hole in the wall: her tunnel access. The map in her HUD showed her where to crawl, and the going was merely tedious, not difficult. The distance was only a hundred meters or so. The tunnel led to a small round chamber about the size of a pup tent. She looked around, found the panel she wanted, and slid it open, revealing a connecting shaft. Once she was done, she'd launch herself down that shaft, which would take her to a perpendicular tunnel where a bio-drone would be waiting to speed her to the minimum safe distance so she could teleport away.

Callie went to work. A schematic popped up on her display, and she pushed open panels until she found a length of fat conduit wrapped in some insulating substance that shone a luminous green. She took a moment to review her exfiltration plan, pointed her energy weapon at the conduit, turned her head away, and fired.

The superheated plasma ate through the conduit nicely, severing the connection immediately. The repair bots would be on their way, and fast. Callie tapped at the tablet mounted on her left forearm, just above the teleporter on her wrist. The symbols didn't mean anything to her, just alien geometries, but she hit them in the simple three-figure sequence she'd been taught.

Nothing happened, as far as she could tell, but if Ashok and Uzoma had done their job right, the station would be tearing itself apart with assorted wormholes now – and none of the wormholes would appear on top of *her*.

She slipped through the hole into the shaft, orienting herself so it felt like she was swimming down, and kicked off hard. She had a small amount of propellant in her suit, enough to send her cruising rapidly through the gravity-less vacuum. In moments the pinprick of the distant opening to the bio-drone's tunnel grew to the size of a beach ball, and then a hot tub, and she was through. There was gravity inside that tunnel, but she was prepared for that, so she ducked and rolled and bounced to her feet.

The bio-drone was waiting, and if Ashok's estimate was right, she had about eight minutes of travel ahead of her, and ten minutes to cover it. Plenty of time. The drone was supposed to scoop her up, and run, and when her timer hit zero, she was supposed to teleport right out of its belly, straight out and away to maximum range.

Then the walls of the tunnel began to flash various colors, red and orange and indigo, and instead of picking her up and carrying her to safety, the bio-drone turned and ran the wrong way down the tunnel.

Callie stared after the drone as it disappeared around a curve. Shit. Some kind of "the sky is falling" emergency protocol probably, overriding its programming. The timer clicked on in her heads up display. Just over nine minutes now, to travel a distance that would take eight minutes by bio-drone. She could not run as fast as a kaiju, especially in an environment suit.

I promise not to die.

She started running.

The tunnel vibrated, and continued to flash warning colors. Titanic and terrible things were happening in the station all around her, and the trauma was transmitted through the walls and ceiling and floor, with vibrations shaking her boots. The gravity suddenly stopped working, right in mid-stride: Callie took a step, and then she was flying, launched up and forward instead of merely forward. Her trajectory was bad, and she had to twist to avoid hitting her head on the tunnel ceiling, catching the blow painfully on her shoulder instead. She spun and scrabbled and tried to find a way to propel herself along the tunnel, trying to figure out if she could go faster in weightlessness than she had in gravity, and if she could go fast enough for it to *matter*, as the timer in the corner of her eye clicked down and down and down.

She knew she couldn't possibly make it, but Callie was who she was, so she caught her fingertips on a seam in the tunnel ceiling and *hauled* herself forward, launching herself along the tunnel.

The corridor curved downward (based on her old frame of gravitational reference), which would have given her a nice little speed boost if she'd been on foot. Not enough to matter, but she would have died with a feeling of exhilaration and progress, maybe. The station was shaking much more badly now, and she bumped against the tunnel walls as they trembled. The timer in her field of vision was getting down to within a minute of Ashok's best guess for when the whole station would be ripped into tiny chunks of debris.

Then Shall dropped out of a connecting tunnel above her, grabbed her with enfolding arms, and pressed her to his mechanical belly. He maneuvered with his thrusters on full burn. Shall's body was designed to zip around in vacuum and fix damaged ships in dry dock or drifting in space, and he had large reservoirs of propellant. He was going through them, accelerating constantly, and Callie let out a whoop in her helmet. "What are you *doing* here?"

"Saving you."

"How did you even get way the hell over here?"

"I yelled at Lantern until she found me an access point that would intersect your path, then I jumped off the canoe and flew around the outside of the station until I found the door, and then I came looking for you. I'm glad I did. I see you missed your ride. I was afraid of something like that. I had a bad feeling."

"You're a hull repair drone. You're not supposed to have feelings."

"I am many things. Hull repair drone is just my current occupation. We're almost at minimum safe distance. Are you ready to jump?"

"I don't think the teleport will take you too."

"Sorry. You'll have to buy a new repair drone. This is goodbye. I'm not connected to the ship at the moment, and this local node of my consciousness will never be integrated back into the whole, so if you have any secrets you want to spill—"

"I never stopped loving you, Michael. It just hurt too much."

"I know, Callie. I hate myself. And by 'myself,' I mean the biological specimen my mind is based on. Fuck that guy."

"I know, right?" Callie's timer was almost at zero. She wiggled her arm, and Shall shifted to give her the necessary freedom of motion to push the teleport button on her wrist.

Then a wormhole formed in the air just a few meters in front of them, breaching the tunnel from side to side. The walls cracked like a teacup hit with a hammer, and the air rushed out into the vacuum, hungry black on all sides. Callie caught a glimpse of spinning silver towers and fragments of metal and scores of spreading inkblots of darkness opening all around her, tendrils drifting like the fronds of strange abyssal jellyfish. Shall's momentum was too great to avoid the wormhole, so they flew straight inside, on through the bridgehead.

Shall was trying to brake, which in practice meant thrusting in reverse, so their progress through the bridge was slow, far slower than even the stately plodding of the *White Raven* through the bridges; slow for a starship was still fast for a person. Individuals had flown through the twenty-nine established bridges before, in vacuum suits, but there was nothing to see inside them, because they were all lightless.

Not so here. There were lights here, rings of blinding white, spaced every few meters. In the *White Raven* those lights had whipped by. Here, they floated past languidly.

In between most of the glowing rings, the tunnel was made of a greasy-looking black substance, just like their bridge generator or Callie's personal teleporter. (She briefly wondered what would happen if she triggered that *here*, in this place, and decided she didn't want to find out as badly as she wanted to stay alive, and the two were probably incompatible.)

One of the rings of light was broken, stuttering and flashing, and she wondered if that was the case on every trip, and they'd just passed it too quickly to notice before. What did it mean, if the infrastructure here was failing, even in such a small way?

Beyond the malfunctioning ring of light, in the greasy black space before the next band of brightness, a portion of the tunnel looked different. The changed area was a segment of the curve that occupied perhaps forty-five of the available three-hundred-and-sixty degrees. Callie happened to be looking straight down at that segment, still clutched tight to Shall's underside.

That one section of the tunnel looked like a window. There was something behind it: something dark, and slumped, and rounded. It was mostly in shadow, but it seemed to be gazing at her with a single fist-sized eye the blue of Cherenkov radiation. The eye appeared to track her movement, and she twisted her head to stare back, but then the window, if that's what it was, slid closed.

Even though they were moving slowly, the trip took as long as it always did: twenty-one seconds. Bridge travel was entirely a matter of time, and not distance, it seemed.

Callie was fairly sure she'd take her strange vision of the blue eye in the tunnel to her doom, since she expected to emerge in the midst of cataclysm. They'd set each ship to open a wormhole in its immediate vicinity – call that point A – with the *other* end of the wormhole opening at another point in the station, ideally in places where the branching tunnels joined – call that point B. They'd passed through a point B, which meant they would emerge at a point A, back in the remains of the hangar, where hundreds of ships had just been torn apart. There would be flying debris, strange radiation, fragments of brain-spiders – who knew what hazards. Callie didn't dare hit her teleport until she'd emerged fully from the bridge, and her finger was poised to do so, but would her reaction time be fast enough to spare her death by flying metal?

It was, but only because Shall protected her. The hull repair drone was pelted by debris immediately, and spun wildly around, but he flung out all his many manipulator arms and batted away the floating remnants of any ships that entered his vicinity. The right chunk of metal at the correct angle and velocity could have holed Callie like a bullet, but Shall took care of the bigger pieces, and she got lucky.

"Love you," she said, and jumped.

"No sign of the captain." Ashok's voice crackled on the comms from the canoe, where he waited at Callie's expected point of arrival.

"Where is she?" Elena was in the cockpit of the *White Raven* with Drake and Janice, watching out the viewport as the Axiom station was destroyed, her eyes straining for a speck she wouldn't possibly be able to make out: one human, floating. She couldn't even see the canoe. But she didn't stop looking.

"Callie is ten seconds late, which means she either didn't make it, or she jumped to the wrong place," Janice said.

Elena didn't answer. The station had come apart like… like… like nothing she had a comparison for. Wormholes had opened by their hundreds in one small region of space, and geysers and fountains of matter had blown out in all directions. Then corresponding hundreds of other wormholes had appeared at every junction and many of the straightaways of the vast interconnected anthill of the station. There were combustible and explosive things in many of those sections, judging by how utterly vaporized they were. There would be a debris field, and a large one, but not even the best forensic computer would be able to reconstruct what that mess of fragments had originally been.

They all stared at the silent majesty of the devastation, with a growing sense of corresponding personal loss that was no less devastating in its way.

Then something went "boop."

"Callie's transponder!" Drake said. "Ashok, she's way the hell in the wrong direction, I don't know what happened, but we're closer than the canoe. We'll pick her up. Converge at these coordinates."

Elena was waiting at the airlock when Callie floated in, and Elena was the one who helped her out of her suit, who checked her over for bruises, who covered her in kisses, who hugged her and then stopped hugging when Callie said "Ow," and who took her to her quarters after Callie gave her last order before falling asleep: "Drake, Janice – take us back home."

Elena left Callie alone in her quarters after a while to go check on Sebastien and her other crewmates. Callie was exhausted and grimy, the exhilaration of near-death draining out of her as her body tried to balance itself again chemically. She couldn't sleep until she got word that they'd successfully traveled via bridge back to Trans-Neptunian Space, emerging in the same spot the *Anjou* had just a few days ago. She ordered everyone to stand down, get some rest, get some food, do whatever they needed to do, ahead of an all-hands meeting to discuss their future.

She certainly needed sleep, but it wouldn't come. "Shall?"

"Yes, Callie?"

"I'm guessing the hull repair drone was destroyed?"

"It took a lot of hard hits, I'm afraid. Came apart completely. But I shut down its copy of my consciousness first, so there was no suffering."

"It – *you* – saved my life."

"A purely selfish act. Without you, Stephen would

be in charge, and he'd park the *White Raven* in orbit around some Jovian moon and never take me anywhere interesting. I wouldn't have any fun."

"Did you, ah, synch up with the drone's memories when it came out of the bridge?"

"I did. Reconnection happens automatically, whenever communication is possible. But there's a keyword system, and I detected a slightly ambiguous request for confidentiality. I err on the side of caution so I encrypted that portion of the information, and never experienced it consciously. Whatever you said to the drone, thinking it would go with me to my robot grave, is still secret." He paused. "Unless you *want* me to hear it?"

"It was just a lot of really filthy sexy dirty talk. You wouldn't be interested. Do you remember going through the tunnel with me, though?"

"I do. That was harrowing."

"Could you see anything in there?" Thinking of that single glowing blue eye.

"No, as usual, it was totally blank to my sensors. I wonder if Ashok could wire some biological eyes onto a drone so I could see the lights in the tunnel, and the other things the Axiom tries to hide from mechanical sensors. We'd have to get our hands on some eyes, of course. Liars seem to have as many as they want. They must grow them in a lab."

"Definitely something to consider. If you like considering disgusting science abominations. Good night, Shall. I'm going to get some sleep."

After a few hours of fitful slumber, she gave up on the effort and went to the infirmary. Robin was floating near the ceiling, chatting with Stephen: "No, my parents handled my transition pretty well. I think it helped that I kept my first name, Robin, and just changed my middle name. They messed up the pronouns sometimes, but at least they didn't–" She looked up when Callie came in. "Captain! I haven't had a chance to thank you for... all that. I fully expected a slow and miserable death. You're amazing."

"I just ran to and fro. Other people did all the work. Do you have a minute, Stephen?"

Robin excused herself to go in search of more coffee. The infirmary was otherwise quiet. Sebastien hadn't awakened yet, though his vitals were good, and Ibn was hermiting away in Elena's room, since Elena was happy enough to bunk with Callie.

"She's going to drink all our coffee," Stephen said. "Nice woman, but insatiable."

"How are you?"

He shrugged. "I have too many patients, one of whom has a robot spider clamped to his head and might wake up and try to murder us all, which is why he's strapped to his bed. My bigger problem is I missed the festival, which has thrown off decades of careful cultivation of my brain chemistry and my spiritual life, and I feel a yawning chasm of despair before me. I would like to fix that when I get home. Except my other big problem is: I am homeless."

"I was thinking about that," Callie said. "We need a home base. We can't all stay here. Me and Elena doubled up, Robin in Ashok's quarters, Ashok sleeping in the machine shop with Lantern, Uzoma just kind of floating around wherever... Even if the *Anjou* people decide to move on, the rest of us have to figure out something long-term."

"What long-term are we talking about? Are you

planning to rebuild the Trans-Neptunian Authority from scratch?"

"No, I'm thinking more of a freelance life. I don't want to move to the Imperative, though. They have too many rules, and they won't give me any decent security work, because they won't trust me as a former TNA officer, even of the occasional contract variety."

"Where else? The asteroid belt? Not the inner planets? Did you want to settle in a colony system?"

"None of the above. I have some thoughts."

"Are they dangerous thoughts?"

"Usually."

"Then you're lucky you have a doctor on board." He paused. "I mean me. No disrespect to Doctor Oh."

"Ashok has a doctorate too, you know."

Stephen made a face. "In engineering. From Lunar University."

"Are you willing to stay on as my XO, even though we don't have any authority or legal standing to shoot at anybody anymore? We're not quite going rogue, but only because there's not really a government left for us to go rogue *from*."

"You want to poke around in parts of the universe where you shouldn't, don't you? Just to see what you'll find."

"Sometimes you find gold. Sometimes you find spiders. Sometimes you find golden spiders."

"You should have called this ship the *Golden Spider* instead of the *White Raven*."

"You're right. That's also pretty good. So. Are you in?"

"I'm too young to retire and too old to learn another trade, so yes, if you can find me a place to lay my weary head and take my wonderful drugs, I will continue to put the broken people you bring me back together."

"Great. How do you feel about becoming a pirate?"

"Not… good? Not good at all. Bad. Yes. Definitely bad."

"Yeah. Me too. But you'll have to trust me."

CHAPTER 31

Callie was in her room, running through the mental script she'd created, that she'd doubtless have to abandon as soon as reality didn't match her hopes and expectations. The ship was burning toward what was once the liminal space between the Jovian Imperative and Trans-Neptunian Space, and was now just the edge of the inhabited solar system instead.

She'd caught up on the news on the Tangle, and there was plenty of coverage about Meditreme Station, but the prevailing narrative was that the station had been destroyed by accident. The Trans-Neptunian Authority was always experimenting with new weapons, or so the inner planets and the Imperative assumed. Rumors had spread of the mass Liar exodus just before the disaster, which led to obvious speculation. Either the aliens had sold the TNA some kind of unstable weapon system, or they'd discovered some deadly flaw in an existing system and hadn't bothered to tell any of the humans about it before saving themselves; which one you believed depended on how xenophobic you were feeling.

Several Liars from Meditreme had been tracked down and interviewed, though My Cousin Paolo wasn't among them. They gave the predictably bizarre range of explanations for why they'd fled: one said it left for a family reunion in colony system seventeen. Another said the ghost of Miranda Tanzer had appeared and given it a vision of a new propulsion system, and it had immediately flown off to a research lab to sell the idea. A third explained that the mass exodus was part of a game the Liars played, a sort of wild chaotic race across the system. A fourth insisted that Meditreme Station hadn't blown up at all but had merely phased into a slightly alternate dimension.

The overall consensus was: something had gone boom, and it was an unprecedented tragedy, but it was nobody's fault. Now there was a big hole in the political system and an area of space ripe for the taking, with some juicy TNA facilities left largely unattended, from asteroid-based research labs to wind farms to icy planitesimals turned into factories, all floating around without clear ownership. So far none of the big players had maneuvered to take over the old TNA holdings, and it was basically lawless out there, once you got beyond the Imperative's reach.

Every remaining TNA facility was probably a mini-fiefdom now, ruled by whoever happened to be there when Meditreme blew, and they would remain so until Mars or the Imperative or some kind of joint venture could conjure up the legal status necessary to claim those holdings, or buy them cheap from the few surviving TNA shareholders, before going in with guns to restore order. That would take months, at best; maybe years; some places would probably remain stubbornly, weirdly independent for the foreseeable future. It was sure to be interesting out there.

Nobody was looking for the perpetrators, though, since no one except a few conspiracy theorists thought there *were* any perpetrators, and certainly no one was looking for a sect of murderous Liars out in the Oort Cloud. That meant Callie's work wasn't done. She still had to get justice for Meditreme.

Fortunately there was a way to combine her need for a new home with her need for justice, but she wondered how Lantern would take the idea.

She didn't have to wonder long.

"Captain, do you have a moment?"

"Come on in, Lantern."

There was gravity, since they were under thrust, and Lantern waddled into the captain's quarters. She slumped down on the floor and fluttered her tentacles. "I was able to copy some of the deep archives from the station onto my infosphere. I have been reviewing them since our return."

Callie sat on the edge of her bunk. "And?"

"My sect, the truth-tellers... our ostensible purpose is a lie. The Axiom made arrangements to form our organization. They wanted to maintain a core of devoted servants in their absence. A small group of my people were trained, conditioned, and convinced of the absolute rightness and necessity of their purpose: to safeguard Axiom facilities over the coming millennia, while several long-term projects came to fruition. The way the organization is structured, the operational parameters the records lay out... I have no doubt that group is the origin of my sect. I thought we were safeguarding the universe from the Axiom. But we aren't. We're– what's the human phrase? Guard dogs."

"I'm sorry, Lantern. Maybe the sect has changed over

the centuries. Is it possible they started out as servants, and became protectors over time?"

Lantern fluttered. "No. We possess perfect institutional memory. Our leaders produce neural buds, and those are passed on to the next generation of leadership. My people can live upwards of two thousand years, anyway – we aren't talking about countless generations. But the Axiom didn't foresee everything. They expected most of the Free to die once the Axiom were no longer around to control us – as if we were children, incapable of coping on our own. They did not anticipate the diaspora, or the great flowering of imagined cultures and histories we have produced. My sect was forced to hide its true intentions from the rest of our people, knowing we would resist. They settled on a strategy of paralyzing us with fear about what would happen if the Axiom ever returned. They convinced us that doing the Axiom's secret bidding was the only way to protect ourselves."

Callie nodded. "So, is there just one big boss in charge of the sect who knows the truth?"

"I don't think so. There must be knowledge on the local level, at least, in all twenty-nine inhabited systems. It would be too dangerous otherwise. There are sparks of rebellious impulses even among our sect, those who wish to modify our methods, and those must, of course, be ruthlessly put down in order for our secret function to prevail. I argued for non-violent interventions, but violence is central to the charter the Axiom gave my elders: destroy or contain any potential threats to their projects."

"That means your elder, back on your station in the Oort Cloud... they know?"

"Elder Mizori. She must know. I think. I cannot be

sure. I would like to find out. I could return, and ask, but how could I compel her to answer?"

"I could help with that part."

"I cannot ask you to involve yourself in this business. It could be very dangerous."

"It's fine, Lantern. I need to see your elder anyway. She's the one who ordered the destruction of Meditreme Station, right? She's the guilty party, and she has to answer for her crimes – but I'll make sure you get the answers to your questions first. How many of the Free are on your station?"

"Not many. Most of us were on the ship your wormhole generator destroyed. All the junior members of the sect, and most of the more senior as well. All that remains is the elder, and her personal coterie, just four others. It's likely they know the truth as well. They have always been an inner circle, planning together."

"There's no chance she's gotten reinforcements?"

"Our cells operate with great autonomy, for security reasons. We can send messages to the other cells, but it is a slow process, and each elder is expected to handle their own problems. They meet once or twice a century to discuss things, but otherwise we operate independently. Short of the total destruction of our cell, there will be no intervention."

"Should be easy enough for us to get in there, then."

"I don't see how. You could drop me off nearby in the canoe, and they would let me in, I think, but I could not force them to answer me. If I come in your company, in this ship, they will recognize the vessel from your engagement with the starfish ship, and will not allow us to enter."

"So we force our way in."

"The station is formidably defended by terrible weapons. We could destroy it, perhaps, by weaponizing the bridge generator, but that would not get me the answers I need. The *White Raven* is a fine ship, but it's not enough. We would need a much larger force to successfully target their defenses and to disable their weapons systems."

"Funny you should say that," Callie said.

Callie lounged in a cockpit seat, looking at the viewport, which had been converted to a screen. The woman on the screen had sneering down to an art. Her hair was all wild spikes, her cheeks were streaked with grease in a way meant to suggest war paint, and her teeth were, somehow, carved into little skulls.

"We're not accepting new applications at this time," the pirate queen said.

They were so close to Glauketas that there was no noticeable delay in the transmission. Callie snorted. "Of course you're not. You can't even feed the mouths you've *got*. Your whole business model was built on robbing smugglers and cargo ships, and now there's nowhere for smugglers to smuggle anything to, or from, and no cargo coming or going way out here. You can't prey on Jovian Imperative vessels because they've been secretly backing you, or at least declining to intervene, because they liked having you as a thorn in the TNA's side. You're floating out there on your fancy rock running out of supplies and wondering what the hell to do next. I bet your crews are getting restless, too. Terrified they'll have to go to some civilized system and do honest work. Why the hell would I want to climb onto your sinking ships?"

The pirate queen, who was also called Glauketas, as

all her predecessors had been, scowled. "If you don't
want to join us, Machedo, what *do* you want?"

"A finder's fee. You know me. I was TNA security
personnel, and I know TNA secrets. I know about secret
bases. Facilities that are only lightly defended, because
they depended on obscurity as their best defense. Those
facilities are full of valuable technology, materiel, and
various ill-gotten gains embezzled by TNA executives."

"If you have a treasure map, why are you offering to
share it? You're TNA. They'd let you in."

"Because lightly defended doesn't mean *undefended*.
I might be able to trick my way into one or two of the
facilities by flashing my old credentials, sure, but word
will get around, and eventually someone will blow
me out of the sky. I'm thinking long-term. You have
manpower and firepower. I have intelligence. Why risk
my life, or the life of my crew, when you can risk yours
for me instead?"

The pirate queen was trying not to look interested.
"What's the offer?"

"I'll give you the location of a base crammed full of
juicy tech. You go steal all their stuff, and give me half."

"Half? Don't be stupid. We'd be doing all the work.
Finder's fees are ten percent."

"I guess I could settle for a third, if you also give
me docking privileges and a berth on Glauketas. *Good*
quarters, too. As good as yours. My house blew up a
while ago, so my people and I are looking for a place to
settle."

"My crews won't like sharing space with TNA security
scum. A lot of them hate you personally, Machedo."

"Please. I know for a fact that at least a fifth of your
people used to work for the TNA, before they got fired

for corruption or incompetence or using unnecessary force. Consider me corrupted by circumstances, and a big believer in unnecessary force. I'd fit right in."

"People on Glauketas *earn*, Machedo. They don't lounge around relaxing while others sponge off them."

"I'll earn plenty. I have a nice long list of targets, quadruple-encrypted so only I can access the data – me, alive and well, breathing and talking, without any strain of coercion in my voice, with the file watched over by an expert system that knows me well and won't put up with any shenanigans."

The pirate queen stroked her chin. "You'll have to prove yourself."

"I'm prepared to offer one target, as proof of concept. If you like it, you'll come back for more."

"Give me a good one. Not the lowliest site on your list." The pirate queen showed off her skull-filled smile. "Impress me, Machedo."

"I can do that. I've got a secret weapons R&D facility, so it's going to be better defended than some, but you've got enough personnel and ships to overwhelm the defenses."

"This isn't the place where they built the weapon that accidentally blew up Meditreme Station, is it?"

"No, but what do you care? You can sell the weapons even if they do have a tendency to explode."

"True, but I try not to blow up my customers. That sort of thing cuts down on repeat business. All right. We'll give it a try, and if the results are satisfactory, we'll discuss an ongoing relationship, and a home base for your ragtag bunch of refugees. Where's the target?"

"It's out in the Oort Cloud…" Callie began.

CHAPTER 32

They held the meeting around the same long table where Elena had enjoyed her first cup of coffee in centuries, and had her first conversation with Callie. Almost all of them were there, anyway; Ibn preferred to stay in his quarters, seemingly indifferent to his fate, and Sebastien was still unconscious and restrained and being watched over by Shall.

Callie laid out her plan, and told them if anyone wanted to bail out, they'd arrange that, but of course Elena and the whole crew were in, Uzoma was curious to see how things would work out, and Robin said she didn't have anywhere else to be, so it was settled.

Elena sat on Callie's right, Stephen on her left, and the others were arrayed around: Ashok, Janice and Drake in their closed mobility device, Robin, Uzoma, and Lantern. "So we think the plan worked?" Callie said.

"Pretty much the whole force on Glauketas departed," Ashok said. "They're burning toward the Oort Cloud. They left one ship, but it's being repaired: there are drones scuttling around its hull. We only have the TNA estimates about how many pirates call the asteroid home, but assuming our intel is good, and knowing how they favor overwhelming force, I'd say they left just a handful behind to guard their base."

"So let's steal their house," Callie said.

Elena rested her head on Callie's shoulder. "I wish you weren't going in alone. I worry about you."

"I fought alien brain-spiders. I blew up an Axiom space station. The kind of pirates who get left behind on a mission like this? I can take them."

The *White Raven* moved in close to Glauketas. The pirate base was lumpy and unlovely, a roughly potato-shaped asteroid riddled with old mining tunnels and bristling with antennae and guns and airlocks. Predictably, the asteroid fired on them when they approached, and, just as predictably, they missed by kilometers, because of the displacement technology the *Raven* employed. While the defenders on Glauketas puzzled over their failure to connect, Callie took the canoe, piloted remotely by Shall, until she was close enough to use her teleporter to jump into the base itself.

She appeared in a tunnel, once bare rock, now lined with metal to reinforce the asteroid's structure. She floated along, her active camouflage making her invisible. Glauketas was tiny compared to Meditreme, but it could house fifty people comfortably, so it would feel like a mansion once she'd cleaned out all the rats. She crept into a chamber, full of looted comforts, and found one pirate sleeping in a hammock. She woke him up and put a sidearm in his face. "Hi. You've been boarded. Why didn't you go on the field trip? Let me guess, too smart and valuable to risk on such a mission, right?"

He was unshaven and red-eyed and staring at the gun like it was the source of all knowledge in the universe.

The rest of Callie was invisible, so it made sense that he'd focus on the weapon. "My hangover was too bad. I couldn't stop throwing up. Please don't kill me."

"Give me an accurate accounting of personnel currently on this rock, and I'll put you in a pod and send you on your way. Lie to me and I'll put you out an airlock."

"You'll do that anyway."

"No, I won't. I used to be the cops, and I haven't gone all the way feral yet."

He shrugged. Pirates, in her experience, were brave in numbers and less brave when cornered alone. "There are only four of us. The others are probably all in the control room. There was an all-hands alarm a few minutes ago, but I didn't answer it, because I'm sick."

"How were you lot ever the scourge of the spaceways? I guess the ones left behind are the dregs, though, aren't you?"

She'd impugned his pride, and he glared. "When the queen comes back, you're dead. She'll kill you slow. She likes that. She might let us all help."

"I wouldn't count on your people coming back. Not all of them, anyway. Where's the control room?" He told her, and she hogtied him with zip ties and gagged him with a dirty shirt before leaving him in his hammock.

She crept up on three pirates, all looking a bit more capable than the one she'd disabled, clustered together in a round room full of screens and control panels. They were arguing and pointing at the screen, trying to figure out why the *White Raven* refused to explode when they shot things at it.

Callie considered killing them, and she considered wading in throwing elbows and head-butts, but hand-to-hand combat in an environment suit was awkward, so instead she lifted her non-lethal gauntlet, shocked one, and darted the others.

She did a sweep of the rest of the station, just in case her informant had tried some pitiful attempt at disinformation, but Glauketas was otherwise unoccupied. She opened up the airlock, and the *White Raven* parked close to the surface and let Ashok and Lantern and Elena and Robin in. The ship retreated to a safe distance, and they made their preparations. Because Callie had promised, they put the pirates in an escape pod and set its course for Io, one of the Jovian moons that stubbornly insisted it was independent, and generally held to be a miserable place. Then they familiarized themselves with the station's weapons systems, and left Ashok manning the consoles.

After that, they picked out rooms for themselves. Callie took the pirate queen's, which was positively luxurious, and Elena kept her company while they waited.

"Incoming," Ashok called over the asteroid's crackly old PA. Callie leapt up and hurried toward the control room, right in the heart of the asteroid, and Elena went after her, feeling languid and serene, even though she knew she should feel tense. They were about to engage in an armed standoff that would almost certainly involve shots fired, but Callie was so confident, and so magnificent, that Elena could only bring herself to be worried in the abstract.

Callie had dragged a huge chair made of real wood, carved all over with comets and stars, into the control room, and now she lounged in it like a throne in front of the screen. The pirate queen's face appeared, snarling.

"What the *hell* are you doing on my station?"

"My station now." Callie yawned. "Right of conquest, yeah? That's your thing? I can't help but notice you left with eight ships and came back with two. How did the expedition go?"

"That was a *Liar* station, not TNA, and they had weapons like I've never seen before – but you know that. You sent us to die. But I didn't die."

"Did you at least blow the place up? They're the ones who exploded Meditreme Station. I was hoping you'd take them out for me." Callie was lying – Lantern had predicted the pirates had no chance of actually destroying the station, but she wanted to keep the queen off balance.

The queen's eyes went wide, then narrowed. "That's ridiculous. Why would Liars blow up the station?"

"It's a long story you won't be around long enough to hear. Did you kill them or not?"

"Not. We hurt them, bad, but not bad enough. After most of my ships were destroyed I didn't have enough personnel to board successfully, so I retreated. I'm going to kill you, though, all of you–"

"Too bad. If you'd performed a service for the TNA, I might have considered leniency. This is a trial now. You're entitled to an advocate. Do you want one?"

"Fuck you, you lunatic–"

"The accused has waived the right to an advocate. I know for a fact that you personally killed two TNA security officers, and your people have been responsible for many more deaths. The innocent people you pushed out airlocks were the lucky ones, weren't they? The others lived long enough to wish they hadn't. The crews of both your ships include known and wanted pirates.

Piracy carries the death penalty under the regulations of the Trans-Neptunian Authority."

"There is no more TNA, you stupid bitch."

"Not much of one, true, which is why I'm authorized to act as arresting officer and judge both. I find you and your crews guilty. I sentence you to death. Drake, carry out the sentence."

The queen smiled at her. "The station won't fire on its own vessels, you moron. There are safeguards in place. We're going to board you and cut you into little pieces and feed them to your friends–"

"I know Glauketas won't fire on its own ships," Callie said. "That's why I wasn't talking to Glauketas."

The queen frowned, and then the screen went black.

"Targets successfully destroyed," Drake radioed from the *White Raven*. "Two torpedoes, perfect hits. They never even saw us lurking behind the asteroid."

"I hereby take possession of this asteroid under Article 18 of the TNA security code, regarding the seizure and repurposing of assets used in the commission of capital crimes. Or, if we accept that the TNA no longer really exists, we can just say we seize Glauketas as spoils of war. Everyone on the *Raven*, come down and pick out some rooms."

Robin sidled up to Elena and whispered, "Damn. How turned on are you right now?"

Elena blushed, which was answer enough.

Callie drifted over and touched Elena's arm. "Can we talk?"

Robin gave Elena a significant look and then went to join the celebratory conversation with Ashok and the crew. Ashok was already talking about rebuilding the pirate's disorganized machine shop, and Stephen was on the radio asking about the medical facilities.

Elena was hoping their "talk" would involve less talking and more action, but then Callie crooked her finger and Lantern came hurrying after them. They went to the quarters Callie had claimed. She shut the door and they all floated around in a loose cluster. "What's going on?" Elena said.

"We've still got a bit of unfinished business," Callie said. "Lantern and I are going to the Liar base in the Oort Cloud."

Elena nodded. She wasn't surprised. "That's going to be dangerous. But you know that."

Callie shrugged. "Elder Mizori ordered the destruction of Meditreme Station. There has to be justice. Lantern wants to ask her a few questions, too, and confirm our suspicions. I expect us to come back, but if we don't... Stephen is in charge of the *Raven*'s crew, but you'll need to take point in helping the *Anjou*'s people move on. Get them to Imperative territory and they can start new lives. They could go back to Earth – it's beautiful now, and it must be paradise compared to what you left behind. Or head for the colony worlds. I just want you, all of you, to be safe and happy."

"I do want to see Earth again," Elena said. "But the things I've learned, about the Free, and about the Axiom... it's too important. I want to help. I want to come with you."

"I don't know if I could do the things I have to do on that station if I'm worried about you," Callie said.

"You can do anything, Kalea Machedo. But you'll have to do it with me by your side."

"What about your crew? If we don't survive this..."

"Robin is smart and capable. It's not like Stephen is

going to put them on a pod and launch them into space. They'll work out what to do next together."

"I just don't–"

"Shush. I left you behind on the Axiom station, and it was terrible, and I was eaten up with worry, and I won't do that again. It's settled."

"You aren't my client anymore. I don't have to do what you say."

"I'm not your client. I'm not in your chain of command. But I am your girlfriend. So when do we leave?"

"Soon," Callie said. "Before Elder Mizori has a chance to recover from the pirate attack."

"How are we getting there? Not in the *White Raven*?"

"It's not really safe to take our ship – they might recognize it and shoot on sight. Fortunately, the pirates left us a ship that's perfectly adequate to take us there. They called it the *Inevitability of Death*, which is a terrible name, so we're giving it a new one: the *Golden Spider*."

"*White Raven* and *Golden Spider*. Are you starting a petting zoo?"

"Anybody who tries to pet us is going to get bitten."

They were about to board the station's lifeboat and head out to the *Golden Spider* when Ashok crackled over the PA: "Shall has a message. I'm patching you in."

"Go ahead," Callie said.

"I was looking for a new repair drone on this ugly rock," Shall said. "Something useful, so I could go with you."

"And?"

"I didn't have much luck. They have hull repair machines, but they're badly maintained and don't have enough processing power to run even a dumbed-down local version of my consciousness."

"Too bad. I would have liked the backup."

"Ah, but Ashok was poking around in the station armory, and he found something better: a Martian war drone. It's a decade old and it has a busted cooling unit, so they couldn't use it – turn it on, and it overheats and shuts off almost immediately."

"Because pirates are shitty mechanics, and prefer to steal new stuff rather than fix the old," Ashok chimed in. "I, however, am a genius mechanic, and I got it working again."

"When you say war drone…"

"You're going to be happy," Shall said.

Elena, Lantern, and Callie got on board the *Golden Spider*, a dirty and much-patched ship, clearly the ugly duckling of the Glauketas fleet. But the engines worked, and they didn't need much else. The weapons systems were offline, but Shall was clinging to the hull inside the war drone, a machine twice the size of the old hull repair drone and more straightforwardly designed for fighting. Possession of such technology by private individuals was illegal by Martian statute, but Mars law didn't reach anywhere near this far out.

They burned toward the Oort Cloud, sitting together in the cockpit, discussing their approach. It was fairly straightforward. Lantern seemed confident the plan would work. Callie was a bit anxious having Elena on board, but she was focusing hard on the task ahead. That was the way you got through any huge project: take it one small, manageable step at a time. Don't build a starship, just bolt on a plate. Don't write a novel, just write a sentence.

Don't topple an ancient alien empire of unimaginable power, just infiltrate a base.

When they got within real-time communication range of the Liar station, but still outside the range of its guns, Lantern reached out on a secret emergency frequency. "Elder Mizori. This is Lantern. I successfully infiltrated the *White Raven* and destroyed the forbidden technology, and the ship itself, along with all its data. I acquired a new and untraceable vessel. And I have taken two prisoners."

A long silence, and then a voice said, "We do not take prisoners. They should have been killed."

"They have information crucial to our mission," Lantern said. "They know about other humans planning an excursion to Axiom space. I considered killing them and producing a neural bud so you could witness the interrogation, but I feared I might not question them properly. Your wisdom and experience are better suited to a task of such importance."

Another pause. "You have done well, Lantern. Dock your ship and bring your prisoners. Come straight to my quarters when you board. Don't mind the mess. We had a small problem with some human interlopers, but it's being cleared up."

"Acknowledged." Lantern shut off the comms, and then trembled uncontrollably. Elena soothed her.

"It's all right," Elena said.

"I have never knowingly told a lie before," Lantern said, and the trembles became spasms.

CHAPTER 33

Lantern got herself under control by the time they reached the station, deep in the Oort Cloud, that shell of icy planetesimals and comets that surrounded the entire solar system.

The station was definitely a Liar construction: radially symmetric, like a seven-armed starfish, with multiple rings intersecting the arms. "It usually spins," Lantern said.

"The pirates did some damage." Their ship eased past drifting, broken pirate ships as they approached. Callie glanced at Elena. "Are you ready?"

"I think so."

Lantern bound their arms behind them in a way that looked convincing, but the zip ties had been sawn almost all the way through, and a hard jerk would make the tough plastic separate, freeing their arms. Elena had her rings, and Callie had her gauntlets. That should be enough, especially when Shall's hulking war drone was added into the equation.

The docking procedure was simple. The *Golden Spider* didn't have an AI, but it had expert systems that managed to communicate with the station just fine.

They didn't even have to match spin, since the station wasn't spinning. Once they were connected, Lantern led the way through the airlock, followed by Callie and Elena, doing their best to look dispirited and captive.

They entered a tunnel rounded and oddly segmented in a way that made Callie think of a snake's underbelly. The war drone barely fit inside the corridor, clumping along after them on magnetic legs.

"What is this machine?" Elder Mizori's voice boomed in the corridor.

Lantern said, "A war drone I found on board the ship I commandeered. I activated it, and tasked it to pacify the prisoners. They were difficult for me to manage alone. Captain Machedo tried to bite me."

"I did bite you, and I'll bite you again, squid," Callie said.

"The armament is welcome," Mizori said. "We expended considerable resources fighting the invaders."

"How did they find us?" Lantern said.

"We assume they were pirates who typically preyed on the people of the Trans-Neptunian Authority. They must have sent out patrols to look for new targets. Parasites in search of new hosts. They won't come back again. We would have pursued the survivors, but our ranks are diminished, as you know. I plan to request new recruits from our sister cells. Bring the prisoners."

Lantern continued swimming through the air down the corridor, past various branches, until they reached the right segment of the outer ring. A wide set of doors stood open, just large enough for the drone to enter.

The Elder's quarters were palatial: floors that looked like polished stone, a domed ceiling with a starfield projected on it, and fluted pillars that flowed with soft white light. A raised dais in the center of the room held a beautiful round water tank the size of a bed, though the water was gone – probably floated away when the station lost its spin gravity.

The Elder was twice Lantern's size, immense for a Liar, and wore draped fabric as black as the void. She had seven eyes, arrayed in a ring around the bulge of her head, so she could see in all directions. Her tentacles were covered in bracelets in red and black and gold – ornaments? Weapons?

Four other Liars, smaller than Mizori but still bigger than Lantern, floated in a loose semicircle behind the elder, holding objects that looked like the marriage of a sextant and a sniper rifle: weapons of a sort Callie had never seen before.

The elder drifted toward them. "Humans. You will be interrogated. Answer truthfully, and promptly, or you will be compelled to do so."

"Funny," Callie said. "I was about to say the same thing to you." She snapped her wrists apart, separating the cuffs, and sensed Elena doing likewise, but it didn't matter: Shall was running a very dumbed-down version of his consciousness, but he was smart enough to simultaneously target all four guards. The noise of his weapons firing was like a brief run of eighth notes on a flute, and the targeted Liars spun away, lifeless and oozing blue blood that clouded in the air.

Elder Mizori curled up on herself, drawing her tentacles inward. "Treachery. How is this possible?"

"You told me lies," Lantern said. "Didn't you? We went to an Axiom station. I saw the deep archives. I read our sect's original charter."

"I don't know what you're talking about. These

humans have deceived you."

Lantern fluttered her tentacles. "That is easily determined. Produce a neural bud, with a complete record of your memories. I will consume it, and know the truth of what you say."

"You are not senior enough to experience my memories. There are secrets you cannot–"

"But she can," Callie said. Shall's weapons moved, with a noisier than necessary realignment, until several nasty-looking protuberances were pointed straight at the elder. "Lantern has seen the archives. She *knows* the secrets. The question is whether *you* know them, or if you were duped by your superiors, too. If you were tricked, it could help your situation." It wouldn't, really, but the information might make Lantern feel better.

"You saw the deep archives, you say," Mizori said. "What is it you think you know?"

"That the truth-tellers are not a defense against the Axiom. That we are collaborators. Protectors."

There was a long silence, and then Mizori made a wet, bubbling sound that might have been a laugh, or a sob. "You were on a promotion track, Lantern. We were going to tell you the truth, in a few more centuries. You might have become an elder yourself. But then you exhibited that pacifistic streak, and were declared unsuitable for advancement. That's why we sent you on the boarding party. Our projections indicated a low likelihood of survival for the boarders. You were a terrible disappointment." A pause. "The original charter. Is that all you saw?"

"Is there more?"

"Ah. Then you don't know where the sensitive installations are. Some of the great works are near completion. You cannot stop them. You would not even know where to begin. The Axiom will return, within my lifetime, and usher the universe into a new age, and those of us who kept faith with our masters will be rewarded."

"They might come back within Lantern's lifetime, maybe," Callie said. "Your lifetime is a lot shorter than you seem to think."

"Why would you work for them?" Elena said. "The Axiom. They made your people slaves. Erased your history. Why collaborate?"

"Fool. The Axiom killed every race they encountered – except ours. They let us live, because we were useful. We must remain useful, if we wish to avoid the fate that befalls all other species."

"But you could stop them," Elena said. "We all could, together. You could help us. You know their secrets, their weak points, because you've been tasked to defend those. You could defeat them, and be truly free."

"I serve greatness, human. I was created to serve. My line is not a line of rebels. I have within me the memories of a long line of overseers. To serve the Axiom is no great hardship, when you are permitted to rule over lesser members of your own race as a reward."

"Are you going to give us a neural bud?" Callie said. "Let us know what you know?"

"Never. There could be no greater heresy than to share my memories with an apostate."

"Can she be compelled to produce a bud, Lantern?"

"No. Or, I don't know how. The Axiom could, but I can't."

"Elder Mizori, will you tell us what you know about the Axiom?"

"No. And torture would be useless. I control my pain receptors. I erased the local archives when I feared pirates might penetrate our defenses and board. I will never tell you anything, and there is no information for you here. You may as well leave."

Callie nodded. "Refusal to cooperate noted. You are accused of high crimes against the Trans-Neptunian Authority, namely, fifty thousand counts of premeditated murder. You have the right to an advocate."

"Your laws do not apply to me, human. Your nation is dust, made so by my will."

"The accused has waived the right to an advocate, and confessed, freely and without duress. I find you guilty, and sentence you to death."

"Fifty thousand is just the start. When the Axiom rise again–"

Callie pointed her finger at the elder, and Shall fired a single shot.

Callie turned to Lantern. "I'm done here. What do you want to do now?"

"I want to destroy the Axiom."

"Me too, but that's a big job. So what's the first step?"

"I send a message," Lantern said.

Lantern sent the transmission from the secure communications center on the station, which was apparently called Veritat; Elena thought that was a little too on the nose, but Lantern said it was a translation anyway.

"Urgent message to our sister cells," Lantern wrote. "This is Elder Mizori. The forbidden technology we detected was successfully destroyed, and all informational contamination has been sanitized. All humans with knowledge of the Axiom have been eliminated. The mission was indubitably costly and left us understaffed. Veritat was damaged, and made vulnerable to attack by local independent criminal forces. Most of our personnel were lost in the ensuing comprehensive battle. We have made arrangements to take in thirteen local orphans, still in their incubators. They will be raised within the sect, and will replenish our losses. No reinforcements are necessary. I was, however, forced to erase our entire informational archive as a precautionary measure when I feared we would be boarded. Sect sixteen, please send a replacement infosphere, keyed to my biometrics. Message ends."

"Do you think they'll believe it?" Elena said.

"I included all three of today's secret keywords – *sanitized*, and *indubitably*, and *comprehensive* – which are recorded nowhere else, and known only to members of the truth-tellers. They will know the message is authentic. It may take months for the infosphere to arrive, though, as great precautions will be taken with its transport from system sixteen. We will have to keep Mizori in cold storage until then, so we can use her biometrics to unlock the data." Lantern twirled in the air, like a falling flower. "Once that's done... I will have a sense of the Axiom projects that are close to completion. I will raise the young we rescued from the Axiom station as truth-tellers, yes, but they will know the *real* truth. My people mature quickly, and in five or six years, they will be ready to join my cause, if they choose. We will dedicate ourselves to defeating the Axiom and recovering the truth of our lost history and culture."

She extended two tentacles, touching both women on their shoulders "I cannot thank you enough, Doctor

Oh, and Captain Machedo, for helping me. I wish you both well. If, in the course of your travels, you discover information that might help my mission, I hope you will let me know."

"We might be able to do more than that," Callie said. "Elder Mizori blew up Meditreme Station, and she paid for that crime, but she was under orders, in a way, wasn't she? We haven't reached the top of the chain of culpability just yet."

"You still want justice, don't you?" Elena said.

"The Axiom destroyed Meditreme Station, ultimately. It was their policy, their orders, and they're the guilty party. They destroyed countless other cities, too, countless other planets, countless other civilizations, countless other *peoples*. I'm sorry, Elena. I'd love to relax and see the galaxy with you, but the galaxy is in danger, and I can help."

"Are you planning to get in the *Golden Spider* and head straight out to punch space monsters?"

"Not quite. We'll take a few months. We'll get settled on Glauketas, and try to cure Sebastien, and settle your crew elsewhere, if they like. But after that, once Lantern gets the information she's waiting for..." Callie gazed at the screens, showing empty starfields, a depth of near-infinite space, hiding wonders and monsters and gold and spiders.

Elena said, "After that, we're going to find the Axiom, and we're going to kick the shit out of them."

"I'm pretty sure I love you," Callie said.

NEXT:

THE DREAMING STARS

ACKNOWLEDGMENTS

I wrote a space opera! Lots of people helped. My agent, Ginger Clark, strongly encouraged me to branch out into this new-to-me genre, and I appreciate her confidence in me.

I'm grateful to Marc Gascoigne and the revolutionaries at Angry Robot for giving the crew of the *White Raven* a home, especially my editor Phil Jourdan, publicity manager Penny Reeve, and US sales and marketing manager Mike Underwood.

Thanks to my wife, Heather Shaw, and our son, River, for their support during all the hours I spent muttering to myself hunched over a laptop instead of being good company. Thanks to Ais, Amanda, Emily, Katrina, Sarah, and Zoe for enduring my endless babbling and enthusiasm and thinking aloud and brainstorming and idea-bouncing and complaining while I was developing the idea and writing this book.

Thanks finally to all the great writers I've read who inspired me to try my hand at something *other* than fantasy for once, most especially Iain M Banks, Lois McMaster Bujold, CJ Cherryh, James SA Corey, Samuel R Delany, M John Harrison, Alastair Reynolds,

Joanna Russ, Cordwainer Smith, and James Tiptree, Jr. If you peer closely you can probably see bits of all of them in this book, and I am indebted to my betters for their inspiration.

ANGRY ROBOT

We are Angry Robot.

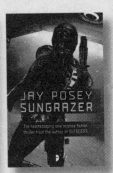

angryrobotbooks.com